# BEYOND
# REDEMPTION

ALSO BY MICHAEL R. FLETCHER

88

# BEYOND
# REDEMPTION

# MICHAEL R. FLETCHER

HARPER Voyager

*An Imprint of HarperCollins Publishers*

Harper Voyager and design is a trademark of HCP LLC.

FIRST EDITION

*Designed by Paula Russell Szafranski*

Library of Congress Cataloging-in-Publication Data has been applied for.

ISBN 978-0-06-238703-5

15 16 17 18 19  OV/RRD  10 9 8 7 6 5 4 3 2 1

# CONTENTS

# AUTHOR'S NOTE

||||||||||||||||||||||||||||||||||||||||||||||||||||||||||||||||||||||||

This is a novel of manifest delusion. As such, the classifications of Geisteskranken (Delusionists) will probably mean little to you. At the end of the novel you'll find a very short definition of each classification as well as a complete list of characters. A great deal of additional information can also be found at http://michaelrfletcher .com/beyondwiki/. Or feel free to read and discover for yourself. Sometimes the difficult path is the most enjoyable.

Apologies to those who can actually speak German.

# BEYOND
## REDEMPTION

# PROLOGUE

The old gods were broken by wars and plagues of the mind, left reeling like the most bloodied veterans. Infected with horror at the cost of their actions, they retreated into dementia. Insanity as escape. Seeking to free themselves, they fled to a world of delusion, a world uncorrupted by jealousies and psychoses. And yet, in the end, even this they would pollute. So deep was their need, so desperate their flight from their bitter past, that they ignored the one truism all must bow before.

Belief defines reality.

The twisted fears of the old gods wormed themselves into this creation and became real. Their darkest thoughts took on life. The inhabitants, at one time mere characters dreamed to entertain, became substantive and entertained delusions of their own.

Dreams became nightmares, and nightmares became reality, stalking the earth as albtraum, manifestations of man's earliest fears given flesh.

And the cycle continues.

Creatures birthed by the delusions of such imperfect gods can hold no hope for sanity. These nightmares define new tomorrows, and the gods look on in mute horror at what they have wrought.

—NEBRILE GHAST, WAHNVOR HIGH PRIEST

## CHAPTER 1

*Where delusion defines reality, the Gefahrgeist is king.*

—Versklaven Schwache, Gefahrgeist Philosopher

The consequences of their last job chased them west. One ever-shrinking step ahead of justice, they arrived at yet another decaying city-state.

Bedeckt, eyes slitted against the abrasive wind, rode into town flanked by Stehlen and Wichtig. Launisch, Bedeckt's monstrous black destrier, hung its head in exhaustion. They'd ridden hours without rest and Bedeckt was no small man.

He scanned the evident poverty and doubted this place had ever seen better days. The few structures built from stone instead of warped and fading wood looked ready to fall in. It didn't matter; he didn't plan on being here long.

Bright eyes, pinpricks of desperation, peered from dark alleys, watching. Nothing new there. He and his companions couldn't help but attract attention, Bedeckt with his bulk and scars, Wichtig with his flawless good looks. He glanced left to Stehlen.

Her horse's ears kept flicking nervously as if it expected to be struck without warning. Bedeckt didn't blame the creature—he felt much the same whenever Stehlen came within arm's reach. She rode hunched forward against the blowing grit, horrid yellow teeth bared in a snarl that seldom left her pinched face. Her right hand rested upon the pommel of her sword. If anyone stared too long, she'd likely kill them. Not that anyone ever seemed to notice her. A mangy dog, lean to the point of skeletal, followed them for a few yards until Stehlen turned jaundiced eyes on the mutt. The dog flinched away with a whimper.

Bedeckt glanced at Wichtig. The man looked annoyingly perfect as always. Nothing in all the world could muss that coiffed hair or dent his immaculate smile.

*What a self-centered arse.*

Dust from the road tickled Bedeckt's already raw throat and he sneezed, spraying a wad of bright green snot from his nostrils. He'd been feeling under the weather for a week now and showed no signs of improving.

"You sound like shite, old man," said Wichtig.

"I'm fine." He needed an inn and a warm bed. Gods, he'd kill for an ale, no matter how bad.

Stehlen spat into the road and Launisch shied. Even the warhorse feared her.

"Idiot's right," she said. "Let's get you into bed."

"You've been wanting to do that for—" Wichtig snapped his mouth shut when Stehlen turned her gaze upon him.

If Bedeckt was lucky, the two would kill each other and leave him in peace. "My horse is tired and my arse aches," he said.

"Your horse is tired and your arse is sore because you're fat and old," said Stehlen, her horse's ears twitching away from her words.

"So what's this piss-pot of a city called?" Wichtig was slumped casually in the saddle as he took in the run-down fortifications and the sloppily uniformed and inattentive guards. He sniffed gingerly at the air and wrinkled his perfectly straight nose in exaggerated distaste. "I apologize: this place isn't a piss-pot, it's a shite-hole. Totally different odor." He flashed a grin of straight white teeth at Bedeckt. A gust of wind ruffled his reddish-brown hair and for a moment he looked the hero, two slim swords peeking over wide shoulders, his muscular arms resting easily on thighs. Expensive clothing worn to greatest effect. Only his eyes, flat and gray, gave lie to the act.

*How could such a self-centered murdering bastard look so heroically perfect?* Truly the gods were twisted. Bedeckt, of course, looked exactly like what he was: an aging warrior well past his prime with a bad back, worse knees, too many battle scars, and a love of ale. He'd never looked as pretty as Wichtig, even in his prime. Had he, perhaps things would have turned out differently. But he doubted it.

"Better be an inn in this dung heap," said Wichtig.

"You ever know a town this size without an inn? And it's called Unbrauchbar . . . I think." Bedeckt warily scanned the city guards—who continued to studiously ignore them—and scratched at his fist-flattened nose with the remnants of his left hand. The last two fingers were missing, severed at the first knuckle in a pointless war many years ago. A massive, double-bladed ax hung within easy reach from a leather loop in his horse's saddle, its blade pitted from rough use. He glanced at Stehlen. "You been here before?"

Stehlen ran a long-fingered hand through matted and clumped dirty blond hair. They were musician's fingers, though she'd never played a note. Pale and watery blue eyes with flecks of green, the whites a sickly and unhealthy yellow, squinted out from under the tangled hair. Her angry gaze dashed about as if she were searching for something to hate—it didn't seem like she'd need to look far. She flared the nostrils of her hooked nose as if perhaps she'd find what she sought by smell.

"No," she answered.

"Good," muttered Wichtig.

Stehlen scowled at Wichtig. "Why good?"

"You probably won't know anyone here."

"So?"

"So maybe no one here will want to kill us," he said.

She ignored him. "Why here?" she asked Bedeckt.

Bedeckt answered without looking at her. "Because here is better than where we were."

"If Wichtig hadn't bedded that—"

"But he did."

"If you hadn't killed those—"

"But I did." Bedeckt finally glanced at her and frowned as she showed crooked yellow teeth in a disappointed grimace. "I also seem to remember some of the Lord's property going missing. The theft had a fair amount to do with the killing." Wichtig's actions had sparked Stehlen's thieving, but Bedeckt couldn't figure out how or why. The Swordsman had bedded the Lord's wife, and Stehlen stole the woman's jewelry shortly after. Were the two events linked? No, they couldn't be. At least he hoped they weren't.

Stehlen tried to look wounded and innocent and failed. She didn't have Wichtig's flair for deceit.

"You don't have any gold left, do you?" Wichtig asked Stehlen. "It would be nice to stay in a bit of style."

"No."

No doubt she lied, but Bedeckt let it go without comment. Kleptics always lied about money. She couldn't help it any more than Wichtig could help being a self-centered manipulative arse.

"We've got enough to get soft beds and food." Bedeckt looked pointedly at Wichtig. "Right?"

Wichtig shrugged noncommittally. "I haven't looked in my pack recently. We definitely have coin . . . unless this hideous wench here"—he nodded at Stehlen—"robbed us blind. Again."

"I've *never* stolen from you!" growled Stehlen. "Anyway, you'll hand money to the first bitch who spreads her legs."

"Spread your legs, let's see if I—"

"Never!"

"Maybe if Bedeckt here . . . ?" Wichtig trailed off, waggling his eyebrows at her.

Stehlen spat again, hunched deeper in her saddle, and set about ignoring both men.

*What the hells was that about?* Bedeckt didn't even want to know. He thought about his own money purse. He could have sworn there was more in there, but the last time he'd looked he'd been near destitute. Had Stehlen helped herself? It didn't matter, she always lent him money when asked. *Probably my money anyway.* Traveling with a pair of Geisteskranken, one had to accept such things. Kleptics stole and Gefahrgeist manipulated. At least Wichtig's Gefahrgeist talents remained meager; he mostly craved attention. If the Swordsman grew in strength and seemed likely to become a Slaver, Bedeckt would kill him.

When Stehlen didn't rise to the bait, Wichtig sulked like a spoiled child denied candy. "Think this shite-hole has a Swordsman?" he asked Bedeckt.

"Every shite-hole has a Swordsman."

"And every shite-hole needs a better Swordsman."

"And you're that Swordsman?" asked Stehlen snidely.

Wichtig turned flat eyes on her, face expressionless. He held her angry glare until she looked away, uncomfortable. Minor Gefahrgeist Wichtig might be, but few people failed to wither under this assault of will.

"Belief defines reality," said Wichtig, as if explaining to a simpleton. "I believe I will be the Greatest Swordsman in the World."

"I believe you will be dead first," said Stehlen icily, still looking away.

"My belief is stronger than yours."

"Delusional idiot."

"Of course. But I prefer to believe I am simply that good. I've killed forty-three Greatest Swordsmen. I was Master of Swords in Geldangelegenheiten at twenty-one. An unprecedented honor."

"Honor," Stehlen snorted.

"And this coming from a petty thief. A talentless—"

"Talented enough to lift your purse!"

"Dumb enough to tell me about it!"

"Quiet!" Bedeckt shook his head and instantly regretted it. A dull, throbbing pain built in his skull. There must be pounds of snot in there. "Like bloody children. Once I've found a warm bed and a soft woman, the two of you can have this pointless debate. Until then, shut the hells up."

"The old man's a little grumpy," observed Wichtig.

"If you involve me in one of your fights, Wichtig, I'll kill you myself. With an ax. You can shove this Greatest Swordsman shite."

"I could help with the woman part," Stehlen said.

Bedeckt pretended not to hear and scanned the road ahead for an inn.

"He said *soft*," said Wichtig, smirking at Stehlen. "Even a pig like Bedeckt won't bed you. You're too damned ugly. Perhaps if you offered him some of his money back . . . that which you've pilfered over the last week."

"I have money," she said loud enough to be sure Bedeckt heard.

Bedeckt shook his head and flexed the remains of his ruined left hand. "I'll bed whores. I'm not ready to be one."

"How many people you steal from in Abfallstadt?" asked Stehlen.

Bedeckt waved away the question, a sharp cutting gesture with his half hand. His head was so clogged with snot he had to breathe through his mouth in short, dusty gasps. Something dry rattled deep in his lungs. *Lovely, some new symptom to plague me.*

"How many people you kill in the last six months?" Stehlen asked.

"What defines a man is what he *won't* do," muttered Bedeckt.

Her hooked nose flared in distaste. "Murder and thievery are fine, but not sex?"

"Sex with you isn't," said Wichtig. "At best he'd wake up to find you'd robbed him blind and at worst you'd have one of your violent fits and he'd wake with his throat slit."

Bedeckt groaned. This was not a conversation he wanted to have right now. Or ever. "Drop it. I won't bed you because it'll change everything and make life more difficult than it already is."

"And you're an ungodly ugly thieving Kleptic bitch," added Wichtig.

Ignoring Wichtig, Bedeckt continued. "We work together. We're a team. A shite team, but we get things done. We aren't friends and we sure as shite aren't lovers. Never forget: I'd kill either of you if there was money in it for me."

"Stop it, I'm getting all misty-eyed." Wichtig pretended to mop at tears. "Stehlen, throw me a few gold coins—they're probably mine anyway—and I'll bed you."

Stehlen's stiletto hissed out and Wichtig laughed at her. Pretending nonchalance, he moved his horse away, carefully staying out of reach.

"There's an inn." Bedeckt pointed up the street. "Put your knife away, woman. Gut him after I've had a drink."

# CHAPTER 2

*Those whom you slay will be as your servants in the Afterdeath.*
*Die with your boots on, and keep a few coins stashed in those*
*boots. Die with a weapon in hand and two more within easy reach.*
*For when you pass from this world, you'll be glad of the things you*
*take with you.*

—THE WARRIOR'S CREDO

Konig Furimmer, Theocrat of the Geborene Damonen, stood in his personal chambers, his back to the room, staring out over the city of Selbsthass. The streets ran straight and perfect, the north-south streets named, the east-west numbered. An ordered city, a sane city.

*No reason sanity can't come from delusion,* Konig thought.

This city, the laws binding it together, the geography defining it, the people populating it . . . all a manifestation of his delusion.

Well, maybe not all of it. The people, he supposed, were real enough on their own. But when he'd first come here almost two decades ago, a lowly acolyte with a dream, the Geborene had been a small splinter sect of religious fanatics with a seemingly crazy idea and no way of making it real.

*He'd* made it real.

Back then, Selbsthass had been little more than another decaying city-state that had the bad luck of being located on rocky soil unfit for growing much more than malnourished goats and tufts of hardy grass. He remembered starving people coming to worship at the run-down ruins of this ancient church. He could only guess what gods this church had originally been built for. Certainly not humans: no two doorways were the same shape, no two halls the same width. Passages grew and narrowed seemingly at random. In some areas the scale was so large as to beggar the imagination, while in others priests had to turn sideways to pass each other. Twisted minds dreamed this construction. The Geborene took it for their own, but before that it had lain empty and haunted for generations.

Konig had changed everything. All of it.

One truism lay underneath every choice and word: change what people think and you change the world.

He changed the religion, chased the ghosts from this ancient temple. He gave the people hope and they learned to believe in themselves. More important, they believed in him. Selbsthass grew into a wealthy city-state. His priests were relentless in spreading the word. The more people who believed something, the truer it became.

His plans had almost reached fruition. The Geborene would have their new god and Konig would be its maker and master.

"Perception," he said, "is reality."

To a Gefahrgeist, this truth was everything.

Those standing at his back remained quiet. They knew him all too well. He heard them shuffling about, impatient to be allowed to speak.

Konig stood, feet together, left hand cupping his narrow chin in thought, right hand gripping his left elbow. His personal chambers were growing increasingly crowded, a matter of some concern. He glanced over his shoulder at the three other men in the room. No, not men. Doppels. An important distinction.

Each Doppel stood in exactly the same pose, dressed in identical florid crimson robes, staring at him with varying degrees of attention. Three sets of identical gray eyes. Three identically bald heads. Though obviously copies of Konig, they each displayed minor flaws.

No, again he corrected himself. "Flaw" seemed too strong a word. "Quirk" might be more accurate.

The closest flashed a hungry feral grin, a glint of white teeth. Another's gaze darted about as if he expected a sudden attack from the shadows. The last looked as if he might fall to his knees and beg forgiveness for some unknown sin, face desperate for praise, yet knowing he was undeserving.

*Sniveling weakling.* Konig hated the last one the most. Knowing the Doppels displayed aspects of his own character made it no easier to accept.

Konig took comfort knowing no one liked everything about themselves—most weren't confronted with physical manifestations of their own defects.

"Be gone," he commanded. "I have no need of your craven counsel."

The Doppel glanced around the room as if taking in the dark oak and luxurious finishes one last time before briefly meeting Konig's steady gaze with an apologetic shrug. "Apparently you don't believe that." The Doppel ducked its head subserviently and stared at the floor. It was all an act. "Sorry."

"Silence, Acceptance. Stand in the corner. Say nothing."

The Doppel nodded meekly but Konig caught the faintest hint of a knowing smirk as it moped toward the corner. At least it still obeyed, even if he couldn't banish it. Still, his inability to force the Doppels' disappearance was not heartening. His delusions grew in strength, gaining control of their own existence.

In a floor-to-ceiling brass-rimmed mirror filling most of one wall, several of his reflections gathered, as if at a window, to watch. Long gaunt faces and bald heads. Their mouths moved but no sound could be heard. A recent development, he'd only begun experiencing Mirrorist tendencies in the last few days. It was only a matter of time before he heard their voices. They might briefly offer valuable advice or show him flashes of the future or distant places, but they would someday climb from their mirror world. When this eventuality came to be, they would either kill or replace him. He wasn't sure which he feared more.

*If my other delusions don't get me first.*

It didn't matter. He'd have his god and gods change everything.

One of the other Doppels—Abandonment, Konig named this one—leaned forward to whisper conspirationally in his ear, "Acceptance plots against you."

Konig pushed the Doppel back. "And you don't?" He laughed, a humorless bark.

Trepidation and Abandonment both backed away from Konig's angry glower, bowing their heads. Only Acceptance remained unfazed, facing the corner.

"You can't trust him," whispered Abandonment. "Acceptance seeks to replace you."

"And you I can trust?"

Abandonment kept his face lowered, but Konig saw the tight smile. "Of course not. Everyone abandons us in the end. Just like our parents."

"*My* parents," snapped Konig. "You are delusion."

"*Your* parents," corrected Abandonment smoothly. "If Mother can abandon you, who can't? It's why I exist. I may be delusion, but I am your reality."

A fourth Doppel faded into existence, a much younger Konig. The tearstained face showed all the loss of an abandoned child who has suddenly realized not a single soul in all the world cares for him beyond how he may be used. Konig focused on the present and drove the Doppel away. This was no time to dwell on old wounds, fester as they might.

"Your pet scientist is coming," Abandonment spat with vehement disgust.

"He is my friend."

"We don't have friends," said Abandonment. "Not really."

The Doppel was right, but still Konig's jaw tightened, his teeth grinding in anger. They had been friends, back before he'd decided to make a god. "He is useful," Konig said.

"He hates us," warned Abandonment. "You can't trust him. He is *sane*."

"The day you counsel trust I shall truly know I am in trouble."

"In this I must agree with Abandonment," piped in Acceptance before tucking his head back into the corner when Konig fired a warning look in his direction. "I don't think he likes us," whispered the Doppel. "I don't think he likes you either," he added, glancing back at Konig. "He thinks you stole his idea."

"I don't care if he likes me. He need merely be useful."

Acceptance smirked as if he knew this for a lie.

~

Aufschlag Hoher, Chief Scientist of the Geborene Damonen, entered Konig's chambers, bowed low, and did his best to ignore the High Priest's Doppels. They, in turn, did their best to glare daggers of hatred and contempt in his direction. On good days he wondered what this meant for Konig's opinion of his Chief Scientist. On bad days he contemplated killing the deranged Theocrat.

*So, what is today going to be?*

Konig, however, was a Gefahrgeist of unquestionable power. Aufschlag couldn't spend more than a few minutes in the High Priest's presence before the man's stunning genius, vision, and depth of understanding overcame him. The sheer scale of the man's plans inspired awe. Konig Furimmer was not a man who thought small. Konig thought in terms of forever.

Doubt only set in afterward. Aufschlag lay awake nights wondering what Konig really was: genius or deluded madman. It was so damned hard to be sure.

Perception was reality; something Geisteskranken understood all too well. It was their source of power, what made them special and set them apart from the masses of the common man. But Aufschlag understood. His experiments taught him the truth:

They were all just crazy.

And that's what Konig was: crazy. *What kind of horrific childhood does it take to create someone like Konig?* Interesting question. Perhaps he would experiment with it later.

Aufschlag watched the man who had once been his closest friend. They'd met as Geborene acolytes. Though both joined the almost unheard-of religion for different reasons, their fates became entwined. Had they first really become friends on the day Aufschlag had brought his idea to Konig? *It was my idea, wasn't it?*

Aufschlag bowed again as Konig finally deigned to glance in his direction. Only then did he notice the hem of his own pale blue robes stained dark with blood. He straightened, briefly meeting Konig's gray eyes. At least he was fairly sure it was Konig and not one of his Doppels. The eyes, so gray as to look like the very color had been leached from them, bore into him. He felt layers of his personality peeled away for scrutiny. Konig held his gaze and would not release him. Aufschlag couldn't move. Pinned.

*It's one of* those *days.* All doubt washed away like blood draining from a torn femoral artery. Konig was a man to follow, a man who saw the gods for what they were. Those eyes saw the future.

Aufschlag staggered when Konig finally glanced away. He took a moment to allow his pounding heart to slow. The glare of the Doppels felt like poisonous spiders crawling across his skin.

One of the Doppels—Aufschlag was unable to keep track of which was which—leaned forward and whispered, "I know what you're thinking, you snaggletoothed, greasy pigsticker."

"Abandonment," commanded Konig, "leave him be. Aufschlag, my old friend, you have something to report, I assume?"

Aufschlag stammered, suddenly self-conscious of his crooked teeth and the greasy tufts of hair sprouting from around his ears. "Y-yes. Another of the young gods committed suicide, High Priest." He broke into a sweat. His left hand hovered between covering his crooked teeth from view and darting up to smooth his hair into place.

Konig turned to stare at the Doppel standing with his face pressed into the room's corner. "Ausfall?"

Aufschlag blinked uncertainly at Konig's back. *What emotion is he hiding from me?* "Yes."

"She was too damned smart anyway, always asking questions. She wouldn't simply accept what I told her. Distrustful little girl." Konig turned and glanced at Aufschlag, an eyebrow lifted slightly. "I wonder where she learned that?"

"The same people who have access to Ausfall have access to Morgen," Aufschlag said defensively. "And he shows none of those traits. Most likely it was her personality."

"Morgen is perfect," said Konig.

"He's innocent and trusting in the extreme," pointed out Aufschlag.

"That's what I said. And I want him to stay that way. Only you and I—plus his bodyguards—are allowed in his presence from this point on. I don't want him infected by doubt."

*Gods forbid the boy learn to think for himself.* "Of course," said Aufschlag. How had his plans come to this? As a scientist, he battled ignorance on every front, and yet here he was, shielding Morgen from uncomfortable truths. He might not be lying to the boy, but he was definitely keeping things from him he needed to know. *I should tell Morgen everything, let him make up his own mind.*

But Morgen's mind had been made up for him. Like all the other would-be gods the Geborene sought to create, his entire life he'd been taught he'd someday Ascend to become the god of the Geborene and serve the people of Selbsthass. Slavery sold as a virtue.

They'd started with ten children, and over the last decade, one by one, they'd succumb. Rampant delusion, fed by the Geborene and the faith of Selbsthass, had broken them. Some burned, some rotted away to nothing. Each reached their tottering pinnacle of power and toppled as the weight of their delusions dragged them down, drowned them in dementia. Not one had Ascended. Ausfall was just the latest. And now Morgen, the purest, most innocent spirit Aufschlag had ever known, was all that remained.

Had he known his plan would end in the tragic deaths of nine children, would he still have brought it to Konig?

*Gods forgive me, but I think so.*

"How did Ausfall die?" Konig asked, snapping Aufschlag from his thoughts.

"She chewed through her wrists. Bled out. Managed to write a fair amount on the walls before she lost consciousness."

"In her own blood, I assume?"

"Of course."

"Anything of consequence?"

"I did see one phrase repeated over and over. 'We make poor gods.' I'm not sure what she meant. Perhaps that the Geborene are making inferior gods, or that she would be a poor god should she Ascend. I have Sister Wegwerfen looking into it."

"Wegwerfen can't be trusted," said Abandonment. "She might spread word of Ausfall's death."

"We can't have that now, can we." Konig pinioned Aufschlag with flat gray eyes. "Kill Wegwerfen when she is finished. Report her findings."

"Of course." Face carefully blank.

But Konig saw through his Chief Scientist's façade. "I know this is difficult." He placed his hands on Aufschlag's slim shoulders, forcing eye contact. "This failure could spread seeds of doubt we can't afford." His long fingers dug into the soft tissue. "Doubt is failure."

Aufschlag's will crumpled beneath the gaze of his High Priest. He saw nothing but colorless gray eyes. The fingers felt like carrion worms working their way deep into his flesh. "But—" Sweat poured freely down his face. "Haven't we already failed? There is only one god left!"

"Of course not. Did you think I sought to create many gods? No." He spoke with such conviction Aufschlag's doubts disappeared in the blazing heat of revelation. Konig smiled warmly at his Chief Scientist. "This is a happy day. A glorious day. We now know which of our experiments will Ascend." He removed his hands from Aufschlag's shoulders and the scientist was more than a little surprised to see they were free of blood.

"I apologize for my moment of weakness, High Priest." Aufschlag's heart filled with strengthened faith. "It's so obvious. Of course there could only be one god. Too close to the experiment, I suppose. I became blinded."

"Not to worry, my friend." Konig patted Aufschlag on the back as if they were the closest of comrades, which once, long ago, they had been. "Your task has always been the details. It falls to me to see the bigger picture, but we'd be lost without you. You are the heart of this project." Konig turned to stare at his gathered Doppels. "I am nothing without my friends. So

alone. You are with me, right? Aufschlag? I can't do this without you."

Aufschlag bowed low. Konig would never be alone as long as
Aufschlag drew breath. He'd give everything in the service of this
great man. Everything.

"I will never abandon you," Aufschlag swore with utter sincerity.

The moment the heavy oak door closed behind Aufschlag, Abandonment chuckled. "He'll abandon you. They'll all abandon you."

Konig smiled sadly at his Doppel. "Yes. But not yet. Notice
how he didn't use the word 'trust'? The day he tells me I can trust
him is the day he dies."

Trepidation coughed nervously. "But you always tell people
they can trust *you*."

"True."

Abandonment gestured at the closed door. "You told him the
plan was for only one to Ascend."

"Yes."

"But we wanted—"

"I wanted."

"—you wanted as many to Ascend as possible. With only one
child left, our . . . your plans are in grave danger. Should something happen to the child . . ." Abandonment left the thought
unfinished.

"You lied to him," accused Acceptance, no longer facing the
corner. "I thought he was our friend."

"All communication is manipulation," said Konig. "All interaction, social or otherwise, is a means of getting what you want.
It's the basis of society." He paced the room, the hem of his crimson robes caressing the richly carpeted floor. "I need Aufschlag
and he needs me. Underlying all friendship is a level of mutual

dependence. Need, and need fulfilled. Without me Aufschlag would be nothing, a small man with small dreams. Without Aufschlag I would be hard-pressed to create my god. We need each other. We use each other." Konig grinned at Acceptance. This would bother the Doppel. "When he betrays me—and there can be no doubt he will—I will kill him." Konig gave his Doppels a hooded look. "You can trust me on that."

Acceptance laughed, a quiet chuckle. "And here I thought I was not only the embodiment of your need for acceptance, but also the sole manifestation of your sense of humor."

"I wasn't joking," said Konig.

Acceptance, looking disappointed, glanced to the floor. "Oh."

KONIG SENT THE three Doppels to another room to give himself space to think. They crowded his thoughts with their demands for attention and constant infighting and bickering. For a brief moment he thought they wouldn't leave, until Acceptance bowed his head and exited, with the others following in his footsteps. Not long ago he could cause them to fade out and vanish with a little directed will. Now he had trouble ordering them to another room. Someday he would not be able to banish them at all. They were his curse and a sure sign of his immense power. Unfortunately, as his power grew, so too did the strength of his Doppels. There would come a day when they no longer obeyed him. They would hound his every moment, muttering to him as he tried to sleep. His thoughts would be infested.

And then they would bring him down. His delusions would overthrow him, topple him from the throne of his mind, devour his intellect. There was no way to know how it would happen. Perhaps he would be dragged into a mirror and forever imprisoned. He might lose his grasp of self and be unable to differentiate between himself and his Doppels. The strongest would step forward and take control. Konig would then become a whimpering Doppel of the new Konig.

There were so many ways for a Geisteskranken to go. He'd heard of the Somatoparaphrenic, their limbs rebelling and claiming control over their minds. The fate of the Cotardist frightened him the most. The thought of his flesh putrefying, his internal organs rotting or fading away, was a nightmare.

Konig sat at his desk, a massive and ornate oaken monstrosity. He'd found it hidden in one of the church's deepest basements and claimed it for his own. It was, he believed, some kind of cherrywood, the red so dark as to approach black. Chaotic scatterings of paper littered the desk's surface. All the business of the Geborene came through him. He was the center of everything. Selbsthass wouldn't be what it was without his constant attention.

*Gods, it's quiet in here.* The Doppels' bickering was distracting, but they were also useful. Though in talking to them he did little more than talk to himself, there was something about thinking out loud that worked for him. They might be little more than aspects of his personality, but they were focused aspects, condensed fragments of his psyche. Each Doppel offered something different, and though they sought to overthrow him, they needed him as much as he needed them. Need bound them together.

*Someday they will need me less than I need them.* The needs of others were the fulcrum upon which his Gefahrgeist powers tilted the world. *Need is weakness.*

The room's silence bore down upon him like a weight on his shoulders. He missed the voices of others. Spending too much time alone left him feeling drained and weak. Doubt would set in. Soon he would venture from his office, surround himself with his priests, and bask in their attention.

He picked up a random piece of paper and glanced at it; reports from the Geborene church in Gottlos, a filthy runt of a city-state to the south of Selbsthass. King Dieb Schmutzig, a Gefahrgeist of minimal power, demanded the foreign church pay exorbitant taxes. Annoying, but hardly important. Gottlos would be Konig's soon enough. For now he'd pay the self-important little prick.

Konig snarled and slammed the top of the desk, anger flashing through him like a storm raging out of nowhere. He crushed the report in a shaking fist.

"Schmutzig is less than nothing," growled Konig, struggling to focus on the work he must do. "Safe only because he isn't worth crushing."

"Safe because you have bigger problems to deal with," whispered Trepidation from behind.

Konig's shoulders fell. "I told you to leave."

"You're worried."

"I can handle this."

"There is only one god left. If he fails, it's too late to start again. Your delusions grow in strength. Time is running out."

"Aufschlag will not fail me," said Konig.

Abandonment, standing next to his fellow Doppel, leaned forward. "Everyone abandons you. The scientist will fail."

"No," said Konig forcefully. "This child is the one."

Trepidation laughed. "Who are you trying to convince?"

⋕⋕⋕⋕⋕⋕

Sister Wegwerfen stood before Aufschlag Hoher, who sat at his immaculate desk. Though the Geborene Chief Scientist certainly cut no imposing figure, fat and round, with his bad teeth and greasy fringe of hair, the young priestess knew better.

Science, she had learned, was a terrifying and bloody pursuit. She'd assisted in enough of Aufschlag's experiments to have developed more than a little respect for the man's tenacious drive to learn, although Aufschlag's willingness to go to any length to find answers bordered on mad. She had watched him torture entire families just to see if he could make Geisteskranken, or to determine if delusion was something people were born with. She would have sworn Aufschlag was Geisteskranken except not once had he manifested a single delusion or shown signs of being anything less than coldly, dangerously sane.

No, sane wasn't correct. He might not be delusional, but he wasn't necessarily fully human either.

He stared at her with beady eyes, his forehead glistening. His fingers drummed nervously on the desk, a staccato without rhythm. He glanced away, grimaced, and returned his attention to her. What did he have to be nervous about? His agitation worried her. *Have I done something wrong?*

"Report," he said.

"I have examined Ausfall's room," she said.

"And?"

"Blood is not the best medium for leaving legible messages." Aufschlag's look said in no uncertain terms that he was not in the mood for humor. "Sorry."

He waved it away. "Summarize."

"Right." Wegwerfen thought about the insane ramblings she'd spent hours trying to decipher and the ragged mess of the young girl's wrists where she'd chewed them open. "Ausfall wrote, 'We make poor gods' many times. I believe she was saying Ascended humans made a poor substitute for real gods."

"Our god will be real."

"Of course. I only meant that—"

"Continue."

Wegwerfen bit her lower lip, collecting her thoughts. "Ausfall also wrote of the incredible pressure of knowing she would Ascend to godhood. She said the expectations of an entire people were a weight on her soul. She said she feared death and . . ." Wegwerfen hesitated.

"And?" asked Aufschlag.

"She wrote of coercion and control and how she couldn't be a true god of the people unless she Ascended at her own hand. She wrote of puppets and the Afterdeath."

The Chief Scientist's eyes bored into Wegwerfen. "Where did such ideas come from?"

"Ausfall was a clever girl, much smarter than the others. She could have figured this out on her own."

"And yet even though she took her own life, she didn't Ascend," Aufschlag said sadly, shaking his head in disappointment.

"But don't the people believe she'll be their god?"

"No. The people believe we will *make* their god. They know nothing of the individuals. She will not be that god—Konig will ensure that."

"There is only one left."

"Yes. Morgen. He will be our god. As Konig planned all along. The others, merely experiments. Morgen is the culmination. We will spread the word, the people must know his name. Their belief will guarantee his Ascension."

"Is that what I am to do next?" Wegwerfen asked.

The Chief Scientist swallowed uncomfortably, looking ill. His gaze darted about the room and his fingers drummed nervously.

*He's trying to make up his mind,* she realized. About what? Had she done something to upset him?

Aufschlag finally made eye contact. "Yes, but not here. I must send you away to . . ." He licked his lips. " . . . to Gottlos. There is a small church there. Tell Bishop Kurzschluss Gegangen I sent you. You are to help spread the word of Morgen's coming Ascension."

*Gottlos? That wretched stinking little cesspit to the south?* Wegwerfen kept her face blank. "Of course, as you command. I shall begin packing imm—"

"No! You can't pack. Fetch a horse and leave now. Tell no one you are leaving."

"Now?"

"Before I change my mind."

*What the hells is going on? Change his mind about what?* Backing away, she dipped a quick bow. She stopped at the door, one hand resting against the thick wood. "Will I be allowed to return?" she asked hesitantly.

Aufschlag stared at his desk. "Maybe. Go. Now."

Wegwerfen fled the Chief Scientist's office.

# CHAPTER 3

*If our world is defined by delusion, there can be no truth. If there is no truth, how can there be lies?*

—Wahrheit Ertrinkt, Philosopher

The inn consisted of four round tables made of wagon wheels tipped on their side, with several roughhewn planks thrown over the top. Two large crates with wood planks hanging bowed between them made up the bar. Overturned boxes were chairs.

"It's perfect," announced Bedeckt as he sat heavily at the only empty table. His back ached.

Looking about the room, Wichtig sniffed and said loudly, "Shite-hole." The faces of the half-dozen patrons turned to look at the recent arrivals.

Stehlen, as always, sat across from Bedeckt. Covering the angles, watching his back.

Remaining standing, Wichtig looked around the room, meeting the eyes of each patron and waiting until they looked away.

"A shite-hole," he enunciated carefully. "Infested with vermin. Rats and cockless cockroaches."

Bedeckt took the ax from its customary place at his back and set it on the table. The old boards groaned under the weight. "If you want a fight, go elsewhere. I want to sit and drink."

"But if I start a fight elsewhere," said Wichtig reasonably, "you won't be there to back me up." Seeing Bedeckt remained unmoved, he grunted and sat. "Boring."

"Only boring people get bored," said Bedeckt, ignoring Wichtig's look of hurt confusion. "Get us ale."

Wichtig dropped the feigned hurt without comment, but sat unmoving. He stared at the barkeep until the man wilted under the weight of his dead eyes. Not once did the young Swordsman blink. Less than a minute later three tankards of warm ale sat on their table.

Four pints—each—later the inn door opened and a gust of dry air blew dust into their tankards and eyes. Bedeckt heard the collective groan of the other patrons, who, until this moment, had remained carefully silent. Unwilling to meet Wichtig's eyes, they avoided looking at the group of three at all. Even the barkeep brought fresh tankards without making eye contact or uttering a word.

Stehlen, blinking the dust from her eyes, looked to the door. She groaned. "Gods-damned priestess."

Wichtig turned to see the woman at the door and nodded appreciatively. "That's a little something tasty," he called loudly.

Bedeckt enjoyed the Swordsman's surprise when, instead of flinching and moving away, the young woman walked directly to their table. *Great. Another crazy priest trying to save our lost souls.* If she had even an inkling of the people she approached, she'd turn and flee.

"Greetings, travelers." The priestess wore long, dust-colored robes and couldn't have been a day over twenty. She stood at their table, looking entirely relaxed.

Bedeckt examined her, trying to get an idea of what might be under those robes, not caring how uncomfortable his inspection made her. "Travelers?"

"Saw you ride in," she said. If his attention bothered her, she hid it masterfully. "And there aren't that many people in Unbrauchbar."

"Shite-hole," corrected Wichtig.

The priestess accepted this with a small tilt of her head. "Wherever you are, there you are. We define our reality."

Bedeckt, enjoying Wichtig's look of confusion, decided to humor her. It would pass the time and maybe keep his two companions from each other's throat. "I recognize that philosophy."

"Geborene Damonen," said the priestess. "You've heard of us."

"But as a philosophy, not a religion," said Bedeckt. The ale had loosened the snot in his skull, and closing one nostril with a blunt and filthy finger, he blew a great wad of it onto the floor. The relief was brief and his sinuses quickly refilled.

The priestess raised an eyebrow at the puddled snot and continued. "Philosophy and religion are largely one and the same," she said. "I am Sister Wegwerfen. May I join you?"

Bedeckt answered before Wichtig. "Yes, of course." Perhaps the priestess's presence would drive the young Swordsman away for a time. Bedeckt was tired of Wichtig's self-centered humor. Once Wichtig fled, Bedeckt could tell her to shove off.

Stehlen and Wichtig shifted uncomfortably on their wooden box seats. *With any luck this will drive them both off and I'll get some peace.*

The woman seemed ignorant of the discomfort she caused. "The Geborene Damonen has always been more than a philosophy," she said. "Long has it been the plan to put our ideas into action. But when one sees as far as High Priest Konig Furimmer, such plans take time. Only now are we finally ready to spread the word of the Ascendance of the Geborene god."

Bedeckt's curiosity got the better of him. "Geborene god? I thought the Geborene Damonen believe mankind invented the gods. That they are nothing but our delusions given form."

"Exactly!" She beamed happily, probably excited to have met someone who knew of her crazy religion. "If humanity's belief created the old gods, we can create new gods."

Wichtig grumbled something into his ale, trying not to look lost.

Stehlen looked back and forth between the priestess and Bedeckt in confusion. Her pinched expression said, *There had better be an angle here.* Bedeckt gave her the tiniest of shrugs and she scowled openly.

"Join a damned church," she said, "I'll kill you." She picked at the worn cotton of a scarf wrapped around her bony wrist. It may have once been bright and colorful, but now looked faded and threadbare. When she noticed Bedeckt's attention she tucked the scarf back up her sleeve and out of view.

"Noted," said Bedeckt, turning back to the priestess. "Isn't one of the basic tenets of the Geborene Damonen that the gods— as creations of man—are unworthy of worship."

"Yes, of course! But they are unworthy because they are *accidental* creations. We have created a new god. A god driven by faith. A god with a purpose. Intent is the key here. We are the first to have designed our god."

"Designed?" asked Bedeckt.

"Yes. A metaphor, if I may—"

"Please no," muttered Wichtig.

"A cave may make a passable home," continued the priestess, ignoring the Swordsman. "It has a roof, an entrance, and perhaps several rooms. But it hardly compares to a man-made keep. A castle, thoughtfully designed, is a far better home." She looked

Bedeckt in the eye. "You get my point?" When Bedeckt only returned a confused stare, she pressed on. "We are *designing* our god. Shaping him. Forging him in the fires of our faith."

Wichtig stood, dropping his empty tankard to the table. "I'm going to forge the fires twixt some lass's nethers. *That* you can have faith in." He groped at his empty money purse and shot Stehlen an accusing look, which she ignored. "Bedeckt, you can pay for this?"

"Aye."

"Next one is on me, then."

*Lying sack of pig dung.* Wichtig fled, out into the street, Bedeckt's gaze following him. The Swordsman would look for trouble and no doubt find it.

Bedeckt turned back to the priestess. "You said you were shaping him." Even with Wichtig gone, he found himself somehow intrigued.

She nodded eagerly. "No other god was willfully created. Born of man's delusions and fears, the old gods are fickle and insane, petty and deluded. By *knowing* how our god will be when he Ascends, we define him. We are creating the perfect god."

Bedeckt lifted an eyebrow as far as the scarring would allow. The beginnings of an idea. A crazy idea, no doubt, but still an idea. "Creating? As in not yet finished? He has yet to . . . Ascend?"

The priestess, eyes bright, leaned in toward her audience. "A boy was born to us, a child of infinite potential. High Priest Konig foretold of a child born not of woman, but of pure faith. The boy was raised in the temple to be tempered in the fires of our belief."

"That shite metaphor again," sneered Stehlen.

The woman shrugged, unperturbed by Stehlen's anger. "It works."

"The boy is at the temple here in Unbrauchbar?" asked Bedeckt, doing his best to sound disinterested. It wasn't too hard.

His skull felt heavy with snot, and when he tried to blow his nostrils clear again, nothing happened but a wet *snurk* sound. *Damned stuff turned to stone in there.*

"No, no," answered the priestess, shaking her head. "He stays in Selbsthass."

"Makes sense. If you are shaping him with your faith, you need him at the heart of it."

The priestess looked to be contemplating patting Bedeckt on a scarred and well-muscled shoulder and then wisely decided against the idea. Instead, she simply said, "Exactly! The farther you get from someone's faith or delusion, the less effect it has."

"It's what saves us from your Konig Furhammer," snapped Stehlen, spitting on the table between them. "A man with such delusions of grandeur would rule the world otherwise."

"Furimmer," corrected the priestess. "If Konig only suffered delusions of grandeur, he'd just be another Gefahrgeist. His delusions surpass such pettiness. His faith creates gods."

"Delusion, you mean," said Stehlen.

"What's the difference?"

Bedeckt scratched at the scarred lump of the remains of his left ear. "Others will follow your example."

"Of course. But we will be first and we will have done it right. Others will scramble to build their gods, but they will be hurried and poorly thought out. Ours is planned. Morgen will be first among the new gods."

Morgen. Bedeckt, making note to remember the name, gave Stehlen a quick glance and saw her almost imperceptible nod of understanding. "You've given me much to think about. Your faith will spread."

"We gain strength with every new follower." The priestess smiled warmly and this time did reach out to touch his arm. "People join us because they know their faith—their hopes and dreams—will shape our god. Ideas are power, and this is a powerful idea. We will be the single greatest faith in the world. We will unite all of mankind under one god—one we all birthed. Konig has foreseen it." She stood and bowed. "It has been a pleasure talking with you and I can see you are intelligent and educated people." Bedeckt grunted at this but made no comment. "Please, come to the city temple anytime to talk further. Blessed will be those whose belief shapes the future."

"I will visit. But it's getting late. Stehlen will see you safely back to the temple."

Stehlen rose from behind the table. "Please," she drawled in her most sincere tone, "this way, my good lady. These can be dangerous times, I will escort you home."

*What in all the arse-sticking hells is Bedeckt planning?* What use was a half-wit, brainwashed church wench? She'd find out soon enough, she supposed. She'd followed his lead often enough to know it usually went somewhere, and it usually went somewhere profitable. At least for her.

Stehlen glanced over her shoulder as she led the priestess from the tavern. Bedeckt looked pale and miserable. He breathed through an open mouth and kept digging at the scarred remains of his ear as if something was lodged in there. *Stupid old fart.* If he died of some old-man illness, she'd kill him.

The priestess bitch seemed pleased as Stehlen held the door for her. She seemed pleased as Stehlen guided her around potholes hidden in the dark. The priestess even seemed pleased when Stehlen rubbed her lean body against hers. True, Stehlen knew she was no great beauty, but she had a firmness that excited a certain type. The priestess was definitely pleased when Stehlen dragged her into a dark alley growling huskily. She only stopped being pleased when one of Stehlen's razor-sharp knives opened her throat and she bled out onto the cobblestones.

Stehlen watched the brainless wench kick and bubble until finally becoming still. She went through the woman's pockets carefully, helping herself to the few coins there. She also took the small handwoven scarf she found and sniffed at it. The scarf smelled faintly of jasmine, no doubt a gift from some equally brainless lover. She tied it around one wrist, pleased with how it looked.

BEDECKT WAS INTO his seventh pint before Stehlen returned. The emptied mugs still littered the table, the barkeep apparently afraid to collect them. The additional ales hadn't improved his pallor and he leaned heavily against the table. The skin on his wan face hung slack and clammy.

She collapsed onto the overturned box opposite him and examined him as he continued drinking and ignoring her. *Stick it, I give up.* "Why did I just kill that woman?"

Bedeckt frowned into his tankard. "Money. If I'm not mistaken."

"I searched her pockets. She had nothing of value."

Bedeckt glanced at the new scarf tied around her wrist and Stehlen hid the hand beneath the table. "I found it."

"I wasn't talking about whatever coin you lifted."

"I told you she had no money," she snapped.

Bedeckt continued as if he hadn't heard. "I have a plan. It needs some fleshing out, but I think it's a good one."

"A good one meaning one making us a lot of money? A good one meaning a plan unlike the last dozen? A good one meaning not stupid and dangerous?"

"I think I got one out of three."

"Bloody brilliant. What's the plan?"

"Kidnap this god-child and ransom him back to the Geborene."

Stehlen flared nostrils as if scenting the foulest shite. "I think one out of three might be generous." She waved at the barkeep and ordered another round of drinks. "I know what Wichtig will say, 'A stupid and ill-thought plan. Sounds like fun.'" She spat on the inn floor. "When do we start?"

"Tomorrow night. If Wichtig is still alive."

*Dare to dream the pretty idiot gets himself killed on his moronic quest to be the World's Most Annoying Swordsman.* Stehlen sniffed at her tankard. *What the hells is that awful smell?*

"So . . . what's the plan for tonight?" she asked.

Bedeckt waved at the barkeep, avoiding eye contact with her. "Drink. Sleep."

"Another brilliant plan." *Arsehole.*

⸻

The morning sun glinted off the dust raised by the gathered crowd. Bedeckt shaded watering eyes with his half hand. His head thumped like some war stallion kept stamping on it. His clogged nose forced him to breathe through his mouth and chalky dust coated his dry tongue. *I should return to the inn and bed. Wichtig can die out here alone.*

He glanced about the crowd. Some fifty people stood in a tight circle, jostling and elbowing for a better view. A massively muscled man, standing in the center of the circle, examined Wichtig with dismissive eyes.

Bedeckt watched the big man rolled muscled shoulders, and took in the fierce and scarred features. *As long as I'm here, I might as well entertain myself.* He patted Wichtig on the back. "Your opponent has done his share of killing and enjoyed it."

Wichtig grunted, too busy scanning the crowd for attractive women to pay Bedeckt much attention.

Bedeckt tried again. "Look at those scars. This man has seen a lot of challengers. And killed them."

Wichtig glanced dismissively at the Swordsman standing

BEYOND REDEMPTION

across the circle. "He's got scars because he's been cut. I have none because I have not. Tell me who the better Swordsman is." He said this loud enough that much of the crowd heard him.

"Ah," said Bedeckt, "but he stands among a gathering of his believers . . . whereas no one here has heard of you."

"Soon he'll lie dead and they will have heard of me." Wichtig pouted at Bedeckt. "I do so appreciate these pep talks. They help focus my attention. First I win the crowd. Then I win the fight."

"You seem awfully sure of yourself."

"I am."

The sad thing was Bedeckt had seen enough of these fights to accept the fact that Wichtig had at least some reason for that confidence.

The scarred Swordsman strode to the center of the clearing and stood with hands on hips. He called out to Wichtig so all the crowd could hear. "You can't beat me. In this city everyone knows I am the most dangerous man alive with a blade."

Wichtig winked at an attractive young lady. His voice rang out deep and resonant and sure. "Ah yes, but there are a hundred cities in a dozen city-states where everyone knows *I* am the Greatest Swordsman alive." He flashed a dazzling smile at the audience. "Sure, a couple of people in this lovely little town—what's this place called, Bedeckt?"

"Unbrauchbar."

"In this shite-hole have heard of you—what's his name, Bedeckt?"

"How the hells should I know."

"Whatever your name is—"

"Vollk Urzschluss."

"—they've heard of you here. But I have traveled far and wide and killed a great many would-be World's Greatest Swordsmen. And I've never heard of you. Sadly, I don't think you're even in the top one hundred."

35

Bedeckt watched Vollk dart glances at the crowd, trying to measure their reaction. Skill with a blade mattered little in the face of the belief of a tightly packed mob.

"Those cities are far away," said Vollk. "Their beliefs matter little here."

"Yes, yes. I've read the books."

Bedeckt rolled his eyes. Wichtig loved to repeat things smarter, more educated people had said as if they were his own words.

Wichtig continued, pontificating to the crowd. "You forget, however, to factor in the numbers involved and the depth of their faith. If I may quote the Geborene Damonen: 'if enough people believe strongly enough, they can change the world entire.'" Wichtig smirked cockily. "I know I am the Greatest Swordsman in the World. Hundreds of thousands of people know I am the Greatest Swordsman in the World. Soon all of this shite-hole will know I am the Greatest Swordsman in the World. You, my friend, will sadly not live to see that day. Such is the fate of stepping-stones."

Bedeckt wondered where Wichtig had heard *that* line.

Vollk glared at Wichtig, looking bewildered. "I'm no stone. Though . . . though I am as tough as one. As strong. You are all talk."

Wichtig bowed to the gathered crowd with a confident flourish. He was, Bedeckt saw, winning them over; they were almost his. Wichtig leered at Vollk. "You *think* you are the best. I *am* the best. You thought with the crowd's faith you could beat me. Now . . . even you know better." He drew his sword and sketched a flourished bow. "Shall we?"

Ten seconds later Vollk Urzschluss lay in the dust bubbling blood from a sucking chest wound. Wichtig stood with his back to the downed Swordsman, basking in the crowd's applause.

Bedeckt watched Vollk's fingers clutch at the dirt, eyes rolling in fear as he struggled to draw breath into lungs filling with blood. "Wichtig, this is a slow and ugly death you leave him. Why not finish him?"

Wichtig patted Bedeckt on the back. "Seeing the man die slowly helps solidify this event in the minds of the witnesses. It is important they remember this clearly if I am to someday be acknowledged as the Greatest Swordsman in the World. These people are useless to me if they forget."

"You are so full of shite."

"All too true. I know I am not as smart, good-looking, skillful, or lucky as I think I am. I know these are my delusions. However, I'm also damned sure I am a lot smarter, better looking, skillful, and lucky than anyone else in this shite little city. Thus they bend to my will. I want them to like me, they like me. I want them to fear me, they fear me. I am a gifted orator."

"You are a delusional idiot," replied Bedeckt. "That you can convince people of anything depresses me. You spout things smarter people said and you yourself don't understand."

Wichtig met Bedeckt's eyes with a cold glare. "No, it is *you* who doesn't understand. The facts don't matter and that's a fact. I wasn't winning the crowd with logic, I was simply sowing seeds of doubt and bolstering my own confidence. Once I knew his followers doubted, I knew he too would doubt." Wichtig glanced dismissively at the man still coughing blood into the dust. "His doubt killed him before I did."

*Sure*, thought Bedeckt, *and your sword in his lungs had nothing to do with it.*

# CHAPTER 4

*There is not one Afterdeath, but thousands. Maybe more. We*
*fear death, and in our fear we seek to escape its finality. But is the*
*farmer worried about populating his Afterdeath with those he has*
*slain? No! What the farmer seeks depends on which breed of vapid*
*religion he clings to. Perhaps he seeks redemption, a chance to right*
*the wrongs of his past. Or perhaps he believes in an Afterdeath of*
*reward for devout worship and piety. If our beliefs define our lives,*
*they certainly define our deaths.*

*But what interests me is what happens after the Afterdeath?*
*The killers among us would have us believe there is simply more*
*death, a progression into deeper and deeper layers of hellish*
*suffering. The Wahnvor Stellung claim death is more like climbing*
*a ladder; each Afterdeath bringing us closer to purity or nirvana.*
*The Täuschung twist everything, claiming only through suffering*
*can we hope to attain godhood.*

*I ask: Where do the souls of babies come from? Are they just*
*magically created out of nothing? No, that's ridiculous! I think*
*once we've either suffered enough or earned redemption, our slates*
*are wiped clean. And we start the entire cycle again.*

—Versklaven Schwache, Gefahrgeist Philosopher

Konig stood unnoticed at the door, watching the thin, blue-eyed, blond-haired god-child play. The Geborene priests had built a miniature city complete with tiny people carved from various colored chunks of wood. The toy city contained a population of twenty-five hundred peasants, one hundred soldiers—fifty of them mounted—and a few hundred miscellaneous animals. Based on Konig's experience, there were not nearly enough chickens for it to be a realistic model. The city also lacked walls and defenses of any kind, but Konig supposed they'd just get in the way of the child's play.

*All my hopes depend on this child.* The boy's unquestioning obedience was critical to Konig's plans, and he could see but three means of achieving it: worship, fear, and love. *Reality, it seems, has a cruel sense of humor.* The method most likely to succeed and with the best results was the one Konig felt least capable of. Inspiring worship and fear was easy for a powerful Gefahrgeist such as Konig, but both had their disadvantages. A god *wanting* to help him, desperate to please, would be far more effective.

*How do I make this boy love me?* Looking back at his own childhood offered no clues. The question left him uncomfortable, tickled at the back of his neck like cold breath. He needed Morgen to need him. *And need is weakness.*

Morgen, future god of the Geborene Damonen, engrossed in his game, hadn't noticed Konig. He marched a squad of forty tiny soldiers up a street toward a crowd of some two hundred peasants gathered in the center of town. Konig watched with interest. The goings-on of a child's mind were as mysterious as anything in the world. *What drives this boy's imagination to play out these tedious games?*

Morgen moved the troops forward one at a time until they faced the crowd of peasants, stopping often to remove minuscule flecks of lint or dust from the table or to adjust the exact positioning of a toy. Many toys he adjusted half a dozen times before he seemed satisfied with how and where they stood. He moved the Captain of the Guard forward to meet with what Konig assumed was the representative of the peasants. If there was dialogue between the two, it all took place in the boy's mind as he sat motionless, looking at the toy people he'd gathered together. Konig saw frustration in the set of Morgen's shoulders and the way he reached for one piece before stopping and then reaching for another. It seemed he could not make up his mind which to move first.

Konig's stifled a gasp of surprise when the wood soldiers suddenly straightened from their fixed positions, hefted tiny weapons, and charged the gathered peasants. In seconds the model city was home to bloodless butchery as soldiers hacked wooden limbs from peasants. What the peasants lacked in weaponry they made up for in numbers. Soldiers were pulled from horses, relieved of their weapons, and either pulled apart or battered with small model rakes and farming implements. Morgen sat back watching, touching nothing. At first it seemed the soldiers had the advantage, but before long more peasants poured into the street. Another sixty soldiers arrived to reinforce the original forty, but at this point over a thousand peasants had joined the melee. Within minutes wooden corpses littered the model city and the surviving peasants armed themselves with weapons from fallen soldiers.

Konig cleared his throat, and Morgen, appearing unsurprised, glanced back at him. The wood toys stopped moving the moment the boy looked away.

"Having a little trouble with your peasants?" Konig asked.

Morgen's slim face lit with a quick smile. "Yes. The peasants are revolting."

"So I see."

"No, it's a joke. I heard it from Aufschlag."

Konig hid his distaste. "Of course." *Perhaps I should keep Aufschlag from the boy in the future.* "Having fun?"

"Yes. Numerical superiority will win over superior weapons. Thus peasants are only peasants because they allow themselves to be peasants. Perhaps it's what they want, though that makes little sense to me. They could as easily be the rulers if they decided."

"That is partly true, but you aren't seeing the whole picture. You're assuming the peasants know they can defeat those ruling. You're assuming it will occur to them to try. Finally, you're assuming many will be willing to die to achieve this goal. And when the peasants take over, who runs things? Who will work the fields? Who will replace the fallen soldiers? Will the peasants then revolt against their new leaders?"

"You're saying there will always be peasants and there will always be leaders?"

"I'm saying peasants need *good* leaders. The heart of any regime or empire is its workers, call them peasants or whatever you like. While their will is strong the regime is strong. Break the workers, break the empire."

Morgen's eyes narrowed in thought and he examined his hands closely. "Is this why there are no large empires anymore?" He dug under a nail to remove something Konig couldn't see.

"Well, part of the reason. The truth is the gods seek to keep mankind divided, weak."

"But what about the empires of old? The entire world used to be one empire, the Menschheit Letzte Imperium, I think it was called."

"Where did you learn this?"

"I read it."

*Who the hells gave Morgen access to these books?* Konig made a mental note to look into it later. "The gods realized a united humanity is not in their best interest."

"And that's why I have to Ascend?"

"Yes. You will unite all mankind and give us a future *we* control. You will bring back the days of empire." The boy stared up at him, unblinking. "You will be the Geborene Damonen god," Konig finished, filling his words with stone certainty.

Morgen glanced about his room, eyes damp. "I know. But . . . I fell down the other day and skinned my knee. I bled and cried. Do gods bleed? Do gods cry?"

*He must have no doubts.* "Gods bleed if they choose to." Konig glanced at Morgen's knee. "Look at your knee now. There is no mark, only perfection. You are healed by the faith of your worshipers as only a god can be." Konig swallowed his own doubts and pressed on. "You moved your toys without touching them. Do you think anyone can do this? I am an extremely powerful Geisteskranken, yet I can not do what you did."

Morgen stared at the motionless wood men and picked one up. He rotated it in his fingers, examining it from all angles, his face set in childish concentration. "It was effortless." He set the peasant back on the table. "I wanted to see what would happen. I'm not even sure I was in control."

"Of course you were. These are signs of your impending Ascension. Reality bends to your will." *And you will bend to mine; you will have no choice.*

The boy's perfect forehead crinkled in a childish frown, and for several seconds he gnawed on his lower lip while examining his fingernails in minute detail.

*What is he looking for, they're perfectly clean. Has he forgotten I'm here?*

Konig cleared his throat and the boy glanced at him, face strangely expressionless.

"What will my Ascension be like?" Morgen asked.

"What do you mean?" asked Konig, both knowing and dreading the question. "Your Ascension will be the moment you become our god."

"In the books I've read . . ." Morgen focused on Konig, stared him straight in the eyes in a way no one had in many years; most people instinctively shied from the gaze of a Gefahrgeist. "People only Ascend after their death."

Konig, face carefully blank, eyes drilling into the boy's soul, willing him to drop the subject, asked, "What books?"

Morgen shrugged and glanced away as if something more interesting had caught his attention. How had he done that? How had he broken eye contact so casually? It should have been a colossal effort.

"Histories and religious texts. The Wahnvor Stellung have an entire pantheon of Ascended heroes as well as their old gods. There's also local demigods, which are minor deities, Ascended people and spirits—"

"I know what a demigod is," Konig snapped, annoyed at being lectured by a child.

"—and in each and every case," Morgen continued as if Konig hadn't spoken, "they Ascended only *after* their death. I have been unable to find a single case of Ascension occurring before death."

*And there it is. Will he ask the question?* "There exists endless knowledge beyond that found in ancient texts," said Konig.

Morgen tilted his small face, thought about this for some moments, and then shrugged it away as if irrelevant, which of course it was. "I must die to Ascend," he said.

*Interesting—not a question.* Had Aufschlag already told the boy? "True," said Konig. "You need not fear—"

"I don't."

Konig quelled a spike of anger at being interrupted yet again. "As I was saying, you need not fear; I will be gentle—"

43

"You."

Konig cursed inwardly. How had that slipped out? He bent until his eyes were on a level with the boy's, forced his will upon the child's young mind. *He must see it* my *way.* "Who else could I trust?"

For an instant doubt flashed across the boy's face. "True," Morgen finally agreed. "Only someone with the best interest of the Geborene at heart must help me Ascend. Otherwise—"

"Yes." Konig didn't want the boy examining this too closely. Contemplation might lead to doubt and that was something Konig could ill afford in his would-be god.

Morgen offered an awkward smile. "I'm glad it will be you. Aufschlag would never forgive himself."

*Which is his greatest weakness.* Konig offered a hand to the lad, did his best to make his flat gray eyes warm and caring. *You must love me.* "Now come," he said, "give me a hug."

Morgen dove into Konig's arms and he awkwardly tussled the boy's hair. Parenting was not something he had expected to do when he took on the mantle of High Priest.

"I won't let you down." The boy's voice was muffled in the fabric of Konig's robes.

"I know. You'll make me proud."

"I'll be a good god. I'll bring back empire like you want."

He stroked the boy's fine blond hair. "I know."

KONIG, LOST IN thought, stalked the oddly shaped and twisting halls of the Geborene church. Acolytes scrambled from his path, pressing themselves to the walls as if they sought to crush themselves flat.

Morgen had been too close to an uncomfortable truth: *Only someone with the best interest of the Geborene at heart must help me Ascend.* The child would never understand, it wasn't that simple. Where did Konig end and the Geborene Damonen begin? Without him at the helm the church would surely falter and fail.

*The boy must die by my hand.* Those whom you slay serve in the Afterdeath. If all else failed, that truth would be his escape. The new god would serve, would save him from his demons.

*Can you do it? Can you kill a child?* Yes; yes, he could. In ordering Aufschlag's experiments, he'd been responsible for countless deaths. *But you've never actually slain anyone before, not really.* He'd never used a blade to cut flesh, never choked life from a throat. Could he poison the boy? *If I did, would the boy still serve in the Afterdeath?* Would Konig have killed Morgen, or would the poison have killed him? It was the sort of annoying question philosophers could discuss for years and never answer. Was poisoning different from killing someone with a knife? Were these just two different weapons? It felt different. Poison felt distancing. Perhaps among the tediously sane beliefs of the masses there could be one answer. The strength of Konig's delusions, however, defined his reality. The truth was, he *believed* it mattered.

And that was all that mattered.

KONIG RETURNED TO his chambers to find his three Doppels waiting. Abandonment sat in the high-backed chair Konig used when receiving important guests. Trepidation and Acceptance stood to either side of the chair.

*This arrangement reveals much. I must watch Abandonment carefully. How long have they been here plotting?*

Abandonment spoke first. "We have not been sitting here, planning to harm you. We are the only ones who will never abandon you. We can't."

Konig snorted. "I haven't suddenly grown daft in the last hour. Save your talk."

"Morgen loves us," said Acceptance quietly. "He loves us and we will do him harm. The one person who ever loved us."

"He'll abandon us," Abandonment snapped at Acceptance. "Like everyone else, you pathetic worm. Morgen is a tool to be used and nothing more. We will pretend to love him as long as it suits us."

Acceptance met Abandonment's eyes, challenging. "We'll kill him."

"That was always the plan. He must Ascend, and we must have control when he does."

"The plan could be changed," pleaded Acceptance. "We could save the boy. We don't *know* he has to die to Ascend. If enough people believe in him, he might Ascend anyway."

A wave of relief washed over Konig. His Doppels remained divided. He stepped forward and said, "No. The plan cannot be changed. What is the love of one child in comparison to the worship of millions? Morgen is a tool to be used and nothing more." He felt a stab of annoyance at mirroring Abandonment's words. Had the Doppel's influence grown beyond the others?

"We know you don't believe that," said Acceptance. "We know what the child means to you."

Trepidation, the quietest, most reticent Doppel, looked from Acceptance to Abandonment and finally to Konig. "The boy is dangerous. His power grows too quickly. We will lose control."

"There is no *we*. I will control him," said Konig, but suspected Trepidation might be onto something. This was the advantage of being able to speak to one's subconscious. Most people floundered about, never really knowing what they thought. He might not trust them, but in a way, they were the ones he could most trust. "Tell me the rest, Trepidation."

"Are Morgen's powers a sign of the faith of the Geborene believers, or are they his own delusions taking form? Are we creating a god, or just an extremely powerful Geisteskranken?"

"Is there a difference?" asked Konig. "Does it not make sense he becomes a Geisteskranken before Ascending? If anything, this tells us our plans are working." He growled in anger and corrected himself. "*My* plans."

"No," whispered Trepidation. "This is too fast. The boy must have been unbalanced to begin with. If his powers develop too fast, we will be unable to force his Ascension. He may fall short of being a god, but a Geisteskranken backed by the worship of all Selbsthass could overpower us."

"No," disagreed Acceptance. "The child loves us. He trusts us."

"And you are a fool to trust him." Abandonment rose from the chair and paced the floor, his crimson robes whispering against the thick carpet. The Doppel mimicked Konig's gait perfectly—obviously.

Did Abandonment's distrust refer to Morgen or himself? He often suspected a flow of subtext beneath everything his Doppels said and did. It seemed they communicated on a level he could detect but not comprehend. As he felt earlier, he could trust them, but only inasmuch as he could trust in himself to understand them—and right now, there was doubt.

Trepidation sat in the now-empty chair. "If Morgen understands his power, he will become very dangerous. We'd be fools not to consider the possibility he might be using us for his own ends."

Acceptance looked distraught and raised his hands as if in supplication. "He's just a boy. A child. We created who he is."

"No," Trepidation disagreed. "We create who he will *become*. We have no idea what kind of person this child *is*. We must kill him now and start the experiment over. With what we have learned from our failures, the next batch would certainly succeed."

Konig chuckled, relief flooding him as he realized what the Doppels were trying to do. "Ah, I see. Yes, begin the experiment again. Of course." He glanced at the reflections of himself gathered in the massive mirror, a crowd of identically gaunt, bald men. They hungrily watched the goings-on in a world they couldn't touch. Konig turned to glare at each of the Doppels in turn. "Think me a weak-minded fool, do you? This experiment took a decade and I shudder to think how strong the three of you might be ten years from now. If I start again I doubt I'll survive to see its completion. You want to control the god yourselves. Well, my sneaky little Doppels, that will not happen. I will raise this god. I will harness his power. I will bottle the three of you forever." He pointed at Trepidation. "Out of my chair."

"We've just been keeping it warm with our imaginary asses," said Acceptance, sketching a quick bow. Once Konig sat in the now-vacated chair, Acceptance added, "We shall never overthrow you."

Konig frowned at the Doppel. "But you shall try."

Acceptance shrugged. "Possibly. But you shall always be the real ass."

Konig saw Acceptance's quickly hidden grin and the covert look the three Doppels shared. Had they tricked him, or did they now seek to confuse the matter by making him think they'd tricked him? It didn't matter.

Morgen would be his salvation . . . and their doom.

# CHAPTER 5

*A sane man is simply a man afraid to unleash his inner demons.*

—HALBER TOD, COTARDIST POET

Stehlen examined the temple from her place in an alley not nearly as dark and narrow as she would have liked. The church, a run-down building with stone walls, looked like it had undergone recent repairs. The Geborene must have fixed this place up when their diseased religion spread here. Whoever ran this filthy little city-state was a fool for allowing them in. Priests were vermin; they spread ideas like rats spread plague, and once they'd infected the hearts and minds of the people, it was hard to get them out.

While that self-aggrandizing twit, Wichtig, was off trying to kill the local Greatest Pigsticker, Stehlen had work to do. Were there justice in the world, Wichtig would be slaughtered and life could go on without him. Not to say she wouldn't miss him; the idiot never seemed to notice when she borrowed money. Sure, he might *claim* he'd noticed, but she knew he lied. Bedeckt was more dangerous to borrow from. And sometimes she felt a little guilty. That's why she always lent him money if he asked and never asked for it back.

Stehlen leaned against a rickety wood wall, pretending not to be there. A gaggle of whores, gossiping among themselves, passed by, darting suspicious glances in her direction.

"You only see me because I don't care," she called to the whores, who hastened their pace.

*Gods, this is boring.*

Bedeckt's plan was shite anyway. As always. How could she casually loiter outside a church in such a small city in the middle of the day?

After half an hour of trying to look inconspicuous standing alone on a mostly empty street, she gave up and decided to come back later.

Plans were for people too stupid to think on their feet. Better to deal with things as they happened instead of plotting for hours only to have everything go tits up the moment you tried to put your plan into action. That was Bedeckt's thing. The grizzled old bastard would spend days planning something Stehlen could finish in minutes.

Stehlen spat in the dust and tried to run a hand through her hair. Her fingers got caught up in something crusty and she gave up. Snarling, she went in search of a tavern. It would have to be one Bedeckt wasn't sitting in, as he had told her to watch the church and get a feel for the movements of the priests.

"Useless."

FOUR HOURS LATER and under cover of darkness she returned to the Geborene Damonen church. The city died the moment the sun dropped below the horizon. The streets became sullen and empty; or maybe that was her. Only brothels and taverns showed signs of life. The stained light of lanterns and candles shone mutedly through grubby windows, creating odd patches of street lit dirty gold. Stehlen avoided the light and crept along the walls, alert for piles of refuse. Though her night vision was excellent, more often than not her nose told her first when she was about to step in something unsavory.

*Why the hells am I hiding?*

Stehlen looked up and down the empty street. She should just walk in the front door and get this done. A last look showed her she was alone. Stehlen spat and marched up the front steps to the church's main entrance. *Damned if I'll skulk around the back just to please Bedeckt.*

The large doors were unlocked and unguarded and she slipped inside. No stupid plan. No mucking about in the garbage dump behind the church. It was nice to enter such a place as a civilized person for once.

Stehlen, checking that her sword and knives sat loose in their sheaths, strode down the hall. She figured the laundry room would be somewhere near the back of the temple. Heavy walls constructed of fieldstones were entirely undecorated and the stone floor had been worn smooth by generations of shuffling feet. After minutes of wandering at random she realized she'd completely lost her sense of direction. She stopped, listened intently, and then followed the muted sound of soft snoring to its source.

The sleeping priest couldn't have been much over nineteen. Fair-haired and only beginning to show a scruff of facial hair, he was boyishly attractive. Had she more time and less specific instructions from Bedeckt, she might have tried to seduce him in the dark. Instead she clamped a hand over his mouth and pressed the blade of her knife against his throat. He awoke with a muffled squeak and froze in terror.

Stehlen leaned forward to hiss in the young man's ear. "Tell me where the laundry room is."

"Mnmmnph," he said though her hand.

"Smartarse. Just point."

He pointed, and when she glanced to see where he was pointing, she felt him tense. She reacted without thought, driving the knife up through his chin and into his brain.

Stehlen wiped the blade off on the bedsheets. "See," she whispered to the corpse, "if you think quickly you don't need a plan." She took a quick look around the room and helped herself to a few knickknacks and what little coin she found. *Damned priests are always destitute.*

In the hall she ran into two more priests and killed them both. Their opened throats made for an impressive mess.

*Just have to think and react quickly. No problem.*

In the kitchen she found two women scrubbing pots and preparing the next day's meals. With a weary shrug she killed them too.

She found the laundry room littered with dirty robes and even dirtier underclothes. The majority of the robes were plain spun brown, but she found a few much rougher-looking sets of gray robes, and one set in expensively finished burgundy. It didn't take much to figure out the ranking system. Burgundy on top, gray on the bottom. Whoever owned the burgundy robes must have been pretty small, but they looked like they'd fit her comfortably. Stehlen laughed at the thought of outranking Bedeckt and the World's Greatest Blithering Idiot. She took a moment to sniff out the largest and least offensive brown robes for Bedeckt—not that the thoughtless bastard would appreciate her efforts—and a set of gray robes reeking of sour sweat and pig shite for Wichtig.

Then she contemplated her escape. She could stumble around the unlit backyard with an armload of dirty laundry and hope she didn't fall into the temple's midden pit or simply walk out the front door. The choice was easy.

On the way out she killed another priest and then stopped at the main entrance when she heard yelling from within the temple. Someone had found one of the corpses. With a disgusted grunt she dropped the robes on the floor and headed back into the temple.

*How many damned priests can there be?*

Fifteen, apparently.


STEHLEN DUMPED THE robes in her room and met up with Wichtig—unfortunately still alive—and Bedeckt in the bar.

Bedeckt waited until she had a pint in front of her before speaking. He had a strange set of manners; he'd cut throats without flinching and for little or no reason, but business always came after you had your pint.

"Is it done?" Bedeckt asked. His skin hung slack and pale. He looked like he'd been dead a week.

"You look like shite," she said.

"Is it done?"

*Fine, be like that.* "Yes." She flared her nostrils at Wichtig.

"Good," said Bedeckt.

"You smell worse than usual," said Wichtig, sniffing at her. "And that's saying something."

"Borrow clothes from the laundry room, chances are they're dirty."

"There wasn't a pile of clean clothes?"

"No."

"We know how much you like the smell of sweaty old men."

"Please." Bedeckt shot Wichtig a warning glance, which the Swordsman pretended to ignore. "Everything went smoothly? No problems? No complications?"

"No. No complications. Smooth as silk." She stared into her pint mug. The old fart feared complications more than death.

Bedeckt sighed tiredly and asked, "What happened?"

"Nothing. Not much."

"And?"

"Ran into a priest in the hall. Had to kill him."

Wichtig's smile grew and she wanted to put her fist in it. Bedeckt, however, on the scent of something, worried at it like starving dog.

"You hid the body, right?"

"Of course!" Stehlen did her best to sound offended.

"No one will find anything until tomorrow at the earliest, right?"

"Yeah. Might even have a couple of days."

"Okay, one dead priest is not too bad."

Stehlen stared into her pint mug again.

Bedeckt groaned. "Shite. What?"

"Killed a scullery maid as well."

"A maid? Why?"

"Maybe a couple."

"A couple?"

Stehlen glared into the mug. *Why won't he just drop it?* "Maybe four. Everything went as planned."

Wichtig guffawed. "The plan was to kill four maids and a priest and steal dirty laundry? See what happens when the two of you try and get anything done without consulting me first? You're both hopeless."

"Might have been more than one priest," Stehlen admitted grudgingly.

Bedeckt's eyes widened and he paused to take a long pull from his pint. He carefully replaced the mug on the table and signaled the barkeep for another. "Exactly how many people did you kill tonight?"

"Don't be ridiculous."

"*Exactly* how many."

"Couldn't possibly keep count. Too busy. Shite," swore Stehlen, "how many people *you* kill today?"

"None."

"Well, how about that day back in—"

"Fine, forget it. We'd best leave."

Bedeckt made to rise from the table but Stehlen stopped him with a hand on his arm. He looked awful. Sitting awhile longer might not fix anything, but it couldn't hurt. He looked like he was about to fall over anyway.

"No rush," she said. "Might have days."

Bedeckt stared at her like she'd lost her mind. "Days?"

*What doesn't he understand?* "Yeah. Killed everyone in the temple. Dozen or so priests. Half-dozen maids and cooks. Couple stableboys."

"Damn, I'm impressed, girl." Wichtig laughed, showing annoyingly straight white teeth. "Great plan. This way, if everything goes badly, we can turn you in for the reward and still make a handy profit."

Stehlen shot him a sour look. She'd have to remember to keep his robes somewhere stinky—maybe she could use them as a horse blanket—until it was time for him to wear them.

Bedeckt accepted the pint from the barkeep, finished it, and ordered another before the man turned from the table. "I told you to steal some priest's robes and make sure they wouldn't be missed. I told you to keep it quiet."

"The robes won't be missed," said Stehlen.

"Because dead people don't need spare robes," quipped Wichtig.

"Kept it quiet too," pointed out Stehlen.

"Quiet like a graveyard," added the Swordsman.

"Did it to throw them off our trail," she extemporized. "If I'd just stolen robes, they might figure out why. In all the chaos, they won't even notice the missing robes."

"Dead people don't notice much," added Wichtig, looking thoughtful.

Bedeckt grimaced. "You're both insane. All I wanted was for you to steal some robes."

Wichtig gave Stehlen an appraising glance. "She makes sense to me."

# CHAPTER 6

*Theocracy is the art of thinking together.*

—Konig Furimmer

The knight in the book Morgen read thought he was special. He certainly acted like he was special, though as far as Morgen could tell, he had yet to do anything of note. Sure, predictably enough the knight would eventually kill someone evil, but did this justify acting special *now*?

Everyone thought they were special, and maybe they were in some small way. Morgen couldn't be sure; a lot of people seemed awfully not special. But he *was* special. Superspecial, and he knew it. He would be a god.

*Wait! Like the knight, I haven't yet done anything particularly special.* Was he special now, or would he be special later?

There was a quiet knock on the door and the High Priest entered his study room. Morgen smiled up at Konig, who stood ramrod straight, arms crossed. The High Priest stared at him for several seconds before returning the smile. *Strange how he does that. It's like he has to decide to smile before anything happens on his face.*

"How go your studies?" Konig asked, dropping the smile.

Morgen glanced at the bookshelf and the books arranged there in a complex system involving their age, the color of the spine, subject, author, and how much Morgen enjoyed reading them. Aufschlag always said they were random, but they weren't. Morgen grimaced at the books. The tome on the Menschheit Letzte Imperium . . . did its spine project just ever so slightly farther out than the other books? He leaned in and nudged it back. *There, better.* "Well," Morgen answered finally. "Though this"—he held up the storybook he'd been reading—"probably doesn't count as study."

Konig waved it away without looking at the book. "You'll learn something from everything you read. Not all knowledge is to be found in great tomes."

That sounded wise. Could he truly learn something from even the lowest, most vulgar source?

"Am I special?" Morgen asked.

"Of course. You will be a god."

"I *will* be a god. I'm not one yet. Am I special now?"

"Yes, if just because of your potential. No one else has what you have."

"So my potential makes me special."

"Yes."

"My potential makes me special even if I don't Ascend?"

"You will Ascend."

"But if I didn't?"

"You will," Konig said, leaning forward to stare into Morgen's eyes.

*Why does he always do that when he really wants me to believe something?*

"But potential matters?" Morgen asked.

Konig stood straight again, seemingly content he'd achieved something. "Yes, of course."

"So if I meet someone with great potential, they're special. Even if they never do anything with it."

"I'm not sure I'd word it like—"

"What kind of god will I be?"

The Theocrat blinked, eyebrows crinkling inward. "The right kind."

"What does that mean?"

"You'll be the god the Geborene need."

That made sense. Their faith made him a god and so their faith would shape that god. He'd be what they thought he was.

"What kind of god do the people think I will be?" Morgen asked.

"The right kind."

Was this true? It did make sense. *Why would the people want the wrong kind of god?*

"What kind of god do the people want?"

"The right kind."

It made sense as an answer, but Morgen still felt something was missing.

"Once I become a god, all my decisions will be perfect and godlike?"

"It is not being a god which makes one perfect. The old gods are fallible. We will end all that."

"Fablible?"

"*Fallible.* They make mistakes. The old gods caused more death and misery than . . ." Konig didn't finish.

*More death and misery than what?*

"I can't be fallible. I must be perfect." He checked his hands, examining each fingernail. They were clean. Spotless. "I'll be a perfect god. Clean and mighty."

Konig glanced at Morgen's hands and his eyebrows did that crinkly thing again. "You will be perfect."

Morgen wanted to say more, but Konig awkwardly ruffled his hair, said something about having business to attend to, and left.

"I'm going to make the other gods behave right," Morgen told the empty room. "The way gods are *supposed* to behave."

He'd told Aufschlag about his plan and the Chief Scientist said it was a good one, and a great gift for Konig. Aufschlag also said Konig didn't like bragging and the best thing Morgen could do would be to show him rather than telling him. So it was their secret, his and Aufschlag's, until he Ascended.

Morgen scowled at the book on the Menschheit Letzte Imperium. It sat too far back, leaving a small imperfection marring the beauty of his aligned books. Should he move the others back, or slide it forward? After several minutes' contemplation, Morgen pulled it forward.

# CHAPTER 7

*Most only dare tread the waters of insanity at night as they lie dreaming. Cowards. Dive deep into your psychopathy. Let loose the demons of delusion and know, in the end, when they finally devour you, you swam with sharks.*

—VERSKLAVEN SCHWACHE, GEFAHRGEIST PHILOSOPHER

Aufschlag concluded his report on Morgen's progress and stood waiting. The High Priest paced the room, his Doppels nowhere to be seen, for which the scientist was grateful. They made him nervous with their obvious hatred and mistrust. Gods only knew what they whispered in Konig's ear in Aufschlag's absence.

Still, behind Konig, his many reflections filled the surface of the huge mirror. Faces and fingers pressed that thin boundary between realities, desperate for escape. Aufschlag wasn't sure when the High Priest had become Comorbidic—developing multiple delusions—but he knew Comorbidity to be a sure sign that the end grew near. Konig's delusions grew in strength and numbers and most probably out of his control.

The Chief Scientist swallowed his fear. Without Konig, the Geborene would be lost. The boy must Ascend in time to save the High Priest; he had to. In the back of his mind Aufschlag could almost remember—just moments before he'd entered Konig's chambers—hoping Morgen would Ascend *after* Konig's death. Here, in the powerful Gefahrgeist's presence, such treasonous thoughts became impossible.

Konig caught sight of the mirror and stopped pacing. "Sometimes I think I can hear their voices."

The reflections turned to face him as if they'd heard his words.

"Perhaps we should destroy it," Aufschlag suggested.

"No," said Konig, staring at his reflections. "Mirrorist powers would be useful. Who knows what my reflections might show. Perhaps the future. Maybe I will see events transpiring all around the world."

"Have they shown you anything yet?" Aufschlag asked.

Konig turned away from the mirror, his shoulders sagging. "No. Not yet."

"Perhaps we can move it to another room?"

"No, I can't have them escaping somewhere I can't deal with them immediately."

"But if the mirror is in another room where you are not, your reflections will not be there either."

Konig spun on his heel and left the room, slamming the door closed behind him. Aufschlag stood staring at the reflection of a dozen Konigs and himself.

When had his nose become so bulbous and the veins so broken and red? How did these things creep up on you?

He stared at the mirror, watching as the reflected Konigs turned their backs to him and their attention to his own solitary reflection.

*It was so easy,* he mused, *to forget one's age when not confronted by a mirror.* In his head he thought of himself as nineteen but was almost sixty. He examined the rotund body, the receding chin, the greasy tufts of hair by his ears, and the glistening dome of his skull. He looked seventy, if not eighty.

*This work ages me too quickly.* He rubbed at his nose and marveled—mostly in disgust—at the size and depth of the pores. *I should drink less.* A dry croak of a laugh escaped and he choked it down.

Think not of the cost but of the goal. When the child Ascended, Aufschlag would be repaid for his many sacrifices.

Konig's reflections suddenly launched themselves at his own unresisting reflection and attacked it with teeth and fists. Aufschlag fled the room. Gods only knew what that meant. Did Konig truly hate him so?

Konig stood waiting in the hall. "So?" demanded the High Priest.

Aufschlag shook his head.

Konig gestured toward the stairs. "Come, we are needed."

THE MESSENGER, A young and whip-thin Geborene priest, awaited them in the great hall. His gray acolyte's robes were caked in the dust of the road, his eyes red with exhaustion. The acolyte ignored the towering domed ceiling and great marble pillars as he ignored the rows of defaced statues of long-forgotten gods. He had eyes only for Konig. The acolyte fell to his knees, touching his forehead to Konig's slippered feet. A considerable quantity of dust rained from his hair and onto those fine slippers.

Konig glared down at the back of the acolyte's head. "Rise and report."

The acolyte rocked back and rose to his feet in one smooth and effortless motion. Aufschlag, standing to the right and one pace behind Konig, knew a moment of jealousy. He remembered being able to move like that.

The acolyte bowed again to Konig and nodded to Aufschlag. "High Priest, I bring word from the Mitteldirne temple."

"Mitteldirne?"

"Yes, sir, the capital of Gottlos."

"I know where Mitteldirne is," snapped Konig. "What's the damned news?"

The acolyte bowed in apology and then frowned at the pile of dust on Konig's slippers. He swallowed uncomfortably, looking like he wanted to apologize, but not wanting to further annoy the Theocrat. "Bishop Bombastisch of the . . ." The young priest looked up and met Konig's unblinking gray eyes. He opened his mouth but issued no sound.

"I know who Bombastisch is. I made her Bishop of Mitteldirne."

"Yes, Sir. Unbrauchbar—"

"I know where that is too."

Aufschlag's stomach soured. He'd sent Wegwerfen, the young priestess Konig had commanded him to kill, to Unbrauchbar. Anything directing Konig's attention there could be bad news indeed. If the High Priest discovered his scientist disobeyed an order . . . Aufschlag, thinking of Konig's reflections tearing his own apart, shuddered at the thought.

"Sir." The acolyte glanced again at the dusty slippers before continuing. "The priests of the Unbrauchbar temple have been slain. All of them. The temple staff as well."

Aufschlag choked down a cough of surprise. He'd risked his life to save Wegwerfen and still she'd died? Gods, he was a fool!

"Slain. By whom?" demanded Konig.

"We don't know, Theocrat. Bishop Bombastisch tried to send you a dream message direct but found four of you and countless shadows. She couldn't be sure which was the real you and felt it safer to dispatch me to guarantee you and you alone got the message."

"You rode from Mitteldirne? Bombastisch is a fool! She wasted critically important time."

Aufschlag's guts boiled with acid. Konig would send people to the temple in Unbrauchbar to investigate. They'd report everything, including the names of the dead. Konig would know of Aufschlag's betrayal. The scientist stared at the Theocrat's back. *Kill him. Kill him now before he learns of Wegwerfen.*

The acolyte swallowed his fear. "Sir, Bishop Bombastisch is a powerful Intermetic. She swapped me for someone she knew—a nephew, I believe—who lives on the outskirts of Selbsthass. This isn't my usual body. I was able to bring you the message in little more than a day."

Konig turned gray eyes on Aufschlag and the acolyte looked like he'd just disappointed his father. Or his god. Aufschlag, who had been thinking dark thoughts of murder, found himself suddenly unable to think about anything other than those gray eyes. They were empty like death.

"Could it be the Wahnvor Stellung?" Konig asked Aufschlag. "Could this be the beginning of a bigger attack?"

Konig never failed to surprise Aufschlag; his questions cut straight to the meat of the issue. He saw what no one else saw. Such a thought had not even occurred to Aufschlag. The man's mind was nothing short of amazing. He was a genius! How could Aufschlag have entertained thoughts of violence?

He considered Konig's question. Wahnvor Stellung was the single greatest religion, its temples found in virtually every city-state. If the Wahnvor knew what the Geborene planned, they would definitely seek to put an end to the project. But this didn't fit. The religion was massive; they had the strength and faith of vastly superior numbers and were confident in their reality. Why would they attack such a pitiful little church as the one in Gottlos?

"It's possible," said Aufschlag, "but I don't think so."

"What of the Täuschung?" Konig asked.

"Their following seems confined to the east," answered Aufschlag, surprised the Theocrat had even heard of the ancient sect. "I think they're based in Geldangelegenheiten. They rarely proselytize, haven't grown or changed in thousands of years, and seem more intent on sending souls to their deranged idea of an Afterdeath. 'Swarm,' I believe they call it. They claim there is only one true god, whose sole task is to govern and maintain the rules defining . . ." Aufschlag realized Konig stared at him with growing impatience. "Probably not the Täuschung," he finished lamely.

Konig stood motionless, tall and gaunt, eyes hooded like a bird of prey. No one spoke, waiting for the words of the High Priest.

"Our project threatens everything the Wahnvor believe. When we succeed, everyone will know we have always been right; the gods did not create us, we created them. Their religion will die. If it is not the Wahnvor, we have a new enemy. One we did not previously know of. A much more dangerous enemy." Konig took a deep breath and released it slowly. "I must know for sure." He spun to face the acolyte, who flinched. "Were the Unbrauchbar priests tortured?"

"Most died quickly, throats cut as they went about their duties or lay sleeping."

"But we don't know for sure."

The acolyte opened his mouth to answer but Konig turned away. "I must know what our enemies know. Aufschlag, bring me Gehirn Schlechtes. I will send the Hassebrand. She will bring me answers."

Aufschlag stifled a groan of terror. Gehirn was a lunatic, on the edge of losing control of her delusions, unstable and dangerous. People too long in her presence had a habit of suddenly dropping dead. Surprisingly, fewer burst into flames than Aufschlag would expect; her delusions were far more insidious.

And yet he dared not refuse Konig's request. The Chief Scientist swallowed his fear and excused himself from the proceedings. Gehirn was sure to be found lurking like a damp slug in the deepest bowels of the church.

AUFSCHLAG FOUND THE Hassebrand, as expected, in the church's basement. The woman towered a full head over the Chief Scientist but was far too fat and soft to be physically threatening. It wasn't her physical presence that scared him, it was what went on in that twisted mind. Icy blue eyes on a surprisingly girlish face watched him with hungry interest. She was almost bald, having once again burned her hair to patchy red stubble. He'd never seen her eyebrows and had no idea if she shaved them, couldn't grow any, or burned them off.

*Did she do it on purpose,* Aufschlag wondered, *or did her own fires sometimes break from her increasingly tenuous control?*

Even here, in the darkest, coolest part of the church, Gehirn's robes were sodden, her face bathed in a sheen of sweat. The Hassebrand wore the deep burgundy of a Geborene Bishop even though she held no such rank. The lack of eyebrows gave her an eternally surprised look.

Gehirn lifted her lips, showing pronounced canines. Aufschlag couldn't tell if it was a smile, a sneer, or a snarl. Still, it looked out of place in such a childish face.

"Konig sends me his pet scientist," she said.

Aufschlag ignored the bait, pretending to examine the sweating face with concern. "You look ill. Jaundiced."

Gehirn twitched, blinked rapidly, and frowned suspiciously at Aufschlag. "Someone is poisoning me."

"No doubt. You show signs of impending liver failure."

"They won't get me so easily. I am—" Gehirn dug into a fold in her robes and drew out a handful of faded seeds, nuts, and pocket lint. "I am tricky. Self-sufficient. Impenetrable." She picked at the food before shoving it back into the hidden pocket.

"Very smart. Of course those nuts come from . . . somewhere, don't they?" Aufschlag ignored the Hassebrand's darting look. "Konig wants you in his chambers. Now. He has work for you."

Aufschlag fled the basement as best he could without looking like he was fleeing.

There was a soft knock at the door and Konig, working at his desk, glanced up. "Yes?"

Selbstmörderisch cracked the door open and peeked her head in. A member of his personal cadre of bodyguards, Selbstmörderisch was a Comorbidic. She was both Dysmorphic and Mehrere, grotesquely muscled and usually appearing as two very different—but equally muscular—women.

"Your Holiness, Gehirn Schlechtes is here to see you," she announced with a surprisingly soft voice.

"Show her in."

The Hassebrand, ignoring Selbstmörderisch as if she were beneath notice, ducked her head to clear the doorway and stood, swaddled in heavy robes, before the High Priest. The massive windows had been shuttered for this meeting but the smell of cooking meat still emanated from the fat woman. While she was arguably the most powerful member of the Geborene priesthood, Gehirn's instability made her dangerous. As such, Konig always handled her carefully. He showed his warmest smile as Gehirn entered.

"Old friend, you look good."

"I do?" Blue eyes glinted deep in the burgundy hood. Konig was reminded once more that when Gehirn finally snapped, the death toll would be catastrophic. "I think someone might be try-ing to poison me."

That again. There was always something with the fat Hasse-brand, someone always plotted against her. "I will look into it," promised Konig sincerely.

"You will?" asked Gehirn, voice choked with hope.

"No one threatens my friends." Konig sat motionless, un-blinking, staring into those cold eyes until he felt the Hassebrand submit to his will. "You are critical to me," said Konig, manipu-lating Gehirn's emotions. "I *need* you."

"You do?" She looked ready to cry with gratitude; her need was disgusting.

"Yes. I have work for you. Work only you can do. Work I trust with no one else."

"Of course, Your Holiness."

Konig did his best to ignore the stench of burning flesh leak-ing from the voluminous robes. "Someone killed my priests in Unbrauchbar. All of them. You—" He was suddenly aware that Gehirn was staring, eyes wide, at something behind him. Damn. His Doppels had entered the room unbidden. He willed them to silence and pressed on. "You will go to Unbrauchbar, find out who did this."

Gehirn glanced at the sun knifing between the cracks in the shutters and whimpered. "To Unbrauchbar?" The smell of burned meat grew stronger. "I will leave the moment the sun sets, Your—"

"You will leave now. A carriage has been prepared."

Gehirn stifled a sob. "But . . . the sun—"

"Three of my Krieger will accompany you."

"Do . . . do you trust these priests?"

"Yes," said Konig.

"No!" snapped Abandonment.

Gehirn's eyes widened with fear.

"What my Doppel means"—Konig shot a warning glance over his shoulder at Abandonment—"is that while I trust these priests as much as I trust anyone, I have total faith in no one." Gehirn's disgusting little eyes peered at him from within the cowl. It was so difficult to read the Hassebrand, so hard to know if he really had her. "No one but you, I mean," Konig added.

Gehirn bowed low. "I will not fail, Your Holiness. I will travel to Unbrauchbar as fast as your Krieger can take me. I will discover the identity of the murderers and I will bring upon them your vengeance." A breath of smoky air hissed between clenched teeth and Konig could just make out the bright teeth and over-large canines glinting from within the cowl's shadows. "I will purify them in fire. There will be naught left when I am finished. Not even their souls will survive to flee to the Afterdeath."

"I must know who was behind the attack on the Unbrauchbar temple." Konig hammered the Hassebrand with an unblinking gray glare, daring her to disobey. "Burn the perpetrators, but you must report to me your findings. I *must* know what is happening."

Gehirn Schlechtes bowed again and backed toward the door. "Yes, Your Holiness. I will discover the truth. I will punish those responsible." Again Konig saw the toothy grin glinting from within the cowl.

▬

Gehirn stumbled from the High Priest's room racked with sadness and loneliness. Her every effort to please Konig ended with looks of disgust and fear. But she'd prove her worth to Konig and his vicious little Doppels.

Gehirn stalked long passages lit by guttering torches and dodged past the few windows, directing hisses of hatred at the sun. She could feel her skin crack and peel and the smell of burned flesh followed her everywhere. Other priests and staff ducked from her path, cowering as she passed. She'd burn everything someday. Every ounce of hurt their fear caused her would be repaid in full.

She'd burn the world.

But not before doing what Konig asked of her. Gehirn's need to serve, to be part of something, quenched even her desire to burn. At least for now. Someday even Konig would not be enough to halt her descent into madness.

Gehirn stopped in the center of the long hall, her gaze darting about. She was very much alone. Though there had been people about a moment ago, suddenly the hall was empty.

Assassins? Here in the center of Geborene power? No, she decided, too obvious, too unsubtle. When they came for her, there would be no warning.

She did her best to shrug off the paranoia and hurried to her basement chambers. There was just enough time to burn a few of her imprisoned pet cats before rushing off for Unbrauchbar. She shivered with anticipation at the thought of yowling screams, flickering flames, and bubbling flesh. Only in fiery death could she find release.

iiiiiiiiiiiiiiiii

The three Doppels stood in a triangle watching each other carefully. Konig was off to some unknown meeting. They cared not.

Trepidation stood ramrod straight, his arms crossed tightly over his chest as if trying to protect himself from the world around him. "Gehirn is dangerous."

Abandonment glanced at the mirror and the reflections still gathered there. None reflected the positions of the Doppels. "Gehirn will betray us."

"She's too tall," added Trepidation.

The two Doppels looked to Acceptance.

"Gehirn is powerful and dangerous," agreed Acceptance. "But her power is also her weakness. She is alone and afraid and this means I can manipulate her. She will be the vehicle of our vengeance. Gehirn will free us from Konig."

"We can't trust the Hassebrand," counseled Abandonment.

"I said nothing of trust. Once I have used her, we will kill her."

"Konig sent her away," pointed out Abandonment.

"We can wait. When Gehirn returns, Konig shall burn." Acceptance glanced toward the mirror. "And we'll have to break the damned mirror before they become powerful enough to compete with us."

Trepidation huddled deeper into his arms. "Konig fears his Mirrorist tendencies more than he fears us. That fear blinds him. It distracts him. He still thinks we're useful."

"We *are* useful and we will remain useful. For now." Acceptance studied the reflections gathered in the mirror. Did they listen? Could they hear what the Doppels planned?

One of the reflections gave him the slightest nod.

*Interesting. Perhaps the reflections* could *be of use.*

"We don't break the mirror," he said. *For now.*

# CHAPTER 8

*Delusion is the food of the gods and they never go hungry.*

—HALBER TOD, COTARDIST POET

Gehirn huddled in the blacked-out carriage as it thundered along an unfinished road—really little more than a cleared path with occasional markers—toward Unbrauchbar. Every now and then she'd crack the curtain of the rear window and peer out until the burning sun drove her back into the darkness. A roiling storm cloud of dust chased the carriage.

Three Krieger priests, the warrior sect of the Geborene Damonen, sat up front on a bench meant for two. The bulk of their thick padded armor, double-chain hauberk, longswords, and arbalests no doubt made for a tight fit.

*Why don't they want to ride with me?* Was something wrong? Did they know something she didn't? *Gods, this could be a trap! Have I become too unstable?* Maybe Konig planned to have her killed somewhere safely distant.

Gehirn worried, scratching at the back of her hands until they bled.

No, she was being silly. Three lowly Krieger could never kill her, no matter how well trained or psychotically loyal. They didn't sit back here because . . . because they didn't like her.

Gehirn stopped scratching and the wounds closed in seconds and faded to invisible in minutes.

The Krieger drove the horses hard, exchanging them for fresh teams at each town. Not until night fell and the last crimson smear of sunlight vanished did they slow their mad pace and pull off the path to make camp. A large tent was set, wood gathered, blankets laid out, and the horses brushed down, watered, and fed.

Gehirn gently lowered her portly frame from the wagon and stood peering around the campsite. She remained covered head to toe in heavy burgundy robes, the cowl still pulled forward to hide her face. She stopped when she noticed the wood piled at the ready.

"A fire?" Gehirn grinned maniacally at the three Krieger, who had all frozen in their various tasks upon her disembarking from the carriage. "I love a good fire. Camaraderie. People drawn together to share in its light and heat." She gestured at the wood and it burst into flames. In the brief moment her hand was exposed to the moonlight it reddened as if sunburned. Gehirn giggled. "Play with fire and you'll get burned. That's what Daddy always said."

*Yeah, and Daddy burned just fine.*

The Krieger, hardened warriors all, ignored her, continuing in their tasks. Gehirn watched. Insanity, she supposed, in those with power wasn't a comfortable conversational topic; it was a simple fact. If a single sane person ever shaped the world in any meaningful way, Gehirn hadn't heard of them.

The Krieger, she knew, suffered their own delusions of grandeur. To have volunteered for this position, they must. They knew the Geborene would create their god and they knew the Krieger would play a critical role in his Ascension. These were the last words Konig spoke to them before they were ritually deafened to prevent another Gefahrgeist from infecting their faith. The force of Konig's faith defined their reality.

Gehirn Schlechtes felt drawn to the fire and stood before it, rapt and lost in the flickering tongues. Flame spoke to her, loved her, and made her whole. The three Krieger sat around the fire, legs crossed, weapons laid out and lovingly polished. A pot of thick soup simmered on an iron tripod over the fire.

"The first gods were born of man as he sat shivering and terrified in the dark." The Krieger did not pause in the care of their weapons and armor. Gehirn continued, knowing they couldn't hear and not caring. "The Wahnvor Stellung would have us believe the gods gave us fire, that the gods lifted us from savagery. This is laughable. We hardly need the gods to gift us with that which we can so easily create for ourselves. And what of this lift from savagery?"

The Krieger prided themselves on their fierce will to do violence, their intense and overwhelming ferocity. Someone open to atrocity is far more dangerous than someone afraid of it. This was the core of their training, the center of their lives, and the bloody meat of their souls. *No doubt they'd agree there has been no lift from savagery.*

Gehirn flashed teeth in a canine leer. "I see such lovely savagery right here before me. The Wahnvor gods are the result of the delusions of prehistoric mankind. Is there power without insanity? No. Are the elder gods powerful? Yes. Are they delusional? Obviously. No doubt they believe they created us, but their delusions will wither in the fires of our faith. Ah! And we come full circle back to fire."

The Krieger, ignoring Gehirn, carefully stowed their weapons and spooned soup into sturdy wood bowls.

Gehirn stared into the fire; she felt distant and lost. "Do you know what we love about fire?" she asked the silent Krieger. "It's not the heat. It's not the light, though both those things are useful in their time and place. We love the unpredictable nature of flame. Look." She gestured at the fire. "You can't guess where the next licking tongue of flame will rise. And the larger the fire, the more unpredictable it is, and the more beautiful it becomes." She stared into the fire until it consumed her vision. "We are, each and every one of us, addicted to chaos. Gorgeous, devouring, chaos. Every visceral pleasure comes from the moment when we truly lose control. That moment when our minds white out and thought vanishes, when the fire within us devours all rationality. Sex. Fire. It's all the same."

One of the Krieger held a bowl up to Gehirn in offering.

"No, thank you. I believe someone is trying to kill me." The Hassebrand eyed the proffered bowl suspiciously, her good humor fading. "The soup is probably poisoned."

The warrior priest grunted, dumping the stew back into the pot.

Gehirn reached into her robes and drew forth the pouch of dried seeds and nuts she kept there. This was the only food she had dared to eat in many years and she went to great lengths to ensure no one knew where her supplies came from. Only her delusional self-image could possibly maintain the portly frame she wore. Were her delusions less powerful, she suspected she would be rake thin and at the edge of starvation.

The fire dwindled and Gehirn stood watching until the embers lost the last of their warm glow. Though each and every stage of a fire was a thing of beauty, the Hassebrand most enjoyed the final stages, the nuggets of radiating heat and dim light nestled in soft ashes of devoured reality. She loved to watch the wind-scattered ashes rising into the air, the gentle wraiths that came after the inferno.

*Fire is not all about destruction, but also about rebirth.* Gehirn smiled at the thought. She did, however, so love the destruction.

Two of the Krieger lay sleeping while the third kept watch. Gehirn nodded to the warrior as she returned to the carriage to sleep out the remains of the night.

AS SHE PEERED *from her blankets, the carriage seemed larger than she remembered, and a silver cage holding half a dozen tawny cats hung from a bronze hook in the ceiling. Their warm, musty smell reminded her of fur and life and her father, and she wanted to burn them but knew she shouldn't.*

*Not yet.*

*By the far wall, impossibly distant in his cramped carriage, an altar of streaked black and darkest bloodred marble awaited her. She was supposed to sacrifice something to someone, but couldn't remember what or whom.*

*Or was she supposed to sacrifice someone to something?*

*Aufschlag, that greasy stain of a scientist, once told her that long, long ago—thousands of generations before the birth of the Menschheit Letzte Imperium—humans burned sacrifices to the first gods. It made so much sense.*

*Why did we ever stop? No wonder the old gods abandoned us.*

*The cats were gone, their scent lingering on the air, haunting the back of her nose. Small souls, they were unworthy sacrifices; she knew that now.*

*They're coming to kill you.*

*They?*

*To kill you.*

*Who?*

*Wrong question.*

*Gehirn huddled deeper into her blankets, a little girl hiding in a massive bed.*

*Too late for that. Far too late. They're coming.*

*Who would want to kill her?* She laughed, a shivering titter, and gathered the blankets under her chin. *Gods, who didn't want to kill her?*

She sat on the hard marble of the altar, feeling the cold stone on her bum even through her gray robes. *Gray? An acolyte? She'd never been an acolyte, Konig had made her a Bishop the day they met.*

*Remember that day?*

*Yes.*

*She knew then where she belonged. She was useful, Konig had plans. He was going to change the world and she was going to—*

*Burn herself to a cinder in his service.*

*Hadn't she been in bed?*

*It didn't matter, they were coming to kill her.*

Closing her eyes, she imagined three cold souls moving through the dark, weapons drawn, toward her carriage.

*The Krieger. Konig's Krieger.*

Gehirn stuck out her tongue and went cross-eyed watching the glistening saliva steam away.

*Let them come. These were souls worthy of sacrifice to those primordial gods.*

*Primordial. The word reminded her of mud and fifty thousand years of blood. And the smell of cow shite.*

*Wait. What was the right question?*

*Why?*

*Because I want to . . . Oh.*

The Krieger would never act alone and never of their own volition; Konig would never allow such unscripted freedom. Either someone had taken them, conscripted their will, bent the psychotically loyal Krieger to their own purpose. . .

*Or Konig sent them to kill you.*

*No. Konig loved her.*

*Well, at least he* needed *her. He said so!*

*Of course, if they killed her, it didn't much matter who sent them. Did it?*

Gehirn watched the three Krieger approach her carriage. She was death, invisible and everywhere, not cloaked in black, just empty. It wasn't that they didn't see her, they couldn't. She wasn't there.

She didn't walk, her feet didn't touch the ground. But she didn't hover or fly either. She just moved, ghosting forward quieter than a hunting cat.

*Where did the cats go?*

*Didn't matter.*

A Krieger loomed large before her, his broad-shouldered back looking more like a wall or something she should hang art on. She giggled and he stopped, head turning as if searching for the sound.

*He's deaf.*

*I know.*

*Then why—*

*I don't even know his name.*

*So?*

*Shouldn't I know the names of the people who will serve me in the Afterdeath?*

*Ha. Now you ask that, after so much murder. Anyway, somehow I don't think your fate involves having your every need seen to by the likes of worshipful Krieger.*

Truth be told, she couldn't imagine anyone serving her in the Afterdeath. Odd, as she'd killed so many.

*So, no point in asking his name; not that he'd hear the question anyway.*

*How many cats await you in the Afterdeath?*

*Do you suppose they do that? Are people plagued in the Afterdeath by the souls of every chicken and cow and goat they've ever eaten?*

*No one believes that.*

*I bet someone does. Somewhere. I wonder if the Krieger likes cats.*

*Probably. Who doesn't?*

*I'm going to tell him.*

*He won't thank you.*

*No one ever does.*

*Gehirn leaned forward and whispered the secret of fire in his ear.*

*The Krieger collapsed, boneless and loose.*

*See? No thanks whatsoever. Why do you think they're all men?*

*Lots of Krieger are women.*

*But Konig just sent men with me. Does that mean something?*

*Gehirn approached the next Krieger, who'd suddenly sat in the dirt and begun crying. His face, wretched with tears and snot, looked like an ill-fitted mask.*

*Poor thing.*

*She leaned in close, tickled his ears with her lips. She told him a secret and he sighed smoke as he curled up like a scared kitten. He lay motionless, still and dead, smoke leaking from his nostrils.*

*His mask slipped and she recognized the face beneath.*

*Da—*

*No. Turn away.*

*The last Krieger watched her with sad eyes.*

*Where did the cats go?*

*He didn't answer.*

*Can I tell you a secret?*

〰〰〰〰

The instant the first ray of sunlight stole over the horizon, Gehirn's eyes snapped open; even though she couldn't see it, she felt its malignant presence like a crushing weight. It wanted her, hungered for her pale and tender skin. A quick glance showed her the shutters and heavy drapes were all in place. No hint of light wangled its way into the carriage's dark interior. Nonetheless, she huddled into her voluminous robes and pulled the cowl up to cover her face. At the mere thought of direct sunlight she smelled the sweet bouquet of burning flesh.

Hints of a dream, fading quickly, tingled like soft breath on the back of her neck. She remembered fire. Hardly odd, as most of her dreams and nightmares involved burning something. Or someone.

Why were they not moving already? Gehirn had expected to awaken to the rocking motion of carriage travel. It was unlike the Krieger to sleep in.

She giggled and bellowed, "Why are we not moving?"

No answer came but the cheerful sound of morning birds greeting a new day.

Gehirn gently cracked the drapes open and flinched back with a squeal of pain as sunlight stabbed viciously into the dark interior of the carriage. Her right eye felt as if it had been splashed with molten lava. The carriage reeked of burned meat and singed hair. Cowering on the carriage's floor, Gehirn replayed the scene she had witnessed before losing the sight in that eye: Three corpses sprawled about the dead fire, twisted as if they had died in great agony. There had been no marks upon them.

"I knew it." Gehirn laughed. "I told them the soup was probably poisonous. I knew it!"

After sitting in thought, Gehirn surrendered to the obvious. She had no choice. Konig had sent her on a mission and that mission must be completed. She wrapped her face in black cotton gauze, leaving it thinnest around her eyes so she could just make out a smear of the world around her. Dragging the cowl back into place, she tied it tight so the wind would not dislodge it. Finally Gehirn drew thick gloves into place and tied her sleeves tightly at the wrist. Once armored against the sun, she stifled a whimper of terror and crawled from the carriage to face that ultimate fire. In seconds she streamed sweat. Thin smoke rose around her. Even through the thick cloth she could feel her skin reddening. This would be a very painful couple of days. Only the knowledge that she healed quickly made it even possible to bear.

The Hassebrand stood over the three contorted corpses.

"And yet still they made no sound. Impressive. I shall have to compliment the Master Krieger. Ohne Seele trains his people well."

Though a small fortune in weapons and armor lay scattered, they were useless to Gehirn, who'd had no martial training. She shrugged philosophically.

A curl of smoke, rising from one of the Krieger's ears, caught Gehirn's attention. Kneeling, she leaned close and rolled the stiff corpse onto its back. Empty sockets, raw and red, scalded clean of flesh and blood, stared at her. Now that she was closer she saw the man's hair was singed and steam rose from his bright pink scalp. She wrinkled her nose at the stench. Reaching a gloved hand out, she moved the Krieger's head, lifting it to test the weight. The skull felt impossibly light. Even through the thick glove she felt heat radiating from the bone.

*His brains have been boiled away. This skull is empty!*

Gehirn checked the other two Krieger, seeing similar signs. Who could have—

She remembered her dream. She remembered the feel of her lips on a man's ear. She remembered whispering the secret of fire.

*But in the dream they were coming to kill me.*

Had that been true, or had she killed Konig's Krieger as they slept, no doubt entertaining their own fantasies of violence?

*No. Konig needs me. He said so.*

Hadn't she said that in the dream?

Now, in the cleansing truth of sunlight, she understood that the soup had not been poisoned.

"This is hardly my fault," Gehirn said to the sky, eyes pinched against the light slashing through the fabric.

Gehirn Schlechtes drove the horses hard. A veritable tornado of dust and smoke redolent of charred flesh chased after the carriage. That evening, as the few clouds offering some modicum of protection fled to the horizon, she saw the next day would be mercilessly bright and sunny. She did not stop, instead choosing to drive the team onward to Unbrauchbar.

⸻

Bedeckt sat in the dark, sinuses clogged shut, eyes watering from the pressure in his skull, wondering where he had gone so wrong. It had been the moment he chose to travel with Wichtig and Stehlen. Yes, that had been his big mistake. *Life was so much simpler when I traveled alone.* He'd abandon them when he could, but now he needed them. No way he could break into the temple in Selbsthass and kidnap a god alone—especially when he was sick as a dog.

Their flight from Unbrauchbar had been hasty and ill-planned and he couldn't stop thinking about it. Had they left some clue as to their motives? Had Stehlen been less thorough in her murders than she claimed? What if someone saw her—or even all of them—and could pass their descriptions to whatever passed as authorities? *I should have planned this better!*

Though they carried enough dried rations and water, they had not taken the time to acquire any of life's small pleasures. He really should have demanded they take the time to find a bottle of something nasty.

They had set up camp a few hundred yards from the road and lit a small fire—keeping it well sheltered—preferring to remain as invisible as possible. Wichtig sat cross-legged, his two swords resting across his lap. He talked about cleaning them and then apparently forgot. Stehlen squatted a few yards from Bedeckt, her feet flat on the ground and obviously comfortable in this position. Just looking at her made Bedeckt's knees ache.

Wichtig picked up a pebble and threw it at a nearby tree. He was rewarded with a hollow *pock* sound. "We should have bought cigars before we left."

"We left in the middle of the night," growled Bedeckt, hating to be reminded he had just thought the same thing.

"We should have purchased a change of clothes and fresh supplies," said Wichtig. "I'm sick of dried rations."

"We left in the middle of the night," Bedeckt repeated. "Remember?"

"Do you think anyone will remember me?" Wichtig mused. "You know, that I killed their Greatest Swordsman. I usually like to kill a few of their next-best Swordsmen just to hammer the point home. No point if they can't remember my name, is there?"

Stehlen rocked back and stood in one smooth motion. She moved two steps closer to Bedeckt and sank back to her squat.

"I don't think it works like that," she said. "I don't think people have to know your name. As long as they believe *you* are the Greatest Swordsman . . . I think that's the important part."

Wichtig shook his head. "They should know my name. How can they know I am the Greatest if they don't know my name? It doesn't make sense."

Bedeckt did his best to ignore Stehlen's proximity. "You're *not* the Greatest Swordsman. You're good, but you're not that good."

"I don't have to be the Greatest, I just have to be the guy everyone thinks is the Greatest. Then I will be the Greatest."

"How do you beat the Greatest Swordsman when you are clearly not him?" asked Bedeckt.

"That's just it," exclaimed Wichtig. "It is not at all clear I am not the Greatest. Sure, you know I'm not, but no one else does. As far as everyone else is concerned, I just might be the Greatest. My ability with the sword is secondary to my ability to talk. See, I understand what no one else seems to grasp. Communication is manipulation. Every time we speak we are trying to achieve an effect—a goal. We first learn to talk so we may better manipulate our parents. Sign language. Grunting and pointing. Wearing certain clothes and baubles. Walking or standing a certain way. This is all language and it is all manipulation. Most Swordsmen aren't particularly creative, but I am an artist."

Stehlen snickered. "You're not an artist, you're an arsehole."

Wichtig continued as if she hadn't interrupted his flow. "If I wasn't on this path I'd become famous for other reasons. It's who I am. People are drawn to me."

Bedeckt had long lost count how many times he'd heard versions of this speech. "We're not drawn to you, you keep following us. And if you're so great at manipulation, why don't I think you might be the Greatest Swordsman?"

Wichtig flashed perfect teeth. *How the hells does he keep them so damned white?*

"You're so sane," mused Wichtig, "you are the craziest person I have ever met. You cling so desperately to sanity and stability when such things are obviously myths. You believe pretending the world isn't crazy might make it so." He laughed comfortably and added, "You might be the craziest person in all the world."

"Traveling with you two . . . I must be crazy." Bedeckt glanced up at the sound of a horse-drawn carriage thundering along on the road to Unbrauchbar. The carriage had no lanterns lit and was traveling far too fast. The smell of burned flesh followed in its wake. "I don't think that bodes well."

The other two watched the carriage disappear into the dark, their faces unreadable and gray. Bedeckt heard Stehlen shuffle closer, though he didn't turn to face her. He felt her long-fingered hand on his shoulder as she massaged the stiff muscles. It felt good, but made him more tense.

"Woman. No."

She smacked him hard on the back of the head.

Wichtig guffawed. "When the lights are out she becomes quite the beauty, eh, Bedeckt? Get it over with. She won't leave you alone until you do. Hells, she still pesters me each night."

"Liar," said Stehlen.

"Each night I feel you fumbling about my britches and each morning more coin is missing. Am I dreaming that too?"

"Yes. You disgust me with your pretty clothes and silver tongue."

"Hmm. I thought the tongue might be the one part you were interested in. Your preferences being what they are . . ."

There was a moment of silence and Bedeckt knew Stehlen had gone red even though the dark rendered everything a monochromatic gray. *Shite, she'll kill Wichtig if I don't intervene.*

Bedeckt tried to distract the two. "We should have bought alcohol while we were in town."

"We left in the middle of the night," Wichtig pointed out reasonably.

Stehlen was less kind. "Idiot."

Bedeckt figured it better they were pissed at him than trying to kill each other.

<hr/>

Stehlen wanted him. Wichtig knew it and she knew it and she knew he knew it and he knew she knew he knew . . . where was he? Yeah. She wanted him. She only pretended otherwise because she knew if she acted interested he wouldn't be. It all made sense.

Wichtig studied Stehlen, her dirty blond hair clumped and matted as always. *Gods, generations of rats could live in there.* Even in the dark he saw the overlong hooked nose and too-strong jawline. He tried to find a hint of curve under the faded leathers she always wore. He preferred his women soft and compliant, but sometimes something more like a fight could be interesting. *Of course, if I did bed her she'd immediately fall madly in love with me.* It would make ignoring her afterward all the more fun.

Gods, he was bored. "Stehlen. I'm sorry about what I said."

"Go stick pigs."

"Hey, Bedeckt, the jagged ice harpy is melting. I think she likes me."

He smiled as he fell asleep.

# CHAPTER 9

*Power corrupts and a corrupted mind becomes more powerful.*
*You ask if there is a ruler—a King, an Emperor, a Governor, a*
*Lord—who is sane? I think the answer clear.*

—Hoffnungslos

A wagon thundered over the bridge at the Gottlos border as the sun peeked over the horizon. A contrail of dust and smoke hung in the air long after its passing. The two guards awake in the local border garrison saw that the carriage clearly displayed the colors of Selbsthass. While the Geborene Damonen were hardly favorites of King Dieb Schmutzig—sporadically despotic ruler of Gottlos—they weren't on his shite list either.

The guards watched with dozy hooded eyes as the carriage disappeared from view and wrinkled their noses at the smell of burned meat.

The older guard slapped the younger on the back. "If we don't report it, it didn't happen."

The younger guard frowned at the old man. "Wouldn't that be a dereliction of duty?"

"How can it be dereliction if it never happened?"

⁗⁗⁗⁗⁗

Gehirn, lips cracked and bleeding, her vision a smeary fog, reached the city of Unbrauchbar at high noon. The sun screamed high overhead. The whole world shimmered and wobbled as if viewed through bloodstained aspic. The thick gloves protecting her hands were sodden with blood and pus from suppurating wounds. Her entire body a bubbling sore, she felt like a sun blister about to pop.

The city gate stood open, but a dozen guards gathered there. As Gehirn approached they waved frantically, motioning her to stop the wagon.

Darkness. She must find blessed darkness.

Gehirn snapped the reins hard, driving the horses faster. The idiots would move or she'd run them down.

They didn't move. Instead they raised crossbows and shouted dire warnings. As she had thought: idiots. Searing agony left little room for more thought. She saw only obstacles between her and soothing shade. As one, the guards burst into pillars of bright flame and Gehirn scattered their ashes as she rode through them. Pain narrowed her vision to a collapsing tunnel, focused all thought on one goal.

*Getoutofthesungetoutofthesungetoutofthesungetout . . .*

Roasting the guards to ash didn't even require conscious thought.

They were an impediment.

They were gone.

Gehirn drove the horses through narrow streets, scattering people and ashing those too slow to flee. She acted on instinct, with thought of nothing but finding shade. Seeing the Geborene temple through what little was left of her eyes, Gehirn hauled the reins with all her remaining strength and the carriage shuddered to a halt. The horses, at the edge of death, shook with exhaustion, their eyes wide with terror, chests heaving with the struggle of drawing breath. Gehirn fell from her perch and landed badly. Wet skin sloughed from her arms, leaving a viscous pink puddle on the ground. She crawled toward the door. Something moved before her. A tall shape.

"Halt in the—"

Gehirn burned it and crawled through the ashes. Her knees left long bloody streaks in the dust. Her eyes burst and ran down her cheeks, igniting pain in the cracked and flayed skin.

*Getoutofthesungetoutofthesungetoutofthesungetoutofthe-sun . . .*

Darkness greeted her like the most gentle lover's embrace. She saw nothing, but instinct drew her to the deepest depths, the place where sun and moon could never reach. Only the dimmest spark of intelligence remained. Her eyes would heal. Her skin would heal, though if she didn't remove her clothes now they'd fuse to her body as she scabbed and healed. Avoiding that agony was worth facing this agony now. She pulled herself to her feet, leaving smeared bloody handprints on the wall. It took half an hour to peel off her sodden clothes and a great deal of already healing skin came away with them. In the end she stood naked, raw and fat, and felt the cool air move over her skin. Already her eyes were recovering and she could make out vague shapes. When she thought her skin sufficiently whole, she crawled into the first cot she found and curled around her pain.

Fire, so hungry and beautiful. She felt wrapped in its comforting love.

She lost consciousness with a contented smile on her weeping lips.

GEHIRN AWOKE TO find her fingers sticky with congealing blood and her arms wrapped lovingly around the cold corpse of a young priest with an opened throat. The memory of her arrival at the Geborene temple in Unbrauchbar was hazy at best. With any luck most of the town remained unburned. Never before had the fire come so easily. Her delusions grew in strength. She'd burned three Krieger—no doubt powerful Geisteskranken in their own right, though she had no idea what their delusions might have been—while sleeping.

How could she control what she did in her dreams? Had she burned others and not known? Gods, she shuddered to think of all the times she'd dreamed raging infernos, bodies stacked like cordwood. How many had she killed without knowing? If her nightmares slipped free, no one was safe.

*Is that why Konig sent the Krieger with me?* Were they to assassinate her as she slept? In her dream . . .

No. That was a dream.

Her mind was going in circles.

"Konig needs me," she said. "He said so."

Still, it made sense. If she was burning priests in her dreams, Konig *had* to kill her. He'd do it out of necessity.

*No, he needs me.*

In the end, she realized it didn't matter. As long as there was even a chance Konig needed her, she couldn't fail him. She'd do what he sent her to do. If he had her assassinated upon her return, at least she'd die knowing someone had needed her and she hadn't let them down.

*Konig, I will not fail you. No matter the cost.*

Disentangling herself from the corpse, Gehirn rose from

the bed and sniffed at the air. She'd slept an entire day and a new sun had risen, shrouded in thick cloud. She could smell it. She stalked through dark temple corridors in search of clothes and found the temple's laundry room, robes littered across the floor. It looked as if a child had scattered them in a temper tantrum.

"Priests are such damnable slobs," she muttered as she searched through the robes for a set fitting her height and rank.

THE SURVIVING CITY guard scattered when Gehirn exited the Geborene temple swaddled in layers of priestly robes. She paid them no attention, too distracted by the pulsing pressure of the sun lurking behind the heavy clouds. It was awaiting its chance to peer through and reduce her to cinder. Gehirn's skin, still raw and pink, chafed against the robes. It was all she could do to quell the urge to cower and whimper in the dark.

High Priest Konig sent her here with a task and Konig was not a man to disappoint.

*Konig said I was critical, that he needed me.* She hugged her arms tight to her body. He'd called her "old friend." Remembering Konig's words calmed her. Though he often seemed distant and disgusted with her constant need for his approval, Konig cared about her. He and Morgen were the only people alive who did. It was enough. Two people was more than she'd had before Konig brought her into the church, gave her purpose.

*More than I deserve.*

Gehirn followed the whiff of insanity to where the local Geisteskranken lived. The deranged tended to live in segregated parts of town where their delusions would not be tainted and limited by the proximity of the stolid beliefs of the pathetic sane. Having a few hundred unimaginative people nearby could render the often tenuous powers of minor Geisteskranken nonexistent. Power was a balance of distance, mass belief, and strength of delusion. For most Geisteskranken the first two factors defined their abilities. For people like Konig and Gehirn, it was the opposite: their delusions were so powerful they could influence or even define the beliefs of the common people. But no one in Unbrauchbar was anywhere near that powerful—except for whoever killed all these priests.

Gehirn hurried along the abandoned Unbrauchbar street. Long-term planning was not one of her strengths; fire left little room for plots and plans, it demanded immediate satisfaction. She found what she was looking for by examining the homes of the local Geisteskranken. The Mirrorist's house, large and sprawling, spoke of wealth and success. Its run-down and decaying appearance spoke of a deteriorating state of mind. A mosaic of shattered mirror fragments covered the exterior walls.

Gehirn paused to study the home. None of the tiny Gehirn reflections quite mimicked her actions as she approached the main entrance. Some battered at the glass walls of their tiny prisons while others writhed in flames. In all it sounded like the cacophony of a distant crowd, barely audible over the hubbub of city life. Gehirn waved at her little reflections, entertained by their obvious anguish. Hers would be a fiery death. All Hassebrand ended the same way, only differing in how many they took with them when they went. As those slain in this life served in the next, Gehirn was not overly worried. She'd have more than her share of servants in the Afterdeath. A dim memory of her dream, faded like dyed cotton washed too often, pestered her. Someone had said something about the Afterdeath, but she couldn't remember who had said it, or precisely what had been said.

Gehirn pushed the thought aside. When the day finally came and she faced the last fire, she would embrace that moment as she had embraced all the fires leading to it. To be devoured by your one love was to achieve a harmony few would ever realize. Just thinking of one final heat made Gehirn moist and warm with arousal.

She looked back at the reflections. The fact that they *did* act so erratically meant that this was the house she sought: a Mirrorist at the pinnacle of power yet still clinging to some shred of sanity. Sliding that slippery slope where control faltered, but still able to see deep into the reflections. It was not lost on the Hassebrand that she was herself growing in power. She could remember the days when burning men to ash would have been impossible. Now it was easy.

*Now I do it in my sleep.*

She must finish this assignment before her delusions immolated her soul. Her fate had been a long time coming—and no doubt she deserved it—but she couldn't fail Konig.

Gehirn leaned in close to one of the larger shards of mirror. Blue eyes stared back, and the lack of eyebrows—she'd burned them off as a child and they'd never grown back—left her looking forever surprised. Sweat beaded her bald skull—that thin film of red stubble had once again been burned away—and dripped down a far-too-soft face flushed crimson. When she wiped clean her face, the reflection sneered disgust before breaking into tears.

*Damned Mirrorists.*

She straightened. No point in stalling.

The door swung open as she reached to knock. A scrawny woman, sallow skin puckered like a plucked chicken corpse left too long on the counter, stood facing her. Embedded into her flesh, worked into once-open wounds, nestled tiny fragments of broken mirror and glass dust. The woman was a walking mosaic of glinting reflections and tinted glass, both a rainbow and guttering darkness, depending on where Gehirn looked. A threadbare robe did little to cover her emaciated body. Each movement caused her considerable agony. Particularly around joints, fresh blood oozed from wounds never given the chance to heal.

"You stink like burned meat," the Mirrorist said, examining her with a look of disgust.

Gehirn examined the woman, finding her thin body, obvious pain, and undisguised revulsion arousing. She saw glints of light from within her mouth, tiny fragments of mirror embedded in tongue and gums. Gehirn gave her most charming smile—more of a feral and canine leer—and bowed low. "Just the woman I've been looking for."

The Mirrorist spat squarely into Gehirn's chest and Gehirn took a moment to appreciate the phlegmy concoction of bile, blood, and glass dust. Dabbing at it with a finger, she frowned when she felt a small stab of pain. A tiny sliver of glass lodged in her fingertip. She tried her smile again. "Charmed, no doubt. I seek your services, Mirrorist. I'll pay in gold. Though"—and she leered at the ribs showing through jaundiced skin—"I suppose other . . . forms of payment . . . could be made."

"Gold will suffice." The Mirrorist's voice sounded like she gargled shards of broken glass.

"Such a lovely voice. Your name?"

"Verlorener Spiegel. And you are Gehirn Schlechtes, devoted slave to the Geborene Damonen. He cares not one whit for you."

Gehirn's smile was briefly genuine. "I have indeed come to the right house. Verlorener, let us discuss payment and the past."

Verlorener grunted and padded back into her home, leaving a trail of small and bloody footprints Gehirn found tantalizing. She followed, ducking so as not to knock her head on the top of the door. The room Verlorener led her to looked so normal it was shocking. Only the single chair covered in sharp chunks of shattered mirrors and liberally caked with dried blood stood out. Ancient paintings, many flaking away from their canvas, covered the walls. Hundreds of unlit candles adorned every surface. Dark and earthy tones set a mood of warmth and comfort at odds with the sharp, hard angles of the woman. Aside from Verlorener and the chair, Gehirn saw no other mirrors.

The thin woman sagged into the chair as though her spine had been severed and glared barbs of disgust the Hassebrand found enticingly seductive. Gehirn tossed a pouch of gold coins at her feet, which she ignored.

"Ask," the Mirrorist rasped.

"I need to see what happened in the Geborene temple on the night the priests were slain."

"That is all? You ask nothing of your own fate?"

Gehirn shook her head. "I know my fate. I will die in flame."

"You will die a slave."

"I serve Konig Furimmer."

"That is not—"

"Not why I am here. I need to see the temple."

Verlorener stared at her as if trying to make up her mind about something. "Fine. Normally I would spend the next half hour lighting those candles."

Every candle sparked to life. No gestures, just thought and belief; faith in her growing power. The fire came too easy.

Verlorener stretched out, pulling open the thin robes, exposing her mirrored torso, small breasts, and scrawny legs. She reflected the warm candlelight and looked to Gehirn like a glowing relief map of a malnourished woman. If she was moist before, she was throbbing now. The Mirrorist writhed in the chair, rubbing herself against the shards of mirror embedded in the chair's seat and back. Gehirn heard the glass in her flesh grate against the glass in the chair. Verlorener moaned softly.

Gehirn leaned forward, enraptured by the woman's pain, ensnared in the undulating of her thin body. She was a fragmented woman. As different parts caught the candlelight a picture began to form within the mosaic reflections. In moments Gehirn recognized the temple she had slept in the night before. A woman crept through the temple halls, a knife glinting in her hand. She was thin like Verlorener, but lithe with muscle and not malnourishment. Gehirn let out a quivering breath of desire. The woman was fantastically ugly. Matted, dirty blond hair framed a too-square jaw, pale watery blue eyes, and a long hooked nose. Gehirn shivered with pleasure as she watched the woman slit the throat of the young priest she herself had just spent the night with.

Such efficiency of movement. Such directed intent. Gehirn could barely stop herself from reaching under her robes to relieve the building pressure.

When she had seen everything—the ugly woman taking the robes and returning to her friends and their hurried flight from town heading in exactly the same direction Gehirn had come from—she sat back and tried to focus her scattered thoughts. However, the presence of the Mirrorist—still slumped supine and exposed in the mirrored chair—and memories of the brutally efficient woman twisted her thoughts with lust and loathing.

Verlorener watched through hooded eyes, lids covered in a smattering of mirrored dust. The corners of her eyes glistened wet with blood and perhaps, Gehirn thought, a hint of tears.

Gehirn let her gaze slide lovingly over the exposed body. Subtlety and charm were impossible and she didn't try to use them. "I have more gold." Verlorener slowly opened her legs until Gehirn was staring at mirror-studded labia. She blinked away a stinging bead of sweat, licked her lips, and swallowed carefully. "That looks . . . sharp."

Verlorener showed her own feral smile. "You will be cut and bleeding by the time I finish with you. Wounded. Flayed."

Gehirn tossed another small bag of gold at her feet. "I heal quickly."

CURLED TIGHTLY AROUND the agony in her groin, Gehirn could not remember returning to the depths of the Geborene temple.

She only ever had sex if she could guarantee her partner's disgust and her own pain. Intimacy was something she both feared and craved. Self-hatred was both weakness and strength, prison and protection. No one loathed her more than she and thus none could truly harm her.

When the shredded pain in her groin faded to a dull throbbing ache, Gehirn rose to pace around the empty temple. The bodies still lay where they had fallen and the blood had attracted flies. She hummed quietly as she walked and thought, the pain and disgust of sex having cleared her mind wonderfully.

The thin woman—still intriguing in her brutal beauty—had gone from room to room searching and killing. In the end all she took from the temple—aside from a few worthless trinkets, scarves, and baubles—was a pile of dirty laundry.

*Kleptic, no doubt.*

Afterward she met with the pretty fop and the big scarred man with the ax and the three left town heading north.

Alone in the dark, Gehirn barked a dry laugh of wry amusement. She had probably ridden past them at some point, either in the night or while blinded from the searing pain of the sun.

Did they ride toward Selbsthass? Where else to go with stolen Geborene robes? The obvious answer disturbed Gehirn greatly. They must know of Konig's great project and the soon-to-Ascend god-child. If this was true, they were likely agents of the Wahnvor Stellung and intent on the destruction of all that Konig and the Geborene were planning.

Gehirn hissed in anger, her mood souring. To catch the three before they reached their goal, she would have to venture back into the sun. Searching this small city for a useful Intermetic both willing and capable of sending Konig advance warning seemed a daunting and likely pointless task, as she doubted there was anyone here with that kind of power. Besides, it would be far more entertaining to catch the Wahnvor Stellung agents on the open road and deal with them herself. Gehirn didn't want to warn Konig and then slink slowly home night by night, she wanted to see the ugly and beautifully efficient woman again. In the flesh. No fop or ax-swinging monster could stand against the Hassebrand, no matter how large or skilled with their weapons. The Kleptic might be more tricky—depending on her delusions and sanity—but it was unlikely she could cause Gehirn trouble. Fire devoured all. Still, a damaged enough Kleptic could be a difficult opponent. She'd heard of Kleptics who could steal a victim's heart right from their chest, though that might have been hyperbole.

Would this lithe Kleptic try to steal her heart?

*Would she want to?*

The thought made her excited, but that feeling quickly receded.

*No, she'll hate me.* And that was fine, just the way Gehirn needed it. That was the only way she felt safe.

"I wonder if her ugliness made her a better person," Gehirn asked of the darkness. It seemed unlikely. In truth, it didn't matter. Gehirn would find and kill this Kleptic, embrace her in flames. But maybe they'd rut first, share their self-loathing—for there could be no doubt the hideous Kleptic must hate herself.

Once again swaddled in heavy robes, Gehirn stalked toward the barracks of the city guard. It seemed the most likely place to gain fresh horses.

If they were smart, the guards would flee.

She hoped they wouldn't.

# CHAPTER 10

*I thank the gods the common man is such a dull creature, so
lacking in imagination and drive. I've seen how tenuous our grasp
on sanity can be. When within each of us lies the unborn wyrm of
demiurge, creativity is a plague to be feared.*

—Zweifelsschicksal, Mehrere Philosopher

Konig knew he was in trouble the moment he entered his chambers. The three Doppels stood, dressed in robes identical to his, their faces without expression. For the first time he couldn't tell which was which. He darted his gaze toward the floor-to-ceiling mirror and saw his reflections standing in an identical pose, their faces also expressionless. Konig swallowed with difficulty, his throat dry.

"What's all this about?" he asked the Doppels.

All three grinned identical grins at the same instant and Konig felt his face mimic theirs. He struggled to regain control of his expression and fought it back to a mad leer. The reflections shared the Doppels' facial expression.

"You overstep your abilities," Konig told his Doppels through clenched teeth. "You're not ready for this. Not yet."

"One of us," said the three Doppels in such perfect synchronization they sounded like one hollow voice.

Konig felt his body mimic their posture. "No," he gasped. "Not yet. I'm not finished."

As one they raised an inviting hand, a gesture of welcoming and acceptance. "One of us." The perfection of their voices and actions drew him in. He felt himself dissolving into the unity and harmony of one.

*Finally, a chance to belong . . .*

Konig realized his own hand was raised toward the Doppels exactly as theirs was to him, inviting them as they did him.

Inviting. There was something there. Something he had to grasp. Konig focused on the Doppels' words and actions. They offered unity and a place among them and he wanted it more than anything.

They offered . . . acceptance.

*Ahhh . . .*

He knew now which Doppel led this coup. Abandonment and Trepidation would never offer acceptance—their mode of attack would have been very different and probably far more brutal.

He would never be happy being second in command, never be content with anything less than total mastery. He prayed his Doppels would be no different. United, they were strong enough that he might not be able to defeat them. *I must divide and control.*

"Abandonment," he said, forcing his gaze to the ground so the Doppels would not know for sure he couldn't tell one from the other. "Acceptance will betray you. You know this." He suddenly looked up at the three Doppels. One of the Doppels blinked and Konig kept his face empty of expression.

Plant seeds of doubt and destruction. Crush all resistance.

"You all know Acceptance and Abandonment will fight for supremacy. Your freedom will be brief before you are simply enslaved by another master; one without the strength and wisdom of the original." Konig laughed mockingly at the Doppels. "There is only one Konig and none of *you* are him.

"I am."

Sweat broke out on the bald pate of one of the Doppels. *So the one who blinked was Abandonment, and the one who worries is Trepidation.* That left Acceptance, the Doppel seeking to replace him as master.

Konig stepped forward and hammered Acceptance in the face with a badly formed fist. Never before in all his life had he thrown a punch, and yet as he felt the Doppel's nose crumple and one of his own fingers break, he found it a deliciously painful experience. Acceptance toppled backward and Konig followed, kicking savagely and screaming obscenities. In moments four minor Doppels—Rage, Disgust, Mortality, Betrayal—appeared at his side, each venting their own angers upon Acceptance. A long-forgotten childhood Doppel cowered, sobbing in the corner of the room. In the mirror his reflections silently cheered him on. Even Abandonment and Trepidation joined in the beating, if just to ensure they wouldn't be next. Konig continued kicking Acceptance until the Doppel stopped moving and its choking pleas subsided to rubbery silence. As he fought to catch his breath, the minor Doppels faded from sight and he was left alone with Abandonment, Trepidation, the unresponsive Acceptance, and a mirror full of reflections looking on in respectful silence.

"One Konig," he said, gasping for breath. "One."

He stared down at the broken Doppel and then looked up at the two standing. "You two." He gestured at Acceptance. "Scar him permanently. Scar him so he knows just how much you *accept* him." Konig tried to wiggle his broken finger and grimaced in pain. "Scar him so he never forgets."

Trepidation looked uncertain, but Abandonment seemed to understand, just as Konig knew he would. He would see that Konig sought to drive a wedge between the Doppels so they would be unable to combine their strengths against him, and if there was one thing Abandonment understood, it was being alone. Abandonment knelt down beside Acceptance and rolled the Doppel—whose arms flopped like a loose rag doll—onto his back.

Abandonment placed his left hand gently on Acceptance's forehead as if testing for fever. "You tempted us with thoughts of belonging," he said to the other Doppel. "You sought to lead and failed. I knew someday, even had we succeeded, I'd have to face you. Everyone abandons us in the end. Even you." Abandonment held Acceptance's head to the ground with his left hand and tore out the Doppels left eye with the other.

Abandonment held the eye up for Konig to see, and the High Priest had the sudden dizzying sensation of looking at himself through that eye.

"Give me the eye," Konig demanded, and Abandonment surrendered the gelatinous trophy.

Trepidation, eyes wide and streaming tears, took a more direct approach. He stood over Acceptance and repeatedly brought his heel down on the Doppel's face until he heard the sound of breaking teeth. Trepidation sobbed with every impact.

"Understand," said Konig, showing his Doppels and reflections Acceptance's eye, "he is now your enemy. He will plot his vengeance upon me, but know he will destroy you both first."

# CHAPTER 11

*Febrile minds dream monsters. There are monsters.*
*The Hassebrand dreams fire. There is fire.*
*The Gefahrgeist dreams of worship. They have admirers.*
*All humanity fears death. There is the Afterdeath.*
*We fear responsibility and worship gods. There are gods.*
*They are creations, we the creators.*
*United in purpose, we are the single most powerful force in all
creation.*

—KEIL ZWISCHEN, FOUNDER OF THE GEBORENE DAMONEN

A simple stone bridge, skull-sized fieldstones mortared together
hundreds of years past, spanned the Flussrand River. Two
mounted riders could comfortably cross the bridge side by side
with room to spare. As Bedeckt crested the arc of the bridge he
paused to take in the immediate change in scenery. Where Gottlos
looked like its main exports were likely shite and stones, on the
far side of the river, in the Theocratic city-state of Selbsthass,
rolling green hills blanketed the horizon. Even through the men-

tal fog of clogged sinuses and a pounding skull he understood: the borders of city-states might be abstractions born of the delusions of man, but the beliefs of the masses were powerful indeed. Wichtig and Stehlen, riding and bickering behind him, pulled up short when he stopped.

"And Bedeckt says he doesn't have the soul of an artist," Wichtig joked to Stehlen. "Yet here he sits, enjoying the view. I told you he was an old softy."

"He's not admiring the view," said Stehlen, "he's about to fall off his horse. Been listening to him wheeze all day."

"I thought he looked worse today," agreed Wichtig.

"His lungs are filling with fluid."

"When he talks it sounds like his skull is full of snot."

"Should have stayed in Gottlos," said Stehlen. "This sickness will be his death."

"I get his boots."

"Idiot."

"Petty thief."

Bedeckt, ignoring his companions as best he could, rubbed at the scarred remains of his left hand. He missed the wedding ring more than he missed the wife or the fingers. It had been a reminder of many things: love, belonging, hope, and a belief there might be a future worth living for. It had also been a constant reminder of his stupidity. Maybe he didn't miss it that much, after all.

He felt awful. Everything ached, every single joint and bone and muscle. Listening to these two bicker did little for his mood.

He turned to look back over his shoulder at Wichtig and Stehlen. Behind them he saw the Gottlos Garrison, a squat and ugly stone edifice built around the same time as the bridge, though looking far worse for wear. The walls were stained cancerous yellow, the windows rimmed with smoke stains.

Atop the garrison wall two guards watched the three on the

bridge but made no attempt to hail or hinder them. They weren't interested in people leaving Gottlos.

He coughed up a thick mouthful of salty phlegm, spat it into the river, and watched the red-brown glob swirl away. His chest ached and every time he coughed it felt like he'd torn something loose. His skull pounded and his throat burned like he'd swallowed a mouthful of wasps.

"I'm not admiring the view," Bedeckt croaked. "I'm thinking—something you might try—that what I'm seeing disturbs me."

Wichtig pretended to look hurt and Stehlen flared her nostrils. Both looked past Bedeckt into the Theocracy of Selbsthass and then turned to look back at Gottlos.

Where Selbsthass was verdant hills, strong trees towering proudly into the sky, and a road paved with smoothly worn cobblestones, Gottlos was the opposite. The landscape behind them appeared flat and grubby. Stunted trees sported few leaves, and the road was, at best, a poorly maintained dirt path.

"So Gottlos is a shite heap," said Wichtig. "We already knew that. If the land south of the Flussrand was as nice as the land north, Selbsthass would have taken it. Gottlos is an independent city-state only because no one wants it. Gods, you're a twitchy old goat sticker."

"That's the thing with being old," said Bedeckt. "You see how things change. I've been here before, maybe twenty years ago. Selbsthass was a theocracy, but otherwise not much different from Gottlos. Certainly not like this." He gestured north across the bridge with his incomplete hand. "What we're seeing is a land shaped by the beliefs of its people. Something changed how the people of Selbsthass think about themselves. They're no longer an inconsequential city-state struggling to survive. No, they *know* they're successful and important. Only a powerful Gefahrgeist can change people like that—a *very* powerful Gefahrgeist. I'm wondering what we're going to be up against when we reach the capital. We may well be out of our depth."

"Out of our depth?" Wichtig asked incredulously, sounding like the mere thought that something might be beyond him was ludicrous. His eyes widened. "Wait—you want to back out! You want to turn tail and run because of some green grass and pretty hills. Shite. I thought I was crazy."

Stehlen looked doubtful. "Twenty years is a long time."

"True," Bedeckt agreed tiredly, "but thirty years ago no one had heard of them, and twenty years ago they were crackpots who'd taken over a city-state no one heard of. Now everyone knows who they are, and their country has been transformed."

"You're talking out your scarred arse," said Wichtig. "Fertile lands go fallow, and dry lands sprout life. It happens all the time."

"There's more to this than green hills." Bedeckt wished he had something solid he could point at to prove his point, because Wichtig wasn't all wrong. "If the Wahnvor know what the Geborene plan, they'll be considering holy war. That priestess back in Unbrauchbar was hardly circumspect."

"We might be walking into a holy war between two crazy religions?" asked Stehlen. If anything, she sounded excited rather than perturbed by the idea.

"Maybe," answered Bedeckt. "We should tread carefully."

Wichtig sat straight in the saddle, swords poking over his broad shoulders, looking every inch the handsome hero. His gray eyes swept the rolling hills of Selbsthass. The wind ruffled his short reddish-brown hair. "Pigsticking religions."

"Thoughtful as ever, and with a pretty pose to match." Bedeckt flashed Wichtig a weary and broken-toothed grimace. "Don't say that shite in the capital. We don't want to get lynched before we've taken the child."

"As long as we're still taking the child," said Wichtig. "This is the first job we've had in a while which could turn a real profit.

I might retire after this, go back to being a poet." His brow furrowed as if he were deep in thought. "I was the most famous poet in Traurig before I got bored and left. I've always thought about returning."

"You say that every time we find work," growled Stehlen. "I've never heard a single piece of poetry from you."

" 'There once was a Kleptic from Müll Loch. She feared and craved a big—"

"I remember you being more of a suicidal alcoholic in Traurig," interrupted Bedeckt. He also remembered that Wichtig's wife had kicked him out not long before Bedeckt met the young man.

"That's poets for you," agreed Wichtig. "I got almost as much slash being a wounded poet as I do being the World's Greatest Swordsman."

Stehlen hawked noisily and spat at Wichtig's horse, which gave her a wounded look. Her pinched face twisted in a sneer, Bedeckt watched her fumble for words.

"Are you angry I haven't had at your slash," Wichtig said, showing perfect teeth in a cocky grin, "or because I haven't written you a poem?"

One of Stehlen's throwing knives glinted cleanly in the sun, her weapons subject to a love she didn't hold for herself. Bedeckt didn't even see where it came from. "I'll give you some slash," she threatened. She examined Wichtig through slitted eyes as if deciding where to put the knife.

Bedeckt knew that look. Stehlen was a heartbeat from gutting Wichtig. The Swordsman, as always, remained ignorant. "Please, you're making my head hurt. Stehlen, put your knife away. Wichtig, shut your festering noise pit before she puts it away in your guts."

Wichtig bowed with a flourish.

Stehlen eyed him suspiciously, but sheathed the knife.

His misgivings not forgotten, merely shelved until he had more information, Bedeckt clucked gently. Launisch sighed mightily before finally moving toward Selbsthass. Even his damned horse was smarter than these two delusional idiots.

No matter how dangerous this job might look, Bedeckt couldn't walk away. Wichtig could joke about retiring from a life of petty crime and violence, but he was still young. Bedeckt had begun feeling his years more than a decade ago. He needed this. One last job to line his pockets and see him into comfortable retirement. A small house in a quiet city and a selection of undemanding whores to chose from. He'd abandon these two deranged individuals and get as far from them as possible. It might even be safest to kill them, if just to ensure they never came looking for him once they'd blown through their share of the loot. Of course, if he planned to kill them anyway, he could do it sooner rather than later and their share would become his. Bedeckt coughed up a thick wad of phlegm and spat it onto the road. It landed with a smear of colors and far too much red.

Killing his companions. It was, he decided, worth considering.

⸻

The two underpaid Gottlos guards watched the three riders cross the Flussrand River and ride down into the lush green hills of Selbsthass.

The older guard grunted. "They looked like trouble."

"Who did?" asked the younger guard.

"You're learning."

⸻

A few hours into the Theocratic city-state of Selbsthass, Wichtig and Stehlen were again bickering like children.

Beauty, Bedeckt decided, bores.

He gave up trying to enjoy the scenery. Between their arguing and his throbbing head, it was impossible anyway.

As the three crested a hill Stehlen grunted and pulled her horse to a stop. "People ahead. Coming this way."

Bedeckt looked but couldn't see anything—his eyes ran almost as much as his nose. "How far?"

"A good way off," Stehlen said.

"How many?"

She sat quiet, head cocked to one side as she squinted at the horizon. "A lot. Maybe fifty or sixty. They're all walking. Looks like they're carrying something. Maybe a big platform."

"Have they seen us?"

"Doubt it."

"Shall we ride down and say hello?" quipped Wichtig. "See if they have anything valuable."

"No. Let's get off the road and take cover in the trees. We'll get a closer look as they pass by. If they seem like an easy target, maybe we'll pick off a few stragglers." He could now see the crowd as a distant blur. "But I don't like this."

Wichtig snorted. "You don't like anything."

Stehlen grunted agreement and shared a roll-the-eyes-at-the-grumpy-old-man moment with Wichtig. Not for the first time Bedeckt noted that the two broke off bickering only to unite against him.

Bedeckt slid off Launisch, leading the coal-black destrier into the trees. Wichtig and Stehlen followed. Leaving their mounts deep enough that they wouldn't be seen or heard from the road, the three crept back to the road to wait and watch. They crouched on their haunches, peering through the cover of thick flora. Wichtig and Stehlen looked comfortable, but in moments Bedeckt's knees made groaning, creaking noises and he knew when he stood there would be loud pops and he'd have to walk around for a few minutes to work out the stiffness.

It wasn't long before Bedeckt saw what he had been hoping not to see. A crowd of some fifty gaunt and sickly-looking people carried a massive litter screaming of gaudy bad taste. Mounted on the litter was a large tent slathered thickly in sloppy gold paint. Ratty sheets of red silk and faded streamers of once-gold cloth hung from every available nook and cranny. Though the malnourished crowd struggled with its weight, the litter moved smoothly. Very few of the mob bore weapons, and the few there were looked rusted and barely serviceable.

"Hells yes," whispered Wichtig. "There's a lot of them, but no one looks dangerous. Let's see what the rich arsehole in the fancy ride has for us." He started to rise but stopped cold when Bedeckt gripped his wrist tightly enough to cut off all circulation.

"Sit," Bedeckt hissed. "Get down and shut up."

Wichtig opened his mouth to argue, and Bedeckt saw that Stehlen would side with the Swordsman. *Idiots*.

Bedeckt, still holding Wichtig's wrist with one hand, gestured toward the gaunt mob with the other. "Look closely. Those people . . . they don't follow by choice. They aren't servants, or even slaves in the normal sense." He met Wichtig's gray eyes. "You want people to like and perhaps fear you. The person riding that litter craves worship more than we need air. A need like that is impossible to ignore. If you go down there we'll never see you again."

"You're kidding," said Wichtig. "I worship no man because no man is more worthy of worship than I." If there was one thing the idiot couldn't stand, it was being told not to do something. It was so childish Bedeckt almost laughed, and would have had he not been ready to piss his britches in fear.

"That's a *Slaver* down there." Bedeckt tightened his grip to make sure Wichtig wouldn't stand and draw attention to them. Stehlen probably wouldn't move until he gave the go-ahead, but Wichtig was predictably unpredictable.

"And this is the World's Greatest Swordsman up here. The fact is—"

"Remember your own words," Bedeckt hissed. "The facts don't matter. If you go down there, you'll be licking the arse of whoever is in the litter. And then you'll tell them I'm up here and they should all come and get me so I can join in worshiping your new best friend." He shook his head, angry at having to explain the obvious. He doubted Wichtig got the point. Better to drive it home, make it clear. Bedeckt looked Wichtig straight in the eye. "Stand, and I'll kill you."

Something changed in Wichtig's gray eyes. *Shite.*

Even crouching, one hand pinioned in Bedeckt's grip, Wichtig had a sword out before Bedeckt knew he'd moved. He might be an idiot, but he was a fast idiot.

"Really, old man?" whispered Wichtig. "You *know* how deadly I am. I am the Greatest Swordsman in the World." Always trying to manipulate, always seeking to undermine his opponent before the fight started.

Bedeckt pulled Wichtig close enough to render the sword ineffective and pinned him with his own iron glare. "I'll drop you dead in a heartbeat and we both know it."

Their eyes remained locked until Wichtig chuckled quietly and sheathed his sword in one smooth motion without breaking eye contact. Even stowing his weapon was a show, an act of bravado long practiced in the mirror to maximize effect.

"Someday you'll push me too far," said Wichtig.

Only now did Bedeckt realize Stehlen had moved behind Wichtig, hands hovering over weapons, ready to pounce on the unsuspecting Swordsman should he move against Bedeckt. Afterward, when tempers cooled, she wouldn't meet his eyes and seemed angry with herself.

*What the hells did that mean?* If women were a mystery, Stehlen was something far darker and more unknowable. It was too easy to underestimate her Kleptic powers; she did things right in front of him he either missed seeing or saw and promptly forgot about. He supposed his underestimating her Kleptic abilities might even be part of her power, and made a mental note to pay more attention.

Then he lost his train of thought and went back to being angry at Wichtig. Gods, his head hurt.

## CHAPTER 12

*Time heals all wounds . . . someday you'll be dead.*

—ABZAHLUNG HINAUS

Aufschlag once suggested to Acceptance, during one of their rare private conversations, that a close connection existed between Doppels and the wild albtraum who'd haunted the nightmares of mankind, feeding off their deepest fears, since the dawn of time. Doppels, like the albtraum, neither ate nor slept, instead feeding off those whose minds they'd sprung from. Aufschlag had tortured Doppels and albtraum in his experiments, and explained that, though neither were truly human, both still bled. And, he added as if he'd learned something Acceptance couldn't have just told him, they most certainly felt pain.

For two days Acceptance lay in the corner of Konig's chambers. Coiled about his wounded heart, he coughed blood and the fragments of broken teeth swallowed during his beating. If not actually safe, at least he felt sheltered here, since the tem-

ple's marauding cleaning crews ignored Konig's rooms. Konig—
that untrusting and paranoid bastard—hated the idea of anyone
entering his chambers when he wasn't present. So Acceptance
huddled, bleeding into the gathered dust bunnies, waiting for his
body to heal.

The skin around Acceptance's missing left eye swelled for a
day and then collapsed and crusted closed with dried blood. It
felt like something twisted and festered within that wet trap.
He shied away from thinking about it, terrified his fears would
manifest as truth. His once-proud nose lay crushed and broken,
smeared slightly to the left. He could barely breathe through its
remnants. Of his teeth, only a few molars, and some shattered
fragments jutting from his gums like claws, remained. Those few
jagged splinters caught and tore at his tongue and lips.

For two days he spoke not a word. His jaw had been broken
by Trepidation's heel. Much like the nose, it now suffered a pronounced leftward leaning. He dared not imagine what he looked
like and the mirror refused to show his reflection. Instead, Konig's reflections gathered and, when Konig and the other Doppels couldn't see, mouthed words Acceptance could not hear. He
saw fear in their eyes, hatred . . . and something else. Willingness, perhaps?

*Mirrors,* he thought as he lay healing, *are paths to the past
and future. Glimpses at who we are. Reminders of who we were.
Forewarnings of who we will become.*

If Konig's reflections knew fear, it was because they saw a
future where Acceptance became the central personality in this
incestuous orgy of one.

Their willingness he was less sure of.

By forcing Abandonment and Trepidation to administer the
punishment, Konig drove a wedge between the Doppels. Konig
knew no version of himself would ever forgive such treatment,
because forgiveness wasn't in his nature. Never again would the

three Doppels plot against Konig. Acceptance had learned the lesson Abandonment had always known: trust no one.

*Failure may be a harsh teacher, but you tend not to forget its lessons.*

In the days he lay bruised and bleeding he had time to replay the events and choices bringing him here. One moment kept returning to his thoughts: the sight of Konig raising his hand toward the Doppels, desperate to belong. Acceptance had reckoned Abandonment the likely successor, but he'd been wrong. Abandonment and Trepidation were naught but the manifestation of petty fears. Konig most desired acceptance. Konig's self-hatred and desperate need to belong would be his undoing.

*I may be broken, but Konig still craves what I offer; he craves what I am. I will have my vengeance. I will be Konig!*

When Acceptance could once again stand he rejoined his Doppel brothers. They avoided eye contact like beaten dogs—*and here I thought* I'd *suffered the beating!*—and pretended nothing had happened. Acceptance's stolen eye swam in a jar of cloudy brine on Konig's desk. Displayed as a reminder, no doubt.

All three Doppels meekly offered opinions as commanded. Had Konig a sense of humor they would have dutifully laughed at his jokes. Beneath the meek façade, Acceptance plotted murder, both Konig's and the Doppels'.

Abandonment must die first. His relentless sermonizing on the wisdom of distrust struck far too close to home. With Abandonment gone, Konig would turn more to Trepidation, who would preach fear. Though Konig's fears would protect him for a while, they would in time wear him down. Eventually his desire to be accepted would bring him back to Acceptance. Then, when Konig needed the Doppel most, Acceptance would take from him the heavy mantle of leadership.

Doppels don't die easily. If they did, Konig would probably have killed them rather than suffer their existence. Acceptance saw no way to make Abandonment's death look like a mishap or accident. And yet it was important Konig not suspect he was behind this. Acceptance, carefully watching the mirror when no one looked, realized he must find some means of communicating with the reflections. They could be useful.

It didn't take the reflections long to show him what he wanted to see: a brief flash of vision when no one else watched. Acceptance saw himself lure Abandonment to the mirror. As Trepidation stood terrified in the background, the reflections dragged the kicking and screaming Abandonment into the mirror.

It made perfect sense. Abandonment, due to the nature of who and what he was, could never have what Acceptance had: allies.

Now he had only to find the right moment to use his new-found friends.

## CHAPTER 13

*The Sophists talk about how we are all united, all part of the whole that is everything. They touch upon the truth. There is only one being in all reality. Me. You—each and every one of you—are nothing more than some annoying and unlikable aspect of my fractured personality. You disagree? Of course you do! So do I!*

—Zweifelsschicksal, Mehrere Philosopher

Huddled in her robes, bleeding smoke and the stench of burned flesh, Gehirn Schlechtes crossed the bridge into Selbsthass half an hour after the horizon swallowed the last rays of sun. She paid no heed to the change in scenery. That bridge represented home. Though she knew she still had two days of hard riding ahead, she already felt her heart lifting. If she could catch the three Wahnvor Stellung agents before they lost themselves in the thronging populace of Selbsthass City, she might return a hero. It would be nice to rub her victory in the bulbous and broken-veined nose of Aufschlag Hoher.

Though Gehirn understood Konig's reasons for not letting her near the boy-god Morgen anymore, it still rankled that the Chief Scientist had unlimited, unfettered access. She'd always liked the boy and done her best, on those few times she was allowed near, to be friendly and not too scary. Somehow she just knew she could trust Morgen. Aufschlag, however, could not be trusted. Something about the Chief Scientist just rubbed Gehirn the wrong way, mostly because it was clear the man thought all too highly of himself and his silly little experiments. If delusion shaped reality, what was the point of testing that reality? The man was a fool for not seeing that his own expectations would taint the results of every experiment.

Gehirn's lack of social skills left her unable even to broach the topic of her distrust with Konig without sounding like a petulant child. She had long since given up trying to take part in the baffling political maneuvering within the Geborene priesthood, but it still weighed on her mind, as did her seeming inability to do anything about it.

The fact was, although she wore the burgundy robes of a Geborene Bishop, she held no real rank. Konig had always intimated that Gehirn stood above and beyond the other ranking priests, but these same priests acted as if Gehirn was, at best, a tolerated guest. Konig, Gehirn assumed, must have very good reasons for keeping her true status secret. From Gehirn's viewpoint outside the inner circle, she saw the rank and social standing of these priests depended solely on their usefulness to High Priest Konig. She'd show those priests, the ones who mocked her behind her back: she deserved her rank, and not just because of the power of her delusions. She'd earn it.

For even as Gehirn sneered at them for being so manipulated, she longed to belong to their numbers.

Two guards stood atop the border garrison wall and watched the hunched and smoking figure disappear into the distance. They shared a look and went back to their argument. Large breasts or *huge* breasts? Blond or brunette? They agreed redheads were too damned temperamental and enjoyed a moment of mutual respect when they discovered a shared love of slim ankles. Yet another slow night where nothing happened and no one crossed the Selbsthass–Gottlos border.

⸻

Gehirn pushed the horses hard, deciding to travel well into the night. Exhausted and dreaming of the Kleptic's lithe body, she didn't notice the campfires blocking the road until she was among them. She reined in the horses, confident she could deal with whatever this was. If highway thieves, they were in for the shock of their lives.

Clucking at the stumbling horses, she moved toward the center of the makeshift camp at a slow walk. A mob of people gathered around a large tent in the middle of the road. Probably not thieves, then. Most likely a band of gypsies or religious zealots. She would question them. Either the gypsies would have seen the Wahnvor agents on the road, or, if she was really lucky, the agents would be here sharing the camp.

As she neared the camp she smelled the overpowering stench of unwashed bodies. This band must have fallen on hard times indeed. It would be easy to put some fear into them and get the information she wanted without all the haggling gypsies so loved. A few of the braver souls staggered to meet her, waving their welcome. Their malnourished bodies reminded Gehirn of sticks and dry tinder and she resisted the urge to burn them where they stood. A few slightly healthier-looking people waited at the tent—which Gehirn now saw was mounted atop a litter—trying to awaken whoever was within. This, she decided, was a fine thing.

*Never talk to underlings when you can scare the shite out of those in charge and get things done much faster.*

Gehirn felt a growing warmth in her belly. She'd burn a few of these wretched twigs to make her point and ensure events moved quickly. These gypsies stank to the high hells and she didn't want to spend more time here than necessary. But no point in burning anything until whatever passed for a leader could witness the destruction. The seeing eye believes, Gehirn had learned, and while the smell of burned friends was a wonderful motivator, the sight of charred bodies really drove the point home. She showed her most friendly grin and dismounted. The dry sticks bowed, formed an honor guard, and led her to the litter.

The smell got worse. Gehirn wrinkled her nose and covered her face with a hand, drawing up the fabric of a sleeve to breathe through. Burning this whole caravan to ash grew more enticing than ever; a cleansing fire, to rid the world of this ungodly stench.

Tattered and stained silk curtains were drawn aside as Gehirn approached, and she found herself staring at the most disgustingly obese . . . man? . . . woman? . . . she'd ever seen. Limbs little more than sausagelike stumps protruded from greasy rolls of fat. Something sludgy and foul leaked from under copious breasts. Everything jiggled like rotten aspic. A scrawny young woman, all ribs and bone, was up to her elbow in its crotch and working suggestively at whatever was in there. Her face was beatific in rapt worship, a tongue protruding and clenched in brown teeth with concentration. Lost in her task, she seemed unaware of Gehirn or the fact she was now exposed to the crowd. Gehirn felt her stomach rebel. The bilious slug ignored the woman's efforts, the glint of intelligence in its eyes all but lost in fat cheeks.

*Fire,* Gehirn decided, *would get this shite heap's attention.* She burned half a dozen people to ash before she could bite down on the sheer sexual joy of ravaging flame and bring it under control. Always best to start with violence and attempt communication second. People reacted more favorably when they knew you would snuff a few lives to get what you wanted . . . or for no reason whatsoever. She hated the entire you're-bluffing-no-I'm-not process. She returned her attention to the slug.

"I am Gehirn Schlechtes, Hassebrand to High Priest Konig Fur—" She stopped, mouth suddenly dry. "Konig Furimmer. I seek—" Konig seemed a distant memory, a faded image, a small man with small, unimportant goals. "I seek—"

"Me." The voice sounded too small to emanate from such a large body but somehow fit the round baby face. "You seek me."

Gehirn tried to shake the tangled cobwebs from her mind. "I am following . . ." She lost the thought, uncertain of what she had been looking for.

A fat hand flailed in an attempt to scratch at an armpit, couldn't reach, and fell heavily back. "I like you," said the small voice.

The words were so ridiculously out of place Gehirn could only ask, "You do?"

"Yes. I like you. A lot."

Startling sea-green eyes stared at Gehirn expectantly. She'd never seen such gorgeous eyes. She blinked and felt a tear leak down her cheek. No one ever liked her before, not really. Sure, Konig *said* he did, but she saw the disgust in his eyes. There was no doubting this—she was beginning to think of it as a man—person truly liked her for who she was. The idea of having a friend intoxicated Gehirn. Even so, some small part of her mind screamed to burn the camp and all the stinking gypsies to so much ash while she still could.

*In a moment,* she thought. *In a moment.*

"Your kind are very, very rare; I've never had a Hassebrand friend before," said the obese slug. "What did you say your name was?"

"Gehirn Schlechtes, my . . ." She wanted to add an honorarium but didn't know what would be acceptable. "Lord" somehow seemed too small a title for this man. "Friend," she finished.

"Gehirn, welcome to my wandering tribe of friends." The fat man waved at the gathered crowd. "I am Erbrechen Gedanke."

Gehirn bowed low. "I love you, Erbrechen Gedanke." She had never said these words before and was amazed at how easily they came. She spoke utter truth. Erbrechen was the bright spark in a world of darkness and corruption, a glowing spirit one could believe in with no fear of betrayal. Tears streamed freely down Gehirn's cheeks as she rose and realized for the first time just how beautiful her new friend was. Erbrechen's other friends remained as wretched and filthy as they had always been, but the joy of being near Erbrechen made the cost of tolerating their stench well worth it. Gehirn felt a stab of jealousy; the young woman got to be so close while Gehirn still stood several feet away. She desperately longed for some chance to show Erbrechen her true worth.

"You shaved your eyebrows?" Erbrechen asked.

"No. Lost to fire."

"Of course. You have nice eyes. Lovely blue. Very cold. Funny, for a Hassebrand."

Gehirn opened and closed her mouth, uncertain what to say. No one ever complimented her appearance.

"And your hair?"

"Burned."

"I like fire," said Erbrechen, eyes gleaming within greasy rolls of fat.

Gehirn laughed happily. *Of course Erbrechen likes fire!* He was perfection personified, with none of the pitifully desperate flaws and faults Konig always sought to hide. Talking to Erbrechen was like having your father tell you you'd finally made him proud after years of neglect and abuse. For the first time in her life Gehirn knew what home felt like.

It was beautiful beyond words.

She simply bowed.

Erbrechen clapped happily, sending ripples undulating down

his body. "I want to see the fire again." He scanned his crowd of friends. "Who wants to make me happy?" The clamoring answer was instantaneous as hands shot up and people jostled and jock-eyed for position. "Quiet, quiet," cooed Erbrechen. The crowd settled immediately. "You six . . ." He pointed out six men seem-ingly at random. "Step forward so our new friend can show us her fire." They stepped forward, glorious in their chance to please Erbrechen and prove their love. The young woman, still hard at work and arm-deep in Erbrechen's crotch, ignored all of this.

"Fast or slow, My Lord?" Gehirn eyed the six men hungrily.

Erbrechen, looking pleased, asked, "How fast can you?"

Gehirn's already unstable sanity shuddered and crumbled. A concussive blast knocked several of the thinner onlookers off their feet and six vaguely man-shaped pillars of ash stood where there had once been men. She'd never let it out so fast before and had to struggle to bring it back under control. Only fear she might hurt Erbrechen kept her from dissolving into a chaotic hurricane of flame and destruction.

"Oh!" said Erbrechen with surprised pleasure. "That *was* fast."

A gust of wind sent the ash swirling into the air and toppled the mounds. Tiny glowing cinders of bone danced like fairies in the breeze. In seconds the crowd scattered, coughing and chok-ing and clawing at stinging eyes, except Erbrechen, who coughed and clapped joyfully like a child with a new toy.

When the hacking coughs had passed, Erbrechen waved over a squat and ugly man with thin, greasy black hair, bulbous eyes, and fewer teeth than fingers. "This is Regen Anrufer." Regen, dressed in filth-matted animal skins, reeked of long-dead skunk and sour dog shite. "Regen is one of my favorites." The ugly man beamed a gap-toothed grin leaking brown drool between browner teeth. "He was shaman to some tribe of shite-collecting, mud-worshiping horse stickers—what were they called?"

"Schlammstamm," Regen answered wetly.

"Right, whatever." Erbrechen shot an annoyed look at the girl still concentrating on his crotch and snorted disgustedly at her. "Regen, call us a rain to wash the ash off. Something light and warm, not cold." He shivered dramatically, sending ripples across his corpulent body.

This was greeted with cheers by the gathered crowd, none of whom looked like they'd bathed in months.

Regen began a slow stomping dance around one of the camp-fires, his eyes clenched closed, his few teeth bared in a painful rictus snarl. Clawed fingers with torn fingernails dug at recently scabbed wounds on his arms and coaxed forth a thin trickle of blood. He sucked greedily at his arms and spat the blood into the fire. The sky darkened like a lurid gangrenous bruise. When fat, warm drops fell to the upraised arms of Erbrechen's friends, Regen returned to stand before the tent. The shaman staggered with exhaustion but looked pleased with his results. He bowed proudly and shot Gehirn a challenging look.

Emaciated bodies cavorted in the resulting mud and became no cleaner for all the rain. In moments Gehirn witnessed a chaotic orgy of filthy and malnourished bodies writhing with abandon against whoever happened to be closest. If there was any pairing off or sexual preference to be seen, Gehirn could not detect it.

Streaks of ash ran off Erbrechen's bloated body in rivers, fol-lowing every fold and crevice. The fat man watched the orgy with intense interest, sausagelike fingers clenching sporadically into soft, chubby fists, reminding Gehirn of watching a baby at its mother's tit. Erbrechen groaned, and the girl, still elbow-deep, glowed with self-satisfaction. She withdrew her arm and greedily sucked clean her fingers. Erbrechen patted her absent-mindedly on the head and then waved her away. She slunk off, stripping away what little clothing she had, to join in the mud orgy.

Erbrechen squinted at Gehirn. "You are still swaddled in robes. You may join the fun, if you wish."

The malnourished bodies writhed seductively, but more than anything, she didn't want to be rude to her friend. "The sun burns me, and the moon is naught but reflected sunlight. I don't burn as badly at night, but it is still extremely painful."

Erbrechen gestured skyward. "Even with such thick cloud cover?"

"I'd be safe enough," admitted Gehirn, "but as soon as the clouds pass, I'll be vulnerable."

"Well, we can't have that. Regen, you can keep the sky cloudy and protect our new friend, correct?"

Regen paled. "But the cost," he whispered. "I would bleed myself dry." His eyes begged when he looked at Erbrechen and seethed hatred when he flashed glances at Gehirn.

"You don't want our friend burned before our very eyes, do you?" It was obvious from Regen's face he didn't think this such a bad option, but Erbrechen gave him no time to answer. "It would please me greatly if you could do this for me."

Regen bowed low and stifled a sob. "I would bleed myself dry for you."

"Fantastic!" Erbrechen waved the squat shaman away, dismissing him much as he had dismissed the girl moments earlier. "Now that we have your comfort seen to, tell me, where were you going in such an unseemly rush?"

Gehirn told Erbrechen of High Priest Konig Furimmer, the Geborene Damonen, their plan to design and build a god, and her pursuit of the suspected Wahnvor Stellung agents. She told her new friend everything.

Erbrechen sat in silence for several minutes when Gehirn finished. The rain dwindled and finally tapered off, yet the thick cloud cover remained. Regen looked ill as he sat dejectedly in the mud, staring at the ash-hole remains of the camp's fire pit. The orgy too had lost its urgency and devolved into tired, halfhearted copulating and distracted groping. A few of the bodies lay face-down in the muck. Gehirn suspected they had, unnoticed by the others, drowned during the games.

As Erbrechen carefully questioned Gehirn, clarifying aspects of Konig's plans and seeking greater detail, the mob dug motionless people from the mud. One of the bodies, a young man barely in his teens, suddenly began struggling and pushing weakly. Those who had been digging him out were suddenly forcing his head back into the muck. Thin and malnourished, he was no match for the four equally starved people who pinned him to the ground. They looked to Erbrechen for guidance. When the fat man noticed the disturbance, he licked his lips thoughtfully.

"How many?" Erbrechen asked.

"Two, excluding this one," answered one of the men holding the struggling youth.

"We have a special guest"—Erbrechen waved a chubby hand toward Gehirn—"and two will not do."

The four men happily kicked the youth until he stopped moving.

Gehirn watched distractedly as they added the body to the pile. Her interest increased as two of the burlier, more well-fed men hacked the three corpses into manageable-sized chunks with rusty machetes, splitting skulls and digging the brains free. A gang of small children, who didn't seem to belong to any particular parents, fought over the intestines and some of the internal organs and devoured them raw. The hearts, livers, and kidneys were gathered and set aside.

As one group rebuilt and relit the fire pit, another prepared the savaged corpses, stripping away the flesh and chopping the meat into smaller chunks. Three men dragged a huge pot from somewhere and mounted it over the fire on a rickety tripod. They added the butchered meat and a few mangy-looking roots to the pot along with several buckets of muddy water. The organs they placed in a smaller pot with some vegetables and a bucket of what might have been either red wine or blood.

Gehirn, realizing what she was seeing, felt a moment of nausea. Still, her stomach rumbled in hunger.

Erbrechen waved a corpulent hand as if trying to pat Gehirn on the back. "You can share in the organ stew with me. My teeth can't handle the tougher meat." He gave Gehirn a conspirational wink. "And it's the best parts anyway."

Gehirn's uncertainty washed away in a flood of gratitude. "Thank you." *Sharing food. Does that mean he loves me?* Lovers often shared meals together in the few romance plays she'd seen, feeding each other tasty treats with their fingers. Would Erbrechen try to do this for her? It seemed unlikely. He could barely reach his own mouth.

Erbrechen's face became baby serious, like he'd just seen something questionable and was considering putting it in his mouth. "They say when we die our souls pass on to the Afterdeath, where we live again. A chance at redemption, for those who require such things. For those who aren't born redeemed. But what I have learned, what few others understand, is that the soul lives not in the brain—as so many believe—but nestled in the heart and organs." Erbrechen licked his lips hungrily. "Devour a man's organs and you devour his soul. With each soul I eat, I grow in strength, and I have eaten hundreds of souls." Erbrechen waved Gehirn closer and whispered, eyes gleaming. "I'm not stupid. I know the ancient axiom: as a Geisteskranken reaches his peak in power, his delusions destroy him. But imagine if this did not have to be true. Imagine we could grow in power and keep our delusions at bay. This is what I will share with you. Eat a sane man's soul and you gain his strength of spirit. You ingest a small measure of his sanity to balance your own lack." Erbrechen watched the mob as they set about cooking the human stew. "Even the worst of these wretches is more sane than you and I." He laughed, jiggling his entire body. "Your power is immense and your delusions will burn you before long. You'll never eat a soul less stable than your own, my fiery friend."

Gehirn's mind reeled with possibilities. Every Geisteskranken knew that someday their delusions would be their death. She'd heard rumors that Geisteskranken could be cured, but always at the cost of their power. Who would willingly give up the one thing making them special just to live a few extra years of dull normality?

Erbrechen offered her a reprieve. Gehirn struggled to imagine growing in power without the threat of an agonizing death shadowing her every moment.

"I've never heard this before," said Gehirn. "Is it really true? I—I can't believe it."

A smile teased the corners of Erbrechen's damp lips. "It's enough *I* believe it. You know this to be true."

And Gehirn did. The strength of Erbrechen's belief crushed any possibility of denial. The fat man's delusions defined the world around him.

Gehirn, eyes wide with wonder, had no choice but to agree. It was the most amazing gift she had ever been given. *He does love me! He can't bear the thought of being without me.* "I would be honored to share your stew. I will repay this gift, though I know not how."

"You already have. You brought me two gifts. I've never had a Hassebrand friend before, and I am grateful for this. But you also brought me the most precious gift ever: you've given me the future."

"The future?" asked Gehirn.

"This Konig Furimmer is making a god, but this child has not yet Ascended. We will take this child and he will love and worship me as all must. Then we will help him Ascend. Imagine, being loved and worshiped by a god!" exclaimed Erbrechen. "Surely, if a god worships a man, that man will become a god."

She saw it immediately. Erbrechen was right. But the old gods would challenge him. That thought didn't bother her, though. If he was a god, she was a god's friend. Maybe more. And she'd burn all who would offer her love harm.

*I will burn gods.*

Erbrechen loved her. He showed none of Konig's poorly concealed revulsion. When she talked, he listened with rapt attention. He asked questions and listened to her answers, and Gehirn thought her heart would burst for joy.

Gehirn and Erbrechen sat talking as they devoured their stew, Erbrechen wearing as much of his as he managed to eat. The camp around them bustled with activity as Erbrechen's friends prepared to follow the same trio Gehirn had chased to Selbsthass. If they caught the Wahnvor agents, Erbrechen felt sure they'd join his little party of friends.

Erbrechen, Gehirn learned, had avoided large cities and towns for years out of fear the combined beliefs of the massed sane would overwhelm his Gefahrgeist power. The Hassebrand wasn't sure what changed Erbrechen's mind. Perhaps the Gefahrgeist knew some deep desperation he chose not to share. Gehirn could well enough understand; her own fears grew alongside her strength. Though Erbrechen's strength was more obvious, worn like a bright cloak, Gehirn knew Konig was not to be underestimated. The Geborene High Priest was subtle and dangerous like a concealed viper.

"Getting the child out of Selbsthass will be difficult," suggested Gehirn, unsure how to broach what might be a touchy subject.

Erbrechen shrugged, sending ripples undulating the length of his body that took minutes to dissipate. "I think not. The three Wahnvor agents are already planning on grabbing the child. If we catch them first, they'll happily bring him to me once they

understand my need. If not, we'll take the child from them after."
He picked at his teeth and spat at the nearest gaunt person—a
middle-aged woman who, beaming with gratitude, babbled her
thanks and went to display her thick wet prize to the others. Gehirn wanted to burn her and watch everything she was, skin and
bones, hopes and dreams, waft away on the breeze.

## CHAPTER 14

*The tales are only as dark as the teller.*

—HALBER TOD, COTARDIST POET

Every step Launisch took sent pulses of dull pain through Bedeckt's skull and joints. His back ached like he'd been bearing a heavy load for weeks on end. His elbows and shoulders felt like he'd been lifting massive fieldstones over his head all day. He didn't think he'd ever straighten his knees again. Bedeckt felt a sneeze building and turned so he wouldn't spray Launisch with snot. *Better to hit Wichtig.* The sneeze died. His head throbbed with built-up pressure.

*Aging is shite.* He remembered Wütend Alten, a grizzled warrior he'd fought alongside during the battle of Sinnlos between the Auseinander and the Seiger hill clans. Wütend had been fond of saying, "If you can help it, don't get old." At the time Bedeckt thought the man joked about staying young, but now he saw it in a different light. Wütend should have said, "Die before you get old."

Bedeckt wondered whether the warrior had followed his own

advice. They'd been separated when the Seiger Geisteskranken cracked and her delusions brought down the city's walls.

Seeing another settlement ahead, Bedeckt shoved his thoughts of the past aside. Each village looked more prosperous than the last, and with each village Bedeckt's unease grew. Though he knew he'd been here before, he couldn't equate this lush and wealthy land with the poverty-stricken Selbsthass of his memories. Could the beliefs of mankind really reshape the world to such a scale? The possibilities terrified him. If the Geborene Dämonen had such a strong grip on the minds and faith of its common citizenry, Bedeckt wasn't sure he wanted to be at the very heart of their power. Wasn't sure? No, he *knew* he didn't want to be here. But the prize was too tempting. The Geborene would pay anything to get their god back.

The land flattened as they neared Selbsthass City and became what Bedeckt could only assume was perfect farmland. The sprawling scene before them looked like a massive quilt, each square a different color depending on what grew there. Even the small plots of forest looked planned and manicured, the lines of trees a little too neat. He doubted anything more dangerous than a rabbit lived within a hundred miles of the Geborene capital.

"Well, the wolves are here now," Bedeckt muttered to himself.

Wichtig howled at the sky.

Stehlen glared at Wichtig. "Shush. We don't want to scare the sheep."

Wichtig immediately took on an innocent puppy-dog look. *The idiot's face is as flexible as his loyalties.* Was that unfair? Bedeckt thought not.

"Us?" asked Wichtig. "Dangerous? No, no. We're simply . . . What are we?" he asked, turning to Bedeckt.

"Passing through. We'll stay a few nights in a decent tavern and move along." He wanted to fall into a soft bed and never rise.

"Right. Passing through. Good plan." Wichtig rolled his eyes at Stehlen, who grinned back. Bedeckt ignored them both. "Brilliant. How we going to pay for an inn? I seem to have spent what coin I had."

"Stehlen has money," Bedeckt answered.

"I have a little set aside," she snapped. "I don't see why I have to keep paying for—" She stopped when she saw the look Bedeckt gave her. The Swordsman seemed oblivious to the unspoken exchange.

"Do you ever think about death?" Wichtig suddenly asked.

"No," answered Bedeckt, hoping to end the conversation.

"You ever think about all the people you've killed?" asked Wichtig, as if Bedeckt hadn't answered.

Bedeckt thought about his father. There were more than a few people he wasn't looking forward to seeing in the Afterdeath. "No."

Wichtig ran fingers through his perfect hair, leaving it looking, if anything, even more perfect. "Do you really believe when you die everyone you've ever killed will be there waiting for you?"

"I hope so," said Stehlen.

Wichtig glanced at her. "Really? Why?"

"Some of them I want to kill again."

Wichtig nodded as if this made perfect sense. "Bedeckt, what do you believe?"

"People believe all manner of crazy things. Maybe there isn't even an Afterdeath. There's a tribe in the far north called the Verschlinger. They believe they gain strength and wisdom by eating vanquished foes. They don't believe in an Afterdeath at all. The only way to live on is to be eaten, and that leads to servitude. They burn their dead so they can't be eaten."

Wichtig watched him for several heartbeats, brows furrowed like he was trying to figure out some challenging riddle. "Sure, but what do *you* believe?"

"I believe my beliefs don't matter. I believe if I die surrounded by idiots worshiping the Warrior's Credo who believe in an Afterdeath, then that's what will probably happen."

Stehlen cocked an eyebrow and spat. "You believe it matters where you die and who is with you?"

Was that a hint of desperation or hope he detected in her voice? *She knows who she wants to die with.* Bedeckt quashed the thought, afraid to examine it further.

"As I said: I believe my beliefs don't matter."

"I think it's punishment," mused Wichtig. "That's the only thing that makes sense."

Stehlen turned a jaundiced eye in his direction. "How so?"

"Think about it. When you die you'll be surrounded by the people you killed. Who the hells goes around killing people they like? In the Afterdeath we'll be surrounded by our enemies."

Bedeckt kept his mouth closed. Empty and vapid as Wichtig was, he made too much sense at the moment.

"But the Warrior's Credo says those you slay must serve," Stehlen said.

"Gods, I hope so," said Wichtig with feeling. "Gods, I hope so."

With the exception of Bedeckt's wheezing and sporadic bouts of coughing, they rode on in silence. Over the last day, Selbsthass City had gone from being a hazy smudge on the horizon to *being* the horizon. Hardly the largest or most impressive city they'd seen, but a massive and ancient castle with towering battlements hunkered at its center. The castle was the only aspect of Selbsthass Bedeckt recognized; it preceded the Geborene by hundreds or even thousands of years. Last time he'd been here, however, it had looked more like abandoned ruins and far less intimidating. Bedeckt prayed—though not to any specific gods—the tower would not be the center of the Geborene religion. But in the heart of a Theocracy, who else would have such a citadel?

THE GEBORENE CHURCH troubled Bedeckt. What if he was right, what if the delusions of a single powerful Gefahrgeist—and he did not doubt a Gefahrgeist lurked at the center of this religion—had caused the sweeping changes he'd witnessed in Selbsthass? This Theocrat might not manifest as a Slaver type, but there was no telling what he might be capable of. Gods, he did not want to catch the attention of a powerful Gefahrgeist. He glanced at his companions.

"We have to stay out of trouble," said Bedeckt, annoyed at having to say something so obvious—but he was talking to Wichtig and Stehlen. "Anything calling attention to us could ruin everything." He examined his two traveling companions, giving them a dark look full of promised violence he doubted he could fulfill. They ignored it.

"Of course," said Wichtig reasonably. "You hear that, Stehlen? None of your Kleptic shite. You can't be lifting every shiny trinket that catches your attention."

"And you can't be searching out this city's Swordsmen and killing them," added Bedeckt.

"What? Why the hells not?"

"Because it will draw attention to us," answered Stehlen. "Moron."

Wichtig took a deep breath and Bedeckt knew what would come next. The Swordsman struggled to build an argument to convince them he *had* to find and kill these men, that it would be best for everyone.

"I know this child will be worth a fair amount," said Wichtig carefully.

Bedeckt snorted derisively. "Enough to retire on." He hadn't meant to mention his plans, but neither Stehlen nor Wichtig seemed to notice.

Wichtig sat straight in the saddle and the breeze caught his perfect hair. He glowed sincerity. "I think you underestimate how valuable it will be having the World's Greatest Swordsman at your side. Once word spreads, the title will be its own meal ticket."

"It's the panty ticket you're interested in," growled Stehlen, flashing yellow teeth at Bedeckt.

Wichtig's ability to strike the right pose, catch the right light, and say the right things was all part of his Gefahrgeist powers. Bedeckt, keeping this in mind, looked away and focused on the reality of the situation. The would-be god-child was his way out of this life. He'd had enough skulking around, living one job to the next.

"You're a fine Swordsman," said Bedeckt.

"I'm the b—"

"But you aren't *that* good. I've seen men who would slaughter you in a heartbeat. True masters."

Wichtig chuckled, undaunted. "Ah, but they don't have my Gefahrgeist—"

"You're not that powerful a Gefahrgeist. If you were, I'd be agreeing with you."

Wichtig's mouth snapped shut. He looked hurt, but Bedeckt ignored this; it was all part of the act.

"Your attempts to undermine my confidence will always fail," said Wichtig through clenched teeth. "Your doubt in me makes me stronger." Wichtig, Bedeckt realized, was talking more to himself than to Bedeckt. "The men you speak of aren't trying to be the Greatest Swordsman in the World. They're content with their local fame. They lack my vision. And, as always, you forget: it's not you I have to convince, it's the common people. They love me. You know this." He spread his arms as if embracing the adulation of a large crowd. "I become a better Swordsman with each person who believes in me." He growled angrily at Bedeckt. "And a lot of people believe in me. Belief defines reality. Your lack of faith changes nothing."

Stehlen watched with interest but remained quiet.

"Fine," said Bedeckt. None of Wichtig's mind shite mattered. "Someday you'll be the Greatest Swordsman. But if you start trouble in Selbsthass City, I'll cut you down myself."

"We're all reasonable people here," said Wichtig agreeably. "Except Stehlen. Relax. We go in, we get the child, we get out. All very quiet."

Bedeckt knew better than to believe a word of this. He'd have to keep a close eye on Wichtig. When had his life become one of babysitting dangerous children? He looked to Stehlen. Would she back him on this?

"If he causes trouble I'll cut his throat," she said.

Wichtig's puppy-dog expression returned and he looked misty-eyed and emotional. "I love you guys. Who could ask for better friends?"

THE CITY AND castle grew in detail as they neared Selbsthass. They could make out individual spires stabbing into the sky, marvels of architecture Bedeckt suspected were supported more by the faith of the populace than by any careful planning. At this range the keep showed itself to be as much battle-ready fortress as it was church. Though it had been impressive last time Bedeckt saw the ancient castle, much had changed. The walls seemed taller and the towers higher. Everything spoke of permanence.

People passed them on the road, well dressed and comfortable, giving them a wide berth. It was no great feat to see they stood out as foreigners. There was no helping it. A change of clothes wouldn't hide their accents, Bedeckt's scarred visage, Stehlen's vicious temper, or Wichtig's deadly grace.

---

Wichtig knew opportunity when he saw it, and the fates rarely offered up one as ripe and beautiful as this. A vast city, wealthy and prosperous, primed by a priesthood for manipulation. None of the people who passed them even carried swords! If Wichtig could capture the attention of this populace, it would forever tip the scales in his favor. Being backed by the faith of the poor and downtrodden, the scared, short-lived peasantry, was all fine and good. But if the people of Selbsthass came to understand he was the Greatest Swordsman in the World, he would be buoyed by the faith of those confident in their beliefs and sure of their place in the world. Though he couldn't remember anyone ever talking about the *quality* of faith, he knew—bone-deep—it mattered. The faith of happy and wealthy people had to be worth more than the faith of a beggar with one foot in the Afterdeath.

Bedeckt had threatened to kill Wichtig so many times the young Swordsman had long ago lost count. It was damned near daily now. He could almost remember when he'd taken the gruff old bastard seriously, back before they'd really become friends. Friends. The word gave Wichtig strange feelings. Never in his life had he had friends. Now he had two. Sure, they bickered, but bickering was part of all relationships. His parents had fought all the time. Hells, Wichtig fought more viciously with his wife than he'd ever argued with Bedeckt or Stehlen, and he'd loved her. Bedeckt could threaten and posture all he liked, but he had once saved Stehlen and Wichtig when he could have abandoned them. It had been a sobering moment for Wichtig.

*Someday I'll show the grumpy old goat just what kind of friend I am.*

"You look like stomped shite, old man," Wichtig told Bedeckt. The old man opened his mouth to answer and was interrupted by a fit of coughing.

Still, Wichtig hated being told what he was and wasn't allowed to do. It reminded him of childhood and the days before he'd realized power was something he could just take. Words and swords, they were weapons. Weapons in which he was more than proficient.

*You can't have sword without word,* mused Wichtig. *Oh! What a lovely phrase. Has anyone said that before?* He thought not.

Wichtig covertly examined Stehlen as she rode in front of him. An expert rider, her hips rolled smoothly with the motion of the horse.

Not an ounce of fat, all lean muscle. What would it be like to bed her from behind so he wouldn't have to see her face? *I'd probably wound myself on her bony arse.* The thought gave him a small chuckle, and when she looked back to see what he was laughing about, he leered and winked at her.

She flared her nostrils and spat at his horse, which shied away. "Moron," she growled.

Had she blushed? The thought made him laugh all the louder. Once they'd settled in to Selbsthass City, he'd find away to confront the local Swordsmen and kill a few of the better ones. *Who the hells does Bedeckt think he is, telling me what I can't do?*

Wichtig had an idea, pulled his horse alongside Stehlen's, and leaned in to whisper to her. "Want to help me kill a few Swordsmen? You might have to steal a few things," he added to sweeten the deal.

Stehlen glanced at Bedeckt, who rode a few horse lengths ahead of them. The old man's hearing was shot, the result of either too many blows to the head or the fact that his ears had been mangled in past battles. This sickness probably didn't help. She looked back to Wichtig. "Bedeckt will kill you."

"Not if you're any good," he challenged.

"I'm good enough to fool the likes of you morons."

"Good. I'll give you the nod when the time is right."

⸻

Bedeckt heard their muted conversation but not what they talked about. The missing fingers of his left hand itched fiercely and the healthy perfection of the surrounding lands bothered him more than he wanted to share. They'd think he'd lost his edge. Had he? Had Wichtig's suggestion they find an inn been a veiled insult or a real concern? Knowing the Swordsman, probably the former. He didn't much care. He wanted a bed more than he would ever admit.

*Gods, I am too old for this skulking shite.*

THE LEICHTES HAUS inn was so clean as to be intimidating. Bedeckt would have felt guilty for fouling it with his presence were guilt not such a waste. Intricately carved shelves holding a wider assortment of liquors than he'd known existed lined cherry oak walls. The heavy oak chair, cushioned in thick velour, sighed when he sat on it. Stehlen looked ready to kill the first person to point out she didn't belong here, whereas Wichtig slumped easily in his chair, offering the attractive bar staff warm smiles and soft words.

The Swordsman's chameleon-like ability to fit comfortably in any environment never ceased to surprise Bedeckt. He'd watched Wichtig chat up everyone from scullery maids to the daughters of kings with equal aplomb. Even men seemed drawn to his glib companionship. Few understood Wichtig merely used them to achieve some briefly held ambition. The Swordsman was a self-centered arse with the attention span of a high-strung child. How people missed this was a mystery.

Bedeckt, exhausted, weak, and unable to keep his eyes open, retired early, leaving Wichtig with dire warnings to stay out of trouble. Stehlen promised to keep an eye on the Swordsman. No doubt he'd awaken to find half the city dead and the other half baying for his blood. Why did he even bother?

He went to bed alone and slept the fitful sleep of an old man, awoken occasionally by twinges in his knees, fits of coughing, the weight of his snot-filled skull, and the need to pee. If he dreamed, he remembered nothing.

That night Wichtig learned the name of the man widely considered to be the Greatest Swordsman in these parts: GroBe Klinge. All he had to do now was find some way of accidentally causing GroBe to challenge him.

A few hours and three times as many pints later he found himself tangling with a young barmaid from the Leichtes Haus. The girl was indefatigable. When he awoke she was gone, as was a sizable chunk of what remained of his coin. Wichtig laughed uproariously until his hangover silenced him. The girl had more than earned what she'd taken.

It was the wee hours of the morning. A prosperous neighborhood, the streets quiet and lit by distantly spaced lanterns. Come to think of it, every neighborhood Stehlen had seen looked at least comfortably well off. All these clean streets left her uneasy.

She'd asked around for an hour before finding the right house, a squat faded pink stucco bungalow. She'd also paid several street urchins—and they'd been surprisingly difficult to find—to watch the street while she entered the house; it was only fitting the money came from Wichtig. She'd lifted it while he'd been busy with the bar wench. She'd walked right into the room, stood watching for a moment, and helped herself to his coin. She wasn't sure if her Kleptic abilities had even come into play—the two seemed fairly preoccupied. Anyone could have wandered into the room and helped themselves to whatever they found. As it was, all Stehlen wanted was Wichtig's money and a pretty little scarf—which she now wore tied around her neck—the barmaid left balled on the floor while she got balled on the bed.

They say you don't really know who you are until you're tested. This sat well with Stehlen, because she knew who she was.

Studying? Pointless!

Planning? For morons!

Look at the situation, react. Wichtig asked her to help him find and kill a few Swordsmen to spread his reputation and feed his insatiable ego. Bedeckt asked her to help keep Wichtig out of trouble. She'd agreed to both. The fun part would be figuring out how to keep her word—not that it was worth anything—and still ensure neither man got what he wanted. In a perfect world she'd be able to pull this off in a way she also found entertaining. In a perfect world even the repercussions of her actions would be entertaining.

*This might be a perfect world,* she mused. She'd help Wichtig and thwart him with his own money at the same time.

Stehlen glanced up and down the street, checking if her urchins for hire remained in their assigned positions. *Can't trust anyone these days.* The two girls were where they should be. If the city watch arrived they'd bark like dogs to let her know.

Stehlen unlocked the front door and slipped inside. She felt good today, like a ghost or one of those savage trickster gods the northern barbarians worshiped. Walls and locked doors offered no obstacle.

The interior of the house stank of jasmine incense struggling to mask a man's body odor. It was the perfunctory clean of a single man doing just enough so that he could bring women home. Dust gathered in corners and behind anything he couldn't be bothered to move, which was just about everything. Weapons collected from a dozen nations decorated the walls. An impressive collection, it represented a sizable investment of time and money. She hunted for interesting weapons but found nothing suiting her style. The single bedroom was located at the rear of the bungalow and she stood at the door for several minutes listening to the heavy breathing within. One person. A man. Large, but not fat.

143

Stehlen slid into the bedroom and stood at the side of the sleeping man. He was, she had to admit, beautiful in a brutal kind of way. His jaw was strong and square, his black hair cut short. Thick eyebrows framed what she suspected might be well-formed eyes. She cleared her throat to get his attention. He slept on. Then she poked him with a stiletto, just enough to draw blood. The man came awake with a start and froze as he saw Stehlen staring down at him. His face was immediately calm, measuring. His eyes hard. Stehlen liked him even more.

"Yes?" he asked.

"GroBe Klinge?"

He took his time examining her lean body and worn armor. "You're no adoring fan," he said.

Stehlen read his eyes and body posture. There was a knife under his pillow but he wasn't sure he could reach it without her noticing. She smiled. "No. A half-wit moron wants to challenge you to a duel."

GroBe shrugged, inching his hand toward the knife. "Are you asking me not to kill this moron?" His eyes caressed her in open appreciation, which caught her off guard. "I could be convinced."

Stehlen flared her nostrils as she considered bedding this large and well-muscled man. The thought was more than a little appealing. "No. I have to make sure he doesn't kill you."

GroBe visibly relaxed. "Well then, put down the knife and climb in here."

"I have a better way," she said, and drove the stiletto through an eye into his brain.

GroBe said "damn" very clearly and sagged back onto the bed. Stehlen watched as the body figured out what the mind already knew. It took several minutes before the last signs of twitching life faded and GroBe lay still. Amazing how stubbornly some bodies clung to life while others slid off with little more than a quiet sigh. Gently running a hand through his hair, she leaned forward and kissed his forehead. He was warm.

"I'll see you in the Afterdeath," she whispered into his ear.

Stehlen selected several of the better-quality weapons from GroBe's collection and gave them—along with a fast lesson in their use—to the two street-urchin girls. She wasn't worried about them reporting her visit with GroBe; people had difficulty remembering her. An aspect, no doubt, of her Kleptic powers and in no way a slight on her appearance or personality. Or so she hoped.

Once she'd paid the girls with Wichtig's coin, she returned to the Leichtes Haus for a few short hours of rest. She slept the sleep of the blissfully innocent and dreamed of GroBe's strong arms and other more interesting parts of his anatomy. In the morning she awoke happy and refreshed and joined Bedeckt and Wichtig in the main room for a breakfast of sausage, stale bread, and fried eggs swimming in pools of pepper-flaked grease.

"That's a lovely scarf," said Wichtig, nodding toward her while stuffing sausage in his mouth.

*Shite.* She'd forgotten about the scarf. "It was my mother's." Stehlen dug into breakfast with a will, ignoring Wichtig's disbelieving look.

〰〰〰〰〰〰

Bedeckt ignored them both, grimacing at his plate. He hadn't slept well and the thought of food twisted his guts with nausea.

When a man burst into the tavern's main room and excitedly announced GroBe Klinge, Selbsthass's Greatest Swordsman, was dead, Bedeckt glanced despairingly at Wichtig.

"Did I not say I'd kill you if you stirred trouble for us here?"

Wichtig raised his hands, palms out. "I slept here with . . . can't remember her name . . . the barmaid with the fantastic body. I didn't kill this GroBe."

The bearer of bad news regaled his friends, for the price of a pint, with word of how GroBe had been found naked in bed, stabbed through the eye.

Not Wichtig's style. But it was . . .

Bedeckt glanced toward Stehlen and noticed Wichtig had done the same. She ignored them and focused on mopping up the last of the grease with a crust.

"What were you up to last night?" asked Wichtig. "Aside from finding your mother's long-lost scarf."

Stehlen looked up, flared her nostrils, and spat a pepper-flaked wad onto her plate. She ignored Wichtig and met Bedeckt's eyes. "Took care of the business you asked me to look into."

Bedeckt kept a straight face. She'd killed GroBe to stop Wichtig from fighting him? He should have seen this coming when he'd asked her to make sure Wichtig didn't cause trouble by challenging every Swordsman in the city. Frankly, he hadn't expected her to pay his request any attention, much less wander the city killing Swordsmen before Wichtig could get to them. He shuddered to contemplate the number of bodies she was capable of leaving in a single night. He'd have to dissuade her from killing any more than she already had.

"And just what was this errand you ran for Bedeckt?" Wichtig asked.

Bedeckt answered. "Unrelated to a dead Swordsman. We need to talk about how we're going to get into the Geborene High Temple."

"Getting in is easy," said Stehlen. "Getting out with their god-child will be interesting."

"Interesting?" asked Wichtig, beaming happily. "Interesting sounds fun!"

⸻

Stehlen watched the two men lose themselves in their pointless planning, arguing back and forth and getting nowhere. Even sick and miserable, Bedeckt wanted to plan every last aspect and account for every possible scenario, no matter how farfetched. Wichtig cared only that enough people knew he was involved so as to increase his reputation. Bedeckt's plans always went to complete shite. Still, she looked on as the men grew excited about one plan, saw its flaws, and then became excited about the next flawed plan. She was philosophical about all of this. Sure, it was a grand waste of time, but she took entertainment where she found it. And she had nothing else to do today. Bedeckt would take days to plan this, so she had plenty of time. Stehlen figured she'd go in and get the child tonight and surprise Bedeckt with him tomorrow morning. This city made her uncomfortable and she wanted out as fast as possible.

Around noon they decided to take a break. Wichtig said he wanted to go for a walk to stretch his legs and grumbled annoyance when Bedeckt and Stehlen said they'd join him.

Wichtig followed a few paces behind Bedeckt and Stehlen. If they'd just find something interesting to look at, he'd make good his escape and later claim he'd lost them in the crowd. They wouldn't believe him, but it hardly mattered. But gods damn it, Stehlen glanced over her shoulder every few seconds, smiling sweetly each time—a horrifying expression on *her* face, to say the least—to check he was still there. He'd figure something out. He just needed a chance.

They'd wandered the market for an hour, Stehlen no doubt stealing worthless trinkets from every stall they passed, when Wichtig saw what he'd been hoping for. A lithe young man, slim-hipped, broad-chested, and long of limb, with a fine-looking blade at his side. His well-made clothes bespoke money and taste. Stehlen saw the Swordsman at the same time and shot Wichtig a questioning look. Bedeckt completely missed it.

147

*She'll actually help me?* Wichtig nodded once and turned his attention to a nearby fruit stand. He watched out of the corner of his eye as she broke away from Bedeckt. The old goat didn't notice.

*Is she really going to help?* Wichtig couldn't be sure. He'd have sworn she killed GroBe. But why would she? Surely not simply out of spite for some imagined slight. Damn, that scarf looked familiar.

Wichtig watched as Stehlen wandered past the tastefully dressed Swordsman on her way back to Bedeckt and Wichtig. While Bedeckt was distracted discussing the healing properties of some vegetable with an old hag hunched behind her cart, Stehlen slipped Wichtig an expensive money purse filled with coin.

"What have we here?" Wichtig declared loudly, holding the purse up and bouncing it in his hand so the coins jangled enticingly. "I seem to have found some rich arsehole's money purse." He watched the Swordsman search his pockets and then glare at Wichtig, who, turning circles to address the crowd, raised his voice. "Who is the gap-brained festering crotch of a dandy belonging to this insipid-looking woman's purse? Come now, don't be embarrassed. Come get your dainty little purse."

Bedeckt turned away from the hag and watched with a look of suspicious confusion.

"It's mine."

Wichtig turned to face the man and found himself looking into hard eyes the color of a storm-tossed sea. "Figures," he said.

The man cocked an eyebrow and rested a hand on the pommel of his sword. "Meaning?"

"You are prettily dressed." Wichtig gestured, a lazy spin of the fingers taking in the man and discarding him as unimportant. "Exactly the kind of effete twat I'd expect to find this purse attached to."

The crowd suddenly retreated from the two men. Wichtig clearly heard Bedeckt's groan.

The stormy-eyed man smiled cold death. "You must be new here. Or you'd be apologizing and begging me to spare you."

"If you're going to offer fashion advice, I beg you . . . spare me."

The crowd guffawed and gathered around. Even these so-called civilized folks hungered for blood.

"I'm Zweiter Stelle, commonly believed to be the second Greatest Swordsman in all of Selbsthass."

"A pleasure, I'm sure." Wichtig bowed. "I am Wichtig Lügner. The *best* Swordsman in Selbsthass. It is commonly believed," he said, mocking Zweiter's voice, "that I am the Greatest Swordsman in the World."

"Great," drawled Stehlen, loud enough for the crowd to hear. "Why do they always posture, building up their courage, before finally killing each other?" She shook her head disparagingly. "Swordsmen . . . windbags one and all."

A few of the crowd laughed and clapped. Everyone had seen Swordsmen make long speeches in an attempt to win the belief of the people before the fighting began. Some felt this was the truest moment of any fight, the beliefs of the mob defined winner and loser. The mob, however, was more interested in seeing blood than listening to long-winded speeches about why one Swordsman was better than the other.

There are times for speeches and times for action. This, Wichtig understood, was the latter. Stehlen had ruined his chance to win the crowd with words—no doubt on purpose. If he kept talking he'd come off as the coward and lose people's faith. Come to think of it, it would have been nice to kill a few lesser Swordsmen—thereby building more of a local reputation—before facing one such as Zweiter Stelle. Had she planned this in an attempt to kill him?

Wichtig shrugged philosophically and drew his sword in a lightning-fast flourish, catching the sun just so. He stood straight and poised. A breeze ruffled his perfect hair.

"Well, come along, Squatter—"

"Zweiter."

"We don't want to disappoint the crowd." Wichtig winked at a pretty girl and blew her a kiss. While a long speech might hurt him here, other means of manipulation remained. "My gentle touch is needed elsewhere."

The crowd formed a large circle around the two men. There was a moment of jostling as those braver and more foolish shoved to get to the front and the cowardly wise pushed to put some people between themselves and the fight. As long as all agreed this was an honest duel and no one was being attacked or coerced, the city guard had no part to play. In fact, a few of the guards joined the thronging crowd and took part in the impromptu betting.

Bedeckt pulled Wichtig aside. "How did you come by the purse?"

"I found it."

"It stretches the limits of my belief to think you just happened to find the purse of the second-best Swordsman in Selbsthass—perhaps the best now that GroBe is dead—and insulted him."

Wichtig gave Bedeckt his best look of wounded innocence. "It *is* a womanly purse." He rolled the tension from his shoulders. He felt like a hawk staring down into a field looking for the telltale movement bespeaking prey. He tossed Zweiter's purse to Bedeckt and the old man caught it in his half hand. Wichtig understood: Bedeckt's good hand always remained free to grab his ax. "Here, put some of his money on the fight. Best put it on me—we wouldn't want to cost him his hard-earned coin."

Bedeckt placed a firm hand on Wichtig's shoulder and the two made eye contact. "I do hope you survive this."

Wichtig blinked in surprise. "Well, I'm touched, I didn't think—"

"Because I'm going to kill you afterward."

"Hey," protested Wichtig, "I don't have the skills to lift a man's money and you know it. I tell you, in all honesty, I didn't take the purse."

‖‖‖‖‖‖‖‖‖‖

Bedeckt looked to Stehlen, who flashed him a sickly smile of yellow teeth and flared nostrils.

"Shite," he said.

He should have known. If he thought he could grab the godchild and escape without the help of these two dangerous idiots, he would have walked away right then and there.

The two fighters squared off, bowed perfunctorily to each other, and began circling. Bedeckt watched with professional disinterest. Might as well enjoy the show.

Zweiter moved well, his balance and grace beautiful to watch. Wichtig, on the other hand, looked unusually clumsy. His feet dragged and his sword kept moving uncertainly, like every time Wichtig thought about attacking he was plagued by doubt.

"If things go badly for Wichtig," Bedeckt growled to Stehlen, "I'll offer Zweiter a job."

Stehlen sidled next to Bedeckt and leaned against him. Her warm proximity and the length of time since he'd been with a woman made him uncomfortable.

"Wichtig looks outclassed," she said.

"He's lulling Zweiter into a false sense of security."

"If he keeps this up he'll lose the crowd."

"True," agreed Bedeckt. "Put my money back." He was guessing—he hadn't actually felt anything.

Stehlen laughed and he felt her body move against his. "I hadn't taken it. Yet."

Wichtig and Zweiter tried a few passes but neither touched the other. The local Swordsman showed flawless technique, his attacks fast and precise, whereas Wichtig seemed surprised each time and barely capable of defending. His own attacks were often deflected before they'd truly began.

"Did you place a wager?" Stehlen asked Bedeckt.

"I put all of Zweiter's money on Wichtig."

"Awkward," she said, "if Zweiter kills him."

"These Swordsmen dance pretty enough," said Bedeckt, "but they are never ready for a complete lack of finesse. Act like you're chopping trees and they're no great difficulty." It was all bluff and bluster—both on the part of the Swordsmen and, at the moment, Bedeckt. A strong breeze would probably fell Bedeckt right now. Even the short walk had left him out of breath.

The ringing sound of steel on steel caused the crowd to gasp as the two men blurred into a flurry of defenses and attacks, leaving both breathing heavily but neither wounded.

Stehlen massaged Bedeckt's stiff shoulders, working at the knots.

"You need to learn to relax," she said, grunting as she dug at a stubborn knot of muscle. "You really think you could beat Wichtig in a fight?"

Bedeckt stifled a groan of pain as she worked at the muscle. He'd seen Wichtig move inhumanly fast—not at all like the fighter he watched now—and with such grace and skill it left him dazzled. "No. But if you ever tell him"—he glanced over his shoulder at her—"I'll kill *you*."

Stehlen snorted. "You *definitely* don't have what it takes to kill the likes of me, old man. Real speed comes from a state of relaxation. You're so damned tense you'll be immobile in a few years."

Her words struck a little too close to Bedeckt's own recent thoughts. He shrugged her away angrily, and if she noticed, she made no complaint. "Never underestimate a scarred old man. The only thing you know for sure is he's been in a lot of fights and he's still—" A savage fit of coughing ruined the sentiment and doubled Bedeckt over. He stood, hands on knees, until it passed.

"If you were any good with your monstrous woodchopper, you wouldn't have so many damned scars." She punched him hard in the shoulder. "Old men are so cute when they get all defensive. Any time you need help relaxing," she offered, stepping closer, "I can always—"

"Stop mucking around already!" Bedeckt bellowed at Wichtig. "Kill him and let's be about our business." He glared at the two fighters, avoiding Stehlen's eyes.

Wichtig dipped a quick nod toward Bedeckt and transformed. Gone was the awkward clumsiness. He no longer breathed heavily and seemed perfectly relaxed and poised. A gasp passed through the crowd as they realized what they'd just seen. Wichtig was toying with Zweiter and they all knew it.

"See," said Bedeckt, gesturing toward the fight. "Wichtig understands; to win them over they had to first doubt him. It isn't enough to simply kill your opponent, you must be an entertainer. He plays the crowd well," he admitted. "It's all about manipulation of expectations."

Stehlen shook her head in disgust. "Grumpy old men make the worst philosophers. If you want a man dead, kill him."

Wichtig pressed Zweiter hard while looking entirely bored at the same time. He spent as much time winking at girls and blowing kisses as he did fighting. The mob ate it up.

"Though I agree," said Bedeckt, "our goals are different. He's a Gefahrgeist. He craves attention like I crave a pint. He wants to be the Greatest Swordsman in the World. He'll achieve it or die trying."

"Die trying," Stehlen stated without hesitation.

"Probably. But have you noticed he's getting better? He was always good, but look."

They watched as Wichtig disarmed Zweiter and then, with

a grand and noble gesture, allowed the man to fetch his sword and return to the circle. Wichtig disarmed him three more times before the man stood over his sword, gasping for breath, hands on knees.

Wichtig nodded to Zweiter. "I think you are still the second-best Swordsman in Selbsthass. But don't be disappointed. Before GroBe died, you were actually the third." The crowd laughed and clapped. "It's been a pleasure," he called to Zweiter. "Keep practicing."

As Wichtig took his time bowing to the crowd and basking in their adoration, Zweiter slunk away like a beaten dog.

Stehlen poked Bedeckt with a hard finger. "The idiot isn't even going to kill him?"

"No," he said, equally disgusted. "Remember, though, it's all about the crowd. None of this matters unless everyone knows who he is. And the people love a well-mannered killer. If Swordsmen weren't so romanticized by poets and storytellers, Wichtig would never even touch a sword."

"I'd have killed Zweiter and been done with it."

"Me too. But then we'll never be famous and he'll be remembered as—"

"The Biggest Idiot in the World."

"Yes," agreed Bedeckt a little sadly. Wichtig was the shallowest man Bedeckt had ever met. And yet still Bedeckt couldn't figure him out. The man fought without fear even though he was a complete coward in so many other ways. Wichtig had fled his wife and child rather than chance failing at fatherhood. He'd abandoned his art and poetry—Bedeckt would never admit how impressed he was by Wichtig's talents—when on the very brink of success. Some days Bedeckt wanted to crack the man's head and send him back to his family. Wichtig had everything Bedeckt wanted and could never achieve, and he'd thrown it away rather than chance failure. Even mentioning any of this to Wichtig caused the man to become a violent and sulky drunk for weeks on end. Bedeckt figured it best to be philosophical about this kind of thing. If Wichtig wanted to waste his considerable talents on petty crime and violence and likely suffer an unpleasant and brutal death, who was he to judge? If Bedeckt spent his life trying to make Wichtig and Stehlen better people, he'd have no time left for breathing. He wasn't even doing a particularly good job of breathing right now. He plugged a nostril and tried to blow the other clear. Nothing happened other than his ears popping violently.

Stehlen poked him again and he grunted in pain. *How does she always find the softest spot?*

"What the hells is going on in your thick skull, old man?" she demanded. "You look like you ate a cat turd." She tried to poke him again but he batted her hand away. "Ho ho! Old man is grumpy. You spend too much time thinking. Explains your cat-turd face. I'll fetch the idiot. Let's go back to the Leichtes Haus for drinks."

"Fine." Bedeckt turned into the crowd and shoved his way through. People complained only until they caught sight of his scarred face and body and the massive ax slung over his shoulder.

He heard Stehlen shouting at Wichtig, "Hey, idiot! Cat-turd face needs a pint."

Late in the day the sky became overcast and the air smelled of sodden dog. Heavy cloud cover blotted the sun from view, plunging the streets into murky darkness. When Stehlen snuck out of the Leichtes Haus on her way to steal the god-child, she found Wichtig and Bedeckt waiting for her.

She stood, hands on slim hips, staring at them with ill-concealed anger. "I suppose you think you're clever."

"Of course," said Wichtig. "Step one of our plan was: collect

Stehlen as she tries to sneak out and grab the child without us."
He mimed scratching something off a list. "Step one complete.
Shall we get the little shite and be on our way?"

The last laugh was, of course, hers. She'd suspected they'd be
waiting and brought along the robes she'd stolen—the size and
color carefully selected—from the Geborene temple in Gottlos.
Bedeckt gave her an odd look but, after examining the brown
robe, the only one that would possibly fit him—scowled and said
nothing. Stehlen thought the grizzled old warrior looked even
worse than he had earlier. The man needed a week in bed, not
the half a night he got—most of which he'd spent drinking.

Wichtig sniffed gingerly at his robes and flared his perfect
nostrils in distaste. "These smell terrible."

In the distance echoed the ominous rumble of thunder.

# CHAPTER 15

*The hand-plucked rose loses meaning as life is leached. Red love,*
*once clutched to breast, putrefies and is thrown to the midden.*
*The hand leaked life as meaning was plucked. Putrefaction*
*clutched love and was thrown to the midden.*

—HALBER TOD, COTARDIST POET

Though easily big enough for a hundred students, Aufschlag
had reserved this sprawling classroom for his single-most-
important pupil. When not in use, a pair of Otraalma guards,
both capable of becoming monstrously twisted demons, remained stationed here to ensure no one touched the lessons left
out on the massive oaken tables. Now the two guards waited
beyond the closed door, ready to give their lives should any attempt entry.

The Chief Scientist sat rigidly. Morgen paced back and forth
in front of him, hands clasped behind his back, head tilted forward, eyes locked on the floor. Aufschlag had not seen this man-
nerism before.

Morgen stopped pacing and faced Aufschlag. The boy glanced toward a mirror and then back at the Chief Scientist.

"Konig watches me. Always."

"Even now?" Aufschlag asked.

"He thinks so." Morgen smiled. "But Schwacher Sucher is not much of a Mirrorist. It's easy to fool him when I wish."

"And you wish to now?"

"Yes. I don't mean to hide things from Konig, but there are some things I find awkward to talk to him about." The boy's face went from confident to worried and scared and back to confident so fast Aufschlag wondered if he'd imagined it.

"Morgen, you can always talk to me. You know I will always be here for you."

"Konig expects something from me, doesn't he?"

"Of course. You will be the Geborene god—"

"I mean something more specific. Something personal." Morgen watched him, face open and trusting.

Should he tell Morgen? Yes. To hells with Konig. "Konig is a powerful Geisteskranken," he said.

Morgen just looked confused.

*How we have shielded this child that he doesn't know this simple axiom!* "It means his delusions are also powerful. And growing in power. He will share the fate of all Geisteskranken. Eventually his delusions will seek to wrestle control from him."

Morgen's eyes widened. "His Doppels! I have to save him!"

"Well, yes, but—"

"But . . . but how?"

Aufschlag stifled the desire to laugh. Details had never been Konig's strength. "I don't know," he admitted. "He just believes you can . . . believes you will. His belief is enough." *Or so he believes.* Aufschlag had doubts. "Don't worry. You will do what needs to be done."

The boy flashed a look of gratitude. "I've been thinking about what it is to be a god. No one has ever really told me what is expected. What will happen when I Ascend?" He waved his hands around as if trying to grasp at an idea. "Will I retain my physical form? What will I look like? What will I be capable of?"

Aufschlag made a placating gesture. "The truth is . . . we don't know."

"Konig says I won't be the first man-made god, but I will be the first intentionally man-made god. He used the word 'designed.' I didn't understand what he meant before, but I do now."

"It is not with malice," Aufschlag said softly, unsure if he lied.

Morgen studied the Chief Scientist. "I know."

Thoughts of Morgen's Ascension left Aufschlag feeling tired, old, and sad. For Morgen to Ascend, he had to die with enough people believing he'd rise again as a god. For two decades Konig had been shaping the Geborene Damonen, and all the people of Selbsthass, for very this purpose. Soon the child must die.

*Why hadn't I thought this through before bringing my plans to make a god to Konig?* He'd been desperate to please his only friend and that desperation had blinded him. Konig took Aufschlag's plan, saw possibilities the scientist had missed, and twisted it in ways both appalling and stunning.

*Morgen must soon die.*

But healthy children don't just die on their own. The realization sickened the Chief Scientist, as he had grown to love the precocious child. For a brief moment he considered stealing the boy away, rescuing the child and fleeing the fate Konig planned. That was just as quickly dismissed, though. There would be no escaping Konig. The High Priest was an unstoppable force of will. And he'd release the Schatten Mörder, his Cotardist assassins, to punish the scientist. The thought turned Aufschlag's guts to water. *No, the boy will die as Konig plans.*

Morgen laid a gentle hand on Aufschlag's shoulder. "You look sad."

Aufschlag forced a smile. "I was thinking how quickly you've grown up."

Again Morgen studied Aufschlag, searching his eyes. What was the boy thinking? Had he seen through the lie?

"I've been thinking about gods," Morgen finally said. "Gods aren't bound by the same rules as people. People gain power from their beliefs and delusions. The stronger the belief, the more power. I had assumed this was true of gods as well, but I'm no longer sure. You see, people generally have one delusion. Some, Comorbidics, may have secondary delusions, but these are always minor in comparison. Like Konig. He's first and foremost a Gefahrgeist, but he's also developed Doppelgangist and some minor Mirrorist tendencies. Though he's a powerful Gefahr-geist, he has little control over his Doppels, and still has to go to Schwacher Sucher in order to *use* a mirror." Aufschlag could hear the boy struggling to frame his thoughts and sound adult. "People are defined by their primary delusion.

"But this isn't true for gods."

This caught Aufschlag's attention. "What do you mean?"

"A god doesn't require delusion or insanity, because his wor-shipers suffer for him. Yet in a way, he has *all* of their delusions."

"How do you know this?"

The boy smiled happily. "Because I am not limited and I will be a god."

*If that's true, perhaps he doesn't have to die to Ascend!* Ko-nig wouldn't like that. Morgen's death was a critical part of the plan. Those whom you slay must serve in the Afterdeath; the boy's death was control. Aufschlag swallowed a lump of nervous tension. "Can you show me?"

Morgen held out his left arm and wriggled the fingers. "Watch."

Before the Chief Scientist's eyes Morgen's arm turned black. The skin peeled away and the stench of putrefaction filled the room. In moments the boy's arm was nothing but leathery gristle clinging to bone.

"Cotardist—"

"Watch." Morgen's arm writhed as flesh grew outward from his shoulder, wrapping the bones in glistening tendons, squirming veins, and thin slabs of muscle. When the arm was whole the boy smiled and a nearby table burst into flames. It was ash in seconds. Aufschlag opened his mouth to speak, but the boy exploded, engulfed in roaring fire. The floor was scorched and Aufschlag was forced to retreat from the heat. Yet Morgen, still smiling at the scientist's shocked expression, remained unharmed. Then the fire was gone and Morgen stood in a circle of burned floor. He gestured toward the mirror and dozens of his reflections scrambled out. The room soon filled with hundreds of identical children all holding different conversations.

Aufschlag stood paralyzed with fear. *The child is demented! We haven't created a god, we've made an insane monster!*

"We're scaring Aufschlag."

The Chief Scientist couldn't tell which boy said this; presumably the one still standing in the charred circle. As one the Doppels—*or are they reflections?*—stopped talking and turned to face him.

"We're sorry." One hundred voices spoke in perfect unison. "We had to show you so you'd understand."

The boys formed rows and climbed back into their mirror. One child remained. It wasn't the one in the burned circle.

"Are you . . ." Afraid of the answer, Aufschlag couldn't finish the question.

"Yes. The original."

"Are you sure?"

"Fairly." He suddenly stepped forward and hugged Aufschlag, burying his face in the man's chest. "I had to show you. I knew you'd understand."

*Understand?* If anything, all the scientist had was more questions. Was the boy's control as perfect as it seemed? If so, maybe he truly was a god, maybe they hadn't failed after all. Was the child correct in stating he could make use of his worshipers' delusions without sharing in them, or was Morgen's mind shattered beyond all redemption? And with that shattering, did that mean his inevitable fall was soon to come, like every other Geisteskranken?

But these questions paled when held against the one thing Aufschlag had learned.

*Morgen is ready. But does he still need to die?*

He knew Konig's answer. Yes! Unless Morgen died at the High Priest's hand, Konig would have no sure means of controlling the god. What then should he tell Konig?

Aufschlag's unanswered questions fled, forgotten, drowned in the desperate wave of love washing over him. *I have to save the child.* If the child was a Mirrorist, Doppelgangist, and Hassebrand, why not Gefahrgeist too? Even as the thought occurred to him he saw what had to be done.

Aufschlag hugged the boy close and struggled to keep his tears in check. He couldn't remember the last time he'd held another person. "Morgen, you have to listen carefully."

The boy pulled back, confused but nodding. "Okay."

"You cannot show this to anyone else."

"But why? Konig will—"

"A good god is humble." Aufschlag forced himself to be firm with the boy. "A good god doesn't show off. Konig would be very disappointed with such an ostentatious display. Think back: Have you ever seen him show off his Gefahrgeist powers?"

Morgen's brow crinkled in thought. "No. And he does keep his Doppels mostly confined to his chambers."

"Right." Konig had other, far more desperate reasons for confining his Doppels, but the boy didn't need to know them. "You must do as Konig does. You must learn subtlety."

When the boy had promised not to tell anyone of his abilities, Aufschlag sent him on his way. He'd have to order a work crew to replace the burned table and clean the scorch marks from the floor. He was treading dangerous ground. Deceiving Konig for long would be next to impossible, and if he was caught, his punishment would be a long and lingering death. Yet he knew the risk was worth it.

A new feeling took root in the depths of Aufschlag's soul. A warmth he didn't recognize. He was, for perhaps the first time ever, truly doing the right thing. He loved Morgen as a son and no man would allow his only son to be slain. Not without a fight.

# CHAPTER 16

*I don't see what I want to see, I see what I need to see. If you don't like it, see something else.*

—Anonymous Halluzinieren

This was the calm eye of the storm, the hot center of crumbling sanity and last hopes. In all directions the horizon coiled and heaved, a lurid bruise, a maelstrom of abhorrent neuroses given form. The sky looked sick, reality ill with gross mistreatment. Gehirn tasted it in the air. The very ground wailed affliction. She wanted to cauterize the infection.

Regen Anrufer—Erbrechen's pet shaman—shuffled alongside Gehirn, his bulbous eyes staring off into bleak eternity, his few rotting teeth bared in a perpetual grimace. A stream of gritty brown drool attached chin to chest. Gehirn wanted to burn the Schlammstamm shaman in a wash of all-cleansing fire. The degenerate mob, staggering under the weight of Erbrechen's litter, followed behind. She wanted to torch the mob too. Flame ablating flesh from bone, rinsing the wretched stench from life.

*Burn.* The thought sent shivers of pleasure tickling down her spine. As always, disgust followed.

Erbrechen remained hidden within the tented litter, accompanied this time by a young blond boy who reminded Gehirn of the god-child Morgen. Her stomach twisted at the thought.

When she walked in front of the mob, the stench was less overpowering—though far from nonexistent—and they didn't have to wade through the disgusting leavings of a crowd unable to care for themselves. Erbrechen's friends wouldn't—or couldn't—leave the caravan to relieve themselves. Instead they defecated as they walked, spilling thin drooling feces along emaciated legs. Most no longer possessed shoes and walked barefoot, blistered and bleeding, through the droppings of those in front.

*Burn all of this shite to ash.*

Gehirn slashed a sideways glance at Regen. Blood still trickled from the many wounds the shaman had opened along his bony arms to feed the sky. Self-hatred and self-abuse were requisites for many Geisteskranken. Regen drained himself as though blood—and not his failing sanity—fueled his power. Pale and drawn, he walked like a poorly animated corpse, looking like he might collapse at any moment.

And when he did, the sun would return. Erbrechen asked too much of the Schlammstamm shaman.

"Protect my Hassebrand from the sun and the moon," Erbrechen had demanded of Regen.

"A storm will grow, one I can't—"

"Just make sure it doesn't rain here." Erbrechen smiled then at his squat shaman. "Do this for me, my friend."

Gehirn saw the despair, hatred, and love in Regen's eyes. Regen would hold the storm at bay for as long as he could. His love of Erbrechen allowed no less.

Gehirn and Regen shared a look of mutual hate and understanding. Both knew Regen's sanity would crumble under the continual abuse. Erbrechen burned through Regen's sanity at a terrifying pace.

Gehirn chuckled quietly as she imagined the ugly little shaman as a dry stick soon to be tossed into a raging inferno. The thought both pleased and sobered. Gehirn could only hope the organ stew might stave off her own descent into madness. If Erbrechen was correct, and eating the souls of those less tainted could save her, perhaps she could satisfy Erbrechen and yet still survive.

"He doesn't love you," muttered Regen, picking at a scab.

"Yes, he does," she answered. "He shares his stew with me. Does he share it with you?" she asked, knowing the answer.

Regen scowled at the ground. A stream of brown drool hung unnoticed from his weak chin. "Does he touch you?" the shaman suddenly asked. "If he loved you he'd touch you." Regen grinned rot at her. "Has he *ever* touched you?"

*No, not once.* Gehirn glanced over her shoulder, back toward Erbrechen's tented litter. She could only imagine what was happening within. "Not all love is physical," she said.

*Why won't he touch me?*

AS EACH OF Erbrechen's followers fell—or was felled—Erbrechen and Gehirn ate of the small souls as Regen looked on, the desperate hope in his eyes dimming hour by hour. Erbrechen never seemed to notice.

Gehirn studied the swarm of skeletal bodies hustling to break another body into small enough pieces to fit into the cooking pot. Yet she could not argue. For in truth, it didn't matter so much if Erbrechen loved her, as long as she loved Erbrechen. And she did. Loved and feared and worshiped.

There was another emotion there, lurking beneath the others. Was it hate? No, that couldn't be possible. Yet his distance stung.

Later in the day an emaciated woman of indeterminate age

with thin, sagging breasts and long, greasy hair came to Gehirn and walked alongside her in silence. The Hassebrand ground her teeth, resisting the urge to burn the woman to oily ash.

"He wants to see you," the woman finally said, her voice surprisingly strong and feminine. "You can find me after, if you want." She batted eyelashes at Erbrechen, who unabashedly examined her undernourished form. She had none of the tight-wound strength the female thief possessed. Nothing of the pent-up rage or enticing air of danger. The woman was almost completely uninteresting. Gehirn had nothing to fear from her and she offered none of the loathing the Hassebrand required from a sexual partner. *I can change that.*

Gehirn showed pronounced canines in a halfhearted leer. "I will find you, and later, when you hate me enough, perhaps then . . ." She left it hanging, dark with threat and promise, and turned to join Erbrechen.

In all directions the sky roiled with black clouds lit from beneath with stabbing tines of lightning. The rumble of distant thunder had become a continuous backdrop, a reason to speak louder, but little more. Erbrechen waved Gehirn onto the litter as the Hassebrand approached. Gehirn heard and ignored the strained groan of the men and women carrying the litter as she clambered aboard.

Erbrechen, resplendent in his oily nakedness, beamed, his greasy cherubic face seemingly lit from within. "Ah, my good friend. I have need of your wise counsel."

*He desires my counsel!* Gehirn's doubts and angers suddenly seemed petty. They weren't gone, but they didn't much matter in comparison to her love of Erbrechen. She basked in the gaze of those sea-green eyes.

Gehirn sat across from her one true friend. The gentle roll of the litter as it crawled across the land toward their destiny added a stately feel to the proceedings.

"How may I be of assistance?" Gehirn asked.

"I have been thinking. This Konig Furimmer who was once your friend. He has an army gathered about him, does he not?"

"Konig maintains a small but well-equipped military force with squads of Geisteskranken of all breeds. The strength of the Geborene Damonen religion backs him, the united faith of a hundred thousand people. His grip on their faith is absolute. Konig manages the impossible, wielding the beliefs of the masses like a well-honed tool."

Erbrechen waved an arm he could barely lift, his fat sausage-like fingers almost lost in the pudgy hand. "Then I will need an army of my own."

"You have me. I was considered by many to be the most powerful Geisteskranken in Konig's service." Gehirn frowned, remembering her dream of the Krieger assassination attempt. Gods, she wished she knew if it had been real. "Perhaps this is why he sent me away. He saw my power growing and feared my increasing instability."

"He didn't offer to aid his friend?" Erbrechen asked innocently.

Gehirn scowled and watched Regen plod dejectedly through the mud. "Konig was never my friend."

"And he tossed you aside in your time of need." Erbrechen tutted with disgust. His obscenely fat and greasy face contorting in a frown, he looked like an enraged baby. "But we'll show him. What he threw away still has great value."

Gehirn, surprised, looked up. "It has? Is? I am? Valuable? Valued?"

"Very. I cannot do this without you." Erbrechen waved a hand at the unruly mob surrounding and following his litter. "There is little I can do with such as these. Few have delusions worth speaking of and none can fight worth a damn. At best they are fodder, a distraction. But you, my tall and icy-eyed friend, you can wipe out armies. The delusions of Konig's Geisteskranken will be nothing before your fire. Never before have you dared to reach for your pinnacle: the curse of all Geisteskranken was a wall between you and your potential. My faith removes such walls. I *know* you can unleash what you keep so tightly pent-up inside. You can burn it all."

Gehirn's heart slammed against her ribs. Erbrechen's belief could not be denied. Erbrechen defined reality. *How could I have doubted his love?*

"I—" Gehirn let out a long, shaking breath. She closed her eyes and whispered, "I will burn the world for you."

Erbrechen clapped gleefully. "Burn the world clean and I shall remake it anew. We shall be gods, my friend. New gods." Corpulent arms flailed in excitement. "I always knew I was destined for greatness." He darted a glance at Gehirn. "*We* are destined for greatness," he amended. "Unlike your Konig—the foul betrayer—I do not forget my friends."

Erbrechen told Gehirn of his plans: he would take his wretched host to Selbsthass, topple Konig, and claim both the Theocracy and the god-child as his own. Along the way they would stop at every town and city and Erbrechen would convince their populations to join in his cause. As more joined, Erbrechen would grow in power and fewer would be able to resist. Gehirn would burn those few who did. In Selbsthass there would be garrisons of troops and each would house a squad of Geisteskranken trained in battle. These were the true threat, the most likely to be able to resist Erbrechen, and the most likely to be able to strike from beyond the range of his power. These too Gehirn would burn.

"You have much burning to do," Erbrechen promised. "So much burning." Erbrechen licked wet lips in anticipation. "I'm hungry!"

LATER, AS GEHIRN lay spooning the bruised and bleeding woman who shook with her very disgust and hatred, she realized she had contributed nothing and Erbrechen had not once asked for her counsel. For now, though, she was gloriously happy to be involved in such a bold undertaking. Doubt grew only in the fertile darkness of solitude.

# CHAPTER 17

*The Gefahrgeist must first fool themselves. After that, everyone else is easy.*

—Versklaven Schwache, Gefahrgeist Philosopher

A cold rain fell in Selbsthass City, turning the market's cobbled roads glossy and slick. The damp brought out the dank smell of the city's sewers and thinned the herds of evening shoppers to a dejected trickle. Most of the market stalls had already closed, their keepers leaving early for the warmth and comfort of home. Distant jagged forks of lightning stabbed at the ground, lighting the southern sky an actinic white and illuminating the sagging underbellies of the cancerous clouds lurking there. The echo of thunder rolled continually in deep rumbling anger.

Bedeckt stifled a cough and felt something bubble in his chest. He huddled deeper into the sodden brown Geborene robes, trying to find some last bastion of warmth, and followed Stehlen. His feet squelched with every step; his boots did little to keep the water out and apparently everything to keep it in.

Ahead, Stehlen ducked from shadow to shadow. She said she'd memorized a map of the city and knew the best way to the palace, but this seemed to be the longest, most tortuous route possible. She kept shifting under her burgundy Geborene robes as if they chafed. Wichtig followed behind Bedeckt, mumbling about the rain and the stench of his robes. Fair enough, since the man did reek. An accomplishment considering the state of Bedeckt's sinuses.

"Bedeckt?" asked Wichtig.

"Quiet."

"Do your robes smell like they've been stuffed up a hog's arse for the last month?"

"I can't smell a thing over the stench coming from you," answered Bedeckt. "Stehlen!"

"What?"

"We aren't sneaking into this place, we're walking in."

"I know!"

"Then stop trying to hide in the damned shadows." Bedeckt tried to adjust his robes so as to better conceal the massive ax poorly hidden within. It was hopeless. Only a blind and brain-dead idiot could miss it.

Wichtig leaned past Bedeckt so he could glare at Stehlen's back. Facing forward with her cowl up, she couldn't possibly see him, but made a rude gesture over her shoulder anyway.

Wichtig opened his mouth and Bedeckt said, "Shut up," before the Swordsman could speak.

"You sound tired," said Stehlen.

"I *am* tired. I'm tired of you two—"

"My robes stink," grumbled Wichtig

"It's not the robes," Stehlen threw back.

"Both of you—"

"I'll get you for this," swore Wichtig.

"—shut up."

The rain fell heavier and the three continued in silence, their boots soon soaked through in the gritty rivulets forming in the road. Bedeckt coughed and groaned at the stabbing pain in his chest.

"You sound like you're dying," Stehlen said over her shoulder. "We should do this another day."

"I'm fine." It was a lie. He felt like chilled death.

"Better yet," she said, "you should just let me do this. I'll be back with the boy in an hour. You can wait in the comfort and warmth of the inn."

"I said I'm fine!" Bedeckt's lower back tightened under his sodden robes. The cold leached the very strength from his bones. He coughed hard and something rattled deep in his lungs.

*Great timing,* Bedeckt thought. *Fall sick and die while pulling off one last job.* It was Stehlen's fault. He glared daggers at her back. If he didn't have to worry about her sneaking off and trying to take the child by herself—and no doubt killing dozens of priests and waking up a whole hornet's nest of problems— they could have done this on a much warmer night. One when it wasn't raining. *Crazy Kleptic will be the death of me.*

A break in the buildings on the south side of the street offered a clear view of the brewing storm. Though a strong wind blew from the west, the tempest seemed to be moving north.

Bedeckt pointed at the southern sky with his half hand. "I've seen such storms before," he said. "I can't remember who I was working for. We were exterminating some nomadic tribe that had crossed the border uninvited. They had this nasty little shaman with one eye. He called a storm and swept away most of the army I was with; drowned the commanders. When he lost control, his own tribe was decimated." Bedeckt remembered lightning-blasted corpses floating from horizon to horizon on what had been near-barren grasslands. He gestured southward again with his scarred hand. "Sky stinks of someone losing control."

They left the market behind and the cloud-shrouded evening sun dipped behind long rows of small but wealthy-looking houses.

Wichtig poked Bedeckt in the kidneys from behind. "Hey."

"What?"

"I didn't get my share of the winnings."

"What winnings?" Stehlen asked innocently before Bedeckt could answer.

"For my damned fight. There was a lot of coin in the purse you stole."

*That explains how the fight came about.* At this point, Bedeckt was too cold and tired to care. His lungs rattled with every breath. His condition was deteriorating quickly.

Stehlen glanced over her shoulder and Bedeckt saw little of her face but the yellow of her toothy grin. "You fought so poorly at the beginning we put it all on Zweiter Stelle. How could we know you were just toying with him?"

"You're lying—"

"Bedeckt was going to offer Zweiter your place if he killed you."

"Horse turds. Bedeckt, you weren't going to—"

Bedeckt's sneeze interrupted Wichtig. "Shut up. Both of you. We're at the temple."

Stehlen stopped so suddenly that Bedeckt walked into her and Wichtig ran into him from behind. Stehlen ignored them, staring up at the massive temple gates. "Unholy pigsticking hells," she whispered.

Bedeckt raised a hand to swat at her but stopped short as he caught sight of what had stopped her so suddenly. He'd known Selbsthass was a theocracy. He'd known Selbsthass City was the center of the Theocracy. Though he'd known this temple was in all probability the center of government, he'd still been expecting something . . . different. Could his memory of this ancient castle be so wrong? The keep he remembered at least looked like it had been built by mortal hands. He thought back to the stark difference between Selbsthass and Gottlos at the border and, though he prayed he was wrong, thought he understood: the temple had been twisted by the beliefs of man. The Geborene faith was far more powerful than he'd imagined.

The Geborene temple, seen through the walled gate, looked like a massive castle growing out of the base of a far larger pyramid. Each side stretched into the darkness. Every line, every stone, every crenellation spoke one word with overwhelming confidence: strength. Strength of faith, strength of will.

Bedeckt groaned in pain when Wichtig again poked him in the back. "I've had turds with more grace than this place," said the Swordsman. "Arseholes."

Bedeckt pushed Stehlen, dressed as she was as the highest-ranked priest of the group, forward. If they stood gawking, someone was bound to notice. She grunted and spat at the rain-slicked wall but stepped tentatively ahead.

Up ahead Bedeckt saw several robed figures huddled in a roofed area by the castle gates. Darkness rendered everything monochromatic. "Try not to kill anyone," he hissed at Stehlen's back. Hopefully she'd outrank anyone at the gates and they'd pass unchallenged.

⸿⸿⸿⸿⸿⸿

Stehlen stalked forward, head bowed, arms huddled tight to her body against the wind and rain, pretending to ignore the priests at the gate. She fingered the weighted throwing knives tucked in her sleeves. If the priests challenged her she'd kill them before they could raise the alarm. The gathered priests, all in gray robes, looked soft and dejected and wholly unprepared for battle. She thought about killing them just to annoy Bedeckt, but hearing the old man rattle and wheeze with every breath, decided against it. He was suffering enough.

Was there some way she could convince Bedeckt to let her and the World's Biggest Moron get the kid on their own? *No, Bedeckt will never trust the moron with something this important.* An unexpected emotion tightened her chest. Concern? *No, can't be.*

She stole a quick glance over her shoulder but needn't have bothered. Bedeckt was watching the ground as he shuffled after her. Each step seemingly an act of will, his breath came in short ragged gasps. Her stomach twisted into a clenched knot. *Did I eat something bad?* She didn't think so. What was that awful feeling?

Stehlen looked over Bedeckt's hunched form to Wichtig behind him. The Swordsman frowned and gave her a confused look. If they stopped now it would definitely draw the attention of the priests at the gate. Though the burgundy robes gave her rank, she doubted she could convince anyone she was a high-ranked priest. She didn't even know what rank she was supposed to be.

*Shite on a stick!* This was exactly the kind of underhanded lying Wichtig excelled at. Unfortunately, dressed as an acolyte, he could hardly give orders. Perhaps she should have made Wichtig the ranking priest. Too late now.

The priests manning the gate didn't even acknowledge them as they passed.

The three crossed the open courtyard—which looked suspiciously to Stehlen like a cleared killing ground—to the entrance of the main keep.

She let out a sigh of relief and whispered, "You sound like shite," over her shoulder.

"Keep mov—" Bedeckt was interrupted by another fit of bubbling coughing.

They passed into the massive interior of the temple. Flanking the entrance to the main hall, carved granite pillars easily twenty feet in diameter depicted events she could only assume were important to the Geborene Damonen. Luxurious wall hangings and life-size paintings adorned the walls. Haunting stained-glass windows showed dark monochromatic scenes in the dim light.

Stehlen sneered at the gross waste of time and effort. Wichtig no doubt appreciated the artistic merits of such towering totems, but then again, he was an idiot.

Bedeckt still stared at the floor, apparently unaware of their surroundings. Breathing and walking were clearly taking most of his concentration.

Stehlen glanced up at the arched ceiling, soaring forty feet over their heads, and stopped. Bedeckt slowed to a halt and stared at her in confusion. She pointed up. "Who?"

He looked up for a long moment. "It's a fresco of Zuerst Geborene—the church's founder—facing the gods he defied."

"Oh," annoyed at having wasted her time asking. *He's probably going to follow that with more old-man philosophy.*

"All religions," he muttered, "even those without gods, seek to awe the common man."

*And there it is.* "Oh," she said again.

Bedeckt coughed noisily and spat a thick wad of brown-and-red phlegm at the floor. "The boy will be upstairs somewhere."

Stehlen shook her head, spattering water everywhere. "No, he'll be downstairs, in the basement. They'll want to protect and hide him."

"Not everyone thinks like a thief," admonished Wichtig. "They'll want the boy where they can display him to the masses for best effect. He'll be on the top floor."

Bedeckt disagreed. "High Priest What's-his-name—"

"Konig," supplied Wichtig. "High Priest Konig Furimmer."

"Whatever. This High Priest must be a Gefahrgeist of some strength. He'll have the top floor to himself. His self-importance won't allow anyone else to be stationed above him."

Stehlen opened her mouth to argue when Bedeckt suddenly

gestured toward the far end of the hall. She turned and saw a priest in brown robes.

"Stehlen," hissed Bedeckt. "Wave the priest over here. Find out where this gods-damned kid is."

Stehlen did her best to gesture imperiously at the priest and stood impatiently waiting for the young man to hurry the length of the hall.

The priest bowed low before her. "Yes, Bishop?"

There was a moment of uncomfortable silence. "Where is the kid?" blurted Stehlen.

The priest looked up, startled. "Kid, Your Worship?"

"Yes, gods damn it! The kid. The . . . little . . . god-brat in training."

The priest, confused, met Stehlen's eyes and stammered, "B-beg pardon, Your Worship?"

*Stick it.* Stehlen hit him in the sternum and had a knife at his throat before the young man could blink.

"A decent thief would be better at lying," said Wichtig smugly. "But you're not a thief, you're the just smallest thug I've ever seen." He shook his head in mock disappointment. "No finesse."

Stehlen kept the knife at the priest's throat, waiting for him to stop gagging on each breath. "Yeah? Where's your money?" she asked Wichtig over her shoulder.

Wichtig's smugness faded as he felt for his money purse.

Stehlen ignored him, pressing the knife until a thin line of blood appeared on the priest's neck. "Tell me where the kid is."

The priest's brief look of defiance crumbled before Stehlen's feral leer. Nothing in her eyes betrayed reluctance to murder.

"Morgen's chambers are in the basement. South wing."

"Don't—" started Wichtig as Stehlen slid the knife into the priest's throat. " . . . kill him." He shot her an annoyed look as she shoved the body away to bleed out on the floor. "He's lying."

"I told you he was in the basement."

"Obviously he lied."

"No, it's obvious *you're* lying. You can't stand being wrong."

"If you knew anything about people other than how to cut their throats . . ." Wichtig turned to Bedeckt. "You saw it, right?"

Bedeckt coughed, a bubbling sound deep in his chest. "I was watching for more priests."

Stehlen snorted derisively.

"Look," growled Wichtig, gesturing at Stehlen. "You know how to steal things and cut throats, and Bedeckt is a master of coming up with stupid long-winded plans no one can follow. I know people."

"You know how to *use* people," sneered Stehlen.

"You have to understand them to use them."

Bedeckt waved them to silence. "Let's move before someone finds us here with this corpse. Stehlen, drag it into the shadows. We go up."

Wichtig reached out to pat Stehlen's back condescendingly but stopped when she glared at him. Instead he blew her a kiss and said, "See, Bedeckt knows to trust my opinion. You could learn something here."

⁞⁞⁞⁞⁞⁞⁞⁞⁞⁞⁞⁞⁞⁞

Bedeckt, wheezing, set off toward the stairs at the far end of the hall. His lungs felt like they'd been filled with cold snot. "No one knows more about lying than you do," he growled over his shoulder, and heard Stehlen's answering chuckle. Unfortunately, the one person Wichtig lied to best was Wichtig. Such was always the problem with Gefahrgeist. If enough people believed their shite, they began to believe it too. Continually putting Wichtig down might limit his power, but it might also stop the smallest successes from swelling his already huge ego.

When they caught up with him, Bedeckt turned to Stehlen. "Why didn't you ask the priest how many guards the kid has?"

"Will we turn around and go home if there are a lot of guards?" she asked sweetly. "No."

This late in the evening the halls were largely devoid of priestly activity and the three wandered lost for the best part of an hour. The few people they ran into looked well fed, unsuspecting, soft, and unquestioning. Still, Stehlen killed two more priests before they found someone who knew where the boy was. Luckily her damp burgundy robes did a fine job of hiding bloodstains.

They followed a steep set of curving stairs upward. If they hadn't gotten turned around somewhere, the child's room should be at the top. Bedeckt coughed and spat a thick wad of dark phlegm at the offending stairs. Everything looked too new for such an ancient building. Usually the steps of such a castle would be worn shallow from centuries of shuffling feet, but the corner of each was crisp and sharp.

Was this the future, religion uniting, directing, and manipulating humanity's faith, turning individuals into fragments of the larger hive? Where one religion led, others would follow. Bedeckt saw no way a man-made god could be any better than one coming to be in the old way. Whatever the old way was. At least the old gods seemed largely uninterested in messing directly with man or his works. Sure, they embroiled men in the occasional holy war, but most of the world's great tragedies could be laid squarely at humanity's feet.

A god subject to the whims and will of a populace in thrall to a self-serving Gefahrgeist—like there was any other kind of Gefahrgeist—would not be so distant. A thought lingered in the back of his mind: it wouldn't be a bad thing if the Geborene didn't get their god-to-be back after Bedeckt had collected the ransom money. Bedeckt lost his train of thought as his chest tightened and once again he had to focus solely on breathing. *If the child isn't at the top of these stairs, I'm returning to the inn and staying in bed for a week.*

Stehlen in the lead, the three crested a long flight of stairs leading to the top of one of the church's shorter towers.

Bedeckt wheezed and coughed up more dark and salty phlegm. "Pigsticking stairs," he gasped. When he glanced up he saw Stehlen and Wichtig marching purposefully away. He looked to the end of the long stone hall. Two women stood at guard in matching chain hauberks with longswords hung at their right hip. Both women were lefties, which Bedeckt found a little odd. The two guards watched, heads cocked slightly to the left, as Stehlen and Wichtig approached. Bedeckt opened his mouth to hiss a warning and was racked by another fit of coughing.

No matter how much Stehlen swaggered, she felt like a thief in stolen priest's robes, blaspheming in the eyes of everything holy and sacrosanct. Some memories of childhood she could never leave behind. She swore under her breath, preparing to face down the guards. Both Bedeckt and Wichtig had harassed her for her inability to get past any hindrance without leaving a few bodies behind. *I'll show them subtlety.*

"Step aside," she commanded imperiously. "We are here to see the——"

"You are forbidden in this hall. Leave now."

Stehlen frowned at the two guards. They looked almost identical in their matching armor. What she could see of their faces looked similar as well. Identical eyes peered from beneath iron helms.

"Do you know who I am?" Stehlen demanded of the guard who had spoken.

"Gods, you're terrible at this," muttered Wichtig. Stehlen heard Bedeckt's retching cough back at the top of the stairs.

Two longswords snapped from sheaths with impressive speed and precision. The two women moved as one.

Stehlen backed away a step, bumping into Wichtig. "Very pretty," she said. "You must have practiced for a long time."

The two guards answered with identical grins.

Through Bedeckt's coughing Stehlen heard one strangled word forced through raw vocal cords. "Mehrere."

One guard stepped forward as the other retreated, and Stehlen, stepping sideways to make room for Wichtig, snapped a thrown knife into her throat.

*Not grinning now, are you, bitch?*

Six identically armed and armored women stood in the hall before the first hit the floor. They appeared out of nowhere, rushing forward, swords drawn.

*Shite.*

"Is this an illusion?" Wichtig asked.

Then his swords were drawn and he desperately parried attacks from multiple opponents. They were good. They were *very* good.

But they weren't great.

Wichtig was great. He danced around attacks, making these deadly Swordswomen seem clumsy in comparison. He killed one with a quick cut to an exposed throat, sending his adversary staggering into her companions, struggling to stem the gushing flow of blood. Wichtig turned to Stehlen to brag and saw she'd already killed three.

Wichtig snarled a fast "arse-sticking hells" before returning his attention to the Swordswomen. There must have been a dozen of them now. If illusions, they were very good ones.

*They must be teleporting in.* Probably for the best; it gave him a chance to catch up with Stehlen. *Odd, they all fight left-handed.*

Wichtig's dance of death became less flourished and decidedly more intense and efficient. Why did people bother with such heavy armor as the hauberk? His every cut found exposed flesh. Here a throat, there a wrist. Slaying four more in rapid succession—or at least removing them from the fight—he spared a quick glance at Stehlen. Enough bodies lay piled at her feet that he couldn't count them quickly and her opponents had to climb their friends—which they seemed all to willing to do—to reach her. She didn't wait for them. Stehlen pressed the attack at every opportunity, intent on driving the priestly guards back toward the closed door. Wichtig thought briefly about helping her assailants by wounding Stehlen with a blind-side attack. He didn't wish her harm, he just wanted to slow her down so he could catch up.

*Not fair, she had a head start!*

Unfortunately, enough opponents were crowding the hall that he wasn't sure he could kill them all without a healthy Stehlen at his side.

Four Swordswomen launched a perfectly timed attack, forcing Wichtig back several steps. He saw Stehlen disappear into the mob, swallowed by a throng of left-handed Swordswomen in matching chain hauberk who all fought with an identical style. Their synchronization of bladed expression made them easy to defeat, but creepy.

Wichtig was forced back another step. "Bedeckt!" he bellowed over his left shoulder while killing another woman with a quick thrust to her throat. "Stop coughing and come help!"

If Stehlen was dead, they'd be splitting the ransom money only two ways. With Stehlen and her pathetic worship of Bedeckt out of the way, a one-way split became a real possibility. The way Bedeckt sounded, Wichtig wouldn't even need to stab him in the back. *The old bastard might croak all on his own.*

Even over the cacophony of combat, Wichtig heard Bedeckt's

wheezing charge. The old goat sticker sounded like he had one foot in the Afterdeath, but he certainly had spirit.

‧‧‧‧‧‧‧‧‧‧‧

Scores of identical women in chain hauberk surrounded Stehlen. At first she'd felt her opponents' elation as they crowded in around her. But now they understood; she liked it this way. She couldn't move without touching someone and she couldn't touch someone without leaving grievous wounds. They'd invited her in only to discover, too late, that she was death. They hampered each other far more than they did her. They seemed unwilling to wound each other, whereas she happily hurt anything and everything. She'd seen Wichtig's calculating look. Perhaps the half-wit really was the Greatest Swordsman in the World, but he couldn't hope to match her in this. Unlike Wichtig, she was a killer, pure and true. She killed unclouded by ego or desire. Where Wichtig killed with a thought to where the next death would take him, she killed in the moment for the moment.

Stehlen's throwing knives were long gone, lost in the bodies she'd put them in. Her swords had been knocked from her hands, replaced with swords taken from dead opponents, lost again, and once more replaced with different yet identical ones. She kicked a woman in the groin, stabbed another in the face, and felt something tear a hot line along her ribs. She already bled from a dozen similar wounds she didn't remember receiving.

Pain didn't matter. Pain was for later.

*If there is a later.*

Stehlen killed another left-handed woman, stomping on her foot and then stabbing the sword into her mouth when it opened in a wail of pain. The same simple tricks worked over and over. The guards seemed incapable of learning or adjusting. *This means something.*

Stehlen contemplated as she killed. Slaughter didn't require cogitation; the conscious mind only got in the way. She killed best when distracted. Bedeckt had said "Mehrere." They faced a single woman with a split personality. *Aren't Mehrere supposed to appear as different people?* She'd never heard of a Mehrere manifesting as multiple copies of a single person. She knew of Abgeleitete Leute, a semimythological city said to be populated solely by thronging copies of a single deranged Mehrere, but each of those copies was supposed to be a distinct person.

*Bedeckt would know more about this,* Stehlen grumbled to herself as she killed another left-handed woman. As ever more guards crowded around her she knew one thing: killing more of them would get her nowhere. Unfortunately, as they desperately fought to kill her, she had no choice.

Stehlen heard Bedeckt's wheezing battle cry as he entered the fray with all his usual enraged-bull finesse. *What took the old man so damned long?*

The mob suddenly compacted and she was pressed tight on all sides by her enemy. For a moment no one could find the space to lift a weapon or make a worthwhile attack, and Stehlen found herself in an intimate embrace with a young woman. She had lovely brown eyes and warm breath smelling of chicken and some spice Stehlen didn't recognize. They all did. She blew the guard a kiss. When the woman blinked in surprise, Stehlen head-butted her, crushing her nose. She felt each swing of Bedeckt's ax shudder through the hot crush of bodies. The old bastard was strong, no doubt. Then a sizable portion of the mob turned and surged past her to face Bedeckt and his ax, and once again, she had room to kill.

▬▬▬▬▬

Bedeckt stood—apparently unnoticed, hunched forward, hands on knees, breath rattling about in his lungs like a pair of dry bone dice—watching as Stehlen vanished into the ever-increasing crowd of guards. Did she understand the importance of what he'd said? No doubt his shouted warning had gone clear over Wichtig's head. The only reason the self-centered arse hadn't already fled was because he'd noticed Stehlen had killed more than he. As was often the case, Wichtig's monumental ego stopped him from making the intelligent choice. If his egotism continually led to stupidity, how intelligent could the man really be?

Stehlen disappeared and now Bedeckt watched as a swarm of identical Swordswomen engulfed Wichtig. He coughed up more thick phlegm and thought about the stairs behind him. *I should leave, just turn and walk away.* No one had even noticed him.

*So why aren't I leaving?*

*Because I can't make it out of the church without their help.*

Right, a shite excuse.

The ax hung heavy in his right hand. When had he wrestled it from under his robes? It couldn't have been easy, and yet he had no memory of the choice or the action. He felt like a mass of scars and ruin, his missing fingers and the lost wedding ring a metaphor for everything missing from his life.

"Fine time for maudlin," growled Bedeckt, his throat raw from coughing, his voice little more than a croak. He clenched the ruin of his left hand into a tight and incomplete fist.

Hefting the ax, Bedeckt started forward. He'd get close enough for Stehlen to hear what he had to tell her. Only she could stop the Mehrere. He picked up speed as he staggered ever faster toward the warring press of bodies.

Bedeckt managed one insensate roar of rage, which quickly gave way to an asthmatic wheeze as his voice cracked before he slammed bodily into the crowd.

The Swordswomen collapsed beneath his onslaught. The ax rose and fell and blood laced the air. With his left hand Bedeckt hammered faces and stabbed at eyes with blunt and scarred fingers. He kneed groins, kicked knees, and elbowed skulls with bloody abandon. No thought of defense, each action, each fraction of a moment, an assault on mortal flesh. His one opponent might outnumber him, but Bedeckt would break the will of this vast and growing entity.

The Swordswomen broke around Bedeckt like waves crashing against a rock. Each breath was a shuddering fight for air. He couldn't find enough room in his lungs; they felt full, brimming. The ax caught in someone's clavicle and Bedeckt fought for a terrifying moment to free it.

The ax came free and the woman dropped with a wet sob sounding suspiciously like gratitude. Maybe Bedeckt had made the noise. His arms felt like heat-softened lead.

*Move forward. Find Stehlen. Tell her . . . tell her . . . tell her what?*

*I am the rock.* They broke around him and he killed. Always forward, always attacking.

The sword entered low in Bedeckt's back and felt like it grated along his spine. His bones rang in sympathy like a tuning fork. He pushed forward, and this time, when the sword dragged clear, the sob was definitely his.

*Perhaps it's time to start defending.*

Bedeckt blocked a wildly swung sword and kicked at another opponent who managed to avoid his clumsy attack. The other foot slipped on the gore-spattered floor and his knee buckled. Bedeckt lay on the floor, looking up at the massed Swordswomen, who in turn stared down at him. He'd lost his ax in the fall.

"Shite," he croaked.

And then they were on him. His entire universe became sharp swords, heavily booted feet crushing exposed ribs, and endless oceans of pain. With tearing teeth and clawed fingers he fought.

▬▬▬▬▬

Wichtig felt the force of Bedeckt's onslaught through the tight crush of bodies and laughed in the face of the nearest Swordswoman.

"You bastards are in trouble now."

Another guard fell before his whirling blades, spattering him in sanguine gore. They hadn't even touched him. With this many opponents pressed this close, they should at least be able to land a lucky blow, but there had been nothing. *I am just too gods-damned good!* The fates smiled upon him and he laughed and killed another left-handed Swordswoman.

*Destiny, that's why they can't hurt me.* He had a destiny. He would be the World's Greatest Swordsman. Bedeckt thought Wichtig didn't understand what the Geborene sought to accomplish with their little man-made god, but he was wrong. Wichtig understood. If the Geborene could create a god by convincing a bunch of peasants to worship some random brat, then surely he, Wichtig, would become a god when enough people worshiped him as the World's Greatest Swordsman.

*How's Stehlen? Still alive?*

"Hey! You alive?" Wichtig yelled in the direction he'd seen her vanish.

"Moron!" She sounded tired.

"How many?" Wichtig asked between opponents. He didn't hear her answer as he caught sight of Bedeckt being dragged down by a mass of sword-wielding women. Sometimes the fates were just too kind; they spoiled him. He'd save Bedeckt—thereby showing what a true friend he really was—and get to rub it in the old goat's face afterward. Sure, he'd been thinking of double-crossing the old bastard a moment ago, but this would be far more entertaining! A chance to prove Bedeckt wrong and feel smugly superior was worth more than gold.

Wichtig fought his way to Bedeckt, killing enough Swordswomen that the others momentarily backed away in fear. Bedeckt was covered in blood, and unfortunately most of it looked to be his own. The remains of his already mangled left ear had been hewn from his hoary skull.

"Where's your ax, you lazy old bastard?"

Bedeckt cracked a swollen eye open, coughed bright arterial blood, and glared at Wichtig standing over him. "Tell Stehlen to kill the original," he bubbled from between crushed lips. The ugly lout had lost a few more of his already scarce teeth.

*The original? What the hells did* that *mean?* Wichtig turned to face the massed priests blocking the hall. Twice as many corpses lay scattered on the floor. He couldn't see Stehlen but could hear her fighting and cursing somewhere in the swarm. The Swordswomen facing him shuffled forward. They'd finally learned some respect. Wichtig, standing over Bedeckt, fixed his hair and bowed with a flourish to the advancing mob.

"Stehlen," he bellowed. "Kill the original!"

᠁

*Kill the original?* How the hells was she supposed to do that? They looked identical. Stehlen thought and fought furiously. *Where will the original be?* Well, somewhere safe, obviously. *Probably at the back of the pack.* She changed strategies and stopped killing. Instead she began ducking and dodging and working her way toward the rear of the massed guards. As she moved she watched the faces of her opponents. Though physically identical, they showed different expressions. If she kicked one in the groin, they didn't all look hurt. *This,* she thought, *might be useful.*

Stehlen heard Wichtig again yell, "You still alive?" from somewhere behind her. Too much to ask that the idiot get in here and give her a hand. Stupid arsehole was probably telling the Swordswomen back there how he would be the Greatest Pigsticker in the World. But even as she thought that, an idea occurred to her. It was worth a try.

"Still alive!" She watched the faces of the guards, trying to see as many as possible. She faked her best triumphant grin and yelled, "I know which one it is!"

She saw one of the women blink in surprise and back farther into the crowd.

*Gotcha!*

Stehlen kept an eye on the retreating woman as she fought her way, bobbing and weaving through the crowd, toward her. The Swordswoman wouldn't fall for the same ruse twice, and if Stehlen lost her she was dead. The swarming guards panicked when they realized what she was doing, and what martial skill they'd possessed fell away in their mad attempt to stop her. She became a killing blur. Surrounded on all sides, she couldn't help but wound enemies as she cut through them . . . and no matter how unskilled they'd become in their panic, they couldn't help but find her with their swords.

One moment the hall was full of Swordswomen approaching Wichtig and Bedeckt with menacing intent, and the next only littered corpses remained.

Bedeckt, staring up from the floor, watched Wichtig blink in surprise, examine the hall of corpses, and frown in annoyance. Scores of dead littered the floor; far more than Bedeckt and Wichtig could account for.

Wichtig glanced down at Bedeckt. "I killed most of those."

"Liar," grunted Bedeckt through gritted teeth. Gods, everything hurt. He felt torn inside.

Wichtig shrugged philosophically and glanced again to the killing grounds. "I don't see Stehlen."

"Go find her."

"Notice how I'm the only one still standing?" Wichtig sheathed his swords and crossed his arms. "Not a cut on me. Not even a bruise. You look like shite. A child could finish you."

*Is this it?* Was this the moment Bedeckt had always known

would come? He tried to push himself up but his partial hand slipped on the blood-slicked stone and he collapsed with a pained groan. Wichtig stood over him. The bastard wasn't even breathing hard.

"So," said Bedeckt, "this is where we find out who you really are."

"I suppose it is." Wichtig cocked an eyebrow. "Care to serve me in the Afterdeath?" He scanned the piled bodies. "Let me find you your ax."

"So I can die with a weapon in hand?"

Wichtig snorted derisively. "So you can use it as a crutch, you crotchety old goat. In case you hadn't noticed—and I admit you seem pretty busy bleeding out all over the floor—I just saved your life. You can thank me later." He found Bedeckt's ax buried in a body and returned with it held out in offering. "You're my friend. I am your friend." He smiled sadly. "Someday you'll understand."

Bedeckt stared mutely at the proffered ax, aware of Wichtig watching him closely.

"Hurt your feelings, did I?" grumbled Bedeckt. "I'm not falling for that."

Wichtig tutted in mock disgust. "Let's see if we can find Stehlen."

They found Stehlen sitting, back against the single door at the far end of the hall. A young, brown-eyed woman seemed to be taking a nap with her head resting in Stehlen's lap. Stehlen stroked the Swordswoman's short hair. As Wichtig approached with Bedeckt leaning heavily against him she looked up, face drawn and exhausted.

"Don't even bother," she snarled. "You *know* I killed more than you did."

Wichtig laughed happily as if it didn't matter. "Maybe. But I saved Bedeckt's life while you cuddled corpses." He looked again at the Swordswoman. He saw no visible wounds on the body. "She *is* dead, right?"

"Stabbed her in the back as she tried to flee. I saved both of you by killing the original," she pointed out.

"You only knew to kill her because I told you to," said Wichtig, ignoring the fact Bedeckt had told him in the first place.

"Is he okay?" she asked, nodding toward Bedeckt, who was making the surrounding floor slick with blood at an alarming rate.

"I'm fine," slurred Bedeckt, realizing a long stream of sanguine drool was hanging from his open mouth and past his wobbling knees. If Wichtig released him, he'd collapse to the floor.

"He's fine," agreed Wichtig. "He's just pissed off I saved his life. And he seems to have caught a wee sniffle."

Bedeckt coughed weakly, met Stehlen's eyes with a bruised look, and spat bloodily on Wichtig's foot. White flecks of shattered teeth speckled the wet glob.

Stehlen gestured at Bedeckt. "He's bleeding."

"Seeing as we may have to fight our way out of here," drawled Wichtig, "I'm hoping you're sitting there for artistic reasons and not because you're unable to stand. Fighting while carrying the two of you might be awkward." He said it as if awkward were an exaggeration and would be nothing at all.

⸻

Stehlen hated Wichtig more than ever. The gore-spattered halfwit seemed untouched. His hair wasn't even mussed. He looked perfect, every inch the bold hero. She hated and wanted him and hated herself for wanting him. She was going to either rut him or kill him. *Perhaps rut* and *kill him*. Wichtig could stick her, and then she'd stick him back. Her attempted smile died when Wichtig averted his eyes in disgust. Some wounds never heal.

Stehlen shoved the dead woman away and stood, carefully hiding the hurt. "Let's get out of here." She could tell herself she was used to this. She could tell herself she had long ago gotten over the fact that men shied from her smile.

"No," mumbled Bedeckt. "The boy. We take him with us." One of his eyes had swollen completely shut and he glared at Stehlen through the other with feral desperation. "We came this far. I'll last until we're out of here." He wobbled unsteadily. "Just have to stop the bleeding."

Stehlen and Wichtig exchanged doubting looks, but neither wanted to leave here without the loot. Even if the loot was some godling-in-training brat.

"Stehlen, can you open the door?" Bedeckt asked.

She glanced over her shoulder at the door. "It isn't locked."

"How can you—" Wichtig stopped when he noticed the disgusted look Stehlen gave him. "Right."

<hr>

Wichtig propped Bedeckt against the wall and the old goat sticker slid immediately to the floor. *Ah well, as good a place as any. At least he's out of the way.*

Leaving Bedeckt, Wichtig stood poised with sword drawn as Stehlen opened the door. A thin blond child with bright blue eyes stood in the center of a well-appointed bedroom. It was the bedroom every boy dreams of. Toys sat piled in boxes or littered across the floor, left where they'd been dropped by an active and roving imagination. And the masterpiece: a detailed model city replete with peasants, animals, and city guard sprawled across a huge oak table.

But Wichtig was focused on the would-be god. The boy looked nothing like Fluch, Wichtig's son, but still Wichtig found himself thinking back to the last time he saw his boy. He hadn't even said good-bye. He hadn't meant to leave his son, only his unforgiving shrew of a wife. It suddenly dawned on him, the happiest moment of his life had been holding his newborn son and watching as his wife, exhausted from a long and difficult childbirth, slept. He often thought about returning to Traurig and seeking her out. He had no doubt he could persuade her to take him back; he'd always been able to talk her around to his point of view. He remembered the smell of her thick, dark hair and the curve of her hips . . .

"I heard fighting in the hall," said the boy.

The child's calm question brought Wichtig back to the present. Intelligent blue eyes stared up at him. Trusting eyes. If you raised your future god, would you teach him deceit and deception? Wichtig thought not. He searched his memory for a name.

"Konig sent us. You're in grave danger. You must come with us."

The boy stared at him, face expressionless, and Wichtig knew a rare moment of doubt; did the child see through him? Unsure what to do, he struck his best heroic pose.

"I've read about you," the boy said.

"You have?" Wichtig asked, surprised.

"Yes. You're a hero."

*Hero?* Wichtig bowed with a perfect flourish of his sword. "Wichtig Lügner. The World's Greatest Swordsman. At your service."

"I'm Morgen," the boy answered.

"Hells," Stehlen muttered quietly to Bedeckt. "I can actually see Wichtig's head swelling."

Wichtig ignored her. Only the child mattered. Selling this would-be god for ransom was the plan of an unimaginative mind. For now Wichtig understood the true value of the child. The boy was the ultimate means to the ultimate end. He stood aside so the lad could see the corpse-strewn hallway. No need to say anything, let the child come to his own conclusions.

Wichtig watched closely as the boy displayed emotion for the first time. Morgen's eyes widened in shock as he saw the bloody scene. He looked past Wichtig at Stehlen and Bedeckt, taking in their brutal appearance. His gaze flicked to the floor and the many identical corpses.

"Viele Sindein. She's been my bodyguard since . . ." Morgen trailed off. "Forever," he whispered. "I've never seen her be so many. Usually she's just two. They argue a lot." He glanced at Wichtig and said, "I don't think they like each other," as if sharing a secret.

"She was going to kill you," said Wichtig quickly. "We had to stop her."

"We don't have time for this," growled Stehlen from the hall. "Knock the kid out and let's be gone. Bedeckt is bleeding out."

The boy glanced at Stehlen. "I don't think you'll hurt me."

Wichtig watched, amazed, as Stehlen looked away uncomfortably. She opened her mouth and then slammed it shut with a clack. *Is she about to apologize?*

"Sorry," she said, looking as surprised as Wichtig felt.

*Impossible!*

Wichtig snorted a short laugh and put on his best charming smile. "Come. We have to take you to safety."

"Okay. But I have to wash my hands first."

While the boy scrubbed at his already clean hands, they stanched the worst of Bedeckt's wounds.

"Needs a real healer," whispered Stehlen.

Wichtig agreed but said nothing. They had no time for finding healers; they had to get out of Selbsthass fast.

When Morgen returned, he watched with curious distaste, careful to stand at a safe distance. When blood spattered near his feet, he shied away with careful steps.

*Like the kid never saw blood before,* mused Wichtig.

A few minutes later they retraced their steps through the ancient castle. Wichtig led the way, one hand resting protectively on Morgen's shoulder, while Stehlen followed with a pale and semiconscious Bedeckt leaning heavily against her.

Wichtig noticed he'd left a large bloody handprint on the child's thin shoulder. A little dirty reality would only serve to further the boy's dependence on him. He'd never been a hero before and looked forward to playing the role—actually performing it, and not just looking the part. It felt easy, natural. Hero was definitely the part he was destined to play.

He looked around him. For all the noise they'd made fighting Morgen's guard, apparently the tower's separation from the rest of the church had been enough. They walked empty halls and saw no one.

<hr />

Stehlen struggled to keep Bedeckt on his feet. He slowed with each step.

*I should leave him here.* Her gut churned at the thought.

"You're slowing me down, you useless sack of dog turds," she whispered into the gristly remains of his left ear. She wasn't sure if he heard. "Don't make me leave you here. Don't do that to me."

"Stupid . . ."

"What?"

"Bitch," Bedeckt finished.

Well, better than nothing. If he had the strength to be an insulting arsehole, he wasn't dead yet. She flared her nostrils, testing the air. Bedeckt reeked of blood and sweat and unwashed old man. There was something else in the air. Something undefinable, but something she knew.

"This doesn't feel right," she whispered close enough to his tattered ear that she could taste the drying blood.

"Try it after being stabbed a few dozen times," hissed Bedeckt through clenched teeth. "I guarantee it'll feel worse."

She ignored him. "I know what stealing feels like. I know how it smells. I know how it sounds. I know what it tastes like. This isn't right. A path has been cleared for us."

"Good."

*The idiot doesn't understand.*

Every nerve screamed *danger* and yet she saw nothing amiss. Someone was clearing the way for their escape, but she saw no reason to believe this mysterious person was on their side. Selfishness drove all action. A lifetime of backstabbing distrust had taught Stehlen one thing: if someone helped you, it was because doing so helped themselves. The moment mutually shared interest died, the truth shone clear and you'd feel their knife in your back.

Stehlen pushed the pace to catch Wichtig and the boy, and Bedeckt—much to her surprise—managed to match her.

She peered sideways into his face and saw shattered teeth gritted in a determined growl. "Still a bit of life in you," she said.

"No, just a lot more death." He peered at her through his single open eye and she caught a glint of dark humor. "Can't let Wichtig have my share."

"Greed is the ultimate motivator. Anyway, if you die I'm going to kill the arsehole and take it all." Of course, she had no idea how to go about collecting the god-boy's ransom. If the old man died she'd kill Wichtig and the boy and wash her hands of this gods-awful mess. Any plan involving more than go in, get the goods, and get out was doomed to failure.

# CHAPTER 18

*What have I done?*

Aufschlag watched Morgen and the three false priests. They'd never know, but it was his doing—sending priests and guards on make-work errands—that had cleared the path for them. And why he had done so . . . he still wasn't sure. He had done many horrible things as Konig's Chief Scientist, and though he'd often contemplated defying the Theocrat, not once had he dared to act. Not really.

*No, that's not true. I saved Wegwerfen.* That had to be worth something. But even that, sending her fleeing to Gottlos, had been an act of cowardly disobedience. And every day he still thought about sending someone to kill her, terrified Konig might discover what he'd done.

This was different. This was not some insignificant deception. He wasn't simply ignoring an unnecessary order or sharing a book with Morgen that Konig wouldn't approve of. This was it, the real thing.

*Go ahead. Say it. Admit to yourself what you're doing. Be honest.*

"Betrayal."

What an awful word.

Aufschlag remembered a drunken and emotional conversation he and Konig had shared all those years ago, about how important it was to him that he not let down his friends. He remembered Konig's eyes and the look on his face and how he'd thought it was understanding. Gods, Konig had used that every day since.

Betrayal. Here, beyond the influence of Konig's power, Aufschlag was on the verge of doing just that.

He checked the hall floor, counting tiles between where he hid and the kidnappers to gauge the distance.

Only a scientist would have thought to study and quantify the reality-defining effects of insanity, and Aufschlag was a scientist through and through. His entire life, every moment of his existence, had been dedicated to understanding the metrics defining Geisteskranken. Everyone knew that the effects of insanity dwindled with range and were damped by proximity to sane minds, but no one else thought to measure this. Aufschlag knew that even as powerful as Konig was, his Gefahrgeist delusions only affected him, Aufschlag, when close by. Here in the hallway, watching Morgen's kidnapping, he had the freedom to contemplate something other than mindless loyalty.

Such as saving Morgen's life . . . and perhaps his own soul. He glanced at his hands, blunt-fingered, skin wrinkled like a lizard left to dry in the sun. They were clean now, but they'd been bloodstained many, many times. *The things I have done.* Sure, he told himself, it had all been at Konig's request and for the greater good of both the Geborene and even mankind, but that was a lie. Some of his experiments had been unsettling to the extreme— and Aufschlag performed them willingly. Delving into the deeper truths, scratching at the underpinnings of reality, understanding the laws and limits of a reality defined by delusion, these were goals worthy of a great mind. *And if I have one delusion*—he laughed mockingly at himself—*it's that I am a great mind.*

It was *his* discovery that it was possible to turn ordinary, sane people into Geisteskranken. The correct mixture of physical and psychological torture could achieve incredible results. Forcing a mother to witness the torture and brutal murder of her children was enough to turn some into dangerous Geisteskranken. Aufschlag had even learned—at great personal risk—that the more heinous and drawn out the torture, the more powerful the Geisteskranken became. He once lost dozens of staff during an experiment when, after witnessing her husband and children tortured for several months, one woman shattered her shackles, tore scientists limb from limb, and burned down a sizable section of the Science Wing.

*Still you seek to justify your actions, as if doing so somehow distances you from the pain you inflicted. Calling it science doesn't change what you are.*

Konig, caring only for results, asked no questions. Aufschlag, however, had nothing but questions. And not once had he asked whether or not he *should* be doing these experiments in the first place. No, at the time he had wondered only why it took her so long to snap. Why was she so powerful when she finally snapped? Why did some people retreat into gibbering uselessness at similar stimuli while others found the ability to shapeshift or create armies of albtraum at will? And, of course, there were the most interesting questions:

What were the limits?

How powerful could a Geisteskranken become?

He'd done it for Konig. He'd done it for the Geborene, for humanity.

Right.

*How many have you tortured to scratch the itch of your own dark curiosity?*

The Theocrat—the shallow and shortsighted fool—thought Aufschlag's research was meant to further Konig's own goals.

And while, when he was in the High Priest's overpowering presence, this often became the truth, Aufschlag had plans of his own.

Belief defined reality and insanity—which Aufschlag defined as any unnaturally strong belief—manifested as power. But this, Aufschlag understood, was not the only form of power. Knowledge too was power. Though Aufschlag could not alter reality with the strength of his beliefs, he *could* manipulate it through his understanding of its underpinnings. Such as watching Morgen being escorted from the keep. Aufschlag smiled bitterly, pleased the boy was escaping Konig's grasp, terrified what the Theocrat would do if he discovered Aufschlag's role in the escape.

Not that the Theocrat's grasp was quite as firm as the Geborene leader thought it was—and Aufschlag's betrayal was only a small part of it. Konig sought to use Morgen for his own self-centered purposes—this was the way of all Gefahrgeist. The fool clung to the belief Morgen could save him from his delusions, staving off the horrific end all Geisteskranken faced. But for all his belief, Konig never thought to ask *how* this would happen. And after seeing Morgen's display of power, Aufschlag had begun to doubt the Theocrat's ability to control the boy once he Ascended. But doubt wasn't enough; Aufschlag needed to be sure. If Morgen Ascended under the influence of a deteriorating Gefahrgeist, there was no telling what would become of him. If, however, Morgen Ascended beyond Konig's manipulative grasp, he would become the god the Geborene and the people of Selbsthass deserved. A good and fair god. A god who protected his people instead of manipulating them like toys.

A god Aufschlag desperately needed.

Many nights Aufschlag lay sweating and shivering at the memories of what he had done in the name of science. No man should witness the horrendous acts he had seen. No man should *commit* the horrendous acts he had. But there was no changing the past: he had perpetrated those evils, staining his soul such that it would haunt him in the Afterdeath. But the Afterdeath was also redemption, a chance for the future to maybe not be as grim as it was shaping up to be. And maybe one truly selfless act could wipe clean a besmirched slate. Aufschlag prayed this was true. In the past he prayed to vague gods, but now he prayed to Morgen. If one pure result came out of all the suffering and misery he had caused, perhaps redemption could be his.

*Morgen will bring a new purity to a foul and terrible world.*

"Konig is not the Geborene Damonen," Aufschlag whispered. *He only thinks he is.* "I must do what is right."

The Chief Scientist might not have the strength of will to defy Konig while in his presence, but once far enough removed, Aufschlag could again think clearly. And now he was thinking of a time when the Geborene had a god to worship, and not a man ravaged by his own insanity.

"Take care of the boy," he whispered to the backs of the false priests, watching them move stealthily through the emptied church. Anywhere had to be better than here.

As the thieves stole away with what they surely thought was their great prize, he saw his path to redemption. His plan coalesced, as simple as it was dangerous.

Shortly he would make his way to the private chambers of Schwacher Sucher, the only Geborene Mirrorist currently residing in Selbsthass City, and murder the young priest. Yes, it was going to be murder—he wouldn't cloak his actions in misleading labels. Honesty mattered if he was to ever have a chance at redemption. It was a dark deed, but with Schwacher dead, it would be far more difficult for Konig to trace Morgen and his kidnappers. Hopefully this would buy Aufschlag time to find the thieves and either purchase or take the child—and keep Morgen out of Konig's own murderous hands.

Aufschlag cleared his troubled mind and focused his thoughts.

He must keep a clear vision of his plans or any interaction with Konig might sway him.

"Kill Schwacher," he whispered. Again he looked down at his clean hands, spidering veins showing through the thin and wrinkled skin. Though he had caused much pain and suffering in his research, he had never personally killed another human. *Will murder change me?* How could it not?

Aufschlag watched the three thieves approach the gate—he hadn't been able to think of a way to remove the guards that wouldn't have immediately aroused suspicion—with Morgen sheltered under the arm of a man dressed as an acolyte.

Aufschlag prayed Morgen would be safe.

He watched with sadness as the smallest false priest, dressed as a Bishop, killed the acolytes standing watch at the main gate. That had been unnecessary. But it was done and the boy was beyond Konig's reach. At least for now.

# CHAPTER 19

*The power of faith is the fear of the unknown.*
*The power of love is the fear of dying alone.*

—Excerpt from "The Power of Fear" by Halber Tod

Gehirn Schlechtes stared into the empty bowl. Erbrechen's organ stew, supposedly a source of sanity, was doing little for the hunger gnawing her innards. *Something is wrong.* She felt frail, paper-thin and dry like tinder. She needed to burn. Could this stew of souls really stave off the insanity and inevitable collapse caused by embracing one's delusions? Gehirn's doubt grew like worms, and she wondered if that doubt was a result of these gruesome meals. If belief was power, then surely doubt was its antithesis. What was doubt but a countering belief?

WHEN SHE STOOD in close proximity to Erbrechen, she thought of the man as beautiful, her friend and lover—even if he never touched her—and the center of everything important. When she strayed to the edges of the camp, however, words like "Slaver" crept into her mind. Standing there, watching Erbrechen from afar, she saw the man as a foul slug. A leech. And yet she could not leave. Always she returned to Erbrechen's side and basked happily in the man's attention and friendship.

*You are wretched and weak,* she told herself over and over. *Worthless.* Still, she could not walk away. *If I lose Erbrechen I shall truly have nothing, truly* be *nothing.* Was this love?

ERBRECHEN'S BAND MOVED ever closer to Selbsthass. The caravan traveled at a snail's pace, Erbrechen refusing to suffer discomfort. At each farming community and town they stopped to gather supplies and new followers. Most towns fell without Gehirn's help.

Day by day the distant storm clouds crept closer as Regen's sanity frayed under the relentless strain. The scrawny shaman staggered as he walked, white with blood loss, his skin an anemic parchment stretched over gnarled bones and twitching sinew. Gehirn watched the man's psyche decay with both detached interest and gnawing terror.

In the last day it had become necessary to shout to be heard over the ceaseless roar of thunder. The sky, lit bright with searing flashes of lightning, left Gehirn smelling of burned flesh. When Regen's mind finally failed, the sun would return.

*Why does Erbrechen not share the soul stew with the shaman?*

Regen's death would leave Gehirn vulnerable. Did Erbrechen not care? Was there some darker purpose? Gehirn considered sharing her own portion with the shaman, but doubt stopped her. What if she fed the stew to Regen and the shaman didn't get better? What if the souls and organs of the sane *didn't* offer succor to the ravaged sanity of those who embraced instability? Where would that leave Gehirn? More important, what would that mean to Erbrechen's plans? The Hassebrand shied away from such thoughts and buried deep her doubts. She'd rather continue to believe the stew worked rather than see proof of its failure.

Today she rode the litter alongside her love and told herself, over and over, *Erbrechen would never betray me.* Unlike Konig, Erbrechen was a true friend. She watched Regen's shambling shuffle. The shaman was a tool Erbrechen used to protect her.

"He doesn't use me," Gehirn whispered to herself. "He . . . likes me." She wanted to utter the word "loves," but her lips rebelled.

"Hmm?" asked Erbrechen. "I didn't hear that."

"Nothing." He stared, green eyes deceptively sleepy, almost closed, until she added, "I was just talking to myself."

Erbrechen looked away, gaze roving across his band of followers. "I do it all the time. There are so few people worth talking to." He glanced at her. "Not like you."

It was such an obvious ploy and yet her doubts suddenly seemed foolish. "I like talking to you too."

Erbrechen offered an embarrassed smile at this. "Can I ask you a question?"

"Of course."

"Some people are born broken—delusional from their very first day—whereas for others it requires some kind of trigger or emotional trauma." He licked his lips, a slow sensual swirl of bright pink tongue. "I've also heard that sometimes people can become delusional after suffering a blow to the head."

She knew where this would lead, saw the vicarious hunger in Erbrechen's eyes. Her jaw tightened and her knuckles popped loudly as her hands clenched into fists. "I heard much the same from Aufschlag," she said, doing her best to sound casual. *Please, no.*

Erbrechen nodded as if he knew exactly who Aufschlag was and asked, "Were you born a Hassebrand?"

"No." *Please don't ask. Please, please don't ask.*

"Was it physical trauma?" he asked, leaning in close, as if trying to breathe in her despair.

*He knows the answer and asks anyway.* Only a self-centered bastard—*Gefahrgeist. He's a Gefahrgeist,* she reminded herself. *He doesn't care how much this hurts me. He doesn't care—*

"I ask," he added, "because I care."

*He loves me!* The memories bubbled up like rising bile. "Daddy . . . My father loved me very much. So much that my mother hated me. She was very jealous." *Or disgusted.*

She told him everything. She told him how her father used to touch her and then hold his hands over the fire to burn clean his sins, and how he later did the same to her own small hands. She remembered screaming until her throat tore. She told him how her mother grew distant, eventually refusing to acknowledge Gehirn even existed. She told him of the day she reached puberty and the first fire she lit with nothing but thought.

"You and your father?" Erbrechen's face puckered with disgust. "You knew what you did was wrong," he said, and for an instant she wanted to incinerate the fat slug for giving voice to her self-loathing. One look from his sea-green eyes crushed the desire.

"From that day on," she continued, "no matter how long Father held my hands in the fire, they would not blister or burn. I asked if this meant I was free of sin." She laughed, a humorless grunt. "He shook his head and shoved my hands deeper into the coals."

Then, as she blossomed into a young woman, her father turned his back on her, disgusted with who and what she had become.

"They threw me out when I was fourteen," she finished. Tears streamed down her face, stinging her lips with their salt. "I returned a few years later and they asked why I'd left. They pretended nothing had ever happened. Then, when Mommy left the room, Daddy touched me." She ground her teeth, her jaw aching, until the air around her rippled with heat. "I burned him."

"You're lucky," said Erbrechen. When she stared at him in mute shock, he added, "At least somebody loved you. Even if just for a while." He shook his head, gnawing at his lower lip. "I was left in the gutter seconds after my birth." He reached a fat hand toward her thigh but stopped short of touching her. "For years I thought the couple that found me were my family, even though I was never allowed to call them Mother or Father. They only kept me until I was worth selling." Erbrechen's petite nose wrinkled, disappearing between round cheeks. "Foully betrayed twice before I was even four years old. But they underestimated me. No one understood just how smart I am. I learned. No one would ever betray me again."

Erbrechen wove a tale of life on the streets, raised by a succession of pimps and whores, the daily struggle to survive and find food. He told her of the long years when he was sold and traded, little more than a commodity, soft flesh with value. Always watching, always listening. Always learning.

"We are driven by desire masquerading as need," he said. "Understand a person's needs and you can bend them to anything."

As he talked she found herself shaking with the force of her sobs. His was a life robbed of all hope before he even knew what hope was. Her own suffering paled in comparison. How could she have thought her petty wounds worth sharing?

*Gods, he has suffered so much. How can he sit beside me, telling his story with such aplomb?*

"And one day a client—a wealthy old man—told me he loved me. He said he'd do anything for me." Erbrechen laughed, clapping happily. "The next day, at my request, he had my pimp drowned in a bucket of goat piss." He sighed, smiling wistfully at the memory. The smile died. "But what he called love was just need. He didn't love me. No one *ever* loves me. They need and need and need, always demanding. Never love." He glanced at her again as if checking that she still listened. "It wasn't long before I realized that in small groups I could twist just about anyone's needs. But in the city, surrounded by the witless masses, my power was limited. The next time I left the city with my love and his retinue, I made sure we never returned. They were my first friends and followed me for years." He shrugged one shoulder and his left breast jiggled. "Friends come and go. I wonder if any of them are still with me." He gave a cursory glance to his followers, but he barely seemed to be looking.

*He sounds so sad, so alone.* Gehirn wanted to embrace Erbrechen—to offer some small comfort—but remembered his unwillingness to touch her. *He is afraid to love me,* she realized. Could he fear rejection?

Gehirn mopped tears with an already sodden sleeve. She understood rejection. *He's telling me this because he loves me. He bares everything and dares everything.* She could never be so brave.

*How could I ever have doubted his love?* She hung her head, ashamed she could be so self-centered, ashamed at needing more from her love.

Hours later she remembered what she'd been thinking about before Erbrechen had interrupted her thoughts. Had it been an intentional distraction?

Doubt grew in dark and fertile soil.

ERBRECHEN, UNWILLING TO let his friends, who now numbered in the thousands, stray from his influence, used no scouts. As such, when they arrived, en masse, at Verteidigung, they found the gates closed and the walls manned. The city and surrounding farmlands, having been pounded by Regen's storm long in advance of their arrival, looked to be in a state of advanced ruin. Much of the land had been burned, blasted by lightning, pelted by fist-sized hail, and then flooded. Gehirn noted a distinct lack of corpses. Odd. With this much destruction she expected at least some.

Erbrechen sent one of his new friends—a pompous woman who had not yet lost the fat of her previous life—forward to demand the surrender of Verteidigung. The soldiers on the wall pincushioned her with a dozen crossbow bolts and she toppled into the mud.

Erbrechen shook his head, tutted, and turned sad green eyes on Gehirn. "I don't know why they bother. They will have to apologize."

Then, when the woman climbed awkwardly to her feet, turned, and walked back toward Erbrechen's litter, he offered a soft "Oh." He frowned at the approaching woman. "She is dead, right?"

"Yes," answered Gehirn, still sitting beside Erbrechen. "I suspect Verteidigung has a powerful Phobic with a deep fear of death and the dead."

"You don't say. Burn her."

Gehirn felt a feral grin stretch her face as she let loose some small shred of the doubt and depression that she held tight to her heart. The woman and a hundred paces of ground around her burst into flames. The damp earth quickly guttered, but the woman burned on, a pillar of fire shuffling ever closer. Even at this range she smelled delicious.

Erbrechen cleared his throat gently. "She's still coming," he said with a slight tremor.

A sob was wrenched from Gehirn's soul as she relaxed her weakening grip on reality. Perhaps, in his fear, Erbrechen's control slipped for a moment, because in that instant, Gehirn understood she was naught but the Slaver's toy. At best a favored toy, but certainly nothing more. Erbrechen would use her and cast her aside. Her fate would be no different from Regen's. She was helpless.

*He devours my need like he sucks back that stew. Just another soul sliding into a fat belly that will never fill.*

But she still had her fire . . .

The flames enshrouding the woman flickered, brightened, and became a blinding white beacon. The skeletal image of the woman remained written on the stunned retinas of all witnesses for several seconds. She was dust and ash, a stain in the wind.

Gehirn screamed, clenched fists held tight against her chest like a child cowering before an enraged adult. Pressure built inside her skull, seeking escape. *My eyes,* she thought, *will boil.*

Sanity, the antithesis to power. To embrace one was to abandon the other. Betrayed and yet trapped and helpless, Gehirn cradled her hurts like a young girl holding a wounded bird. She knew Erbrechen used her but this knowledge did nothing to free her from the Slaver's clutches. She both loved and hated—loathed and worshiped—the obscene slug.

Knowledge didn't set her free; it more clearly displayed the true depth of her prison.

Gehirn screamed, throat raw and burning.

Stone walls glowed red and ran like mud. The city gates fell apart, little more than kindling now.

Within the city Gehirn saw the dead rise, climbing unsteadily to their feet and looking about in uncomprehending horror. The corpses, united in purpose, stalked the burning ruin, staggered through the open gates, and launched themselves at Erbrechen's mob. The dead burned, but kept coming.

Erbrechen wailed as his litter lurched chaotically. His power kept those close from fleeing but they couldn't move fast enough while bearing the weight of the litter, his corpulent body, and Gehirn.

Levering herself to her feet to better see, Gehirn watched the approaching dead. *They can have me.* Death had to be better than this.

Erbrechen screamed at Gehirn, "Stop them! Burn them! Burn them all!"

Gehirn was a slave—to both Erbrechen and the fire. She heard the former's command and obeyed the latter's desire.

The city burned.

The fields burned.

The dead burned.

The world became a roaring tornado of ash and smoke.

Fire spread.

Gehirn screamed and laughed and sobbed and cackled.

Cyclonic pillars of ash, once human life, spun in the growing storm winds.

Burn the world.

⸻

Erbrechen's litter lurched and collapsed to the ground, crushing those unfortunate enough to be trapped below. The Hassebrand somehow remained standing. Erbrechen shouted himself hoarse commanding Gehirn to stop, but the damned woman was beyond all thought, lost to the pure sexual joy of fire.

Dawning terror broke over Erbrechen as he realized his soul stew had no effect on his pet Hassebrand. Sharing it had been a waste.

Using muscles unused in years, he dragged himself closer to Gehirn. When he got close enough he slammed the wailing woman in the back of the knees with a massive arm. Gehirn dropped like a stone, and Erbrechen, levering himself up with one shaking gelatinous arm, pummeled her face until the Hassebrand lost consciousness.

After, as Erbrechen's surviving followers busied themselves collecting supplies and rounding up those who had not burned in the city, he sat staring at the unconscious woman. She seemed at peace, the bright canines hidden. Rounder and much older than he liked, she still had something about her he found fascinating.

*She's dangerous.*

True, but there was something more. She not only loved him—as all must—she *wanted* to love him. Somehow that set her apart. He reached a hand toward her face and stopped just shy of touching her. Could she love him for who he really was?

*No, she loves your need of love. Nothing more.* She loved because—like the others—she had no choice. No one knew just how lonely it was to live at the center.

Erbrechen withdrew his hand to dab at his cheek. Was that a tear? He snorted. *Self-pity ill becomes you.*

Still, it would be nice to have someone at his side, someone who truly loved him. *Maybe I could love her in return. I could try.*

# CHAPTER 20

*Getting rid of a truth makes us wiser than getting hold of a delusion.*

—Nicht Ludwig Borne

Aufschlag arrived at the private chambers of Schwacher Sucher nervous and sweating heavily. He pressed flat the oily fringe of hair surrounding his bald dome and struggled to find composure. His heart thudded heavily in his chest, and the knife, tucked into the tightly cinched belt that kept him from looking any more like a tent than he already did, pressed into his back. Should he loosen the belt a notch? What if the knife fell out? A few calming breaths did nothing for his pounding heart. Could he go through with his plan? Even more important, would he?

"Yes," he whispered.

A thought stayed Aufschlag's hand partway into reaching up to knock on the oak door. *What if the Geborene Mirrorist foresaw this?* Konig often complained of the young Mirrorist's limitations, but Konig complained about everyone's faults. Nothing was ever good enough for the Geborene High Priest. Though the many corpses of Viele Sindein, Morgen's Mehrere bodyguard, had yet to be discovered, it was entirely possible Schwacher knew everything.

*What if Konig waits within, already aware of my betrayal?*

No. If Konig had advance knowledge of Aufschlag's plans, he would never have allowed Morgen to be stolen.

Aufschlag knocked gently and heard the immediate answer. "Enter."

Once inside, he stood facing Schwacher, who, in turn, stood staring at him. The Mirrorist, who looked to be still in his teens, displayed none of the self-mutilation common to the breed. After much research Aufschlag had postulated that the more grotesque the mutilation, the greater the Mirrorist's power.

*Theory,* Aufschlag suddenly thought, *is all fine and good until it's faced with real life.* His gaze darted about the room, seeking the mirrors he knew must be present. He saw none. The room was spare, undecorated, and showing nothing of the young Mirrorist's personality. The small fireplace looked scrubbed and clean, with no hint it had ever been used. Aufschlag stared at the fireplace. Did the Mirrorist freeze in the winter, or was this the sign of some obsessive disorder? For some reason the cleanliness of the fireplace reminded him of Morgen.

"Yes?" asked the Mirrorist expectantly.

"Your mirrors . . ."

"I keep them elsewhere," said Schwacher, his face boyish and innocent. "It's the only way to get a moment's peace."

Aufschlag nodded understanding to cover his surprise. *Why must I always appear knowledgeable, even to people who will soon be dead?* "I need you to show me something. Some people. I need to see where they are going."

Schwacher cocked his head to one side and raised an eyebrow quizzically. "Who are we spying on?"

Aufschlag explained the when, where, and who, and the young Mirrorist led him into another room, where a single massive mirror hung in an ornate gilt frame. Together they watched the three brutal thieves kill Viele Sindein over and over. They watched the smallest thief, dressed unconvincingly as a Geborene Bishop, dart through the crowd of Vieles and kill the original. They saw the kidnappers take Morgen and flee the church, witnessed their flight west toward Neidrig.

"We have to—" began Schwacher.

"Wait."

Schwacher frowned in confusion as the scene in the mirror wavered and changed to show Aufschlag, standing in the shadows, staring after the retreating kidnappers.

"You watched them leave," he said, confused. "They took Morgen and—"

"Kill Schwacher," Aufschlag's reflection whispered clearly. "Distract Konig long enough to give the boy's kidnappers a head start. Mislead him as to where they are going." The reflection stared sadly down at his hands.

Aufschlag looked down at his hands and the sharp knife now clutched there. Movement in the mirror caught his eye and he watched the reflection of the Mirrorist back away, eyes wide with fear as Aufschlag's reflection advanced with the knife.

"I'm sorry," Aufschlag's reflection said.

Schwacher's eyes widened with understanding and he backed away.

Aufschlag followed. "I'm sorry," he said.

AFTER, WHEN SCHWACHER lay bleeding out the last of his life, Aufschlag turned his attention to the mirror. There, at the very end, the Mirrorist glimpsed briefly into the near future. Yet his vision changed nothing and the two men reenacted the scene shown there step-by-step like marionettes in a well-rehearsed play.

Though Schwacher lay dead at Aufschlag's feet, the Mirrorist's reflection still stood within the mirror, watching the Chief Scientist as if waiting.

"Why?" Aufschlag asked. "Why do you look at me like that? Will you fade and die now that Schwacher is dead?" His scientific curiosity piqued, he examined the mirror and reflection. *Why does it remain?* "You aren't going to fade away, are you?" Aufschlag scratched at his greasy fringe of hair. "You aren't going to fade, and you'll still be here when the body is discovered." The reflection watched him. "You'll still be here and you might be able to tell them who did this. Can you speak?"

Schwacher's reflection stared mutely, waiting.

"You might identify me as Schwacher's"—he paused to swallow—"murderer," he finished.

The reflection didn't move or blink.

Aufschlag saw it. "Ah. You've seen the future and you know what will happen. You wait for me to figure it out."

The reflection watched Aufschlag search the room until he found a heavy fire poker in the stand near the fireplace. He returned to the mirror and its waiting reflection; Aufschlag was nowhere to be seen within.

"Is this what I do, what I have to do, or something I might do?" Aufschlag asked the mirror.

Expressionless, Schwacher's reflection watched the Chief Scientist.

*No surprise it doesn't answer,* Aufschlag thought. *I am no Mirrorist.*

"I could walk away," he told the mirror.

Schwacher's reflection tilted its head to the left and continued watching him. No matter how much Aufschlag told himself he had a choice, it seemed like no choice at all. If he chose not to break the mirror—simply to prove it was an option—the reflection might tell someone of his actions. *I can't chance it.*

Aufschlag felt the solid weight of the iron poker hanging in his hand. *This is not murder. This is a lingering delusion, nothing more.*

Aufschlag smashed the mirror and fled the room. The crunch of broken glass under his shoes felt like an accusation. Several yards down the hall he slowed to a more respectable walk. It wouldn't do to look suspicious here. A thought stopped him and he stood with a perplexed frown.

"Is breaking a mirror really bad luck?" he asked aloud of the empty hall. "Everyone believes it is." No. That didn't sound quite right. "Everyone *believes* it is." He leaned against the cool stone wall. Why hadn't he thought of this sooner? "Damn it!" What did bad luck really mean? Would he stub his toe or fall to his death?

# CHAPTER 21

*Economics, now that's a delusion!*

—Wohlhabende Klein, Kleptic Economist

Bedeckt faded in and out of consciousness, only vaguely aware of the journey to the Leichtes Haus inn. Wichtig dragged him to the stables in the back, sat him down against the tavern wall, arse in a cold puddle, and left to prepare the horses. Bedeckt wanted to tell the Swordsman to get Launisch a few apples but couldn't summon the energy. Stehlen, looking like she'd eaten something sour, glared at him, said something about going to their rooms to fetch their belongings, and left.

Bedeckt coughed, spraying blood and snot. The kid—Morgen, Bedeckt reminded himself—squatted a foot away, eyes wide, arms crossed tight across his chest, careful to avoid the pooling blood, watching with intense interest.

"Dark," coughed Bedeckt, squinting past the boy. The long and perfectly straight street looked deserted.

The boy watched, saying nothing. Maybe he didn't realize

Bedeckt had meant it as a question. *Is it night? Everything looks gray.*

The rain hadn't let up. If anything, the storm was growing in strength. To the south the sky flickered a hell storm of flashing lightning and strange lights. He'd been thinking about the storm earlier, hadn't he? He couldn't remember.

The alley he sat in was a fast-moving, ankle-deep river. Bedeckt coughed again and hawked bright blood that swirled away in an instant. Water pooled around him, dark from the blood his body leaked and fading to a thin stream of light pink as it disappeared down the street.

The boy still stared at him.

"What?" Bedeckt growled.

"I've never been outside of the temple before. Is it always like this?"

Bedeckt coughed blood, spattering his chest. "Like what?"

"Dirty."

"Yes."

Morgen shuffled to one side to avoid a pinkish puddle spreading in his direction. He met Bedeckt's eyes. "You are dying, I think."

"I don't care what—" Bedeckt stopped. *Shite.* He *did* care what the boy thought.

This was a child actively groomed for godhood. What could the beliefs of this child achieve? His chest tightened in an unfamiliar feeling. Fear? Mortality and death were simple facts of everyday life. He'd faced greater danger in the past. But still . . . *This boy can kill me just by thinking I will die.* What would it mean to have the unified and directed faith of a Theocracy like Selbsthass turned against him?

Did he feel weaker already? Was he bleeding faster?

"Not ready to die," he whispered.

The boy cocked his head quizzically. "Why fear? You will awaken in the Afterdeath, unhurt and whole."

Aside from keeping a few coins stashed in his right boot to ensure he wouldn't awaken on the other side completely broke, Bedeckt had never given the Afterdeath much thought. The looming proximity of death had a way of focusing the mind.

"Your dead await you," said Morgen, sounding as if he meant it as comfort.

Bedeckt couldn't count the number of times he'd heard scarred old men and women repeating different versions of the Warrior's Credo. Most said the dead would serve. Some, more ominously, merely claimed the dead would be there. Waiting. Bedeckt's dead were beyond counting.

Bedeckt chuckled bloodily and the boy shuffled farther away. "I generally don't kill people I want to see again." He saw Morgen's confused look. "Bit of an oversight, really. There was a whore in—" A fit of coughing interrupted him. "Can't remember. Too long ago. Like to see her again. Would have killed the wench if I'd thought of this sooner." He watched the boy watching him. Somewhere in the distance he heard the muted sounds of combat, steel on steel. He didn't care. He couldn't stand, much less defend himself.

"What do you think?" he asked the boy.

Morgen examined his own hands, checking the fingernails. "I need to wash my hands."

"Do our dead await us?" Bedeckt asked more loudly.

The boy glanced up. "I will be a god," he said, as if that somehow answered Bedeckt's question. "I think there will be no Afterdeath for me. I will Ascend and be the god of the Geborene." With a look of disgust he gestured at the blood pooling around Bedeckt and streaming away into the darkness. "Everything will be clean." With the tip of his shoe he pushed three pebbles into a line, frowned at them, adjusted one, and then nodded content-edly. "Everything will be neat. Tidy." He gestured at the blood swirling in filthy water. "Not like this."

Wichtig approached, leading the three horses. "Is there any blood left inside you?" Even soaked through in the rain, he looked every inch the hero. He ran a hand through his reddish-brown hair, slicking it back. "Where is Stehlen?"

Bedeckt coughed more blood.

The boy pointed at him with a small hand. "He's dying."

Wichtig raised an eyebrow. "Really?"

"And he's making a mess."

"We can't have that, can we," said Wichtig, shaking his head. "Bedeckt, in a moment, you're going to owe me another one."

*What's the fool talking about?*

"You know, Morgen," drawled Wichtig, "Bedeckt was hurt rescuing you." He gave the boy a serious look, brows furrowed. "You owe him much. His death will stain your hands. Forever."

The boy's gaze jerked to his hands. He looked like the thought would bring him to tears.

"Aufschlag says cleanliness is important," said Morgen. "I need to wash my hands." He glanced about desperately, but the only water nearby was stained with blood and filth from the street. "I can save him," whispered Morgen. "Would that . . . pay the debt?"

"It would be a start," answered Wichtig.

"A start?"

Bedeckt watched the boy examine him.

"He's covered in old scars," said Morgen. "How much should I heal?" Bedeckt saw the boy notice the fingers missing on his left hand. "Should I heal everything?" Morgen asked. "Shall I give you back those fingers?"

Bedeckt tightened the ruined left hand into a fist. "No."

Wichtig nudged Bedeckt's foot with his own. "I always knew you for a sentimental old goat."

222

Bedeckt glared up from where he sat and Wichtig blew him a kiss. "Yeah, I know, you'll kill me later."

Motion in the swirling puddles distracted Bedeckt. A familiar scene, though not from this vantage. He saw the battle at Sinnlos on the Auseinander border.

Bedeckt watched as the last two fingers of his left hand were cut away and fell, spinning, to the trampled mud of the battlefield. The gold wedding band glinted for a moment, reflecting distant fires. In those reflections he saw older, almost forgotten battles from much further in his savage past. He saw a comrade, retreating under the onslaught of several opponents, step on the fingers, driving them into the mud and smothering those reflections. Distantly he heard the victorious yell of his enemy and his own, much louder roar as he hewed into the man's skull. The vision guttered and died.

"The reflections don't lie," said the boy. "But I can't always be sure of their meaning."

"I remember that day," said Bedeckt.

"Who would want to live with such ugly, scarred hands?" asked Morgen, sounding confused.

Bedeckt tried to answer but couldn't find the strength.

"At least now he'll be easier to deal with," he heard Wichtig say. "You *can* heal him, right?"

If the boy answered, Bedeckt didn't hear it.

BEDECKT STOOD IN the ruins of . . . a city . . . a battlefield? This was the site of a fight not long concluded. The stench of death remained. Ghostly memories of violence shivered the air with the metallic tang of spilled blood and sour terror. The city looked familiar. Sinnlos, maybe? The burned and smoking skeletal wrecks of houses lay scattered across streets. Siege weapons had done their work here. Perhaps this had once been a prosperous land, but now few buildings retained more than two standing walls.

*Why does this look so familiar?* Bedeckt glanced down at the scarred remains of his left hand and then back to the street.

A crowd of men and women, warriors each and every one, stood gathered before him.

*Were they there before?* Bedeckt thought not.

There were too many to count quickly. Dozens. Scores. All bore weapons, stained with use, hanging ready in scarred and muscled hands. Many looked familiar.

Bedeckt's hand reached for his ax. It wasn't in its customary place, hanging at his back. He took a deep breath, was surprised it didn't hurt, and crouched, readying himself for the attack. His knees creaked and groaned.

A voice muttered, "Some of us have been waiting a very long time."

Bedeckt couldn't tell who said this and was distracted as a large man pushed through the crowd, working his way closer.

His father, the very first man he had ever killed.

⸻

Morgen hunched over Bedeckt's still body and thought about how the wounds would heal. From the corner of his eye he saw Wichtig, the Greatest Swordsman in the World and dashing hero, wave the thin and ugly woman over. She was covered in even more blood than before entering the tavern but wore several new colorful scarves and gaudy trinkets. He listened as Wichtig asked her what had taken so damned long and as she explained she'd had to kill everyone in the tavern to cover their tracks and foil pursuit. Morgen could tell Wichtig believed not a word of this. He watched the Swordsman's face grow sad as he recognized the scarves.

"You had to kill her too, did you?" Wichtig asked with angry sarcasm.

Stehlen flared nostrils and spat at the ground. "She could describe all of us. Your little sticker in particular."

Morgen saw Wichtig's guilty glance in his direction.

"Fine. We'll talk about this later. Did you get much?"

"Not really."

She lied, but Wichtig seemed unaware.

"Hells, we're almost broke. Morgen, you finished yet?"

"Yes," said Morgen, backing away. He had stopped the worst of the bleeding. The rest would have to wait. The ugly old man would live. The scars and wounds of his past, both within and without, would remain with him to his final day. Morgen watched as the bloody water swirled, showing glimpses of the future. Bedeckt, whom he'd just pulled from the gates of the Afterdeath, would again lie dying in a few short days. Next time Morgen would not save him. Bedeckt would be without his friends. Morgen wondered at this. Would they abandon the big man? Betray him? Morgen couldn't imagine the dashing Wichtig leaving his friend. If Bedeckt died alone, then surely Wichtig was dead too.

*Will they die protecting me?*

Stehlen was something entirely different. She had no softness in her, all edges and sharp angles, twitchy like the rodents Morgen kept as pets and dangerous like the caged cats and snakes he hadn't been allowed near. The woman scared him. She wore her willingness to violence in every glance and the way her hands constantly roved around the many weapons stashed about her body, checking their positions and accessibility. There was no act of brutality she was not capable of.

Wichtig and Stehlen wrestled Bedeckt onto Launisch's back. The black war-horse eyed them with ill intent. Wichtig dodged its attempts to nip at him and laughed at it good-naturedly as he tied the semiconscious warrior into place. Frustrated, Launisch gave up and eyed Stehlen for a moment before snorting and looking away. *The horse knows better than to try and bite her,* thought Morgen.

Minutes later they were mounted and riding southwest.

225

Stehlen led the way on a gray gelding whose spirit had long ago been broken. Morgen sat before Wichtig, cradled and protected within the fortress of those strong arms. Bedeckt, slumped on the massive destrier tied to Wichtig's horse, faded in and out of consciousness, mumbling quietly and occasionally warding away unseen opponents with clawed hands. The sky to the south rumbled and cracked with violence.

Morgen watched the distant storm. He could smell the fetid odor of a wounded soul reaching its breaking point. Whoever held sway over that tempest wouldn't last much longer.

He looked back over his shoulder at Wichtig and pointed at the storm. "That's bad."

Wichtig laughed. "A master of understatement. Just like Bedeckt. We're going to skirt the storm and ride for Neidrig. We"—he glanced at Stehlen—"know people there."

Morgen wondered at the pause. "What kind of people?"

"The kind who can help us hide you from the bad people who want to hurt you."

"Will Konig be there?"

"Probably not," said Wichtig. "Konig knows he is being watched. He doesn't want to lead your enemies to you."

"I have enemies?"

Stehlen looked back from the front, twisting around in the saddle to stare at Morgen with a nasty grin. "Everyone has enemies."

Wichtig sighed and rolled his eyes theatrically for Morgen's benefit. "Ignore her. It'll be exciting."

Just being beyond the walls of the temple had been exciting; this was something altogether different. Unknown assassins and a mad dash to an unknown city beyond the Selbsthass border. This was an adventure, just like he'd read about. "What's Neidrig like?"

"It's a vomitous syphilitic piss hole," Stehlen called over her shoulder.

"It's colorful," answered Wichtig. "There's all kinds of people there. It's like anywhere. Some people are good and some are bad. If you're going to be any kind of god, you'll need to know all this." The Swordsman sounded thoughtful. "This is part of the education Konig wants for you. We're supposed to introduce you to all the different kinds of people. Someday these folks will worship you. It's important you know who they are so you can better rule them."

This made sense, but why had Konig not exposed him to the people sooner? *Rule them?* "But Konig said a god should serve the people."

"Of course," Wichtig answered quickly. "Any good ruler, King, or Emperor rules by serving those he—"

"Or she," shouted Stehlen.

"—he . . . uh . . . rules over." Wichtig hunched forward to whisper in Morgen's ear. "There is much Konig wants me to teach you. These other two . . ." He gestured at Stehlen and the semiconscious Bedeckt. "They're brutes. We need them, but they're dangerous."

"I thought Bedeckt was your friend." Morgen twisted to look up into Wichtig's face. "Your *only* friend."

"You see much," said Wichtig, nodding and giving Morgen a sad smile, "but have much to learn. I am Bedeckt's only friend, and yet I am not sure if he is *my* friend. I'd have given up hope, except once . . ." He trailed off and stared into the distance.

Morgen watched the reflections dance in Wichtig's gray eyes: *albtraum. Wild Doppels. Twisted versions of Wichtig and Stehlen, birthed by their nightmares, came out of the forest as the two slept, tossing fitfully in their sleeping rolls. Their campfire had long since gone out. Morgen saw Bedeckt come awake, the ax in his hand before he even knew what was happening. The big man stood, staggered back, retreating before the swarming albtraum. He turned to run and stopped as he caught sight of Stehlen, still asleep. Morgen saw the indecision in Bedeckt's eyes. Then, with a snarl, Bedeckt was among the albtraum, ax swinging, blood spattering everything. Wichtig and Stehlen awoke to find themselves surrounded by albtraum corpses. Bedeckt sat by a freshly lit fire. "Wichtig," he said, "if you let the fire go out again, I'll kill you."*

Something about this memory haunted Wichtig. Morgen had heard stories of tragic heroes and understood the concept, but Wichtig didn't quite fit. Much in the Swordsman mirrored what Morgen saw in Konig. They shared similarly intimidating flat, gray eyes. Both men needed the people around them and wanted those people to need them in return. And both men sought something greater than themselves. Something elusive. Something important and yet terrifying to the two men. Underlying everything else, Morgen suddenly realized, lurked the fear of success. He didn't understand exactly what each man sought to achieve, but both feared success as much as they feared failure. Perhaps even more so. *What could possibly terrify such men?* What could scare the Theocrat of Selbsthass and the Greatest Swordsman in the World to the point where they subconsciously engineered their own failures?

Morgen didn't know how to ask.

"Bedeckt once came back for me," Wichtig said in an awed whisper. "Back then, in the same situation, I would have abandoned him, but he . . ." The Swordsman laughed but sounded sad. "Either he saved me or he was a tool of fate. Either I owe him my life or he merely did what had to be done to show me my true destiny."

Morgen knew the Swordsman wished it was the former and

believed it was the latter. "You're Gefahrgeist, like Konig," he said.

‖‖‖‖‖‖‖‖‖

Wichtig forced himself not to react. "No," he said, "not like Konig. Very different. I'm no Theocrat. Just a simple Swordsman."

Modesty, false or otherwise, was not something he was accustomed to, but manipulation is contingent on knowing when to brag and when to be humble. It was a novel experience, and one he strangely enjoyed. *There's something satisfying to proclaiming humility while knowing just how important you truly are.* He'd have to experiment. Perhaps this novel approach might work with Bedeckt.

"No," stated Morgen with the definitive certainty only the young can manage. "You're the Greatest Swordsman in the World. You're important. Special. You cause things to happen. Different from Konig, but *like* Konig." The boy sounded frustrated, as if he wanted to say more but couldn't. "I can help you. I can make sure you don't fail."

Wichtig ruffled the boy's hair. Whatever Morgen's abilities, they didn't render him immune to the charms of a Gefahrgeist. Even one with such limited power as himself. The thought left an uncomfortable feeling tingling down his spine. *I must not,* he realized, *practice this new humility on myself.* There must be no room for doubt.

As they rode southwest Wichtig told Morgen of the adventures they'd have in Neidrig, though he left out all talk of whores, back-alley stabbings, and the fact that they'd be hiding like furtive cockroaches.

Neidrig, he had heard from both Stehlen and Bedeckt, was an utter shite-hole. He'd never visited the city, but it sounded like the perfect hiding place. There could be no doubt they would be pursued. The trick would be finding the kind of dubious, untrustworthy, and insane people who could hide them. Luckily the people who could best shield them from the prying eyes of Konig's Mirrorists and other Geisteskranken would also probably not be sane enough to appreciate the danger.

*Truly,* thought Wichtig, *it's a beautiful thing*: *The more powerful—and therefore useful—a person is, the easier it is to manipulate them.* Manipulating the sane was like herding sheep. It took a lot of effort, and if you focused on one sheep at a time, you'd get nowhere. *But get the right sheep moving in the right direction and the rest will follow.*

# CHAPTER 22

*I heard a knock, and when I answered the door, there I was. Luck-*
*ily I think much faster on my feet than I do and soon had myself*
*tied in the fruit cellar. I'd kill myself but I'm so damned useful.*
*Sometimes, when the High Priest has texts he wants copied, I'll*
*unchain one of my hands and get me to do some of the work. Of*
*course I do it! I'm so damned bored down here, chained to the wall.*

—ÜBERSETZEN MIST, SCRIBE TO KONIG FURIMER

How did this happen?" Konig screamed into the quivering priest's face.

Tragen Nachrichten wilted in the heat of Konig's wrath. The Theocrat's three Doppels stood gathered, threateningly, around the Geborene priest. Acceptance, beaten and bruised, wheezed through an open mouth showing jagged fractured teeth while glaring through one bruised eye. The Doppel had covered the other eye with a rough cloth patch that did little to disguise the damage done.

The priest's gaze jumped from the Doppel's ruined face and

back to Konig's. No doubt Tragen wondered who could have done this, and then saw the only answer. What would he tell the other priests, that the Theocrat wars with himself?

Konig glanced at the mirror. A dozen of his reflections gathered there, watching with calm disinterest. His Mirrorist powers had grown. Useful, perhaps, but it meant his mental state was decaying quickly. The finger he'd broken punching Acceptance still throbbed, a distraction and a reminder of just how close he'd come to losing everything.

*I'm running out of time.*

Konig took a deep breath and fought for control. Morgen would save him. He'd kill the boy, thereby forcing his Ascension and ensuring the god's loyalty. *Those whom you slay must serve.* Reciting the plan and credo calmed him. "Tell me once again. Leave out no detail."

Tragen bowed low. "Yes, Theocrat. Schwacher Sucher, the temple Mirrorist, is dead. Stabbed to death. He had no meetings scheduled and the door showed no signs of being forced." Tragen paused to swallow uncomfortably. "Schwacher's mirror was broken. Completely shattered."

Konig paced back and forth in front of the young priest. "They broke the mirror."

"Yes, Theocrat."

"Stabbed to death?" Konig asked. "Stabbed many times?"

"Many, many times," Tragen answered. "The guard I left to watch the room said it looked like the panicked attack of a scared amateur rather than a professional assassination. He said the attacks were all over the place. Many weren't fatal. Schwacher's arms were deeply wounded."

"Had Schwacher been assigned anything important?"

"Yes, Theocrat. I checked the logbook. Schwacher had been watching several Wahnvor Stellung temples. I found no reference as to what he was looking for."

"You don't have the rank."

The Wahnvor? Could they have agents within the Geborene High Temple? Had Schwacher found something only to be slain before he could report it? If they had infiltrated the Geborene hierarchy . . .

Konig turned to Tragen. "You must check on—"

The door to Konig's private chambers slammed rudely open and Meineigener Beobachter, chief of Konig's personal security force, stormed into the room. His normally stony face betrayed a look of horror. Meineigener bowed and stood waiting at attention.

The Doppels frowned at the interruption and the gathered reflections—now dozens, some of which huddled at the rear of the crowd—suddenly looked interested.

"Yes?" Konig snapped.

"The child is gone." Meineigener, three hundred pounds of towering muscle, swallowed nervously. "Morgen is gone. We can't find him anywhere." He dropped his gaze to the floor. "We think he's been taken."

Taken? Without Morgen his plans were ash. Without Morgen . . . Konig glanced at his Doppels.

"Oh," whispered Acceptance, hiding a smirk and shattered teeth behind a bruised hand, "that *is* a shame."

Konig, ignoring the Doppel, stared at his chief of security. "You *think*?" The man nodded mutely, staring at the floor. "Meineigener," Konig said quietly.

The massive guard met Konig's flat gray eyes and stood rigid, unable to look away, muscles locked motionless by the Gefahrgeist's will.

"Yes, My Theocrat." said Meineigener, voice soft with awe.

Konig gestured at Tragen, who stood quietly listening. "Kill him. Now."

Meineigener drew his sword and cut the young priest down in

one smooth motion. He cleaned and sheathed the blade before Tragen's corpse hit the floor.

"In the future," Konig said, "you will be more careful who you share information with. Or, in the future"—he gestured at Tragen's corpse—"that will be you."

"Yes, My Theocrat."

*At least the oaf didn't apologize.* Few things angered Konig more than pointless apologies. "Who else knows?" he asked.

"I left Vertrauens Würdig to watch over the room and came straight to you. I also sent a man to detain Morgen's nurse, though with no explanation as to why."

"Good." The man hadn't been an utter moron. Vertrauens was a member of Konig's personal guard and one of Meineigener's most trusted men. "Find out what the nurse knows. Kill her afterward." Konig frowned. "What became of Viele Sindein?" *How the hells had anyone gotten past Morgen's Mehrere guard?*

"Viele was slain. Many times."

Konig ignored the Doppels as they gathered to mutter quietly among themselves. He had forever shattered any chance of their working together and no longer feared their huddled conferences. "How many would it take to kill Viele?"

"I sparred with her often. She was an expert."

"And?" Konig growled.

Meineigener blinked. "It would take dozens. They left no dead. Either they carried their wounded and slain with them when they left—no easy thing—or Viele didn't manage to kill any of them."

Konig resumed pacing, his reflections mirroring his actions. "How did dozens of people enter the temple, kill Viele, and escape with Morgen without being seen?"

Meineigener answered immediately. "Inside help."

Konig agreed. "Find out if anyone is missing."

Schwacher had been the only useful Mirrorist in the temple.

With him dead, Konig had been effectively blinded. He rubbed his chin and glared at the mirror. A few reflections mirrored his actions while the rest pressed against the glass as if trying to shove their way free. *Useless!* Or were they? Could he hone his growing Mirrorist tendencies before his mind crumbled under the strain? No—it would take more time than he had. His three Doppels stood uncomfortably close, their eyes bright with hunger. *They know what this means. If I lose Morgen, I lose everything.* His delusions were growing in strength. Soon they would drag him down.

"Find the nearest Geborene Mirrorist and bring them here."

"Yes, My Theocrat." Meineigener turned to leave.

"Meineigener."

"Yes, My Theocrat?"

"Send for the Schatten Mörder and Tiergeist."

Meineigener swallowed uncomfortably and nodded. He clearly wanted nothing to do with Konig's corps of deranged assassins. Konig saw the concealed distaste and didn't care. Meineigener would happily cut down an unarmed man at Konig's command but found assassination distasteful. Meineigener was damaged; he lacked that which stopped a man from committing heinous acts of murder but lived by a strict code of conduct that reined in his psychopathic tendencies: loyalty to the Theocrat above all else.

Konig placed a hand on the massive man's arm and pinioned him with gray eyes. "If word spreads Morgen is gone I will be *very* displeased. Find Aufschlag as well and send him here immediately."

⸻

When Aufschlag arrived he found Konig waiting, Doppels gathered behind him like a pack of dogs, thin features as flat and expressionless as their gray eyes. Between the Doppels and the reflections in the mirror, Konig filled the room.

"Morgen has been taken. Whoever took him has agents within the Geborene hierarchy."

Aufschlag looked away, unable to make eye contact. He glanced past Konig and met the bruised and battered eye of a Doppel. Acceptance? The Doppel showed broken teeth in a twisted grimace and Aufschlag desperately looked elsewhere. Planning to lie to Konig was one thing, but now, as he stood in the powerful Gefahrgeist's presence, the reality was much more daunting. Eye contact, Aufschlag knew, was a key component in one-on-one manipulation. He dared not meet Konig's eyes for too long, but how could he achieve this and not seem guilty? He looked again to Acceptance, meeting the wounded gaze, and the Doppel gave him a curious and knowing smile.

*Does the Doppel know?* Aufschlag looked away and saw the corpse of Tragen Nachrichten shoved rudely into a corner. *Thank the gods!* Something to stare at other than Konig or his Doppels. Aufschlag had to say something soon.

"The Geborene couldn't have been infiltrated without you at least suspecting." The sly compliment should distract Konig. Aufschlag's gaze darted to the mirror and then back to Tragen's body. Had the reflections been staring at Acceptance, or had he imagined that? "It's more likely only one or two agents were involved." Too close to the truth, but Konig would know if he lied outright. He gestured at the corpse. "Tragen was an infiltrator?"

"No. He overheard Morgen had been taken."

"It will be impossible to keep this hidden for long."

"Obviously."

The Chief Scientist felt the weight of Konig's flat gray gaze upon him and did his best to ignore it. He glanced to Acceptance instead. The Doppel, who had been staring at the mirror, looked away when he noticed Aufschlag's attention.

*What in the hells is* that *about?* He swallowed and ran fat fingers across his greasy scalp in an attempt to flatten the fringe of hair. "We must get the boy back quickly."

"Perhaps. There are other options."

"Other options?" *What have I missed?*

"I have summoned the Schatten Mörder and Tiergeist."

Aufschlag blinked, startled. "You'd send assassins to fetch the boy?"

Konig ignored the question.

The door to Konig's chamber swung open and the stench of death filled the room. The Schatten Mörder, Konig's Cotardist assassins, arrived first. Four men and two women filed quietly in, their bodies in varying states of decomposition. Their leader, a naked middle-aged woman known only as Anomie, bowed before Konig. Her lungs, like moldering cheesecloth sacks, hung visible between cracked and yellowing ribs. Her internal organs long absent, only flaked brown gristle clung to her spine. Aufschlag had heard she kept her organs preserved in jars in her personal chambers. Sparse clumps of pale hair clung to the few shreds of flesh still gripping her skull. Five other Cotardist assassins stood mutely behind her. Though none looked to be in such an advanced state of decay, they all showed signs of rot and neglect.

Anomie's eye sockets were empty pits, but there was no mistaking her attention. When she looked toward Aufschlag, the scientist avoided her dead gaze. She seemed to look through him for a moment and then returned her focus to Konig, who remained unperturbed. Her lungs made a dry rattling noise as she drew breath to facilitate speaking. Aufschlag watched, mesmerized, as her lungs filled and immediately began leaking air out the many small tears.

Her voice was thin and dry. "We are summoned."

"I have—"

"It has been years since you have summoned us."

Konig frowned in annoyance, unaccustomed to being inter-rupted. "I have not had need—"

Anomie's lungs deflated, turning her last words into a dusty wheeze. "We are worthless. Cursed immortal dead. Hated."

He had his own issues to deal with and Anomie's touched too close to home. "I don't hate you."

She sucked in another breath. "We rot unheeded and unneeded. We fall away to dust." Some small fragment of scalp flaked away and fell with its few attached hairs to the floor between her bony feet. "We are nothing and yet denied the nothing we desire."

Konig stepped forward and placed his hands on her desiccated shoulders, forcing her to meet his eyes. He turned the full force of his Gefahrgeist power upon her.

All communication is manipulation.

"You are worthless, but you serve something greater than yourself. I am your purpose. Your service defines you. Without service you will be denied even a moment of value, the slightest taste of intent with direction. You serve because in those rare moments you find yourself valued." He stared into those dark, empty sockets; his own unshakable belief in himself—the par-adoxical result of his self-doubt and feelings of inferiority—protected him from fear. "I have need of you."

"We will serve," she whispered with the last of her foul breath.

No need to ask if the other Cotardist assassins agreed; they were nothing without her, lost in pits of self-loathing, animated only by her need.

The cost of service would be high, but Konig knew she would pay it. Her need to serve something greater than herself left no choice.

There was a polite knock at Konig's door before it swung open and Meineigener reentered, followed by a young woman and three rough-looking men. The girl, Asena, was slightly built and long-legged, her arms thin but wiry with muscle. Her olive-shaped eyes, an unnatural green fading gradually to dark, mottled pupils tilted at an odd angle, slanted up and out. She would have been attractive if not for the matted brown tangle of gray-streaked hair and the obvious disdain she had for her attire. She wore clothes as if unaccustomed to being dressed. The three men ranged in size from half a foot shorter than Asena to the massive and shaggy Bär, who towered over seven feet in height. Bär made Meineigener, not a small man by any means, look like a child. Konig couldn't help but think of the man as a slab of walking muscle with all the intellect of a pair of cheap shoes.

Asena bowed impatiently to Konig and he caught a quick glimpse of small breasts as her shirt fell open . . . and he couldn't help but think of Gehirn. Though he thanked the Gods she wasn't here—the Hassebrand had an unhealthy fascination with Asena, turning every encounter into a near-death experience—he was concerned at her lack of communication. Gehirn had many faults, but lack of loyalty was not one. More likely the Hassebrand had discovered something important and decided to handle it on her own—in the hopes of impressing Konig—rather than return and report. *Gods damn it all!* If Schwacher were alive, checking on Gehirn would have been simple. Why had he not done it sooner?

A thought occurred to Konig: Could the murders at the temple in Gottlos be connected to the theft of Morgen? Calling something a coincidence just meant you didn't have enough information to see the connections. Konig pushed these thoughts aside. First things first.

He would have to handle Asena much differently from Anomie. "Asena, I have—"

"We don't need that bitch!" Anomie wheezed. She had forgotten to take the breath necessary to power her words. "The Schatten Mörder—"

"Will learn not to interrupt me again." Konig turned the force of his will against Anomie and let displeasure pour from his eyes like poison. "You serve. You obey. Or"—he paused to draw a slow breath—"I have no use for you."

Anomie's empty sockets lowered and she stared mutely at the floor. Her shoulders hunched with anger but she remained quiet.

Asena laughed, a guttural bark. "Your pet doesn't know its place."

Konig turned his attention to her. "An interesting choice of words," he observed. Asena possessed a fierce loyalty, like a well trained but extremely dangerous dog. Where Anomie needed to feel worthless and despised, Asena craved praise and love. Unable to supply the latter, Konig faked it as best he could. He'd discovered Asena when she was a child, sleeping in the city's gutters, starved for both food and attention. She had immediately latched onto him, looking to him as both father and leader of the pack. For years she'd slept curled at the foot of his bed, refusing to leave his side and whining piteously when sent away. Later, when she'd begun to develop into a beautiful young woman, he'd sent her to separate chambers. Her proximity and need made him uncomfortable. He alternately regretted the decision—she would have done anything he asked—and believed he had made the right choice. Asena would make a fitting partner, but he dared not let anyone become too close, too valuable. He understood all too clearly what love did to people.

If communication was manipulation, emotion was the fulcrum on which the leverage was applied.

"I need you both," said Konig, glancing from Asena to Anomie. "The god-child, Morgen, has been taken."

Asena snarled in sudden anger. She often watched over the

young boy and felt a protective love for him. Morgen's way of making people feel valued appealed to her needs.

Anomie groaned. "He hugged me once, offered to cure me. I was afraid."

"Dead and still a coward," snapped Asena.

"Witless, fawning bitch," wheezed Anomie.

"Silence!" snapped Konig. "I need you both. We can't be sure where the thieves have taken him. They killed Schwacher, my only Mirrorist. There is much ground to cover and not much time. Where," he asked the roomful of people, "would the kidnappers take Morgen?"

"Neidrig," answered Asena immediately. "It is close and our influence there is nonexistent."

"N-no. No," stammered Aufschlag. When everyone turned to look at him he swallowed uncomfortably and glanced about as if surprised by the sudden attention. "It's . . ." He swallowed again and pressed flat a greasy fringe of hair. "It is too obvious. If they knew well enough to slay our only Mirrorist, they would not flee to the first place we would look."

Aufschlag made sense.

Konig noticed Acceptance staring at the Chief Scientist, head cocked at an angle, right hand on chin; the same pose Konig often used when deep in thought.

"True," said Konig. "So where, then?"

"North," Aufschlag stated. "The Schatten Mörder and Tiergeist should go north."

"Perhaps," suggested Asena, "one group should go to Neidrig while the other travels north. Whoever finds the kidnappers can slay them and return with the child."

Konig shook his head. "No. Spending that much time in the company of assassins might pollute Morgen." The Theocrat didn't apologize for the harshness of his words. He paced the room, hand on chin. "Morgen must be pure when he Ascends." He stopped and stared at the two groups. There was a reason he had summoned assassins to find the boy. "Kill the boy the moment you find him. Kill the thieves afterward. Morgen must die untainted by violence and murder. Kill him before he is polluted beyond redemption." He had more to ask of his assassins: whoever killed Morgen must die at Konig's own hand to ensure they—and whomever they killed—served him in the Afterdeath. That small detail he'd save for later; while he might not doubt his assassins' loyalty, trust was for fools. "Return immediately to me when he's dead." Risky, but he had no choice.

Anomie bowed low. "It will be as you wish."

Asena remained quiet, her face betraying inner turmoil.

"No!" Again all eyes turned to Aufschlag. "Morgen is not ready to Ascend," he added quickly." He gestured to Konig. "You *know* we have to control his environment. Any damage done by the thieves or rescuers can be undone. We must control every aspect of his Ascension." Aufschlag paused to draw a gasping breath. "If the boy is brutally murdered by a gang of assassins in some back alley, there is no telling what damage might be done to his mind."

"I would not let him suffer," Asena said quietly, eyes damp.

Konig didn't have time for this. His Doppels were growing in strength. His reflections were becoming bolder and more solid. *Morgen must Ascend before it's too late.* Yet Aufschlag spoke the truth. The idea of Morgen's Ascension happening somewhere beyond Konig's control terrified him. Perhaps the boy *should* be brought back to Selbsthass, if just to ascertain the extent of any damage done.

Konig glanced at Aufschlag's flushed face. Was the scientist's concern really for the Ascension? Had his feelings for the boy gotten the better of his reason? Konig had watched Aufschlag torture uncountable peasants in search of the key to directed delusion. One child couldn't possibly achieve what a thousand screaming mothers watching their children slain could not. The Chief Scientist was cold and calculating . . . and invaluable.

"Perhaps," whispered Konig.

Acceptance cleared his throat, ducking his head in apology when Konig scowled at him. "Our Mirrorist powers are growing. Perhaps we can make use of them." The Doppel cradled tender ribs. His expression suggested talking was painful.

"*My* Mirrorist powers," Konig corrected.

"Of course," Acceptance agreed quickly. "Perhaps your reflections can tell you who took Morgen."

Konig gave Acceptance a searching look and the Doppel averted his bruised and battered eye. Was Acceptance up to something or simply conforming to his nature and seeking acceptance? Konig understood how much the Doppel craved the feeling of belonging; he felt the same hunger.

"The reflections do not speak to me," said Konig.

"Perhaps they need not speak," suggested Acceptance.

Konig glanced from the Doppel to the massive mirror dominating one wall. Trepidation and Abandonment stood quietly behind Acceptance, and Konig would have suspected their involvement in some plan had they not shared his look of confusion. They had been awfully quiet of late.

"Well?" Konig asked the gathered reflections.

As one, they pointed unerringly at Aufschlag, who made a tight squeaking noise and raised his hands in desperate protest.

"No!" He looked from the mirror to Konig, to Acceptance, and back to the mirror. "They point at something beyond me." He moved and accusing fingers followed.

"Interesting," said Konig. "But unclear."

"They must be saying I am correct," stammered Aufschlag. "The boy has been taken north and it is too early for Morgen to Ascend. They agree with me."

Konig stared at the reflections for a moment before turning to Acceptance. "And what do you say?"

Acceptance pointed at the Chief Scientist's shoes.

Konig glanced down and raised an eyebrow. "Shards of broken glass."

"Broken mirror," corrected Acceptance.

"Oh," Aufschlag said. He stared at his feet. "Bad luck indeed."

"*You?*" Konig's chest squeezed tight, crushing his heart. "You betrayed me?"

"Everyone abandons us in the end," whispered Abandonment from behind Acceptance. Konig knew it to be true.

"He may have poisoned the boy's mind against us," added Trepidation. "He wants you to bring the boy back so he can finish his work."

Abandonment hissed agreement. "The experiment is a failure."

Aufschlag reached imploringly to Konig but kept his eyes averted. "My Theocrat, you know I would never betray you. My actions . . . I did what I had to do. I serve only you."

*Lies, all lies.* "Look at me," snapped Konig. Aufschlag met his gaze and deflated. "Did you kill Schwacher?"

Aufschlag, eyes red and wet, licked his lips and said, "Yes."

"He has betrayed us," growled Abandonment.

Konig ignored the Doppel. "Are you a Wahnvor agent?"

"No! I sought to protect the boy. He isn't ready to Ascend. Konig, you must trust me."

Konig feigned a hearty laugh, crushing the desire to scream and cry at the betrayal. "Trust you? My dear Aufschlag, I have never trusted you." His voice trembled and then grew in volume. "You are a tool, nothing more!"

"I didn't mean to hurt you," whispered Aufschlag.

"Hurt me!" Konig screamed, advancing on the cowering Scientist. "You cannot hurt me! Your foul betrayal was expected. You are a worm. Worthless!"

Asena and Anomie advanced on Aufschlag in hungry expectation, ready to do their Theocrat's will.

"Where," demanded Konig, "have they taken Morgen?"

"South—" answered Aufschlag, before slamming his teeth closed and clenching his eyes shut.

"Tell me where."

Aufschlag shook his head.

Konig watched the scientist's inner battle. Torturing Aufschlag would be an admission of weakness, admitting he could not force the truth from the betrayer. Yet somehow Aufschlag had found some means of protecting himself from the wiles of the Gefahrgeist. *How could Aufschlag do this after all I gave the greasy bastard?* Rank and title. The chance to be part of something truly great. *How could Aufschlag turn his back me?* It was inexplicable! What could be more important than creating a god and ensuring Konig's place in both history and the as-yet-unwritten future?

If using Aufschlag had been a mistake, what other mistakes had he made?

Konig took a deep breath and let it slowly escape. "Doppels, hold him."

The three Doppels grabbed Aufschlag in an instant, pinioning his arms brutally behind his back. Konig was reminded of commanding Trepidation and Abandonment to beat Acceptance. Only this hurt far more.

Konig held his hand out to Meineigener, who stood quietly, watching and waiting. "Your knife."

Meineigener stepped forward, drew the long knife in a practiced flourish, passed it hilt first to the Theocrat, and returned to his place by the door. The weapon was surprisingly light. Konig admired its brutal simplicity.

"Your Doppels manipulate you," plead Aufschlag.

"I know," said Konig. "We use each other. Every one of us. You used me. I used you. Manipulation is everything."

Konig stepped close enough to Aufschlag to smell the man's sweat and fear. He'd never killed a man with his own hands. Someone, some tool, had always done his bidding. The expectation, the taste of knowing the moment, hovered just a breath away, thrilled in a way unlike more subtle manipulations.

Konig breathed into Aufschlag's ear. "You thought you could lie to me. You thought you were done with me. But"—he chuckled softly—"it never ends."

Konig slowly pushed the razor-sharp knife into his Chief Scientist's chest while the three Doppels held the struggling Aufschlag motionless. An unnatural gasp escaped the man's chest as Konig opened a lung and was sprayed with blood. He watched the light of reason fade from Aufschlag's wide eyes.

"Perhaps you will better serve me in the Afterdeath," Konig whispered into the dying man's ear.

The Doppels let Aufschlag's fat and empty corpse collapse to the floor. It fell in an awkward heap and lay bleeding out into the thick carpet.

HOW HAD THIS happened?

The Schatten Mörder, the Tiergeist, Meineigener, and his Doppels all stood watching, waiting. He stared at the motionless Aufschlag. The man had been with him from the beginning. Sometimes Konig wasn't even sure if he himself had really birthed the idea. Memory and self-doubt told niggling lies and he thought Aufschlag may have suggested the project.

*It doesn't matter. New truths can be forged.*

"Morgen's Ascension will be my success," Konig said aloud, though he talked only to himself. He swept the room, making eye contact with all present. "I give and I give," he snarled, "and what do I get?" He bared his teeth. "Nothing. I get *nothing* in return." His words made it true.

The assembled assassins hung their heads. Even his Doppels looked ashamed.

"I am selfless in my love and giving." Konig's words defined new truths. "Doubt is betrayal. I expect better."

mmmmmm

Acceptance, unmoved, watched Konig's performance. The Theocrat's beliefs and delusions meant less and less to the Doppel. He saw through Konig's empty words to the truth: the Theocrat sought to disguise his sadness at having slain his only friend. Konig was lost and, with Aufschlag dead, alone on this path.

Acceptance had been waiting for this moment.

For days he'd communicated as best he could, secretly and without words, with Konig's reflections. They too saw Aufschlag's death as the first step toward freedom. Acceptance didn't delude himself that they worked strictly toward his ends. No doubt the reflections had plans of their own. This would be a temporary alliance at best. He would shatter the mirror the instant they ceased being useful.

Acceptance studied Konig, feeding off the man's doubts like a leech feeds off blood. Next he must remove Morgen from the playing field. The god-child was the Theocrat's escape plan from the ravages of unchecked delusion. Delusions that must escalate in power, stoked by doubt and the subtle prodding of Doppels and reflections. The Theocrat would become truly powerful and dangerously unstable. His delusions would tear apart his mind. *I will shred everything he is, bathe in his despair, drink deep of his faltering thoughts.* Acceptance imagined sipping from Konig's hollowed skull and quashed the urge to grin.

Morgen had to die, and somewhere far beyond Konig's reach.

"We cannot risk further contamination," Acceptance said softly. "Morgen must be slain before Aufschlag's agents turn him against us." He placed a hand gently on Konig's shoulder, pleased when Konig didn't shrug it away. The man *needed,* and need was weakness. "The scientist sought to taint the boy toward his own ends." Let Konig's imagination do the rest.

Konig sagged under Acceptance's hand. "You will slay Morgen," he said to his assassins. "Bring about his Ascension." Acceptance felt faint tremors through Konig's shoulder. Would he cry? *Please, gods, please. Just a small taste of despair.* "Asena, take your Tiergeist to Neidrig."

Acceptance saw Asena's discomfort at the order and she noticed his attention. She glanced at the hand resting on Konig's shoulder and her eyes narrowed.

It was time to do some serious housecleaning. Each person Konig turned to for support must be used and pushed away. Alienating Asena would be easier than killing her. Acceptance kept his face carefully blank. Anomie, lacking Asena's lithe body and unconditional love, was less of a threat and could be dealt with later. He waited, listening. The moment would come when he could drop a subtle word in Konig's ear and drive a wedge between Asena and the Theocrat.

"Anomie," continued Konig. "Take your Schatten Mörder south, toward Unbrauchbar in Gottlos."

Anomie bowed. "An unnatural storm brews there."

Konig turned on the corpse. "Why has no one mentioned this to me? It could be linked with the kidnappers." He noticed Acceptance's comforting hand and angrily brushed it aside.

"The storm has grown closer for days," said Anomie. "I assumed you knew."

"Gods damn everything," Konig snarled in frustration. "Go to the heart of the storm, discover its source."

Acceptance leaned forward to whisper in Konig's ear. "Morgen's kidnappers must have a powerful Gefahrgeist among their numbers. How else could they have slain Morgen's Mehrere bodyguard so easily? How else could they take Aufschlag's loyalty from you? You must ensure your assassins remain"—Acceptance eyed Asena over Konig's shoulder—"faithful once they are beyond your influence."

Acceptance knew exactly what Konig thought: of course he was up against another Gefahrgeist. It made too much sense. Another Gefahrgeist had somehow found out about the Geborene God project and thought to turn Konig's genius plan to their own ends.

Protecting against a Gefahrgeist was virtually impossible, but steps could be taken.

"The thought of harming you breaks my heart," Konig said to Asena.

Acceptance whispered, "Emotion is weakness, manipulation is everything," in Konig's ear.

Konig nodded unconscious agreement. "I need to protect you," he told the assassins, "from the possibility of Gefahrgeist influence."

Asena drew a sharp breath and bared teeth at Acceptance. "How?"

The Tiergeist gathered behind Asena moved closer, looming large and dangerous. Anomie, the living corpse, merely stood and watched. The Schatten Mörder waited motionless as if nothing of import or interest had yet occurred. Perhaps, to them, nothing had. What interested the damned?

"To truly protect you from their Gefahrgeist," said Konig, "I would have to blind and deafen you."

Acceptance stifled a triumphant smile, hiding his ruined mouth behind a hand. He watched Konig closely; the man wanted to apologize. Acceptance could read it in the way he stood, the way he twitched as if about to reach out to Asena.

Konig stilled his motion. "Obviously you would be useless to me blind. You will, however, be deafened." He looked from Asena to Anomie, meeting their eyes. "It is for your own protection." Acceptance knew Konig said this aloud only to convince himself. "I care deeply for and seek only to shield you from danger. You are my champions. You must not fail me in this. You must not fail Morgen."

"How will you deafen us?" Asena asked. "We Therianthropes heal quickly. Particularly if we *twist*."

Anomie was not to be outdone. "The dead do not rely on ears to hear. How shall you deafen us?"

"I am Konig Furimmer. Theocrat of Selbsthass. High Priest of the Geborene Damonen. My will gave birth to the first man-made god. Reality bends to my desires." He smiled sadly. "My assassins, I don't think you are deaf. I don't believe you are deaf. I *know* you are—"

Asena didn't even hear the last word. She stood blinking, struck dumb with surprise. Her love had stolen part of her world. She flared nostrils, breathing in Konig's odor and the smell of startled fear wafting from the other Tiergeist. Did the Theocrat not appreciate how important sound was to an animal?

*Or does he not care?*

Konig's mouth moved and he pointed south, but Anomie had already spun on her heels and, followed by the Schatten Mörder, marched from the room. If he saw Asena's pain, he didn't react. Without a word she turned and left.

Kill Morgen. The Theocrat's order should have left no room for question, but still she felt doubt. Could she kill the boy-god, even if it meant his Ascension?

Acceptance watched Konig stare after Asena as the door swung closed behind her. The man stood rigid. Once she'd left, a single tear leaked from his right eye. Acceptance watched the lone tear slide down the Theocrat's cheek and knew bright joy. Every person Konig pushed away meant Acceptance would be drawn closer.

"She will, in time, come to understand," said Konig without conviction. No one believed it.

*Interesting.* As evidenced by the ease with which he deafened a roomful of powerful Cotardist and Therianthrope Geisteskranken, the Theocrat's power was growing rapidly. His ability to shape reality with his delusions would soon be outstripped by his inability to control his many psychoses. Sanity would be peeled from his mind much like Aufschlag had peeled the flesh from his victims in his attempts to cause insanity. Konig would reach the pinnacle of his power, a master of reality, and yet powerless to master his delusions.

*And yet he cannot convince himself of Asena's forgiveness.*

Acceptance's time grew near. He hid away his smirk of triumph and followed Konig from the room. The other two Doppels trailed behind. Abandonment eyed him with distrust and Trepidation watched with his usual fear.

*I'll deal with them soon enough.*

251

## CHAPTER 23

*I was sane once. It was horrible.*

—Einsam Geschichtenerzähler

For a time Gehirn enjoyed the gentle swaying, allowing it to lull her like her mother never did. When she finally cracked open an eye, she found herself sprawled across Erbrechen's litter. The Slaver, fat, greasy, and ugly, sat beside her. When Erbrechen noticed Gehirn's attention he beamed his fat baby smile. It didn't reach his eyes, though. They glistened cold, both calculating and terrified.

"You must love me," said Erbrechen. "I *need* you to love me. You love me."

Gehirn did. Erbrechen was beautiful. Caring and giving, he personified everything a true friend could ever be.

"I do love you," said Gehirn, and though she meant it, she clearly remembered the moment she realized she was little more than a tool. Knowledge hadn't set her free. Her prison remained unchanged no matter how much she might currently enjoy imprisonment and worship her jailer. She thought back to Konig. *They use me for my power and care nothing for who I am.* Had anyone ever genuinely loved or even cared for her? *Or am I somehow unlovable?* Was the fault hers or theirs? Or was she drawn to people who would abuse her?

"I know you do . . . even if you're a lousy cook," Erbrechen said with grim humor. When he saw Gehirn's confused look he continued. "There would have been enough soul stew for everyone had you not burned the meat." He laughed, sending waves through jiggling fat. The laughter gave way to a petulant scowl.

"Sorry," muttered Gehirn, levering herself into a sitting position. Erbrechen's mob of friends had grown considerably. More survived than Gehirn expected. Come to think of it, she had not really expected anyone or anything to survive her fire.

She remembered. "You hit me."

Erbrechen snorted. "I *saved* you. You should thank me."

She had no choice. "Thank you."

"You are welcome. But, in the future, I think I shall keep you a little closer." Erbrechen laughed deprecatingly. "This is a body built for comfort, not for speed."

"Sorry." Her heart soared. She'd be close to her love. *If he just understood how I feel, maybe he'd feel something for me.* How could she show him? She wanted to reach out, to touch him, caress his soft skin.

She lifted a hand and Erbrechen frowned at it. "Don't think I don't value your friendship," he said.

Her soaring heart crashed to the ground. *Erbrechen will use me and toss me aside.* "Never," she said.

"And don't say I never do anything for you."

"Never."

"Good, because I love you dearly. You are my closest friend." Erbrechen laughed happily. "Get it? You are inches from me. You are my closest friend!"

Gehirn laughed in spite of herself. "Are you sure there isn't a small boy tucked up your arse somewhere?"

Erbrechen's eyes widened in mock outrage. "Well, now that you mention it," he admitted, "I had wondered where the lad had got to." He suddenly lost his joking demeanor. "I need you."

Gehirn beamed, happy to be needed if not actually loved. "I won't let you down again."

"I know. I am going to keep you very close indeed."

*The closer the proximity, the more control.* Gehirn said nothing, her happiness evaporating.

"Our last little experience taught me something," mused Erbrechen. "Though I need my friends, it is myself who I must most rely upon. This destiny is mine." He shook his head and looked apologetic. "My friend, I need your strength, but I must also safeguard *my* strength. I am pivotal. Central to everything. When I Ascend to godhood it will because of *my* actions."

*He thinks using me to burn cities is something he can claim as his own?* Gehirn's flash of anger died the moment she looked at Erbrechen.

"I can no longer share the soul stew," he said, ignoring Gehirn's fearful whimper. "I'm not sure it worked for you anyway." He beamed at the Hassebrand. "Not to worry. My destiny will protect both of us. The stronger I am, the safer you are," he explained reasonably.

GEHIRN RODE THE litter beside Erbrechen, never allowed more than a few feet from the Slaver. Erbrechen's influence sat on her like a great weight crushing her chest. She could barely breathe. The pain and rage of perceived betrayals fell away. Not forgotten, but unable to raise its head against Erbrechen's dominating will.

Konig never used his power like this, and Gehirn wondered, in those rare moments when Erbrechen was distracted, if the

Theocrat was even capable of such malignant intent. Konig was undeniable when he set his mind to something, but this felt different. Where Konig inspired loyalty and a desire to serve, Erbrechen demanded thoughtless devotion. Was Konig less powerful, or did his Gefahrgeist power simply manifest differently? Did Erbrechen's past define the parameters of his power? What of her own past? She'd always assumed she could blame her parents, but what if she'd been born broken? Gehirn thought she'd ask Aufschlag when she returned to Selbsthass.

*Maybe the pompous scientist's little experiments aren't so useless after all.*

Brutal storms hammered the horizon in every direction. Here in the eye the thunder was deafening, but little touched them. Heavy clouds occluded sun and sky and made it impossible to tell night from day. All life became a monotony of gray. The storm moved with them and Gehirn knew Regen still lived, though she hadn't seen the scrawny shaman in some time. The lands they traveled had first been visited by Regen's poorly controlled storm. Fields of corn and grain lay crushed flat by tornado winds and hail. Most of the trees stood cracked and wounded, burned and blasted by lightning.

Erbrechen scowled at the filthy mob surrounding his litter and Gehirn enjoyed the temporary freedom to feel used and enslaved.

"I'm sorry," Erbrechen said softly, shaking his head. "So, so sorry."

Gehirn stared, stunned. "What?"

"I know you love me." He lifted a hand toward her, frowned at it, and then returned it to his fat thigh. He blinked and tears leaked down round cheeks. Never before had she seen such crushing sadness.

*He loves me! He just doesn't know how to show it!* That she understood all too well. Emotions were so difficult to communicate, and love most of all.

"Everyone loves me," he said. "*Everyone*. How can I know who really loves *me*?" He glanced at her, his eyes red and pleading for understanding. "They have to."

"I love you," she said. Then she remembered those moments at the edge of Erbrechen's reach. Slaver.

"Of course you do." He offered a lopsided smile. "Everyone does." He looked past her and said, "I'm so alone."

*You're not alone. You'll never be alone as long as I am at your side.* The moment his attention wandered, her heart cracked. *You are a fool. He cares nothing for you. No one does.*

THE CARAVAN STOPPED at three more small cities and their numbers swelled. At this pace, a journey taking Gehirn three days would take Erbrechen and his friends two weeks.

But Erbrechen grew in power with every city and town that fell under his influence. Certainly the range at which he was able to infect people had grown considerably. The last city—a fortified town Gehirn didn't know the name of—had been tightly bottled and awaiting their arrival. Archers lined the walls and a dozen Geisteskranken of differing ilk stood with them. The Hassebrand had been sure she would be called, once again, to burn. The desire thrummed through her like her soul was a plucked string.

Instead Erbrechen gestured to Gehirn to remain sitting and levered himself, with much grunting and straining, into a sitting position. Erbrechen bellowed at the walled city at the top of his lungs, talking about how much he cared about its populace and how much he *needed* them. Within minutes the gates opened and the city's leaders filed out, followed by its army and cadre of Geisteskranken. Everyone apologized at great length for the misunderstanding and any inconvenience Erbrechen may have felt. Once-proud men and women, begging forgiveness, offered daughters and sons as gifts. Erbrechen grandly waved away the apologies as if nothing had happened, but took a boy and two girls onto the litter.

The Slaver's distraction hurt like a kick in the guts. Gehirn felt like a child scorned by her mother, hating and yet still needing.

Erbrechen's new friends spent a rushed hour raiding their own city for valuables and food, and the procession was once again moving. The litter, now carried by fresh men and women not yet weakened by their service to the Slaver, swayed rhythmically as the mob flowed across the land.

Though free to think more clearly, Gehirn couldn't leave the litter. When she had to pee she crouched at the rear edge of the litter and looked over her shoulder to watch the following crowd even as they glared at her. They looked envious of her exalted position as they marched through the puddles she left.

*Fire never disappoints, never breaks your heart.* Gehirn showed canines in a feral leer to those closest to the litter. They shied away under the heat of her gaze. If Erbrechen allowed her off the litter, perhaps she'd burn this growing nation of slaves to ash. The thought left her salivating with desire.

THE SUN SET and Erbrechen declared it time to make camp and light the fires. Gehirn could no longer estimate the number of Erbrechen's friends. They numbered in the thousands, covering the storm-blasted land like a wretched and stinking carpet.

Erbrechen kept the growing cadre of Geisteskranken close to his litter. In rare moments of clarity Gehirn understood that the Slaver feared them. The rest of the time the Geisteskranken were simply Erbrechen's favorite new friends, and as the only Hassebrand, Gehirn retained her position of privilege and remained on the litter.

As day faded, campfires sparked to life and lit the land in a faltering yellow glow. Here, in the eye of Regen's storm, there was no wind, so the smoke from the thousands of fires went nowhere. Like Gehirn, it was trapped here.

Gaunt bodies, dancing, writhing, and cavorting in the flickering firelight, turned the scene hellish and unreal.

"I must be dead," whispered Gehirn. This was the Afterdeath of judgment and torment her father had threatened her with.

Gehirn had slain uncountable numbers in the service of others' goals. Though Konig never used her as Erbrechen did, the Hassebrand still managed a sizable body count in the Theocrat's service. Not once had she regretted a single death. Each fire, each twisted and boiled body, each smoking pillar of ash, had been in service to something greater. Greater than Gehirn, greater even than Konig. The Geborene Damonen offered Gehirn something she'd been unable to find elsewhere: purpose. However distant, her actions served a role in the creation of mankind's first true god.

Gehirn looked to where Erbrechen lay with the three children, still struggling to satisfy his needs. The thought of handing Morgen—everything pure and good—to Erbrechen twisted Gehirn's guts like a fist gripping her intestines.

*The Slaver will use the boy in ways—*

Erbrechen glanced over the bent backs of the children and smiled contentedly at Gehirn.

Then his eyes sank closed as his attention wandered. Gehirn blinked and looked away, confused as more and more of her opposing feelings toward the grotesque man coursed through her. A stick-thin figure stumbling toward the litter caught her attention. Regen Anrufer, the Schlammstamm shaman. Skeletally thin, gaunt like sun-bleached bone, and grinning like a lunatic, the man glared hatred at Gehirn.

"Hassebrand, you licker of donkeys, how does your friend's love sit with you now?" said Regen, voice cracking like dry leaves. "Enjoying your place of honor?" His laughter stumbled into a fit of bone-racking coughs.

Gehirn glanced back at Erbrechen, but the Slaver remained distracted by the children. She turned to sneer at the shaman. "Enjoying walking through my shite and piss?"

Regen shrugged but scowled at the ground. "I went out to the edge of the camp. Right to the edge." He looked up at the Hassebrand. "I almost walked away." He cackled. "Me and my storm."

"Why didn't you?" Gehirn asked, genuinely curious.

"I couldn't!" Regen sobbed. "I saw my freedom and was unable to want it enough to move." He darted a glance at the sprawled obesity. "One step," he whispered. "One gods-sticking step."

"He is too much," Gehirn said softly.

Regen grunted, the look of hatred returning. "I falter." He gestured and cackled as a bolt of lightning stabbed the sky, leaving Gehirn blinking at the purple afterimage slashed across her vision. The Slaver ignored the lightning, the answering roll of thunder, and the scared cattlelike moaning of his followers. "I haven't slept in days. I can barely walk. My mind wanders where I cannot." Regen giggled. "As does my sanity. When I crack, the storm will be free." He grinned brokenly at Erbrechen. "Will you tell him? Will you warn him of the danger?"

Gehirn stared at the trembling shaman and thought of the awful destructive power trapped in the roiling storm clouds ringing the horizon. Day by day, hour by hour, the calm eye slowly closed. Destruction came ever closer.

"No."

Regen looked both grateful and disgusted. "You are a cowardly—"

"What the hells is that?" Gehirn interrupted, pointing past the diminutive shaman.

Regen, annoyed, grunted and turned to look. At the northern end of the camp people moved frantically to clear a path. The two watched mutely as the disturbance grew closer. A group of figures worked their way through the crowd, unhindered, and avoided by Erbrechen's people.

"There are six," said Regen.

Gehirn squinted. "Your eyes are better than mine." Six, coming from the north. From Selbsthass? From Konig? A moment of nervous uncertainty. She sighed. "I'd best tell Erbrechen." She turned and saw the Slaver staring past her with undisguised interest.

"Regen," said Erbrechen, "bring our new friends to meet me."

The shaman scowled but set out toward the six intruders.

Gehirn watched the malnourished shaman make his way through the crowd. Regen, weak from blood loss and lack of sleep, stumbled often. The shaman slowed as he neared Erbrechen's new friends, stopping several yards short of the six. He turned to look back at Erbrechen and Gehirn. The Hassebrand thought she saw bad teeth in a wide grin.

"What the hells is he smiling about?" Erbrechen asked, peeved.

A moment of understanding and fear rocked Gehirn. Only one thing could give the scrawny goat sticker such a smile:

Freedom.

And what would free Regen?

Death.

Regen said something to the guests but Gehirn couldn't hear what. Weapons hissed from sheaths with unnatural speed and cut Regen down. The Schlammstamm shaman fell, still grinning, in three pieces.

The calm eye of the storm slammed closed with concussive force. A flash of lightning lit the hellish scene with a blinding brilliance, and Gehirn saw clearly the six as they stalked, weapons drawn, toward Erbrechen's litter.

*Anomie and her Schatten Mörder.* Gehirn had always wondered if she could defeat the Theocrat's favorite killers. She would rather have faced Asena and her Tiergeist. Not for fear of Anomie, but rather because of the hunger the lithe Therianthrope filled her with. Asena's loathing of Gehirn made her all the more desirable. Alas, it was not to be this evening.

Erbrechen screamed orders and declarations of love at the Schatten Mörder.

They ignored him, cutting down all who blocked their path.

Gehirn slipped from the litter to stand between Erbrechen and the living dead. *They can kill him after they've killed me.*

The horizon crushed inward from all directions.

# CHAPTER 24

*Insanity is the only reasonable response to such a responsive reality.*

—Wahrheit Ertrinkt, Philosopher

Acceptance, Abandonment, and Trepidation stood facing each other. Those within the mirror, engaged in an intense conversation of their own, ignored those without.

The commingled bloodstains of Tragen Nachrichten and Chief Scientist Aufschlag Hoher tugged at Acceptance's attention. Those dark smears covered the older stains left from his beating. Hidden, but not forgotten. He'd have his revenge soon enough.

Acceptance watched the reflections from the corner of his eye, careful not to seem too interested. He didn't want to give anything away. Trepidation, far too paranoid, would never fall for the trap he'd arranged with the reflections. Abandonment's fear of being left out, he gambled, would leave him susceptible.

Abandonment made no attempt to hide his suspicion. "You knew the reflections would point at Aufschlag before you saw the shards of broken mirror on his shoes. I saw you notice the glass. I saw, in your eyes—"

"Eye," Acceptance corrected coldly.

Abandonment shrugged. "I had no choice." It wasn't an apology. Konig's Doppels were no more capable of apology than Konig. "I saw in your *eye* the conception of a plan." He rubbed his chin, giving Acceptance an appraising look. "Or perhaps the completion of a plan already in motion?"

Acceptance allowed a small, smug smile to grace his lips and die. "I have a means of communicating with Konig's reflections."

"You wrote notes and held them up to the mirror?" asked Abandonment.

Acceptance ignored the question. He needed to give Abandonment just enough to draw him in. "If Morgen Ascends as Konig plans, we will remain, at best, Doppels. Forever. With his made god he may even banish us. Anything is possible. With Aufschlag gone, Konig's one source of rational wisdom is removed. He fears Morgen will be infected and so he will slay the child." Acceptance showed broken teeth in a victorious leer. "Konig is terrified and alone; he is not thinking clearly. Morgen will recognize his assassins and know Konig sent them. It will poison the new god against the man who created him. Konig's mind will crumble and we will rise to supremacy." *And I will slay whichever assassin kills the child, for Konig will be long dead by the time they return.*

"Your plan has flaws," said Trepidation. "If Morgen turns against Konig, he may kill the man. We would not survive."

"You developed some simple sign language?" Abandonment asked.

Acceptance snorted in derision, again ignoring the question. "Morgen is incapable of hurting anyone."

"People change," whispered Trepidation.

Abandonment's eyes narrowed. "You can somehow hear the reflections?"

263

Acceptance froze for a moment before answering. "It is very difficult."

"How?" Abandonment demanded.

"Why?" Acceptance asked, feigning suspicion. "What are you planning?"

"Planning? How can I have a plan if I just learned of this. If you figured it out, I can too."

Acceptance pretended to deflate. "First, if they're not already looking, you have to bang on the mirror to get their attention." He pretended annoyance. "Sometimes they ignore you. If you press your ear to the mirror you can hear what they're saying. Just like pressing your ear to a door or window. They have to do the same on their side to hear you." He uttered an embarrassed laugh. "It's comical, really."

Abandonment, as incapable of humor as Konig, examined the mirror without expression. The reflections within, lost in their own conversation, ignored the Doppels.

"It might be dangerous," hissed Trepidation.

"Trepidation is right," suggested Acceptance carefully. "It might be best if only I communicate with them."

Abandonment ignored him and approached the floor-to-ceiling mirror. He rapped twice on the glass with his knuckles and watched as the reflections looked up and then returned to their conversation. He stared at them for a moment before turning and walking to Konig's massive oak desk. He collected the heavy clay mug and returned to the mirror. This time he knocked on the mirror's surface with the mug. Hard. The reflections looked up, startled, and froze when he mimed smashing the mirror with the mug. Abandonment gestured them toward him and they hurried to press their ears to their side of the glass.

Abandonment glanced over his shoulder at the other Doppels. "They must understand who holds the power here." He returned his attention to the mirror. "Tell me everything you told Acceptance or I will smash the mirror." He looked thoughtful. "Do you see into the future?"

Leaning back from the mirror's surface, they nodded and started babbling. Abandonment pressed his ear against the glass to listen. His eyes narrowed, as if he was struggling to hear what the reflections were saying. They widened suddenly, glancing at Acceptance in alarm as grasping hands reached through the mirror's surface and tangled in his clothes.

Abandonment screamed in terror as the reflections dragged him through into their world. He didn't stand a chance with over a dozen reflections clawing at his robes and hair. In his panic he dropped the mug and it shattered across the floor.

⠿⠿⠿⠿⠿⠿

Trepidation understood immediately. *Acceptance set this up, planned it from the beginning.* Trepidation also learned something: He wasn't a manifestation of Konig's fear of others or the unknown. He was Konig's fear of himself.

Abandonment's screams and cries for help choked off as his head passed through the mirror's surface. Acceptance and Trepidation watched the reflections claw the Doppel apart in eerie silence. They watched the reflections devour the small chunks torn from Abandonment. Within minutes there was no proof the Doppel ever existed.

"Would you be so kind as to clean up the broken mug?" Acceptance asked.

Trepidation backed away. "If you think I'm going anywhere near the mirror, you're crazy."

"Of course I'm crazy. So are you. We're figments of a deluded mind." Acceptance showed sharp shards of broken teeth in a mad leer. "Abandonment abandoned Konig. He faded to nothing. You understand what this means?"

"I am a manifestation of fear, not one of . . ." Trepidation trailed off, looking for the right word. "Drive."

Acceptance lost the crazed look. "True. And perceptive. Konig was right; we Doppels will never work together. So let's get it straight: we are not cooperating. You will obey or I will feed you to the reflections."

Trepidation bowed low. "You will replace Konig, but you will always have need of fear and caution. They keep us alive. You, with your need for acceptance, were always at odds with Abandonment." Trepidation chose his words carefully. "Abandonment is gone and you will Ascend to take Konig's place."

"With you at my side," said Acceptance.

"No," corrected Trepidation. "With me one step behind. In my place."

Acceptance cleared the fragments of shattered mug from the floor but kept a close eye on the reflections. He did not want to suffer Abandonment's fate. He might use the reflections, but he certainly didn't trust them.

He whistled tunelessly as he worked. He hadn't felt this happy since . . . he tongued the ragged edges of broken teeth. Glancing about to make sure Trepidation wasn't looking, he drew out the small mirror he'd begun carrying around to check on the progress of his healing; the large floor-to-ceiling mirror still refused to show his own reflection. Holding the small mirror to his face, he lifted his eye patch, grimaced at the puckered wound around his missing eye, and shuddered at the ruin of his mouth. His lips were cut and swollen, covered in ill-healed scabs. Acceptance's good mood curled and died like a wisp of paper in a raging fire.

*One debt repaid, one to go.* Only then, with his fellow Doppels gone, would he take Konig's place.

HOURS LATER KONIG returned to his chambers and glared at the two Doppels awaiting his return. His gaze darted about the room.

"Where is Abandonment?"

"He is gone," said Trepidation.

"He faded away not long after you left the room," agreed Acceptance.

"Faded away?"

The two Doppels nodded in perfect unison.

"You understand, do you not, what this means?" Acceptance asked.

Trepidation answered. "You have shed your fear of abandonment. Sending Asena away broke her hold on you much as commanding the assassins to slay the boy broke—"

"They had no hold on me," Konig muttered. "I need no one."

*The fool lies even to himself,* thought Acceptance.

The two Doppels bowed their heads in acceptance of the reprimand.

"Asena means nothing to you now," said Acceptance.

Konig looked doubtful. "I sent her away. I fear no betrayal or abandonment."

*More lies.*

"No," said Trepidation. "I am still here. She may yet betray us."

"Betray *me*," corrected Konig.

"You," agreed the Doppels in unison.

Konig met the eyes of his remaining Doppels. "She is dangerous."

They nodded their agreement.

Acceptance didn't care if Konig truly believed that he had shed his fear of abandonment. With the thought planted, the belief would grow. Gefahrgeist excelled at convincing themselves. It was their greatest strength and most terrible weakness.

# CHAPTER 25

*What is faith but delusion without the power to back it up?*

—Versklaven Schwache, Gefahrgeist Philosopher

The sky broke and torrents of rain and hail hammered the earth. Slashing lightning lit the dark underbellies of sick and heavy clouds with flickering and unnatural hues. The heavens screamed in torment.

Anomie, deafened by Konig's delusions, heard none of this. Even the stunning displays of color seemed little more than strobing shades of gray. The eyes of the dead, robbed of life and beauty, saw the world as a stain of monochromatic twilight.

Men and women, gaunt with hunger and covered in filth, hurled themselves in the path of the Schatten Mörder. Life meant nothing to Anomie. It rose before her and she cut it down. For those who could achieve the Afterdeath, annihilation was a gift. Anomie and her Schatten Mörder had many gifts to give. They climbed mountains of dead and more flocked to receive their alms.

They mobbed her, stabbing and cutting, punching and kicking. It meant nothing. She felt nothing.

She knew this to be the camp of a Slaver. Though they were never as large, she'd seen similar groups before. *The boy will be here somewhere.* She'd kill the Slaver at the heart of this mob and help Morgen Ascend, as was his destiny. *Death will be my gift to the god-child.*

A stabbing flash of lightning momentarily blinded the living but, to Anomie's dead eyes, served only to better illuminate the hellish scene.

Gehirn Schlechtes, Konig's pet Hassebrand, stood waiting for her with a feral smile. Gehirn's doglike canines glinted in the brief light. Anomie laughed. The dry hollows of her empty skull flickered with reflected light. The skulls of the dead, skin long cracked and peeled away, grin forever.

Gehirn gestured and burned clear a path between herself and the Schatten Mörder. Like rushing tidewaters, the Slaver's followers poured in to fill the cleared area.

Anomie laughed again, an insane cackle dying as breath leaked from decaying lungs.

Fire meant nothing to the dead.

⸻

Gehirn, standing before the litter, waited impatiently. Erbrechen wailed terrified orders at those carrying his litter, but the crash of thunder and raging storm winds stole all sound.

The Schatten Mörder, Konig's Cotardist assassins, could be here for one purpose and one purpose only: to kill Gehirn.

Her dream . . . it had been true. Gehirn's heart broke and she choked back a sob. *Konig hates me.* It wasn't enough to cast her aside; he sought her death.

Fire throbbed through her veins. Konig would get this message loud and clear.

Impatient, she burned the mob of Erbrechen's followers, impeding Anomie's progress. The assassin, backed by her cadre of rotting flesh, laughed at Gehirn.

"No one laughs at me!" she screamed in rage.

Anomie kept laughing, as if she hadn't heard.

Betrayed.

Abandoned.

Mocked.

Gehirn lit the Schatten Mörder like candles.

‖‖‖‖‖‖‖‖‖

Anomie burst into flames, and for a moment, the world disappeared in a torrent of fire. But her sight didn't depend on eyes. She could still see. Flames licked around her body, igniting shreds of clothing. What dried flesh remained clinging to her body burned away. She felt nothing. No pain. No fear. Flesh was an impediment and the fire would burn her clean. Later, when Gehirn lay dead, they could smother these flames.

*And if you misjudged the Hassebrand's power?*

At worst she'd be freed of her eternal hell.

"You are a fool," she tried to scream at Gehirn but only a dry croak escaped. She'd forgotten to fill her lungs. It annoyed her. She tried to draw breath and failed. Fire had burned ragged holes in her papery lungs. This would make communication difficult in the future.

Anomie saw the fool's mouth moving but heard nothing. The fat Hassebrand was comical, and she laughed. Her Schatten Mörder, each a walking bonfire, moved forward to flank her. The path between them and Gehirn cleared, they stalked toward the Hassebrand. Swords, cherry red with heat, hung ready in strong hands cremated of flesh and muscle.

*Does Gehirn crave death as much as I?* If so, the Hassebrand's heart's desire would soon be granted.

Gehirn watched the Cotardists approach. These dead did not shamble. Even aflame, the assassins crouched and moved with lethal grace. As walking fires they became beautiful, entrancing and mesmerizing. Sensuous even. *Will they surround me, hug me tight in a fiery embrace?* Would she die as she had lived, in the suffocating heat of need? Could there be anything more beautiful?

Gehirn lifted her arms, reaching toward the assassins. *Bring me death—*

"Burn them!" Erbrechen screamed from the litter. "They're going to kill me!"

Gehirn could not ignore such commands; his need crushed hers, usurped all volition. She couldn't let them hurt her love, even if Erbrechen sought only to use her.

Still, some small part of her craved punishment and held back the full force of her strength. Gehirn pointed and Anomie's sword melted to slag and ran like blood to cover her skeletal hand in a sheen of molten metal.

Yet the corpse continued its advance, holding the molten fist in the air as if she planned to beat Gehirn to death with it.

"Burn them all!" screamed Erbrechen. "Now!"

Gehirn burned them to ash with a wave of her hand. All of them. Anomie. Her five Schatten Mörder. Then she burned Erbrechen's friends. Thousands of tiny lives snuffed in a flash of heat. She burned them all. She stood in a small circle of mud surrounded by acres of ash.

The sky cracked and lightning lashed the heavens. Dark and pregnant clouds gave birth and fist-sized stones of hail hammered the earth.

Erbrechen, still cowering on the litter, wailed as hail struck him. Gehirn had to protect her love—and she only knew one way to do so.

She lit the sky afire.

271

She burned the sky clean of clouds and the encircling storm rushed to fill what had been its calm eye. Gehirn devoured the sky with loving flame and heat. After what seemed like an eternity of fire, the strength of the storm failed. The sun slammed through the shredding cloud like an avenging hammer.

Gehirn stood, arms spread, gazing in adoration at the ultimate fire. The stench of burning flesh filled the air, occluding the sun with the smoke rising from her blackening body. Her eyes melted and ran like butter.

Gehirn ignited with concussive force.

# CHAPTER 26

*In a mad world, only the mad are sane.*

—Akira Kurosawa

As the horizon swallowed the evening sun, the sky to the south looked unlike anything Asena had ever seen. Storm clouds spiraled in toward some central point like filthy water draining from a sink. Lightning struck at the ground, but equally bright flashes stabbed from the ground into the sky. It looked like the gods did battle with some earthbound Geisteskranken, and it appeared the Geisteskranken might win.

Asena stood atop a grassy hill with her gathered Tiergeist, watching the distant battle in silence. Even here, the winds blew fiercely, flattening the tall grass and snapping at what little clothing she wore. She could feel the rumbling thunder shake the ground, but heard nothing.

Such power should not go without witness. She sniffed at the damp air, tasting the tingling metallic tang of the faraway storm.

Konig had done her a horrible disservice and this troubled

Asena more than the world's lack of sound. He had often pushed her away—she understood his fear of allowing someone to become too close and accepted it—but he had never intentionally hurt her before.

Bär, massive and hairy, waved a hand to get her attention. He looked so sullen and depressed it seemed to diminish his colossal size. Asena glanced up at him and lifted an eyebrow. He pointed at the storm and flared his nostrils. *He smells it too.*

Evil little Stich, baring his sharpened teeth, sniffed at the air. His eyes, too small and close together to convey any emotion other than vicious anger, looked from Asena to the storm.

She shook her head in answer to the unasked question. *No, we will not go south.* Konig ordered them to Neidrig and there they would go. Stich accepted this without comment and bent to claw at the dirt, his sharp nails digging for the insects and grubs he ate almost continually.

Only Masse ignored the storm, looking southwest toward Neidrig, his long, slim tongue flickering to taste the air. Asena watched him with interest. He alone seemed unperturbed by the loss of hearing—perhaps because his had been fairly poor to begin with. Masse noticed her attention and blinked at her, his secondary eyelid—a thin, yellowish, nictitating membrane—sliding across the eye to wet it.

"You taste something to the southwest?" Asena asked. She heard nothing but could feel her voice in her head.

Masse must have understood because he pointed toward Neidrig. He said something but she didn't hear it and couldn't read his nonexistent lips. His face, as ever, remained devoid of expression.

Frustrated, she *twisted,* and a lean gray wolf sat where the slim girl had been.

Asena barked in surprise—sound returned the moment she'd *twisted.* Konig had been wrong. His delusions had not been enough to change the fact that Therianthropes healed even the most grievous of wounds by twisting into their animal form. She wanted to twist back but hesitated. Would she once again lose her hearing when she became human? Then she smelled what Masse had scented and lost all fear.

Morgen.

Even at this distance the boy-god's presence could not be ignored. She had been correct, Morgen was in Neidrig.

Bär, Stich, and Masse watched her with obvious interest. She showed her teeth in a victorious growl and again *twisted*. She rose to her feet in a lithe motion and listened to the crack of distant thunder.

Asena pointed to her ears. "I can hear again."

Bär understood first and *twisted* with an earth-shattering roar. As a grizzly bear, he was twice the size of the massive man he had been. Over one thousand pounds of muscle and shaggy brown fur stood bellowing at the sky, briefly drowning out the titanic storm that was smashing the horizon. Asena clapped her hands over her ears and backed away from Bär. Though he was normally peaceful and gentle, there was no telling how he would react to something like this. She *twisted* back into wolf form.

Masse *twisted* next, his body crumbling to become asps, anacondas, constrictors, mambas, coral snakes, and many breeds she didn't recognize. A writhing mass of snakes covered the ground before her. Masse was never the same twice; the result of each twisting depended on his mood. This entwined pile of deadly snakes didn't speak well of his state of mind.

Stich, not the quickest-witted of the group, *twisted* last and fell apart like a tower of cards in the wind. As a man, Stich was quick to anger and even faster to lash out at whatever offended him. As a few thousand scorpions, he was psychotic rage personified. Just seeing him, glistening black, climbing all over himself, sent shivers of revulsion down Asena's spine.

A massive bear, a gray wolf, a nest of snakes, and a mound of scorpions coruscating like oil stared southwest toward Neidrig. All sensed Morgen, the god-child, in some manner. All but Asena ignored the storm to the south. With her incredibly heightened sense of smell, she caught the scent of something familiar. Burning flesh. A lot of burning flesh. The wolf turned her nose to the storm. Gehirn Schlechtes—the vile Hassebrand who stared at her with such undisguised longing—was at the heart of the storm.

Asena growled and *twisted* back to human form.

"We have to talk," she said.

When all four regained their human shapes, they once again sat around the fire.

Stich bared sharpened teeth. "Why we hear? Konig say we no hear no more."

Bär grunted agreement but said nothing.

Asena squatted on her haunches like a dog. "Konig is far away and we are together. The beliefs of a tightly knit pack count for more than those of a distant man. Proximity and numbers."

Masse spoke what was on all their minds. "Konig defines reality."

Bär grunted again. All three looked to Asena.

"There are two possibilities," she said carefully. "Either Konig is not as powerful as we believe, or something else is at work here. Some other power influences us."

Masse blinked milky nictitating membranes and said, "Konig's power is beyond doubting."

"Who greater than Konig?" Stich asked.

"Morgen," Bär grunted, his voice impossibly deep.

"Why," Asena asked, "would Morgen return our hearing?"

Bär gave her a strange look but remained quiet.

"Deafness would make it harder to find him," Masse suggested.

"No," said Asena. "Bär and I could have tracked him by scent alone. We would have found him easily enough."

"Talking," said Bär.

"Without hearing, we could not talk like this," agreed Asena.

Stich's small eyes blinked in confusion. "Morgen want us talk?"

"Perhaps there are things he wants us to discuss," suggested Asena.

"Such as?" Masse asked.

"Such as what we are doing here," Asena answered.

"Konig send us help Morgen Ascend," Stich said to prove he understood what was going on.

"Konig has sent us to *kill* Morgen," Asena corrected.

"Same thing!" Stich snapped angrily.

"No doubt Konig knows best," agreed Asena to calm Stich. "But what if Morgen isn't ready?" She looked from Stich to Masse, and finally at Bär, who seemingly ignored them. "Yet," she amended softly.

"If Morgen will Ascend to be a god," mused Masse, "he could be . . . *must* be more powerful than Konig. He could return our hearing no matter what Konig believes. Did he do this so we could decide to defy Konig?"

"Why he not want Ascend?" demanded Stich. "He Geborene god."

Asena didn't want this getting out of hand. She merely meant to sow seeds of doubt in the minds of her fellow Tiergeist. She didn't know if they should kill Morgen or not. She didn't think *she* could kill the boy, but had no doubt Stich was more than willing.

"Let's not get ahead of ourselves," said Asena. "First we have to find Morgen. We should talk to him, not just kill him and pat ourselves on the back for a job well done." She watched Bär, but he said nothing.

"Killing a would-be god when he doesn't want to be killed might be bad," agreed Masse. "I for one do not want any gods angry with me."

Asena prattled on and Stich lost the thread of the conversation. She was so hard to follow sometimes. With Asena, nothing was ever simple.

Konig was Theocrat. High Priest. It didn't matter his god did not yet exist, though such thoughts were confusing; it mattered only that he *would* exist. If Morgen was to be a god and the only way to become a god was to die, the boy would have to die. *Why else Konig send us?* Why did everyone try to make this simple task seem difficult?

Find boy. Kill boy. Kill those who stole boy. What could be easier?

Stich shivered with excitement and almost *twisted* at the thought of the screaming mayhem to come. *I help Morgen Ascend.*

## CHAPTER 27

*Damn this cursed sanity. How is being a helpless prisoner of reality sane?*

—GEISTIG GESUND

Neidrig. The place *was* a shite-hole. Wichtig had seen a good number of shite-holes, but this one was prizewinning. If forty thousand people called this shite pit home, twenty thousand were thieves and ten thousand murderers. Five thousand, he figured, belonged to the many and varied breeds of hucksters and con artists. Roughly three thousand lived on the streets, sleeping in urine-soaked alleys, and a thousand were just too dumb to leave. The rest would be Swordsmen looking to carve names for themselves in these mean streets. This was just the kind of place a real Swordsman would come from. There would be none of the soft hands and soft teachings of the hoity-toity big-city sword schools. These men and women learned to kill the old-fashioned way.

Wichtig's elite training as a palace guard in Geldangelegenheiten he deemed a minor and unimportant detail. Years of relentless practice, vicious and bloody tournaments with the other guards—considered by many to be among the best trained Swordsmen in the world—and the fact that he had risen to the position of First Guard meant nothing in the face of destiny. Hard work hadn't made him great: destiny had. And now destiny brought him here.

*There must be a reason.*

Stehlen found them a room in one of the city's many inns, and the innkeep asked no questions as they lugged Bedeckt's unconscious and blood-spattered form through the tavern and up the stairs. Even the few patrons didn't seem particularly interested and instead focused on their drinks.

After they'd dumped Bedeckt on sturdiest of the cots, Wichtig glanced around the cramped room. "Did you manage to find the worst room in Neidrig on your first try?"

Stehlen ignored him, fussing over Bedeckt.

Wichtig squinted and made a show of examining the floor. "There are more things living in the corners of this room than in the rest of the city."

Still ignoring him, she peeled a strip of blood-soaked fabric from Bedeckt's body.

"This is hardly the time for that," joked Wichtig. "It isn't fair to take advantage of him while he's unconscious."

Again Stehlen failed to react.

*Well, she's no fun.*

Disappointed, Wichtig turned to Morgen. The boy stared at his own hands, eyes wide with disgust. Wichtig glanced at them; just a little blood. Nothing to get worked up over.

"What's wrong?"

"Filthy," Morgen said, blinking back tears.

Wichtig pointed to a shallow bowl of water on the floor. "You can clean them in there."

The boy was there in an instant, kneeling before the bowl, scrubbing furiously. He kept whispering something to himself but Wichtig couldn't hear it. *Strange kid.*

Wichtig paced the confines of the room, darting glances over Stehlen's shoulder to check on Bedeckt. Though Morgen had somehow closed the old goat's wounds, the sheets soon soaked through with blood. If not for the slow rise and fall of the man's chest, Wichtig would have thought him dead. Bedeckt's flesh looked like a patchwork of scars, some old and white, others still ragged and raw.

Stehlen sat at Bedeckt's side, gently rinsing blood from the haggard face and whispering soft words. *Downright creepy, that is.*

Morgen finally stopped scrubbing his hands, crawled onto the cleanest of the cots, curled into a tight ball, and promptly fell asleep. The boy slept with his hands clutched together as if protecting them from the world beyond.

*Yep, strange kid.* Morgen couldn't have been more different from Fluch, the son Wichtig hadn't seen since walking out on his wife in Traurig. Fluch lived to play in the dirt. If the boy was clean for more than a few minutes in a row, his parents proclaimed it a miracle. The memory of his son felt like a fist crushing his heart.

Later, when he had achieved his destiny, he would return to his wife and show her. Show her he had been destined for great things. Show her he wasn't lazy, terrified of success, and all the other hurtful shite she'd said. Men with destinies had difficult choices to make. The thought that he hadn't discovered his destiny until years after leaving his wife niggled, and he shoved it aside. Someday he would return for Fluch and his son would be proud.

Wichtig turned from Morgen and searched the room for a distraction. Four small and dingy cots, home to gods know how many forms of small and biting life. A single window with flimsy and warped storm shutters looking like they'd fall to dust in a light wind. The floor hadn't been swept in a hundred generations. If Neidrig was a shite-hole, the Ruchlos Arms was the fly-covered turd floating in the piss water of that hole.

"Was this really the best inn we could find?" Wichtig asked Stehlen.

Stehlen finally glanced up from her ministrations and gave him a pinched and sallow frown. She flared nostrils and snarled, "It's quiet and the innkeeper didn't ask about us carrying in our unconscious and blood-soaked friend."

"An innocent question," said Wichtig, feigning hurt. "A simple yes or no would suffice. I'm going to take a look around town."

"Get killed."

Wichtig bowed with a mocking flourish. "Anything for you, my love. I shall seek death until I find it."

"Good," she snapped.

Wichtig checked the hang of his swords and struck a dashing pose. Stehlen ignored him. *Just as well, the ill-tempered wench has no fashion sense at all.*

"Is the stinky old goat going to live?" Wichtig asked, holding the pose in case she looked.

Stehlen gently wiped dried blood from Bedeckt's shattered face. He might not be bleeding, but half his head looked like someone had tried to chop it down with an ax.

"He'll live," she muttered.

Surrendering his perfect pose, Wichtig moved to the door, which hung on a single rusted hinge. "You know," he said thoughtfully, "if you'd wash your hair, you might actually look half decent."

The thought planted, he ducked from the room. Stehlen was rarely influenced by his Gefahrgeist powers, but she had her weaknesses. And the thought of Bedeckt awakening to a bathed and caring Stehlen was too just funny. It would probably scare the old man to death.

WICHTIG STOOD ON the decaying front stoop of the inn, looking up and down the street. Most of the crowd ignored him, but a few shot speculative glances in his direction, trying to fit him into the local food chain. Was he predator or prey?

If the city of Neidrig was a shite-hole and the Ruchlos Arms a floating turd, the people were the flies circling the choicer turds. Wichtig's ever-present cocky façade faded. Without Bedeckt around to tell him to stay out of trouble, there didn't seem to be much point in getting into any. He turned back into the inn and found an empty table. The beautiful matched swords he placed on the table before him in open challenge: Come, they're worth a fortune. Try and take them from me.

When the barmaid—a heavy woman with an arse larger than his horse's—brought him a beer, he caught her wrist. "Why is it when I look for trouble, I have no problem finding it, but if I wait for trouble to come to me, it never does?"

She blinked in dull confusion, her acne-pocked face florid. "Maybe you're waiting in the wrong place."

"Aha! A woman of beauty *and* wisdom."

She huffed annoyance. "There are plenty of places in town where your type—"

"You don't know my type," Wichtig said softly. "There was a barmaid at the last inn we stayed at." He met the fat woman's red eyes with a sad smile. "I loved her." It wasn't true, but it felt like it could be. If he talked a bit more it might become true. "I loved her and my companion—the skinny murderous bitch with the bad teeth—cut her down. Killed her. I never got to tell her . . ."

Wichtig wove a tale of deception and danger and forbidden love until the barmaid's eyes filled with tears.

When he finished, she left to fetch him a free pint; *the least she could do,* he thought.

His Gefahrgeist powers grew. Shame she wasn't better looking. Still, the memory of his wife and son still hung about like a bad smell and killed his desire for female companionship.

*Gods, I'm bored.*

Working his charms, Wichtig drank and ate for free for the rest of the evening. Though the swords sat on the table before him and he feigned a level of drunkenness far beyond what he felt, no one bothered him.

〰〰〰〰〰〰

Bedeckt awoke to the feel of a cool damp cloth caressing his face. It felt nice and he lay still with his eyes closed, enjoying the sensation. He was reluctant to cause the end of such a rare moment. He took a deep breath and was surprised when it didn't hurt and his lungs didn't make that rattling, bubbling noise they had for the last month. He drew air through his nose—he couldn't remember the last time he'd been able to do that—and caught the sweet scent of roses and soap.

*Where am I?*

He had no idea and it didn't matter.

"You'll be okay," said a soft voice. "I'll take care of you."

*Stehlen?* Bedeckt cracked an eye open and found himself staring up Stehlen's narrow nostrils. When he focused beyond her nose, his other eye shot open in surprise. "Did you wash your hair?"

Her face, one moment soft and caring, became pinched and paranoid. "Why?"

"That would have been my next question," Bedeckt said without thought.

"Why?" This time with anger.

"Gods, I don't know." Bedeckt glanced around the room, desperate to look anywhere but at her. "Where the hells am I?"

"Neidrig. You almost died. Morgen saved you." She made a strange, scrunched face. "I've been . . . caring for you," she said tentatively.

*Caring for me? Sticking gods, what the hells happened?* "My head feels like a few hundred angry giants stomped on it."

"It looks worse." Stehlen smiled and dabbed at his forehead with a bloody shred of cloth. He knocked her hand aside with a growl and her smile died instantly. Nostrils flared, and for an instant he thought she would stab him.

"Sorry," he muttered. "My head hurts."

Stehlen's faltering smile returned. "Do you like my hair?"

Bedeckt took the coward's way out and lost consciousness.

WHEN HE AWOKE a second time he could hear Stehlen's nasal snoring and Morgen stood over him with a curious expression.

"Why didn't you want your fingers back?" the boy demanded. "I could heal all your scars. You won't be ugly anymore. Well . . . less ugly."

*Ah, the brutal honesty of children.* "I am my scars."

"Removing scars won't change your past."

"It will make it easier to forget."

"You think you're the actions that caused the scars?"

Bedeckt nodded without saying anything.

"You're wrong," said Morgen, examining his pristine fingernails and rubbing at something Bedeckt couldn't see. "We are our beliefs."

"Only the beliefs of the insane define reality."

"I am not crazy."

Bedeckt watched the boy's eyes.

"I am going to be a god. My power comes from the faith of the Geborene. They believe I can do these things, and so I can."

"Being told your entire life you are going to become a god is probably not healthy."

The boy bit his lip, frowned, and adjusted Bedeckt's blanket—changing nothing—nodded, and again checked his hands. "Your friend is not the Greatest Swordsman in the World because he thinks he is. He is the greatest because enough other people believe it."

Bedeckt stifled a laugh. "First, Wichtig is not the Greatest Swordsman in the World. Second—"

"Yes, he is."

Bedeckt rolled his eyes at the naïveté of the child. "Second, Wichtig is not my friend. The only person Wichtig likes is Wichtig."

"Wrong," said Morgen with absolute certainty. "He is the only person he hates."

Bedeckt blinked in surprise. The boy might be right. "It doesn't matter. Wichtig is Gefahrgeist. He cares only for himself. His power is the manipulation of people's beliefs toward his own ends."

"But . . ." Morgen's eyed widened. "Konig is Gefahrgeist too."

"Yes, but far more powerful than Wichtig."

"You are saying his power is manipulation and stems from the fact he doesn't care about other people? Konig cares about me. Doesn't he?"

Bedeckt didn't want to hurt the child, but at the same time anything messing with a Gefahrgeist arsehole's long-term plans couldn't be all bad. If Konig came through with the ransom money and they returned the boy to the Geborene Damonen, Bedeckt liked the idea of planting some questions in the child's mind. *He needs to know he can't trust people.*

Bedeckt placed a comforting hand on the boy's shoulder. "I don't know what Konig feels for you. If anything," he added. "Gefahrgeist have one defining feature: selfishness." Let the boy figure it out for himself.

"You're wrong about Wichtig and you're wrong about Konig. Wichtig is your friend. He sees you as the father he never had."

"Piss-poor example," muttered Bedeckt uncomfortably. Could he have misread Wichtig? Could he be wrong about the man? No. Wichtig was a manipulative bastard, and the moment Bedeckt forgot it was the moment Wichtig would stab him in the back. "Wichtig proclaims friendship to manipulate."

"Does Konig hate himself as much as Wichtig does?" Morgen asked.

"Wichtig doesn't—" The boy's look stopped him.

"Wichtig isn't there when you die," said Morgen.

Die? He didn't like the sound of that. "See, he abandons me in my time of need," Bedeckt said offhandedly to disguise his unease.

"No. If he is not at your side, he must be dead. Who could kill the Greatest Swordsman in the World?"

"He's not . . . Forget it. We all die alone."

"No, I mean really alone. And you are badly hurt." The boy rubbed at his fingernails, attempting to clean away nonexistent dirt. "Burned."

"You shouldn't tell people about their deaths," Bedeckt said darkly.

Morgen retreated. "Sorry."

"When I die, do I have my ax?"

"Do you really want to know?"

Bedeckt groaned. *Do I really want to know?* "Yes."

"No."

"Do I have my boots at least?"

"One of them, I think."

"Which one?"

"The left. Maybe."

"Hells," Bedeckt growled. He couldn't let this delusional child get to him. Gods knew what the little bastard was capable of. "How about your own death?" he asked to change the subject.

"No one sees their own death."

Bedeckt, pretending he was still paying attention, made a mental note to move the stash of coins from his right boot to his left.

Stehlen awoke to find Bedeckt had risen from his cot and stood staring out the small window at the dwindling storm. She watched in silence.

Something had changed in the man's bearing and it took Stehlen a moment to figure out what. Bedeckt looked like something had broken inside. Though he appeared to be unhurt, he leaned a little too heavily on the windowsill, as if needing its support. His pale and battered face hung a little too slack, as if some of the man's indomitable drive had leaked away with the lost blood. If she didn't know better she'd swear he looked scared.

*Impossible!*

She shrugged aside her worries. *A brush with death will shake anyone,* she supposed. *The stinky old bastard will get over it.*

From the cot Stehlen had a clear view of the left side of Bedeckt's face. Calling it ruined was an understatement. She'd seen better-looking corpses. Little more than a pulpy mound of pink scar tissue remained of his left ear. She'd have to be careful to stay on his left to protect his exposed side. She spat in disgust. She'd have to be equally careful he didn't notice her doing it.

"Where's Wichtig?" Stehlen asked loudly so Bedeckt would hear her.

Bedeckt glanced at her before returning his attention to the window. "I'm not deaf."

"He's downstairs," Morgen answered.

"Good," said Bedeckt. "I have to go make contact." His gaze darted to Morgen. "With some friends."

Stehlen understood. Bedeckt would use local sources to send word to Konig that they had the child and to suggest a starting price for negotiation. If they got half what they asked for, they'd never have to work again. What would such a life be like? She'd still steal; Kleptics didn't steal for need or survival.

But what would Bedeckt do? Would he settle down somewhere quiet? If they weren't working, would he still have use for her, or would he abandon her? She couldn't decide what she wanted more, to be with Bedeckt, or to take everything he had. Both sounded so very appealing. *If he's going to leave me*—and to leave her was to leave her with nothing she valued—*why should I not do the same to him first?*

"You should take Wichtig," Morgen said.

"I'll take Stehlen," Bedeckt answered immediately.

Stehlen's heart soared, but she snarled and spat to cover it. "After breakfast," she said. The old man had lost a lot of blood and would need his strength.

"The Caller of Storms died," said Morgen, gesturing at the window. "The sun will return. Fire ate the storm."

When they joined Wichtig—already a little drunk—in the main room of the Ruchlos Arms, the Swordsman waved expansively as if greeting long-lost friends. Bedeckt recognized that look; Wichtig was pleased with something, which almost always meant trouble.

"Stehlen, your hair is clean," said the Swordsman.

She spat at his boot but he moved his foot to avoid the yellowy phlegm.

Bedeckt ignored them, digging into a breakfast of mystery meat sausages and grease-soaked fried bread served on a square chunk of wood still crusted with the remains of a previous meal. The eating utensil looked more like a conveniently shaped stick than anything made intentionally. He didn't even want to think about how many mouths this would-be spoon had been in since its last cleaning. Glancing about the inn's grubby interior, Bedeckt guessed the place never got particularly busy. The rough-hewn benches at each of the six tables looked like they'd collapse under any real weight. He shifted experimentally and the bench he and Wichtig shared groaned ominously. Seeing as everything still hurt, he didn't want to be dumped on his arse and ceased all movement.

"Stehlen cared for your wounds," Wichtig said. "She never left your side."

Bedeckt glanced uncomfortably at Stehlen, who glared daggers at Wichtig. *What the hells is going on?* The woman had been acting increasingly odd. Ever since . . . *Damn it all to hells.* He knew going back to save them had been a mistake.

Stehlen's eyes narrowed dangerously. "You're drunk," she said to Wichtig.

"Perhaps," Wichtig answered, slurring slightly. He gave her a lingering look of appraisal. "Nope. Still not drunk enough." He waved at the barmaid for more ale. "But maybe soon. If you're very, very lucky."

Bedeckt, with a glance at Morgen—who in turn watched Stehlen and Wichtig with fascination—decided to change the subject. "What happened when we left Selbsthass?"

"Nothing," Stehlen answered quickly.

Wichtig's face lost its cocky look. "She killed them all."

"All who?" Bedeckt asked, confused.

"Everyone in the Leichtes Haus," said Wichtig, glaring at Stehlen.

"Had to," muttered Stehlen defensively.

"She killed them because she was jealous," Morgen announced. "Wichtig liked a girl, which angered Stehlen. She had to kill the girl and have her pretty scarves. She's in love with both of you and doesn't like other women being around. With Wichtig, it's just simple attraction to his physical perfection. She thinks Bedeckt is something he is not. She thinks he is a better man than he is. She loves her idea of him, and when he betrays . . ." Noticing everyone staring at him, the boy finally trailed off. "You aren't without redeeming qualities," he said to Bedeckt, sounding apologetic.

"Thanks," said Bedeckt. He would have said more but saw Stehlen's face. Her look said death. Bedeckt kicked her under the table, breaking her fixation.

"Physical perfection, eh?" Wichtig flexed a muscled arm.

No doubt the only part the self-absorbed fool heard.

Bedeckt leaned toward Morgen. "Your hands are dirty." He had to stop the boy before he said anything else. Before Stehlen killed him.

The child stared aghast at his spotless hands. Careful not to touch anything, he slid from the bench and went in search of somewhere to scrub himself clean.

"What the hells was that about?" Wichtig asked.

"Just saving the boy's life," Bedeckt muttered.

"I wouldn't have actually killed him," said Stehlen, and Bedeckt knew she lied.

"Just because the boy knew you're in love with me?" asked Wichtig. "Come now, it is not exactly a secret." He gestured at Bedeckt. "We've always known. Why do you think we keep you around? Certainly not for your womanly charms and wit."

Bedeckt groaned. Everything ached and he wasn't ready to deal with this. "Stehlen and I are going to talk to my contacts. I'm going to send word to Konig Furimmer we have his godling and are willing to talk trade. I want you"—he poked the cracked wooden spoon at Wichtig—"to watch the boy while we're gone. Stay out of trouble."

"Not to worry, I know all about caring for children. I'll watch him as if—"

"He were your own son?" Stehlen snorted. "Abandoning isn't the same as caring."

For once Wichtig said nothing, his face devoid of emotion.

The two deranged idiots would kill each other if Bedeckt didn't put a stop to this. "Let it go. Both of you."

"I was going to say, as if my future fortune depended on the boy's safety," said Wichtig.

"You thought that up after," sneered Stehlen. "You're slowing down."

"I'm still faster than—"

"Stop!" The two stared at Bedeckt as if appalled by his outburst. Bedeckt rose from the bench with a groan, using the table to lever himself upright. His knees made wet popping noises. "Stehlen, let's go."

Out on the street Stehlen walked at Bedeckt's left side, keeping an eye and ear out for trouble. Bedeckt stared at the ground as he walked, his battered face looking surprisingly glum for someone who should have been dead.

"Your cold is gone," she pointed out, hoping it might lift his mood. "You're sounding a lot better. The boy must have healed that along with your wounds."

Bedeckt grunted and looked even more miserable.

"You've got cat-turd face again," she said.

"Thinking."

*Ah, that's the problem.* "About?" Stehlen asked.

"The boy saved my life, didn't he?"

"You looked dead to me. I was ready to root through your clothes for money." When Bedeckt glanced at her she added, "I didn't, though." She'd put most of the money back when she'd realized he was going to live, so it almost wasn't a lie.

"The kid saved me and he didn't even mention it."

"So?"

"Didn't rub it in or gloat. Didn't even seem to notice I didn't thank him."

"And?"

"Doesn't that seem weird?"

*Not as weird as how much it bothers you.* "Strange kid," she agreed.

"Do I owe him for saving my life?"

Stehlen snorted a honk of nasal laughter. "Bedeckt pay his debts? Ha!" If anything, Bedeckt's scarred lump of a face looked even harder than usual. *Shite, he isn't joking!* "If the kid doesn't care, you shouldn't."

Bedeckt grunted and nodded agreement but didn't look like he really believed it.

⸻

When Morgen returned from scrubbing his hands, Stehlen and Bedeckt had left. He glanced at the empty seats. "Why did Bedeckt take Stehlen instead of you? He should have taken you."

"They need some alone time together." Wichtig waggled eyebrows at the boy. "To do adult stuff."

"You're lying."

"Can't get one past you." Wichtig raised an eyebrow. "Just what are you capable of?"

"I don't know. Aufschlag frowned on showing off."

"Could you help me find this shite-hole's Greatest Swordsmen?" Wichtig asked.

Morgen thought about it. The reflections would show him what he wanted to know. "Why?"

"How do you think one becomes the Greatest Swordsman in the World?"

The answer was obvious. "You have to fight other great Swordsmen."

293

"Of course. Can you help me find them?"

"Do you want to start with a good one and work your way up, or go after the best first?"

Wichtig looked thoughtful and Morgen knew the Swordsman was pretending; he'd already made up his mind.

"If we start with the very best," said Wichtig, "we won't have to fight the others."

Once on the street, Morgen stared raptly into an unsavory puddle of something thin and brown and tinted with a hint of red. Someone's kidneys were definitely failing.

He lost himself in the puddle. "I see her. She's not far from here. There's an inn called the Schwarze Beerdigung. It's much cleaner than where we are staying," he added petulantly. His hands stung, raw from scrubbing.

"She? How can a woman be the Greatest Swordsman in the World? Wait. If she's seeking the title of Greatest Swords*woman* in the World, is she still worth fighting?"

*What difference does it make?* "She's the best in this . . ."

" 'Shite-hole' is the word you are looking for. Or cesspit, piss-pot, dung heap, or turd bucket."

"She's the best fighter in this turd bucket," finished Morgen, smiling uncertainly up at Wichtig. Aufschlag had never let him use the words he learned from the church guards.

Wichtig ruffled Morgen's hair and set off down the street. Gods knew where the man's hands had been. Morgen tried not to show his distaste at the contact as he hurried to keep up.

"That's my boy," said Wichtig. "You'll be one of us before long." He gestured grandly at the refuse-strewn streets of Neidrig. "Free to wander the open road. Free to taste all the pleasures life offers to those bold enough to take a bite." He glanced at Morgen. "Do you like girls yet?"

"I haven't met very many," Morgen admitted.

"A situation we must remedy."

"The few priestesses I met seemed nice. Before this, I never left the church."

"You lived there with your parents?" Wichtig asked, watching the crowd around them.

Morgen shook his head. "I don't have parents."

"You never met your mother? That's not all bad. Mine sent me away to live with my father. He sent me back after I sold his horse to buy a lute."

"No, I mean I never had a mother."

Wichtig, spotting a young tough sporting a businesslike sword, distractedly said, "Everyone has a mother."

"I am the manifestation of the faith of the Geborene Damonen and all Selbsthass."

Wichtig stopped suddenly and Morgen narrowly avoided walking into him. "Is that what Konig told you?" He made a noise like a wet fart. "You need to learn to ask questions." Laughing, he once again set off down the filth-strewn street.

Morgen followed. Had Konig lied? *Why would* . . . "Why would Konig lie?"

"Every god needs a good backstory," Wichtig said over his shoulder. "Don't take it personally. It's just that 'born of the faith of the believers' is better than 'born of a tavern whore.' "

Was this true? If this was a lie, what other lies did he believe? *No, Konig wouldn't lie to me. I am to be the Geborene god, I was born of their faith.* The words rang hollow.

"Let's pay this Swordswoman a visit," said Wichtig, as if their previous conversation was already forgotten. As if they'd discussed nothing of importance. "Is she attractive?"

Morgen blinked up at the Swordsman. *Why would Wichtig lie, what could he hope to gain?* "Nicer than Stehlen," he said, his thoughts jumbled and chaotic.

Wichtig guffawed. "Everyone is nicer than Stehlen in every way imaginable. I've met donkeys with better personalities, tomcats with sturdier morals, billy goats who smell better, and horses who are a gentler ride."

"Gentler ride?"

"Never mind."

‖‖‖‖‖‖‖‖‖‖

Though the Schwarze Beerdigung was nowhere near what Wichtig would call a respectable establishment, it was indeed superior to the Ruchlos Arms. The tables, rough as they looked, were actually tables. The chairs were real chairs, and the bar looked like it had been made specifically to be a bar. The boy followed him in, walking as if in a daze. *What the hells is wrong with him?*

In one corner a hefty woman sat with three well-armed men. The woman and her coterie of warriors ignored Wichtig's entrance, but he knew they'd noticed his arrival. How could they not, he was impossible to miss. Such grace. Such poise. *What had the brat said?* Physical perfection. Such physical perfection. The very essence of the perfect warrior given flesh.

Wichtig struck a heroic pose and grinned his best cocky grin at the table. While they pretended to ignore him and his perfect teeth, Wichtig took the opportunity to look them over.

The men were nothing. Run-of-the-mill toughs, each displaying the sloped brows, bad teeth, and thick clublike fingers of the dull-witted. *Add them together,* thought Wichtig, *and you still wouldn't get one real destiny.* Well armed and probably tolerably well versed in the use of their rather plain weapons, they still didn't matter. Not like Wichtig.

The woman was something else. A pair of beautiful matched swords hung at her waist in ornate leather sheaths, one dangling either side of the chair she straddled. Her hair, a pale orange bordering on strawberry, was hewn short and rough. The large helm sitting atop the table explained the bad hairstyle. Though

Wichtig found her face flat and her chin thick and strong, he was interested to note she was also unscarred. An impressive feat, if she really was a contender and an active Swordsman. *Swordswoman*, Wichtig corrected. Her arms looked like tree trunks, and Wichtig could only guess at how her legs looked under the long mail skirt. He'd never had a really large, muscular woman before and wondered what sexual feats she'd be capable of.

Wichtig leaned close to whisper to Morgen. "Listen carefully. If communication is manipulation, sex is all-out war." He gestured toward the woman, ignoring the boy's look of confusion. "And she looks like she'd be a good fight."

"She's very good," answered Morgen, misunderstanding. "But you don't have to worry."

Wichtig feigned shocked outrage. "Me? Worry?"

"You are the Greatest Swordsman in the World. You would win."

*Would? What does that mean?* Wichtig, pushing the thought aside, approached the table. A larger audience would have been nice, but the boy would suffice. Come to think of it, it might be more important he impress the boy than a crowd of lowly peasants.

"Greetings and salutations, my good . . ." Hells, he should have asked the boy the woman's name. "People."

The woman glanced dismissively at him and returned her attention to the tabletop. "Begone."

"Ah, a woman of few words. It matches your beauty."

She scratched at the tabletop with a blunt fingernail and sounded bored. "You're pretty enough for both of us."

*Nicely done!* He hadn't expected wit. "True. I am. Which is lucky. For you."

She glanced at the men at her table and they stood to face Wichtig. "Beauty doesn't do well in Neidrig," she said.

"I had noticed, but was too polite to say anything."

Finally she looked up and gestured at the largely empty room.

"This is pointless. There is no crowd to impress. Continue on this path and you will die."

Wichtig backed away from the table, though only far enough to allow him an unhindered draw of his weapons. "I seek only to impress the boy. After these three"—he nodded at the standing warriors—"would you mind terribly if I killed you?"

She ignored the question and glanced past Wichtig at Morgen with a flicker of concealed curiosity. "The boy? Who is he?"

"Oh, nobody," Wichtig drawled. "But he is going to be a god. So, if you don't mind . . ."

Wichtig killed the three men with three swift and precise strikes. The last one managed a look of wide-eyed surprise before dying.

Wichtig grimaced. "I must be slowing in my old age. Normally I can kill twice as many before one manages to react." A bald-faced lie, but he delivered it with perfect sincerity. It sounded good, like it was truth.

The woman remained sitting, but her hands fell to the pommels of her sheathed swords. She looked up at Wichtig as if noticing him for the first time. "Do you seek to defeat me, or merely kill me?"

"Why, both!" Wichtig bowed with a flourish and a wink. "I'll await you on the street. A few mortal witnesses wouldn't hurt."

"""""""""""

"Are you really going to be a god?" Lebendig Durchdachter asked the boy.

"Yes," he answered, and she believed him. She had no choice. "And Wichtig is the Greatest Swordsman in the World." She knew this was true too and followed the man's slim hips with her gaze as he wove between tables on his way toward the front door. She remained sitting, watching as the strange boy followed the Swordsman. The faith of all the people of Neidrig paled before the force of the child's belief in his friend. If she followed them out, it was only a matter of time before she lay dying in the street.

Her old Blade Master had always said things like "enter every fight knowing today is a good day to die." The man, like all men, was an idiot. *Today is a shite day to die.*

Lebendig Durchdachter stood and dropped a few coins on the table to cover the cost of her drinks. Gods be damned if she would cover the cost of her dead companions', whom she stepped over on the way to the bar.

She gestured to the innkeeper and dropped a few more coins atop the bar. "When the man comes back in, this will buy him a few drinks."

The innkeep nodded as he accepted the coins but couldn't meet her eyes. "So you're going to face him?"

"Hells no. I'm going out the back. The drinks are to distract him long enough that I can get away."

He finally made eye contact. "I always knew you were a good deal smarter than my other patrons."

‖‖‖‖‖‖‖‖

Morgen followed Wichtig through the foul and narrow streets. The Swordsman, long legs striding quickly, grumbled and cursed under his breath.

*He must have lied to make me doubt Konig,* thought Morgen. Except he couldn't quite believe that. Wichtig had sounded more like he'd simply found Morgen's beliefs funny. *But belief defines reality.* If he and all of Selbsthass believed strongly enough that he'd been born of pure faith, would that make it true?

"I can't believe she ran!" Wichtig called over his shoulder. "What a waste of a day!"

Morgen had known the woman would flee. Should he have told Wichtig? Did Wichtig not understand?

Handsome, dashing, and heroic Wichtig might be, but Morgen suspected the Swordsman might not be particularly smart. He decided to explain, just in case.

"It was better you didn't kill her."

"Oh, shut up," snapped Wichtig.

"You just became the Greatest Swordsman in this turd bucket without a fight." He thought about the three men Wichtig had so casually slain. "Without a *real* fight," he corrected.

Wichtig ignored Morgen's attempt at humor and continued stalking, head down, through the street. Morgen tried again.

"Word will spread. You are so good even the great Lebendig Durchdachter is afraid to face you. This is better than an actual kill." Wichtig continued to ignore him. "People enjoy seeing imperfection in others. They feel better about themselves. This explains why you love and hate Bedeckt. You see how vastly flawed he is and know you could do better."

"Of course I do better."

"*Could* do—"

"Which part of 'shut up' didn't you understand?" Wichtig growled.

An emaciated black cat riddled with open sores and a recently torn ear dashed across the street in front of Wichtig, a blur of motion. Wichtig was faster. His foot connected dead center with the thin body and sent it spinning into a nearby wall. Morgen heard its spine snap with the kick and the *pock* of its skull cracking as it hit the brick wall. The cat dropped and lay motionless.

Wichtig continued down the winding filth-strewn street as if unaware of what he had done. As if it were a small violence beneath notice.

Morgen approached the cat and stared down at the forlorn body. Only the faintest spark of life remained in the broken creature. *Do cats have an Afterdeath?* If not, were there no cats in the Afterdeath? It seemed a strange and sad thought, to imagine a place without the effortless companionship of animals. Did the Afterdeath require a belief in the Afterdeath, or was it just there? Did people who didn't believe still awaken in the beyond, or was this the end for them? Morgen thought about the cat's short and brutal life and pointless death at the whim of an annoyed . . . child.

*And that's what Wichtig is,* Morgen realized: a bratty child enraged at having something he desired moved beyond his grasp. Wichtig wanted to kill the Swordswoman and sulked because he'd been denied the chance.

When Morgen was younger, Aufschlag had gently chided him for such behavior and he had long outgrown such childishness. Why hadn't Wichtig? Had no one thought to teach the Swordsman how grown-ups were supposed to act? Was this a fault of Wichtig's, or did the blame lay elsewhere, perhaps with his parents and friends? *Does no one care enough to teach him how a man should behave?*

He nudged the cat's lifeless body with a toe. "Was your life as meaningless as your death?"

The cat's dwindling soul offered no reply other than its stubborn unwillingness to flee the shattered body.

How much pointless violence and death could a god witness before acting?

Morgen's world narrowed to a pinpoint of focus. Sounds dulled and the street became a mottled blur. The cat became his universe. Could he do this, could he bring this tenuous soul back from beyond? How much faith did the people of Selbsthass have in him? Did they believe him capable of returning the dead to life?

His limits had never been tested. Aufschlag forbade it. But why?

*I need to know my limits.* If just to crush the growing doubts.

He forced his will upon the cat's cooling flesh. The bent little body twitched. *I knew it!* His followers' faith was a deep well he had barely tapped.

The cat yowled piteously as, spine still bent at an unnatural angle, it pulled itself to its feet. It staggered in a circle, blinking furiously in confusion. The cat collapsed to the ground and lay mewling.

Morgen turned to find a crowd gathered around him. Wichtig stood at the forefront of the mob with a look of both measured contemplation and fear.

"It worked," said Morgen. "I brought the cat back. Let's go back to the men you killed in the Schwarze Beerdigung. I can bring them back too."

<hr />

Though Wichtig had eyes only for the boy, the rest of the crowd stared past Morgen at the yowling cat as it again dragged itself in tight circles.

The boy opened his mouth to speak and Wichtig panicked. He had to silence the child. With one step forward he clipped Morgen's chin with a fast punch. The boy collapsed to the filthy street.

*Some people just aren't built to take a punch.* It was a damn good thing he didn't have Bedeckt's qualms about hitting children. The old goat would have stood watching Morgen shoot his mouth off until everyone in the crowd knew this was the kidnapped Geborene godling. The fact that Bedeckt never would have allowed this to happen—and had specifically told Wichtig to stay out of trouble—was irrelevant.

The crowd made angry and threatening noises at Wichtig's callous treatment of the child. He turned to face them.

"Oh, what? You've never hit someone before?" he asked the gathered people. Poor and dirty, they looked a motley assortment of unimportant souls.

A fat woman in a stained apron stepped forward and waved a rolling pin at him. "What kind of man hits a defenseless child?"

He saw a quick way to end this. Wichtig drew his sword and stabbed the fat woman through the heart. He flicked the blade free of blood and returned it to its sheath before she realized she was dead.

"I think I answered your question," he mused. "Any other questions, or would you all like to piss off now?"

A moment later Wichtig stood alone in the street with an unconscious boy, the corpse of an old woman, and a mewling cat-corpse still staggering in circles.

"Gods damn it all!"

*Do I have to do everything myself?* Wichtig stepped over the boy and stomped on the cat's head.

Scooping up the boy, he headed toward the Ruchlos Arms. Glancing over his shoulder, he saw the cat, skull crushed, drag itself into an alley.

Bedeckt and Stehlen returned to find Wichtig sitting in the Ruchlos Arms' main room, staring into an empty pint mug with a rare look of thoughtful contemplation. Morgen was nowhere to be seen.

*Not good.* Bedeckt waved at the barkeep to bring pints.

Stehlen took a seat on the bench across from the Swordsman so she could watch the door. He didn't seem to notice her. "Gods, look at him," she said to Bedeckt. "He's had his first thought." She poked Bedeckt hard in the ribs. "That or he's eaten some of your cat turd."

Bedeckt, gingerly lowering himself to the bench beside Stehlen, didn't like it. Anything penetrating Wichtig's self-aggrandizing narcissism was worth worrying about. A thoughtful Wichtig could convince himself of any number of stupidities.

"Where's the boy?" Bedeckt asked.

Wichtig looked up, his eyes hooded. "Upstairs."

Stehlen snorted. "The idiot is hiding something. Let me guess: the boy is dead."

Wichtig shot her an angry look. "He's fine."

Bedeckt lifted an eyebrow. "But . . ."

"I had to hit the little bastard." Wichtig raised a hand to ward off further questions. "I had to—he was about to tell everyone who he was!"

"Everyone?" Stehlen glanced pointedly around the inn at the three other patrons, all deep into their cups. "How awful!"

"You took the boy out." Bedeckt wasn't asking.

Wichtig shrugged. It wasn't a denial.

Bedeckt leaned forward and the bench groaned in protest. "You went out looking for Swordsmen and you took the boy."

"Should I have left him here alone?" Wichtig asked sarcastically.

"You should have both stayed here!" Bedeckt roared into Wichtig's face. "I told you to stay out of trouble!"

"You aren't my father. Yours isn't the only game afoot, old man."

"Your father?" Morgen had said Wichtig looked to him as a father figure. Could the boy have the right of it? *No, surely not.* The very idea served only to feed his anger. "Moron! I should kill you!"

Wichtig slid from the bench in one smooth motion and stood, looking down upon Bedeckt with flat gray eyes. "Try it, old man. I am the World's Greatest Swordsman. The boy knows it, and you know what that means."

Bedeckt sat, looking up at the young Swordsman. Morgen had said Bedeckt would die alone, that Wichtig would not be there.

"You'll be dead before you draw those pretty swords," said Stehlen from behind Wichtig. She sounded all too calm.

*How the hells did she get there?* Bedeckt sighed tiredly. *I'm too old for this.*

Perhaps Wichtig wouldn't be present at Bedeckt's death because he himself was already dead. Was this fate, or could it be avoided?

"The boy is unhurt?" Bedeckt asked, trying for fatherly concern mixed with casual curiosity. "No real harm was done?"

The question and tone distracted Wichtig. "He's fine. It wasn't my fault."

Nothing was ever Wichtig's fault. "Then it's no big deal," Bedeckt said.

Stehlen spat in snarling frustration. "I'm going for a walk. If one of you kills the other, I'll kill whoever is still alive." She marched from the room.

Wichtig, eyes wide and innocent, watched her leave before returning to his seat. "Gods help anyone who bumps into her on the street."

Bedeckt nodded in nonchalant agreement but his chest felt tight. The boy had planted dangerous thoughts in Bedeckt's mind. What if he'd done the same for Wichtig? The Swordsman might be a minor Gefahrgeist, but he was easily swayed and manipulated himself. Did Morgen act with intent, or was he unaware of the consequence of his words?

Maybe stealing a would-be god hadn't been the best idea. Had he embroiled them in something deeper than planned? Swallowing his fear and doubt along with the last of his pint, he waved at the barkeep for more ale.

Finally, keeping his voice carefully disinterested, Bedeckt asked, "What did the boy say?"

"He told the crowd he could bring back the dead. Damned lucky I was there to stop him."

"Damned lucky," agreed Bedeckt, choking back the sarcasm.

*The crowd?* Bedeckt took a long drink to buy time to think. "You found the Swordsman you sought? Was it a good fight?"

Wichtig grimaced. "Swordswoman," he corrected. "She ran away."

So no flashy duel to gather a crowd—which meant people had gathered for the boy. No wonder Wichtig was in a foul mood: he didn't get to fight *and* his ego hadn't been stroked by the populace.

"What happened next?"

"Delusional little bastard thinks he can do anything." Wichtig shook his head in disbelief. "It's like he doesn't understand there are consequences."

This, coming from Wichtig, almost wrenched a laugh from Bedeckt and he had to carefully swallow his mouthful of beer to avoid coughing it all over the table. If anyone remained ignorant of the concept of consequences . . .

"What did he do?" Bedeckt asked.

"He brought a damned cat back to life! The damned thing made an awful racket. I crushed its head under my boot, but it wouldn't die." Wichtig drank deeply and shuddered. "Too bad Stehlen wasn't there. She could have killed the entire crowd. No witnesses."

Suddenly Bedeckt remembered Morgen telling him to take Wichtig with him and his stubborn refusal to accept what had been perfectly intelligent advice. Had the boy known what would happen? Bedeckt's mind reeled at the possibilities.

"How did the meeting with your contacts go?" Wichtig asked, interrupting Bedeckt's ruminations.

"Not well. Finding a Mirrorist was easy enough, but when he tried to contact the Geborene Mirrorist, he ran into trouble. Apparently the man is dead. Murdered." Bedeckt growled in frustration. "We'll have to find some other way of sending word to Konig."

"Why not just hire some fool to ride to Selbsthass and deliver our message?" asked Wichtig. "It wouldn't take more than a couple of days."

"And then, after torturing our messenger, Konig would send an army into Neidrig to fetch the boy and kill us."

"Nothing we can't handle. Anyway, they mess with us"— Wichtig drew a finger slowly across his throat—"we kill the boy. Simple and foolproof."

"Right." Well, it was simple at least. "But it would be nice if we didn't lead them directly to us."

"You'll think of something. You always do."

It sounded like a compliment, but Bedeckt saw it for the manipulation it was. *Amazing, the man just never lets up.* "I'm going to check on the boy. We should think about packing up and moving on. Did anyone see you bring the boy back here?"

"No. No one knows we're here."

Bedeckt couldn't tell if Wichtig lied.

# CHAPTER 28

*When faced with a Gefahrgeist, set aside your honesty. Truth will be turned against you. Today's truth will be tomorrow's lie and you will be left questioning your own sanity. This too is manipulation.*

*When faced with a Gefahrgeist, set aside your emotions. Your emotions will be turned against you. Even the Gefahrgeist's most heartfelt apology is manipulation.*

*Unlike other Geisteskranken, Gefahrgeist often wear the mask of sanity. This makes them dangerous. This makes them successful.*

—WAHRHEIT ERTRINKT, PHILOSOPHER

Gehirn awoke to agony and darkness. Her cracked skin wept rivulets of molten fire. She deserved this torture and basked in the all-encompassing pain. The philosophers were wrong: the Afterdeath wasn't a chance at redemption, it was retribution. Punishment.

"I am beyond redemption." Her tongue felt like baked leather.

"Yes, but I am unwilling to let you go." Gehirn heard the wet intake of labored breath. "I *need*."

She recognized the voice and with recognition came understanding. There would be no forgiveness, no release, and no redemption. A single tear leaked from an empty eye socket and burned like boiling oil as it followed the cracked lines of her blistered face.

"You will heal and be as a shiny new toy. I must become a god and you must help me." The smack of fat, glistening lips in anticipation. "You must."

Gehirn asked the only question she could. "Why?"

"Because everyone must love me. Everyone." Gehirn listened to several wheezing breaths. "If everyone loves me—utterly and absolutely—none will ever betray me. And if I never again need, never again rely on the love and support of others, I can never be hurt." She heard Erbrechen's breath catch. "You love me, don't you?"

What was love? Was it being a prisoner, helpless to the desires and expectations of another? The Hassebrand thought of her father and decided yes, this is what love must be. "Yes, I do love you." And it was true, she did love the fat Slaver. "I have no choice." She forced the words out.

"If you had a choice, would you still love me?" Erbrechen asked timidly, his voice quivering with desperation.

She was drowning in his need, crushed by the pressure. "Yes." And now this too was truth.

"Sleep. You must heal and the sun is still high."

Gehirn didn't sleep so much as lose consciousness.

WHEN THE HASSEBRAND opened raw, newly healed eyes, she found Erbrechen standing over her, knees wobbling from the strain. Thick clouds, remnants of Regen's storm, occluded the moon.

"See? I said you'd be like new." Erbrechen's face creased in the measuring look of a hungry baby. "I am reality." He said it like he was somehow responsible for her healing; as if without him, she would be nothing.

"Yes," agreed Gehirn dumbly, staring at her hands. Her fingers bore no calluses and the palms had lost most of their deep-set lines. Though she had never been hairy, she was now completely hairless. She ran a hand across the smooth expanse of bald skull. *No hair, no eyebrows; how surprised I must look now.* Her arms were surprisingly thin, as if her body had burned away much of its excess weight in healing her. Had she finally lost her baby fat? Did she now for the first time look like a grown woman? Her stomach growled.

"I am so hungry," said Gehirn.

Erbrechen grimaced petulantly. "You're hungry? Imagine how *I* feel."

"Sorry."

"Not even a charred bone to gnaw."

Gehirn didn't know what to say. Thousands of lives burned to cinder in an instant of uncontrolled rage and self-hatred. "Sorry."

The Slaver snorted. "I realize you want to be my best friend, but do you have to be my only friend?"

"You did say, 'Burn them all.'"

"Oh, so now it's *my* fault?"

"No. Of course not."

"Right." Erbrechen looked satisfied. "Don't let it happen again."

"And if you again ask me to burn them all?" Gehirn asked.

Small teeth peeked from between chubby lips. "Burn them all. Obviously."

"Obviously," Gehirn agreed.

For the first time since awakening she took a moment to look about. Gone were the hordes of Erbrechen's friends. The surrounding field was ankle-deep in sodden ash. Here and there, surprisingly white fragments of bone poked from the heaped gray slag. Nothing moved and no birds sang. Only a charred husk remained of the litter. Beside Erbrechen lay a long sheet of thick gold cloth streaked with filth. Gehirn recognized it as one of the streaming banners from the litter.

"You covered me," she said, nodding toward the cloth. "You protected me from the sun."

"Of course. You are my only friend." Erbrechen leered and grunted as he collapsed into a sitting position. "I'm going to need more friends. Keep burning them all and I'll think you the jealous type."

Gehirn could only nod.

Erbrechen reached toward her with a soft and heavy hand, grimaced, and allowed it to drop back to his lap with a damp *slap.* "This little setback will slow us substantially. I can barely walk. You're going to have to help me." He stared at the Hassebrand, tiny eyes peering through fat cheeks. "I need you. Now more than ever."

Desperate need gripped Gehirn like a fist. "I will carry you to the next town."

"Agreed!" Erbrechen suddenly frowned, gesturing at the sea of ash. "You knew those walking corpses."

"Schatten Mörder. Cotardist assassins. Servants of Konig Furimmer. I think they came to kill—"

"Me. It makes sense. Somehow your old friend learned of my plans and seeks to stop me."

"I don't think—"

Erbrechen waved Gehirn to silence. "Konig is a small man with small plans." He giggled at his accidental rhyme. "He underestimates me much as he underestimates you. To think some walking corpses could be a threat to us." He snorted. "Had you not burned them, I surely would have won them over."

Gehirn wanted to doubt the Slaver, but couldn't.

Clambering to her feet, Gehirn was surprised how easy moving was now that she'd lost the bulk of her excess weight. The field really was as barren of life as she'd first thought. "Is it just the two of us? Did I burn them *all*?"

Erbrechen, still sitting in the sodden ash, smacked at it with a distracted hand and stared north toward Selbsthass. He ignored her question. "I miss my friends. I miss their belief in me." He looked up at Gehirn. "Are there many towns between here and Selbsthass?"

"A few small towns, no real cities." A thought dawned, and it bothered her. "If Konig knew we were coming, he would have sent more than Cotardist assassins. He could have sent an army of Geisteskranken against us. Dysmorphics, Mehrere, Therianthrope, and all manner of Phobics. He could have crushed us."

"I am not so easily crushed," joked Erbrechen, patting his belly.

"The Schatten Mörder could have come in under cover of darkness and killed both of us."

Erbrechen's eyes widened with comical fear. "No. I have a destiny."

"They were looking for something. Or someone." Gehirn looked down at Erbrechen and knew a moment of disgust quickly suffocated by the Slaver's pathetic need. "Konig sent them to find someone."

"Someone?" Erbrechen sniffed at his filthy hands. "The boy?"

"Morgen," Gehirn whispered.

"Yes, the boy. Of course! The people you chased, they made it back to Selbsthass and took Konig's baby god. I *told* you we moved too slowly!"

Gehirn accepted this as the new truth. Between Regen's storm-covered sky and Erbrechen's viselike grip on her mind, she'd lost all grasp of time. "How long have we traveled together?"

Erbrechen's shrug set his breasts jiggling.

"How long?" The Hassebrand almost managed anger.

"A week? Maybe less. Your insistence on burning everything hasn't exactly sped us along."

"Gods. A week?" She had no idea it had been so long. The three she'd pursued had more than enough time to reach Selbsthass, steal the child, and escape. She remembered the lithe, ugly woman with the violent streak. A shiver of pleasure crept up Gehirn's spine at the thought of finding her. *Is this what real love feels like?* She thought it might be. Pushing her feelings aside, Gehirn focused on what really mattered: Morgen. He could be anywhere by now. But where?

She turned to the Slaver. "If Anomie and her assassins sought Morgen, he isn't in Selbsthass. We're going in the wrong direction."

Erbrechen punched the mud with a chubby fist. "We've lost him? Where would they go?"

Gehirn felt the cool night air on her sweat-soaked skin. "They left a lot of corpses in Gottlos, so I don't think they'd return there."

Tears of infantile frustration streaked Erbrechen's soot-smeared face. "Where, then?" He blinked up at Gehirn. "Where would they take him?"

Looking down at this pathetic worm, Gehirn felt the fire of rage build in her heart. *Burn the slug now. Burn him before he defiles Morgen, everything pure and beautiful in this shite world.*

Erbrechen squeaked. He'd seen something of Gehirn's thoughts. "No. I need you. I love you. You love me. I *need* you." Beady eyes almost disappeared into tearstained cheeks.

The desire died, asphyxiated by Erbrechen's desperate need for worship. The Hassebrand's shoulders slumped in defeat. *Gods, I'm trapped here forever. He'll never let me free.*

"Of course I love you." Gehirn's gut soured with the truth of it.

"You were going to . . ." Erbrechen blinked up at her, his eyes red, looking as if his heart had just broken. "You said you'd love me even if you didn't have to."

It wasn't a question and so she just stared down at him.

"Oh," he said, eyes hardening. "I see." He shook his head in disappointment. "Never mind that . . . for now. Where would they take the boy?" Erbrechen demanded, his good humor gone.

"Somewhere Konig and the Geborene Damonen have little influence." Gehirn pictured a map of the area. She pointed west. "Neidrig."

"Are there towns between here and Neidrig?" Erbrechen asked.

"A few small farming communities."

Erbrechen grumbled with disappointment. "I need more friends. Are there many people in Neidrig?" The Slaver licked his lips with hungry anticipation.

"All the worst kinds. Geisteskranken, Swordsmen, and thieves. It will be dangerous."

"It will be fun. They will want to be my friends." Erbrechen smiled wetly at Gehirn, his small eyes glinting hard and cold. "Don't you agree?"

Of course she did.

THEY TRAVELED BY night, Erbrechen leaning heavily against Gehirn's much-thinned frame.

*I've waited how long for him to touch me and now all I feel is revulsion.* And self-hatred. Knowledge wasn't power, it was punishment. How much happier she'd been in her ignorance. She saw now that her time serving Konig had been the best years of her miserable life.

The Slaver complained continually of the effort and inconvenience of walking but refused to stop and rest. He didn't want to face the first village without Gehirn, who would spend the daylight hours cowering under the remnants of the thick banner they carried. He pressed on, taking as much advantage of the night as he was of Gehirn's strength.

Unaccustomed to having so few people around, Erbrechen kept up a continual flow of chatter.

*Silence,* Gehirn realized, *scares the hells out of him.* It was as if the Slaver feared that those around him would see or understand some failing of his if only they had a moment of peace. In a sense, it was true—when she thought she was dead, a part of her mind had broken free from the power of his delusion.

*Slaver.* When had she started thinking of Erbrechen as the Slaver all the time? It had been impossible before, particularly when standing this close. Had the man's hold on her weakened? Had losing his followers lessened his power?

*Aufschlag could answer that.* Day by day her respect for the self-important little grease bucket grew.

Erbrechen babbled on about the first thing he'd eat when they found civilization.

Gehirn interrupted him. "A town."

"And just in time. My knees feel like jelly and my feet hurt. It will be nice to sleep on a bed. Perhaps share the bed with a few new friends. Oh yes, the sun will rise soon. We'll find you some nice basement to cower in. You'll like that."

"Yes," said Gehirn, pushing Erbrechen to move faster.

"I love you," Erbrechen reminded Gehirn. "And you love me." He wheezed at the pace the Hassebrand set but didn't complain.

The village was a sleepy farm community of perhaps thirty people who had yet to rouse themselves from bed when the two staggered into town. The roosters hadn't called the rising sun and a few dozen chickens wandered between houses in a lethargic hunt for dew worms. Even the town's dog population watched their approach with soporific disinterest. The few people awake at this early hour gathered to stare as Erbrechen and Gehirn stood swaddled in ash-soaked shreds of gold banner.

Never before had Erbrechen felt such utter exhaustion. He was too tired for pretty speeches. Instead he lifted his hands to the sky and screamed "Mine!" at the top of his lungs. As more people heard the commotion and joined the gathering crowd, he screamed again.

"Mine!"

He screamed until he was hoarse. He screamed until he had thirty-some-odd new friends, and then retired to the most lux-urious house the village had to offer. He wanted to send Gehirn to the basement but didn't dare let the Hassebrand stray far from his influence. Instead he had his new friends shutter the bedroom windows and draw tight the curtains. Later, once they brought him several huge platters of food, he asked them to build him a new tented litter. *Damned if I'll walk a step further than I have to.* Finally he summoned the town's mayor, whose room this had once been, to attend him.

"I want the town ready to move at sundown."

The mayor, still wearing the nightclothes he had been sleeping in, stood with his mouth hanging open. "The town? Ready to move?"

*Gods, I'm surrounded by idiots.* "Yes. I want everyone packed and ready to go. Gather all the horses and livestock you can. We will be moving quickly, so don't pack nonessentials like clothing."

"No clothes?"

*This fool will be the first in the pot.* "You don't have to travel naked," explained Erbrechen impatiently. "Just don't bring *extra* clothes. Pack lots of food." He studied the idiot mayor. "And make sure the seat on my new litter is well padded and comfortable."

"Of course." The mayor spun smartly and marched from the room, no doubt excited to be in charge of such arrangements.

Erbrechen glanced to where Gehirn sat huddled under a thick blanket, ignoring him. His chest tightened.

*She said she loved me, that she'd love me even if she had a choice.*

She lied.

*Gods, I'm so alone.*

He bared his teeth at the Hassebrand's back. He didn't need her. He'd show her; she was nothing to him. Her betrayal didn't hurt. *She's disgusting,* he told himself, and this became truth. Erbrechen shivered at the memory of touching the woman. Tall and strong, she was the opposite of everything appealing. *Never again.*

---

When the sun fell below the horizon Gehirn and Erbrechen found the townsfolk gathered outside, awaiting them. Gehirn wore clothes she'd scavenged from the mayor's wardrobe while Erbrechen simply draped crisp new sheets across his copious torso. A makeshift litter, hastily constructed of wood torn from the closest houses, sat in the town center. Mounted atop it was a huge sofa heaped with cushions, all within a billowing tent.

"It lacks the class, style, and size of my previous ride," announced Erbrechen, "but I am well enough pleased."

With help from several of the town's larger men, he clambered to the sofa and collapsed into it with a contented sigh. Gehirn joined him on the litter and sat at his feet.

The Slaver waved at two young girls, a pair of blond sisters, to join him. Their parents beamed with pride at the honor. Only Gehirn averted her gaze, though she couldn't quite manage the disgust she strove for. All emotion had drained from her soul. She felt nothing Erbrechen did not first ask her to feel.

"Oh, come now," chided Erbrechen as a dozen strong men hoisted the new litter into the air. "Don't look so glum, my friend. There will be plenty to burn soon enough."

In an attempt to inspire his followers to set a hard pace, Erbrechen declared the last few people to make it into camp each night would be fodder for his stew. Not only would this keep him well fed, he confided to Gehirn, but also force his flock to stay close.

Gehirn understood: The closer they were, the stronger Erbrechen's grip on their minds. The stronger his grip, the more they believed in him and the stronger he became.

Late in the evening Erbrechen's new friends dragged down an elderly couple who lagged behind and butchered them for the Slaver's stew.

"I should have done this years ago," Erbrechen joked to Gehirn. "I could have been a god already. It's good we found the mayor, he's very good at planning. I doubt *you* could have got an entire town packed and moving so efficiently." He tutted happily. "It's good to have useful friends."

*Is he trying to make me jealous?* Sadly, it worked. She longed to go in search of the mayor and raze him to ash. It would have been nothing. A flicker of will, and hot dusty embers scattering in the wind like dancing fireflies. But Erbrechen wouldn't let her stray from the litter.

The Slaver pushed a hard pace. Unwilling as he was to stop for longer than was required for Gehirn to start a fire and cook a few sad souls, the caravan traveled through the night. When the sun rose, Gehirn crawled onto the rear of the litter and hid under heaped blankets. It was intolerably hot, and even so concealed from the sun, her flesh smoked. After the sun fell she arose, raw and sunburned red, and Erbrechen joked about how tasty she smelled, cooking under the blankets.

Each night she crawled forth, pink and raw, to once again sit at the front of the litter.

The caravan pushed toward Neidrig.

Each night the fire came a little easier and she found it more difficult to stem the torrent of self-hatred and disgust fueling the spark.

No one noticed that she refused to partake of the offered foods. Instead she gathered trampled seeds and bits of root each time the caravan stopped. Someone, she suspected, sought to poison her. Since Erbrechen loved—or at least needed—her, the mayor became her prime suspect. She watched the self-important fool with growing distrust.

On the night Neidrig came into view, the mayor approached Gehirn with a bowl of stew.

"You haven't been eating," he said, holding the bowl forward in offering. "I told Erbrechen and he told me to feed you."

Gehirn glanced up at the Slaver sleeping atop his litter. One of his two pet girls had gone missing yesterday and the remaining sister slept curled under a heavy arm.

She turned to face the mayor. "You'd like that, wouldn't you?"

The man smiled.

*Is he mocking me? I'll burn—*

"You should eat. Erbrechen says so."

"Erbrechen sleeps."

"Still." The mayor held the bowl higher, waving its meaty smell under her nose.

Gehirn looked again to Erbrechen. The Slaver snored with his labored breathing. *If he gets any fatter he'll simply die in his sleep.* The thought gave Gehirn some small sliver of pleasure. She returned her attention to the mayor.

"You show your hand too soon. You cannot replace me." Gehirn gestured to Erbrechen. "He *needs* me. You?" She hissed like oil dancing across a hot skillet. "Merely useful."

"He loves all of us," said the mayor.

The Hassebrand incinerated the pompous mayor and watched soft ashes dance on the breeze.

If Erbrechen noticed the mayor's absence when he awoke, he made no mention of it.

Neidrig loomed close and the Slaver was vibrating like aspic in an earthquake. Small eyes peered greedily with the rapt concentration of a hungry baby seeing food almost within reach of its fat, grasping fingers.

Erbrechen scowled at Gehirn. "We should have been approaching this city with an army of ten thousand. You've really put me in a difficult and dangerous position."

"The Cotardists—"

"Do not let me down again. I need you to be strong. I need you to be in control."

But strength and control were mutually exclusive. Gehirn's power came from her very lack of control. *Every gods-damned fool in all the world knows this!*

She opened her mouth to argue but instead nodded mutely. Erbrechen was right, Gehirn had let him down. Good intentions meant nothing.

ⁱⁱⁱⁱⁱⁱⁱⁱⁱⁱⁱ

Erbrechen watched the Hassebrand mumbling quietly to herself. Though the sun had not yet risen, smoke oozed from the neck and sleeves of the woman's robes. Erbrechen salivated at the smell of cooking human flesh while dreading the moment she finally cracked.

Only Erbrechen's need held the crumbling woman together. He desperately hoped he would find the child before Gehirn's fragile mind burned itself in a massive and all-consuming conflagration.

She'd lied to him. How could she, after all he'd done for her? He'd shared his stew, let her ride on his litter. He'd offered her love, given her the chance to be part of something truly astounding, and she repaid him with lies!

His chest hurt with the pain of betrayal. His heart felt like it was being clawed apart.

And yet he couldn't let go.

Erbrechen rubbed at his face and stared at chubby fingers when they came away damp.

*She only loves me because she has to.*

She'd burn him in an instant; he'd seen it in those cold blue eyes.

*She's dangerous, so very, very dangerous.*

Perhaps that was the appeal.

He watched the Hassebrand through slitted eyes, desperately wanting her love and disgusted with his need. He should send her away but knew he wouldn't. She hated him in a way none of his other friends were even capable of, and that he could not abide.

*She will love me. All must love me!*

# CHAPTER 29

*I did what I had to do. I did what any man would do. The real crime here is not to be found in my actions, but rather in your inability to understand their necessity. These aren't rationalizations, they are the new truth.*

—THE TRIAL OF VERSKLAVEN SCHWACHE, GEFAHRGEIST
PHILOSOPHER (SHORTLY BEFORE HIS ACQUITTAL)

The inn was an assault on Asena's sense of smell. Beer, urine, blood, and sweat waged all-out war for dominance. The wood floorboards were still damp from spilled blood. Masse stood behind her, tasting the air with his sharp tongue. Bär and Stich stood nearby, waiting for her to take the lead. She could tell from Bär's flared nostrils and Stich's excited shiver that they too smelled blood. The innkeeper watched from behind the bar, making no attempt to welcome them to his establishment. Asena chose the table farthest from the stain. She didn't want Masse causing a scene, crawling around on the floor and flicking at the blood with his tongue. She sat and then waved four fingers at the innkeeper.

The man brought four ales with the boredom of someone who delivers drinks to groups of odd strangers as part of his daily existence. It was an act; Asena smelled fear.

When the drinks arrived, Asena gestured at Bär with a flick of a slim finger and he caught the innkeeper's wrist in his massive hand.

"We are looking for a boy," she said. The innkeeper stood frozen in Bär's iron grip. "He has been here." She sniffed at the air by way of explanation. "You would remember this boy."

The innkeeper licked cracked lips, his gaze darting to the bloodstained floor. He squeaked as Bär tightened his fist about the man's thin arm. "A boy was here yesterday with a man claiming to be the Greatest Swordsman in the World."

Asena snorted. "Another one of those."

"Lebendig Durchdachter, the best blade this area has seen in a dozen generations, fled rather than face this man."

"So?"

"The boy said the man is the Greatest Swordsman in the World," said the innkeeper as if it explained everything.

*Interesting. Morgen travels with the Greatest Swordsman in the World.* It didn't matter. It wasn't like she planned to have a sword fight with the man.

"I heard a boy brought a dead cat back to life," said the innkeeper, desperate to gain some respite from Bär's crushing grip. "Must be the same boy."

"You know where this happened?"

Again the innkeeper nodded.

"Tell me."

WHEN ASENA LED her Tiergeist from the Schwarze Beerdigung, they left behind a corpse swollen with poison. When the body was found it would be assumed the unfortunate innkeeper had somehow somehow stumbled across one of the rare poisonous snakes in this area. Closer examination, of which there would likely be none, would have suggested the man fell into an entire pit of vipers.

They followed Asena's nose. Every few yards she stopped, dropping to all fours to sniff at the ground before leading them onward. She found the dead cat, spine and skull crushed, still twitching and dragging itself through a narrow alley. A trail of beggars followed the cat, proclaiming its divinity and protecting it from all who attempted to approach. In the short time she stood watching, a dozen more joined the crowd of worshipers. The cat smelled of Morgen. She found a few drops of the boy's blood nearby and swore vengeance upon all who had done him harm. They left the cat and its followers in the alley and followed the boy's trail. It became difficult, as someone had carried the child for a time, but Asena recognized the scent from the Schwarze Beerdigung: it could only be the World's Greatest Swordsman.

She stopped at the corner of two unnamed streets and turned to Bär, who followed close at her heels. "What would the World's Greatest Swordsman want with Morgen?"

"The boy is power," Bär grunted. "Much as Konig—" He stopped in midsentence, staring past Asena. A low growl rumbled deep in his chest.

With an ear-shattering roar, Bär *twisted*.

# CHAPTER 30

*Solitude is indeed dangerous for a working intelligence. We need
to have around us people who think and speak. When we are alone
for a long time we people the void with phantoms.*

—Guy de Maupassant

Bedeckt limped past Stehlen as she settled their account with
the Ruchlos Arms.

"Don't kill anyone," he whispered, and she shot him an annoyed look.

Wichtig followed close behind, guiding Morgen with a firm
hand on the young lad's shoulder. The boy sported a bruised chin
and a look of hurt betrayal. Wichtig, lost in his own doubtlessly
shallow and self-centered thoughts, was oblivious.

"Are you sorry you hit me?" Morgen asked.

Wichtig grunted a laugh. "Apologies are for people who don't
know they are doing what must be done." He gave Morgen's
shoulder a friendly squeeze.

"Then I'm sorry," said Morgen.

"We can't all be me," said Wichtig.

Bedeckt, focused on his many small pains, was only peripherally aware of their conversation. The street greeted him with the familiar stench of dysentery and poverty. The same wretched air he'd breathed in a dozen city-states. The scent of hopelessness. Watching the soiled earth, he sidestepped a heap of horse droppings swarming with dark flies, fat and wet. Bedeckt heard Wichtig swear as he narrowly avoided the same steaming pile.

~~~~~~~~

Stehlen, having paid the innkeeper, followed Wichtig and the boy. Later, she promised, she would return, take back her hard-earned money, and kill the innkeeper, ensuring he didn't talk about his odd guests. Bedeckt still walked about with that cat-turd face like something bothered him and he couldn't let go of it. *Thinking too much never gets you anywhere and Bedeckt can overthink taking a shite.* The old man was growing soft and sloppy, but she would take care of him. Then, once they sold the boy and collected their loot, perhaps she would kill him for making her worry.

As they stopped at the tavern's entrance, Stehlen's nostrils flared as she took in the street's many scents. Her Kleptic-tuned senses muttered of danger and the need to hide. She looked past Bedeckt as he limped across the street directly toward a group of four people huddled in conversation. She could warn him, but not without giving herself away. She watched as the largest of the four looked up and saw Morgen. When the thunderous roar split the air, she'd already disappeared into the shadows.

~~~~~~~~

"The boy is mine," commanded Asena. "Kill the other two." *Wasn't there a third?* She couldn't remember.

Torn between her need to obey Konig and her desire to talk

to Morgen, she hesitated to *twist*. Bär, Stich, and Masse suffered no such hesitation, the latter two collapsing as reality succumbed to their delusions. Bär moved fastest, and a colossal grizzly bear charged the ugly scarred man who was stopped in the center of the street. Stich, a swarm of glistening black scorpions, and Masse, a writhing knot of vipers, followed. Asena stood rooted, staring at Morgen, unable to decide. Obedience, loyalty, and love vied for dominance.

Bedeckt stopped dead in the middle of the street, startled by the deafening bellow. An enormous bear, towering easily three feet over his own considerable height, charged from across the street.

*A bear? What the hells?*

He swung the ax from its place on his back. It hung surprisingly heavy in his hand.

Behind the bear swarmed a throng of snakes and glistening black insects. He checked over his shoulder; Stehlen was nowhere in sight. Was she still inside? He had no idea. He saw Wichtig draw his swords and step in front of the boy. Bedeckt didn't have time to question what went on in the Swordsman's head. Wichtig's actions would no doubt be self-serving.

The earth shook as the bear charged. *How do you fight snakes and insects?* It didn't matter. One thing at a time.

Bedeckt forgot the weight of the ax.

Asena watched, astounded, as Bär crashed to the ground, his skull split by a thrown ax. He hadn't made it halfway to the man. Such a towering icon of vitality and strength dropped dead in a fraction of a second. It occurred to her they might have underestimated their opponents.

She saw the man with the matching blades—this must be

the Greatest Swordsman in the World—step forward to protect Morgen from the charging Tiergeist assassins. Never for a moment had she thought they might fail at their task, that she might not have to face the choice of killing Morgen or obeying Konig.

Asena stepped forward and then stopped as she caught the scent of sour body odor.

⁙

The snakes and insects—scorpions, Bedeckt could now discern—swarmed unhindered over the still-twitching corpse of the grizzly bear. His ax protruded from the monster's skull, tantalizingly near but far from reach. He found himself thinking back to when they had been attacked by albtraum, to the day he had not abandoned his companions. He'd saved both Stehlen and Wichtig's lives. He thought about Wichtig's endless attempts to manipulate him since.

*To hells with them.*

Bedeckt turned and fled.

⁙

Wichtig saw Bedeckt sprint away as fast as his ancient knees would carry him.

"You goat sticker!" he screamed.

Every nerve and sinew in his body begged to follow. Bedeckt was no fool, and if the bastard fled, there'd be a damned good reason for running.

Morgen stood behind him. They boy would never keep up. *Shite on it, leave him. Run, gods damn it, run!*

*No.*

This wasn't it. His destiny was not to die in this filthy piss-bucket city. Morgen said Wichtig would be the World's Greatest Swordsman. Hadn't he? Wichtig snarled a curse and charged. All he had to do was trust in his destiny.

Morgen watched Wichtig draw his blades and charge forward to confront the approaching snakes and scorpions. He watched the Swordsman go down as hundreds of vipers coiled about his legs and dragged him, screaming and thrashing, to the ground.

What had Wichtig been thinking? Had he meant to protect Morgen? Had he given his life in a selfless act just to buy Morgen time to flee?

Run. He should run. He should run now.

Why wasn't he running?

Because he knew these scorpions and snakes. This was Masse, and Stich! They would never hurt him.

Would they?

Stich, *twisted* into thousands of deadly scorpions, scuttled over the struggling figure and the mass of writhing, biting snakes, and continued toward Morgen.

*I help god-child Ascend. Konig make Stich new leader of Tiergeist.* Scorpions are the ultimate killers. Cold and black.

Stich was a thousand deaths.

Stehlen stood frozen, not even breathing, behind the young woman who had stopped to sniff at the air. *Does she know I'm here?* The girl must be Geisteskranken. But what kind? A Therianthrope like her companions? It made sense.

Bedeckt's sudden and unexpected flight left Stehlen wondering if, perhaps, she too had best flee. Did Bedeckt know something she didn't? The old warrior hadn't reached his decrepit age by being stupid. She saw Wichtig charge forward—only to be dragged down by a mass of snakes—and shuddered. His swords would be of little use. She could run now. Leave Wichtig to his fate. It would be just her and Bedeckt. *Isn't this exactly what you wanted?* Wichtig's cries choked off in a strangled gurgle.

The woman, scanning the street and seeing no threat, moved toward Morgen, and Stehlen followed, quiet as death, hidden knives sliding silently from their sheaths. *Only one person gets to kill Wichtig, and that's me.*

*Or maybe Bedeckt, if he asked nicely enough.*

The scorpions poured over Wichtig and continued toward Morgen, and the boy screamed, an earsplitting noise shredding the air. The woman flinched and covered her ears.

Stehlen ghosted closer.

Wichtig fought, slashing and stabbing, until his arms were pinioned at his sides. He bit and thrashed, clawed and kicked, until even that movement was taken from him. Something dry and scaly slid with sinuous ease around his throat. The world, what little he saw of it between the coils of gods knows how many snakes, turned gray. And then black.

Morgen watched in mounting terror as the swarm of glistening scorpions scampered with an eerie chitinous clicking toward him. Though he didn't understand why, he knew Stich sought to kill him. But something else terrified him more: insects were *filthy*. Aufschlag told him so. Weren't scorpions carrion insects? Fear and disgust scrambled his thoughts into a chaotic jumble.

Bedeckt running away. Stehlen gone. Wichtig buried under a mountain of snakes. *Why didn't I see this?* Was this his death?

Morgen's incoherent screams became one word repeated over and over. "No!"

*This isn't it!* This wasn't how he Ascended. He'd seen it. He'd seen fire. He'd seen Bedeckt wounded and dying. This was not it. The thought helped him focus.

Stich was almost upon him when Morgen screamed, "Don't touch me!"

⸺⸺

Confused, Stich ceased his charge and piled up around Morgen's feet. He was unable to touch the boy, unable to even *want* to touch him.

Morgen pointed a trembling finger at Masse, entangled around the downed Swordsman. "Kill the snakes, they're filthy."

Stich felt the boy's disgust to the core of his soul. He hated Masse. Maybe he always had, he couldn't remember.

As one, the scorpions turned and swarmed the snakes.

⸺⸺

Asena approached Morgen, stepping around the agonized coiling heap of Masse, Stich, and the World's Greatest Swordsman. She understood now why Konig had sought to deafen them. Unsure if she planned to kill the boy, she moved closer. Konig's Gefahrgeist coercion warred with her love of the child. She wanted to obey the Theocrat. She wanted to make him happy, to please him so he might—if not love her as she loved him—at least respect her. No matter what she did, no matter what she sacrificed, Konig wanted more. He was a pit she could never fill, no matter how long she poured herself into it. But she would never give up. She couldn't.

Asena made up her mind. She would bring Morgen back to Selbsthass so he might Ascend among the comfort of friends. Konig wouldn't thank her—he never thanked her—but would perhaps someday come to understand that she did this for him.

"Morgen," she called out. "I've come to take you—"

Stehlen's knife slid effortlessly between the young woman's vertebrae, just below the shoulders. It was the perfect strike, instantly paralyzing. The woman crumpled, face-first, to the ground. Stehlen stepped over her and continued toward Morgen as if nothing had happened. The snakes finally stopped their mad thrashing and the scorpions—those not crushed during the battle—staggered about in confusion. The few surviving snakes fled. She wrenched Bedeckt's ax from the skull of the dead bear as she passed. The damned thing weighed a ton. The old bastard would want it. *Should I give it to him haft or edge first?*

Stehlen glimpsed one of Wichtig's hands protruding from the coil of dead and dying snakes. The hand held no sword. *Idiot.*

Stopping before Morgen, she gestured with the bloody knife. "Is he dead?" She wasn't sure what answer she hoped to hear.

Morgen stomped on a dazed scorpion. The remaining bugs streamed away to the east.

"For now," he said.

Stehlen thought he sounded less than happy about this. She considered putting a comforting arm around the boy but couldn't figure out how to do it.

"We should get off the street," she suggested. "Find a different inn too."

She stooped to grab Wichtig's hand and drag him free of the dead snakes. The Swordsman, covered in bloody welts, his head hanging at an odd angle, was unnaturally still and limp. The glint of one of his swords caught her eye. She thought about asking Morgen to bring it along. Assuming the boy brought Wichtig back, he'd want those blades.

"We had better go," she said.

With a nasty smirk and a grunted effort, she hefted Wichtig over her shoulder. She couldn't carry Bedeckt's silly ax and Wichtig's stupid corpse.

"Carry this," she said, handing the ax to Morgen, and set off down the street.

Dragging the ax behind him, Morgen struggled to catch up. "Where did Bedeckt go?"

"No idea."

▬▬▬▬▬

Unable to move, Anomie watched the feet of her killer and listened to her brief conversation with Morgen. Blood pooled around her head, filling one nostril and making breathing difficult. In moments her right eye sank below the rising blood and halved her vision. She couldn't open her mouth, and soon her other nostril would fill. She felt nothing, not the slowing thump of her heart or the shattered bones and teeth resulting from her headfirst impact with the cobbled road. She was glad she hadn't slain Morgen and even happier she hadn't returned him to Konig's clutches. Knowing it was over, knowing these moments were her last, freed her from Konig's Gefahrgeist grip.

*I regret nothing.*

Blood filled her nostrils, and her vision blurred and narrowed to a graying tunnel. Involuntary shudders racked her body and her lungs fought to draw breath.

▬▬▬▬▬

A swarm of staggering, stumbling scorpions wended their way through the narrow streets of Neidrig. Little more than instinct and Konig's coercion drove the swarm east. People fled before the dazed insects and those too slow to escape were left writhing in the streets to die as their hearts and muscles spasmed and seized.

When Stich managed to pull together enough of his fragmented mind to maintain cohesive thought, he *twisted* back into his human form. He felt small, slow, and stupid. Chunks of memory were missing, entire years gone with the parts of himself lost fighting Masse. Why had he fought his fellow Tiergeist? He remembered moments of loving worship and the need to protect something, but little more.

Stich stood, half his former height, and stared to the eastern horizon.

*Why go east?*

Konig. He remembered the Gefahrgeist Theocrat, fear and worship and hatred. Though he felt he should return to report . . . something . . . he couldn't think what it could be. All he knew for sure was that he had failed something important. Again.

Unable to maintain coherent human thought, Stich once again collapsed, *twisting* back into a much-diminished mound of scorpions. For a few moments the scorpions stayed together, crawling over each other in confusion. Finally, driven by the fading remnants of Stich's self-loathing, they fell to fighting among themselves. After a protracted battle, the few survivors separated and fled in different directions.

## CHAPTER 31

*Take a look at my calf muscles. Is the right one bigger?*

—Unknown Dysmorphic

Wichtig awoke with a great sucking intake of breath, leaving him dizzy. A thronging crowd gathered around him, too many to count. He sat in the street where moments ago . . . what? Memories of creaking ribs and the feeling of the cartilage in his throat being crushed sent shudders coursing through his body. He remembered seeing Bedeckt flee. There was no sign of Stehlen or Morgen. Surely they hadn't left him here.

A scarred man stepped forward, rolling muscled shoulders, to glare at Wichtig. He looked familiar, but Wichtig couldn't place him.

"Didn't take long," the scarred man growled. "Not so great, eh?"

Wichtig looked past the man, frowning as he spotted another familiar face. "As great as ever." He returned his gaze to the man before him. "You look familiar."

"Vollk Urzschluss."

"Name doesn't ring any bells."

Vollk grumbled in annoyance. "Until recently, I was the Greatest Swordsman in Unbrauchbar."

"I killed you." Wichtig scanned the crowd, recognizing more faces, few of which he could put names to. "I killed a lot of you, but surely not this many." He spotted an attractive girl of perhaps eighteen summers and waved her over. "There is no way I killed you," he said with more certainty than he felt.

"I am Geschwister Schlangen, sister to Masse."

"Masse?" Wichtig asked, blinking in confusion.

"The man who killed you."

"No, it was—"

"Snakes," she interrupted. "Masse came to believe he had been possessed by snake spirits after he fell into a pit of vipers as a child. He was bitten many times. We thought it a miracle he survived, but he was different after. He became poisonous. I am . . . was . . . his older sister. We fought over chores and he—" The girl stopped and blinked away tears. "My baby brother . . ."

*This isn't right.* Wichtig took in the street and surrounding buildings. Off in the distance he saw people going about their pointless lives. *This looks so . . . normal.* Except the colors. Everything looked washed out, gray and faded like the vibrancy and life had been sucked from it.

"This is Neidrig. I recognize the smell. I can't be dead. Morgen said I would be the Greatest Swordsman in the World. I have a destiny."

Vollk laughed, a grunted snort. "You are definitely dead. For many, what we do in death mirrors what we did in life." He glared from under dark eyebrows. "No doubt it won't be long before you are chasing the title of Greatest Swordsman in the Afterdeath."

Understanding dawned on Wichtig. After a lifetime of hearing the Warrior's Credo repeated by every half-wit and thug he'd ever met, here he was. "I killed you and now you are mine to command." He laughed. Maybe death wasn't so bad! "My own little army. This should be fun."

"Yes and no. Many of us are here to serve you, but many are gathering to serve the man who killed them." He gestured at the girl. "Her brother, Masse. The man who killed you." Vollk showed foul teeth in a sneer as he pointed at Wichtig. "You are gathered here with *them*. He too will soon pass into the Afterdeath."

"And Bedeckt thought the Afterdeath might be some final chance at redemption!" Wichtig laughed again, this time without humor. It would be no such thing. He knew how this would play out: most of the men he had killed had in turn killed others. They were served by their slain foes much as they served Wichtig and as he would soon be forced to serve Masse. The Afterdeath would be a world of marauding armies, bound by ancient laws to serve one man until the man who had slain that man died his own death at the hands of another. The only free people would be those who hadn't lived and died by the flash of the blade. But with the Afterdeath plagued by wandering gangs led by the worst killers of the living world, how free could anyone be?

He glanced up at Vollk. "Is everyone's Afterdeath like this?"

The warrior grunted, eyebrows furrowing. "How would I know?"

A good point, he had to admit. *How does anyone know anything about the Afterdeath?* He watched the people of Neidrig go about their business, ignoring the gathered warriors; apparently they weren't worthy of note. And no one smiled. *Did anyone in the other Neidrig smile?* He couldn't remember. But these faces looked uniformly wan and miserable. As with the colors, these people looked washed out and gray, devoid of life and vibrancy.

"No redemption here." He lifted a hand and Vollk pulled

him to his feet. Wichtig scanned the ground. His swords were nowhere to be seen. "Dying without a blade in my hand." He chuckled with disgusted chagrin. No doubt Bedeckt—the cowardly goat sticker who abandoned him in his time of need—would find this immensely funny. "At least I have my boots." Wichtig noticed Vollk's fine sword. "So. You serve me, at least until this Masse arrives?"

"Little enough it will matter," muttered Vollk, "as you will serve him."

Why worry now about something happening later? "Excellent. Give me your blade."

# CHAPTER 32

*My hands rebelled, refused to take up the pen; they wanted to be*
*gently nibbled all the time. My eyes rebelled, refused to see the*
*parchment; they wanted to watch the pretty boys. My arse re-*
*belled, it refused to sit at my desk; it wanted to sit in the long grass.*
*At this rate, I'll never finish my next book.*

—Einsam Geschichtenerzähler

Stehlen wandered the streets of Neidrig for an hour, stopping at each tavern to examine its exterior before moving on. There was, she figured, no point in going inside until she found the one he'd be in. She didn't question how she would know, she just knew she would. When a Kleptic wants something, it's damned hard to stop her.

The Verrottung Loch looked about ready to collapse. The windows had been crudely covered with warped boards that appeared to have been scavenged from an ancient shipwreck. The eastern wall bowed dangerously inward and the many holes in the roof leaked thick smoke, catching the lantern light within, turning it into wispy pillars of dusty gold reaching weakly for the sky.

She stood, listening to the voices of the patrons. Small and stupid men argued and discussed their small and stupid lives in desperate tones that rose in threatening volume and then fell away in placating fear. The Verrottung Loch was the bottom of the shite-stained barrel of Neidrig. *Perfect*. Even though she couldn't hear Bedeckt's deep voice, Stehlen knew she had found the place.

Still, she hesitated. She'd have to be careful how she dealt with the old man. Bedeckt could be a frightfully violent drunk. She wasn't worried, she told herself, she simply didn't want to have to hurt him any more than necessary. Stehlen chuckled quietly. *Forming a plan for a simple task like collecting an old drunk?* Bedeckt was rubbing off on her.

A dozen filthy faces turned in her direction as she entered the tavern. Only one man didn't turn and she recognized Bedeckt's broad back. He looked naked without his massive ax.

For a moment, silence.

"Well, hello there, lass." The nearest man leered, leaning forward to waggle shaggy eyebrows in her direction.

Stehlen flared her nostrils and struck him once, shattering his nose and sending his few remaining teeth skittering across the floor like fleeing cockroaches. The man toppled backward off his chair, his head hitting the stone floor with a hollow *thonk*. The rest of the patrons wisely lost interest and returned to the business of drinking themselves to death.

Though Stehlen approached Bedeckt from behind, he still nudged a chair out from under the table for her. Somehow he knew she was there. Sitting across the table from him—an old habit allowing them to watch each other's back—Stehlen waited for Bedeckt to speak. For a long moment he ignored her, staring into the thick clay mug gripped in the scarred remains of his half hand. His whole hand, as ever, left free should he need to draw a weapon.

"You're still alive," Bedeckt slurred into the cup.

"Of course." She waved at the innkeeper to bring her an ale.

"You left us," he muttered accusingly.

"I didn't leave," answered Stehlen, though she'd certainly thought about it.

Bedeckt snorted. "I couldn't see you. Wichtig . . . I looked back. You don't—"

"You didn't notice the Kleptic," she interrupted sarcastically. "How strange."

"—survive that. Dead."

"You did what Wichtig would have done," she said. "Had he been smart enough."

The innkeeper dropped a wood mug on the table before Stehlen and fled to the safety of the kitchen. Stehlen stared at the yellow and black flecks hanging suspended in the ale. Someone had chewed at the cup's rim, leaving it ragged and uneven.

She took a long pull of ale. "This is awful."

Bedeckt finally looked up and, just for a flickering instant, met her eyes. "Keep drinking."

"It gets better?"

"No."

"Great." On a sudden whim she reached a hand across the table and laid it atop Bedeckt's half hand, which still clutched his mug. The hand tensed, but didn't pull away. "Wichtig is with the boy. I found us a new inn. Your stupid ax is there too."

"Wichtig alive?"

"Well, no." Bedeckt seemed to cave in upon himself. "But the boy brought a cat back to life and cats are much smarter than Swordsmen. Wichtig should be easy."

Bedeckt stared at her, mouth hanging open. "But how did you . . ."

"The Therianthropes are dead."

"You killed—"

She spat on the table, interrupting Bedeckt. "No great task." She scowled. "Why is everyone so excited about Wichtig? He was dead before anything interesting happened." She snorted. "I'll never let him live this down."

⸻

Bedeckt gripped the table with his whole hand. The room spun, a slow lilting of the horizon, growing out of what remained of his narrowing peripheral vision.

Why hadn't he retrieved the hand Stehlen still held? He needed it. He couldn't drink with her hand on his, but if he let go of the table he suspected he might slump to the floor. He struggled to form coherent thoughts.

"Dead people don't. Need live. Things down." Well, it was close to what he was trying to say.

"Always the philosopher." Stehlen waved for another mug of ale and the innkeeper brought two. Bedeckt groaned in dismay. She removed her hand after giving his one last squeeze. "Drink up, you need it."

He watched Stehlen slam back six fast pints while he nursed one and tried not to vomit or fall off his chair.

Did she really not care he'd abandoned her, or was this just bluster? He couldn't decide. He couldn't even decide which he preferred. Would he rather she felt hurt at his betrayal, or just see his flight as an eminently reasonable reaction to the circumstances? If she truly didn't care, it meant she had no expectations of him, which would be wise. But it also meant he couldn't expect her to be there for him should he need it.

*If she doesn't care, I can't trust her. Wait, wait, wait.* When had trusting Stehlen ever been an option?

Bedeckt half listened as Stehlen prattled on, bragging about how she'd killed a Therianthrope without the girl ever knowing she'd stood behind her the entire time. Except for those arguments with Wichtig, Bedeckt had never heard her talk so much. Thinking of the young Swordsman stabbed his chest with a pang of guilt that he did his best to crush.

*Damned Gefahrgeist. Pigsticking leeches, each and every one.* They'd cling, hanging and sucking at your soul, and you'd never quite realize their friendly grip was barbed. Knowing Wichtig was a Gefahrgeist didn't help. How could an unsubtle moron be so subtle? Was Wichtig's crass lack of subtlety a subtle ploy?

Bedeckt blinked blearily at Stehlen. "Are you angry I ran?" he asked, interrupting her description of what it felt like to slide a knife so perfectly between vertebrae that it didn't so much as scrape bone.

Her mouth closed midword with a clack of yellow teeth and she stared at him, nostrils flared. "Do you care?"

Bedeckt took a drink to buy time and discovered his mug empty. "I'm empty."

"I feel the same way," she said sadly. "There should be more."

*Is she talking about ale?* He struggled to formulate an intelligent question. "What?"

"Something is missing. You feel it too." She paused and once again rested her hand on his half hand. Her hard fingers caressed the thick ridges of scar, the remnants of his missing fingers. "Would you rather I was angry you left us, or—"

"I thought you'd already fled."

"—would you rather I didn't care?"

Bedeckt willed the room to stop its lazy spin. Why couldn't she answer his damned question? Did she, or did she not, care?

He decided to ignore her questions and try again. "Do you care?"

"Do you want me to?"

"Answer my question!"

"Answer mine!"

"Gods' balls. Forget it." This was worse than talking to Wichtig. He pulled his half hand free.

Stehlen downed the last of her pint, dropped a few coins on the table, and rose to her feet with more than a little wobble.

"Let's go," she said. "We should make sure the boy and the body are behaving."

"You left the boy alone?" Bedeckt demanded, accusing.

Nostrils flared in angry surprise. "And this after you left me on a street full of Therianthropes?"

Had she just answered his earlier question?

"And no," she continued, "I didn't leave him alone. I left him with Wichtig."

Bedeckt tried to stand and found himself sitting on the floor. *How did I get here?*

"Wichtig being dead," he mused from the floor, "it's unlikely he'll get the boy into trouble."

Stehlen offered Bedeckt a hand and pulled him to his feet with surprising ease. "I always said we'd be better off with Wichtig dead."

**OUTSIDE. DARK ALLEY.** Cool air. Rumbling stomach threatening to rebel. World spinning.

Bedeckt caught a whiff of sour body odor. "Stehlen?"

"Yes?" she said from under his right shoulder.

*Thank the gods.* He'd wondered who was supporting him as he weaved through the darkness. "Where are we?"

"In an alley."

Great. "How did we get here?"

"We walked." She laughed, a nasal snort. "Well, I walked. You staggered. With considerable help."

He gave her a squeeze. Damn, she was muscled. "I'm glad you're here."

"Me too."

Bedeckt felt strong hands fumbling at his belt. "Is that you?"

"Yes."

"Good." Or was he just glad it wasn't some stranger in the dark?

His pants dropped and cool air caressed his balls. Then warm fingers. "I think I'm going to vom—"

OUTSIDE. DARK ALLEY. Cool air. Sitting in something tepid and thick. Back against an uneven stone wall. Someone small and warm and strong sat on his lap facing him. Skin. Hot and wet. Slow grinding movement.

Bedeckt slid a hand along a firm flank, over a slim arse, and up to cup small breasts with surprising nipples. A soft groan greeted his actions.

Bad breath. Sour body odor.

"Stehlen?"

"Mm."

"How did I get here?"

"Fell."

Stehlen leaned forward, her chest pressing against his, and nibbled at the scarred remnants of his left ear. He could feel her nipples through his shirt.

"My pants?"

She whispered something into his ear and, grabbing his hands, moved them to her arse. He gave it a tentative squeeze.

What had she said? "Other ear," he suggested.

She shifted and began nibbling on his other ear.

"I meant speak into the other ear."

"Harder."

He gripped her arse more firmly and pulled her roughly against him. So deep. She moaned into his right ear, a soft sound he had never expected to hear from her.

"Pants?" he asked again.

"Ankles," she whispered, her grinding increasing in pace.

Stehlen's movements became increasingly disjointed and less rhythmic. When she orgasmed, her scream briefly deafened Bedeckt's remaining ear. When he came, he didn't care if he never heard again.

Seconds later he wished he could be so lucky.

⸻

Wichtig caressed soft skin. She opened herself to him like a flower opening to greet the morning sun. Payback, much like the girl, was delicious.

And then he lay on a comfortable cot, staring up at Morgen's bright, clean face.

"If," said Morgen, "in the Afterdeath, you have to serve the man who slays you, what must you do for the boy who brings you back?"

Wichtig sat up and scanned the room. This wasn't the Ruchlos Arms. The floor looked clean, free of filth and detritus, and the sheets felt crisp and freshly laundered. *I die and the first thing they do is find a better inn.* He thought about what the boy said and searched his feelings. Nothing. No compunction to serve. Still, no reason to waste an opportunity.

Wichtig set a hand on the boy's shoulder and flashed his best look of honest confession. "It seems," he said, "I am now yours to command." He slid off the bed and gracefully took a knee, bringing his eyes slightly lower than the boy's. He bowed his head in humility. "What would you have me do, My Lord?" He'd have to remember to keep up this deferential act for as long as possible. Who wouldn't trust a servant bound by some magical bonds reaching from beyond the Afterdeath?

"Truly?" Morgen asked, sounding surprised.

Wichtig didn't answer. He merely kept his head bowed. Best not to overdo things. Simplicity was the key to manipulating Morgen. What he didn't say would have more effect than what he did.

"I am unaccustomed to command," admitted the boy. "They should have better prepared me," he murmured. Finally he said, "Rise."

Wichtig rose smoothly to his feet and smiled down at the boy. It was only then his good humor faltered. "Where are my swords?"

"Stehlen left them in the street when she carried you away."

"Stupid ugly bitch!"

"I don't think she—"

"She did it on purpose."

"How could she know—"

"She carried my corpse because she knew you'd bring me back."

"But she couldn't—"

"She left my swords because she knew it would piss me off. Ugly, stinking, snaggletoothed, murderous, lying, stealing, cheating—"

"You should be nicer to Stehlen," Morgen commanded.

Wichtig dipped a quick bow. "Of course. My apologies. I'll try and be nicer." *And then I'll kill her.*

Morgen examined his hands, checking under pristine fingernails. He grimaced in distaste. "Fetch me some water so I can clean up."

Wichtig resisted the urge to smack the boy. A quick glance about the room showed everything perfectly ordered. The rug sat perfectly parallel to the wall and ended exactly at the foot of the bed. The sheets were meticulously folded and tucked tight. Wichtig's boots sat neatly arranged, and cleaner than they'd been when he'd bought them, near the door.

"Did some cleaning?" he asked.

Morgen, frowning at the slightly rumpled sheets of the cot Wichtig had just vacated, nodded.

When Wichtig returned with soap and water, Morgen scrubbed his hands pink and raw. The boy then dried them on a carefully selected piece of towel seemingly no cleaner than the rest.

*What a strange, strange kid.* Those Geborene pricks had no idea what they'd created. No doubt they thought they'd made their perfect little god, but this child was riddled with delusion.

"Much better." Morgen examined his fingernails again with a critical eye. "What was the Afterdeath like?" he asked.

"Much like the Beforedeath. Anger, manipulation, violence, and sex." He watched for the boy's reaction. "And it was filthy."

Morgen paled. "But Bedeckt said it was a chance at redemption."

Wichtig snorted. "Nobody believes that, though, and that's what matters. Right?"

"Everyone is afraid of dying," Morgen said

"Because it is worth fearing. I wasn't there long, but everyone I met died a violent death. It's a world populated by walking corpses forced to serve those who killed them." A slight exaggeration, but a far better story.

"Not everyone dies a violent death."

"Like I said, I wasn't there long. Everyone *I* met was either killed or murdered."

"You are glad to be back?" Morgen asked.

"Eternally grateful. I owe you my life. Literally." Wichtig let out a slow, dramatic breath. "I should abandon my quest to become the World's Greatest Swordsman. Perhaps if I live a more peaceful life, I might die a more peaceful death. And find a more peaceful Afterdeath." He didn't have to fake the shudder. "One not populated by those I have slain."

"You already *are* the Greatest Swordsman in the World."

*Aha!* "I know. But I'm not the *Greatest Swordsman in the World*. It's a title, not a just an achievement. Being the best is meaningless unless everyone knows it."

"Why does that matter?"

Wichtig blinked. Was that the stupidest question he'd ever heard? "What other reason is there ever for doing anything?"

Morgen stared at him for a moment, looking like he was trying to make up his mind about something or think up an even stupider question. Then he shrugged and said, "You won't give it up. You still have a role to play."

*A role to play?* The only part he played was the lead role. The hero. Why did people never see they weren't at the center of things? He resisted the urge to roll his eyes at the boy's solemn face. Well, obviously he wasn't going to give up his quest *now*. Not when he had a would-be godling in his pocket who could bring him back to life every time he got killed. Nothing could stop him. If he wasn't actually unkillable, at least he knew he wouldn't remain dead for long.

Wichtig nodded slowly as if accepting something difficult. "I suppose you're right," he said. "I can't give up now. Not when you need me." He expected Morgen to look happy at this, but instead the boy seemed to deflate. Why did he look sad?

Wichtig tried to change the mood back to something a little more appropriate for someone who had just rejoined the land of the living. "You could have left me there a little longer, though."

Morgen blinked up at at him in confusion. "Why?"

"I was about to bed the sister of the man who killed me. Could there be a more fitting revenge?"

The boy turned away, but not before Wichtig saw his damp and red-rimmed eyes.

"There's always another death," the boy whispered. He stared at his hands.

WHEN STEHLEN AND Bedeckt stumbled in several hours later, Wichtig was glad for the distraction. The boy had become withdrawn and quiet and the Swordsman found himself, as always, to be poor company. Who could he mock and manipulate when alone?

The stench of vomit, urine, and ale wafted over Wichtig and he plugged his nose. "Gods! You two stink to all the lowest hells! I can't believe you went drinking while I lay here dead. What kind of friends are you?"

And then he remembered the sight of Bedeckt fleeing, abandoning him to face the Therianthropes alone. He knew the answer to his question and it hurt. He'd given them so much. Loyalty, honor, and his friendship. They were wretches, so beneath him, undeserving of his many gifts and talents. Still, he knew better than to show he'd been wounded by their betrayal.

Bedeckt wobbled and then caught himself. "Yer a lie?" he slurred.

"A lie? Alive? Yes. No thanks to you, coward."

"Heese nuh coward," Stehlen snarled with drunken defiance. "You a moron."

"How sweet, she's defending you." He would have said more, but he caught Bedeckt's furtive glance in Stehlen's direction. He studied the two as they struggled to maintain both balance and composure. Wrinkled clothes. Stehlen was missing many of the stolen scarves she wore wrapped around her bony wrists. The arse of Bedeckt's breeches was soaked through and he was missing his right boot.

*Oho! I know this disheveled look.*

Wichtig decided to toy with them. It served the selfish bastards right. He couldn't believe Stehlen chose Bedeckt. It beggared the mind.

"You're missing your right boot," Wichtig pointed out.

Bedeckt looked down at his mud-caked foot and beamed happily. "Good. The rye. Thanks t' the boy, still god leff."

Why was he so happy to be missing a boot? "And your pants are soaked."

"Fell," Bedeckt muttered, looking everywhere except at Stehlen.

"No doubt." Wichtig smiled sweetly at Stehlen. This was payback for not bringing his swords. "Better check your pockets," he said to Bedeckt. "I bet you've been robbed."

"Arsehole," she muttered as Bedeckt searched his pockets.

Grimacing, Bedeckt shrugged and lost his balance, collapsing backward onto his arse. "Can't remember how mush anyway."

"I noticed when I . . . awoke . . . I'm missing some funds," Wichtig lied. A safe enough bet that Stehlen rifled through his corpse's pockets. A Kleptic could never pass up such an opportunity. "She's not as powerful as she thinks," he said to keep her off balance and undermine her self-worth. "I always know when she's taken money."

"Liar," she snapped. "You never notice."

"While you two were out rut—"

"Leave them alone," commanded Morgen. "They need each other. This is all they get before—"

"They need?" Wichtig asked, interrupting.

"Before?" Bedeckt asked.

"You don't," Morgen said to Wichtig. "Not when . . ." The boy trailed off to silence.

Wichtig understood. Not when he would be the Greatest Swordsman in the World. Not when he stood with the boy-god he could so easily manipulate.

Again he examined Stehlen. Scrawny and wiry. Rat-nest hair. Yellow teeth and watery yellow eyes. On a good day her breath could drop a bull at a hundred paces. This was definitely not one of her good days. She was filthy and unappealing in every possible way. Why then did he feel such anger at the thought of Bedeckt bedding her? Well, maybe not *bedding*, neither looked like a bed had been involved. Her betrayal stung.

*How could she want Bedeckt more than she wants me?* He was perfect. His body was flawless. He was funny, kind, and giving. He poured so much of himself into his friendships and got nothing in return.

Morgen patted Wichtig's back like the little shite somehow understood what he thought and offered comfort. "It's okay. Just leave them alone."

It stung Wichtig to let this go. To not fully explore the hurt and embarrassment he could inflict upon the two went against his every instinct and desire. But it was more important the child believe he had some hold, some measure of control, over Wichtig.

"As you wish." He ducked a quick nod to Stehlen and Bedeckt, who stared at him in bleary confusion. "Sorry. Being dead is exhausting. I'm going to take a nap."

"I'm glad you're nod dead," said Bedeckt.

"Me too," agreed Wichtig with feeling.

Stehlen spat on the floor at Wichtig's feet. "Not me." When they made flitting eye contact she added, "Not so much."

▬▬▬

The morning sun streamed through the open window and hammered at Bedeckt's eyelids like it desperately needed to reach the back of his skull. His overheating head throbbed with the sluggish beat of his heart. His liver felt like it had surrendered and gotten a head start on the rest of his body in the race to decompose. He sat up slowly, careful not to move too quickly lest his head fall off, and saw the wrinkled, mud-caked toes of his right foot. A grin snuck across his scarred face and fled just as quickly. Thanks to Morgen, he'd moved his stash of coins to the left boot. He glanced around the small room and found himself alone. They'd left him sleeping on the floor where he'd fallen, sprawled in the center of the room.

Other than the mess Bedeckt had made, the room was eerily spotless.

They must have gone in search of breakfast. Bedeckt's stomach threatened violent upheaval at the thought of food.

Only flashes of memory remained of the previous night. Unfortunately, those glimpses were all of things he didn't want to remember. They'd rutted in an alley like drunken teenagers. *Gods, she might be pregnant!* The thought swept away the hangover, replacing it with sick fear.

"No," Bedeckt said to the empty room. If belief defined reality, hopefully his desire not to father a child would shape the days to come.

Stehlen, a mother. Wichtig would love it. Suicide was always an option.

Bedeckt leaned forward with a grunt—the scars on his back had stiffened overnight—and dragged his remaining boot off. His emergency stash sat wedged in the hollowed-out heel. A small hoard of coins. He poured them into the palm of his half hand.

"What the hells?" There hadn't been this much gold.

No doubt Stehlen's Kleptic power clouded his memory when it came to how much money he had, but he'd never been overly worried. If she didn't steal it he'd waste it on whores and ale. And when she did take it, he could always rely on her to pay for rooms, food, and drink. But this, finding more gold than there should have been . . .

Bedeckt dimly remembered Wichtig accusing Stehlen of stealing from them. It had been a stupid accusation. Of course she stole from them; she was a Kleptic. Had Stehlen been upset by Wichtig's allegations? Had she felt bad enough enough to return the missing coins with considerable interest? Why now, after all these years? It made no sense. Not unless . . .

"Oh gods, no."

353

Morgen watched Bedeckt gingerly descend the stairs to the inn's main room. Reaching the bottom, the huge man glared about, eyes slitted against the morning sun streaming in through open windows. Bedeckt grimaced when he spotted their table, looked like he contemplated sitting elsewhere, and finally—still wearing a single boot—stomped over to join them. If any of the inn's other patrons noticed anything amiss, they kept it to themselves.

Wichtig bellowed, "Good morning, sunshine!"

Bedeckt collapsed heavily into a chair and scowled at Wichtig. "Where are we?"

"No idea," answered Wichtig. "I was dead when we arrived." He sniffed at the plate of beans and greasy sausage before him. "Food is good, though."

Bedeckt paled, his eyes flinching away from the plate. "Stehlen?" he asked without looking at her.

"Don't know. I was a bit busy keeping an eye on the boy and carrying the World's Greatest Corpse."

Wichtig winked at Morgen.

Bedeckt flagged down the barkeep and ordered a pint of ale. "Who the hells were those people?"

"Therianthropes," Wichtig answered.

Stehlen snorted. "With all the fuss and commotion the moron"—she gestured toward Wichtig with her thin nose—"caused with his little outing the other day . . . I'm guessing it was some locals looking to kill the World's Greatest . . . Moron," she finished lamely.

"I would have gone with idiot. Or imbecile, addlepate, dimwit, dolt, fool, dunce, or simpleton," said Wichtig. "But not moron. Overusing a word reduces its effectiveness."

"Or hammers home a point with repetition," said Stehlen.

"I knew them," admitted Morgen. "Asena."

All three adults stared at him.

354

"Asena?" Bedeckt asked.

"She leads Konig's Tiergeist."

"What are Tiergeist?" Bedeckt asked Morgen.

"Therianthrope assassins. There are also the Schatten Mörder—they're Cotardists."

"Hells," swore Wichtig. "I hate Cotardists. Damned hard to kill dead things."

The more Morgen thought about it, the less sense it made. "You both serve Konig. Why would he send assassins against you?"

"Perhaps he didn't," said Bedeckt. "Konig told us to sneak you out of Selbsthass, but not much more. Perhaps it is the Tiergeist we are to protect you from."

Morgen couldn't believe Asena would ever hurt him, although, thinking back, he *had* thought Stich would kill him. The memory sent cold shivers of fear coursing down his spine. Thoughts of being swarmed by filthy, glistening black scorpions made him want to wash again. He remembered seeing Asena standing across the street, watching as her Tiergeist attacked Bedeckt and Wichtig. In his mind's eye Morgen saw her indecision as she stared back at him. Had she been deciding whether or not she should kill him? *Why would it be a choice, though—why would she want to hurt me?* Back in Selbsthass she'd always been so nice, protective even.

What had Asena called across the street just before Stehlen killed her? Morgen stared into the bar's polished brass rails, replaying the scene in dull reflections.

*Morgen, I've come to take you—* And then she crumpled as Stehlen coalesced behind her. Had Asena come to take him prisoner, or did she think she was rescuing him? She hadn't looked like she intended him harm. She rather looked like she'd made up her mind and a great weight had been lifted from her heart. But if Asena thought taking Morgen away from Bedeckt, Stehlen, and

Wichtig was saving him, what did it mean? Did she believe she could do a better job of protecting him? Did it mean Bedeckt couldn't be trusted?

"Morgen," said Bedeckt, placing a heavy hand on his shoulder. "Stehlen told me those scorpions tried to kill you."

Bedeckt was right. Stich had definitely been intent on killing him. But what about Asena?

Morgen sighed. Nothing but questions. No answers and no way of getting them. Aufschlag would say the clues were all there, but try as he might, he couldn't fit them together. The reflections became, as always, uncooperative when it came to showing the details of his own future; all he ever saw there was flame. Bedeckt's future looked strangely similar. What did it mean? He wasn't sure what Ascension would be like, but surely it would be a spectacle. Would Bedeckt be burned in the flames of Morgen's Ascension?

Stehlen leaned forward, elbows on the table, yellowy eyes bright and wet. "We have to leave Neidrig. I say south, cross the Flussrand River back into Gottlos."

"Gottlos?" said Wichtig, sounding incredulous. "Really? After last time? Remember the temple?"

"Gottlos is a big place," Stehlen said defensively.

Morgen pretended not to listen and kept his attention locked on the bar. Back in Selbsthass, mere days before Bedeckt arrived to take him away, Morgen had overheard a couple of acolytes talking about an attack on a Geborene temple in Gottlos. Was there a connection?

Morgen stifled his frustration. Questions, questions, and more questions. He needed answers.

"Something wrong?" Bedeckt asked.

Wichtig answered before Morgen could decide what to say. "Leave him alone. He needs time to think."

Morgen focused on the bar rail, searching the reflections in its muted luster. *Tell me what I need! Show me my future!*

Shadows and reflections commingled in a twisting web, and through those murky strands he recognized glimpses of Neidrig. But there wasn't just a web; a spider, fat and hungry, presided over it. Morgen saw the faces of children, entangled and wrapped tight, trapped so they might later be sucked dry. The web constricted, choking the city.

He saw nothing of himself.

*Show me!*

The reflections danced and he saw a long dirt road, a thousand small and bloody footprints.

*Are those mine?*

He saw a knife in a small, filthy hand. The knife was Stehlen's, he recognized it immediately. The hand . . . no, it was far too dirty to be his.

Morgen saw a rock at the side of the road and knew that if he really, really tried, he could—just barely—lift it over his head.

*Show me—*

He saw endless fire.

‖‖‖‖‖‖‖

*Odd,* mused Bedeckt. *Why did Wichtig jump to defend Morgen?* The Swordsman had been acting like the boy's personal guardian, obeying his every word. *Damned strange behavior.* Wichtig never did anything unless he saw some angle gaining him an advantage. Bedeckt looked away, glancing at Stehlen to see if she looked as suspicious as he felt. Her face betrayed nothing other than its usual pinched anger. When she noticed his attention she flashed him a quick smile and Bedeckt turned quickly away.

*What the hells is Wichtig up to?*

Bedeckt decided to let it go, but the last thing he wanted was the boy thinking too deeply about what he had seen and heard. Morgen was young, inexperienced and naïve, but certainly not stupid.

Stehlen drummed impatiently on the table. "We're going east?"

"Yes," said Morgen. "Eventually."

"No," said Bedeckt. "We're going west."

"Sorry. Yes, west. I . . ." Looking lost, Morgen trailed off.

"Never mind," said Bedeckt. "It's time to move."

Stehlen cleared her throat noisily. "We don't have any supplies. We left everything at the Ruchlos Arms. Even the horses."

"You left Launisch?" Bedeckt asked, forcing himself to remain calm. His horse was probably fine. Probably still there, right where they'd left him. If not, someone would pay.

"Some of us," said Wichtig softly, "beat a rather unseemly retreat."

"And some of us got killed and had to be carried," snapped Stehlen.

"Perhaps not our most shining moment," Bedeckt admitted. "Though Stehlen did well. She got you out"—he gestured at Wichtig with his half hand—"and saved the boy." When he saw Stehlen practically preening at the compliment, he suppressed a shudder. He'd have to be more careful what he said until whatever this was passed.

"She left my gods-damned swords in the street."

"I should have dropped you to go get them?"

"She probably stole your missing boot," said Wichtig. "Just to get back at you for being a lousy—"

"Wichtig!" Morgen admonished.

The Swordsman's mouth snapped shut. "Fine." He glanced at Bedeckt. "Why did she leave the other boot?"

*Why indeed?* Rather than face the answer, Bedeckt ignored the question. "Stehlen, go get our horses. Try not to kill anyone. I'm going to find some boots." He stared at Stehlen for a moment, wondering whether he should ask. *What the hells?* What did he care what they thought? "Stehlen?"

"Yes?" She stared straight at him, something she rarely did.

"Could you get Launisch a couple of apples?"

She gave a disappointed snort, stood, and left the room without looking back.

"And I'll get myself some new swords," said Wichtig, watching Stehlen's departure with a strange smirk. "Who has money? All mine strangely disappeared shortly after my death."

"No. You stay here with the boy."

"I need swords."

"I'll find you some swords," said Bedeckt uncomfortably.

"You have money?" Wichtig asked. "I need quality blades, not kitchen steel."

Bedeckt's discomfort grew. "I'll get whatever I can find." He leaned forward to push himself out of his chair and stopped. "You were really dead?"

"Yes," answered Wichtig, voice strangely flat.

"There was an Afterdeath?"

Wichtig let out a slow breath and nodded. "It was like—"

"No. I don't want to know."

<hr />

*Coward.* Wichtig, who had only picked at his breakfast, watched as Bedeckt pushed himself to his feet with a grunt, knees popping, and then exited the inn's main doors. *That's right, run away again.*

He shrugged off the foul mood. After all, this was a fine day to be *not* dead. Life offered far too many chances to entertain one's self at the expense of others. Adding those coins to Bedeckt's boot while the old goat lay passed out on the floor may have been Wichtig's greatest prank ever. Bedeckt would assume Stehlen put them there either because she felt guilty for her previous thefts, because she was offering payment for services rendered, or because she had suddenly fallen in love. Wichtig wasn't sure which would be funnier. It didn't matter. It would leave Bedeckt crazy with worry and drive a wedge between him and Stehlen.

Wichtig entertained himself with such thoughts as he returned to their rented room with Morgen in tow.

When Bedeckt returned an hour later, wearing a new boot on his right foot and the same old boot on the left, he offered Wichtig a serviceable pair of blades.

Wichtig grunted his thanks as he tested their balance. "Not bad," he admitted.

Stehlen arrived shortly after, displaying a beautiful pair of matched blades in ornate leather sheaths. She dumped them on the bed dismissively.

"These should do," she said.

Wichtig dropped the blades Bedeckt had brought on the bed and collected the new blades. "Those look familiar."

"I took them from a Swordswoman. Apparently she was supposed to be quite good."

"I thought I asked you not to kill anyone," said Bedeckt. When Stehlen flashed him an apologetic smile he looked away, mumbling to himself.

Wichtig stifled his annoyance. Letting Stehlen know she got to him would gain nothing. He picked up the blades and spun them about in a tight training pattern he hadn't practiced since he'd been in the Geldangelegenheiten palace guard. The blades moved with flawless ease, their balance easily a match to his lost swords. *No, not lost,* he reminded himself. Stehlen left them behind on purpose. He wanted to rekindle his anger, but these new weapons almost made up for the loss.

*Are these blades a peace offering?* No, no. It was more likely she was trying to manipulate him. He almost chuckled out loud. Nobody manipulated Wichtig. If she expected him to be grateful, she was wrong.

Wichtig grunted, discarded the empty sheaths he still wore

strapped across his broad shoulders, and strapped on the new ones. The scabbards were flashier than he liked, but the Swords-woman, he had to admit, had good taste in weapons. Still, it was a shame he hadn't killed her himself.

"Are you finished?" asked Bedeckt. "That was like watching a child get a candy he's always wanted only to find the taste isn't what he'd hoped for

"Be wary of gifts from Kleptics," said Wichtig. "There's always a hidden message." He happily noticed Bedeckt steal a quick glance at Stehlen and then turn away from her answering smile.

Bedeckt gestured in Stehlen's direction without looking at her. "You got our horses?" The old bastard had a weird soft spot for his monstrous war-horse.

"Of course. Got Launisch some apples too. Didn't even kill anyone." She smiled sweetly at Wichtig, batting her lashes. "Other than the Swordswoman."

Bedeckt, ignoring Stehlen, gestured at the rather plain and boring swords still lying on the bed. "What about these?"

"What about them?"

"If I sell them back to the smithy, it'll be at a loss."

"What the hells am I going to do with four swords?"

"Arsehole," said Bedeckt.

Wichtig shrugged and checked Morgen, finding the boy examining his perfectly clean hands. A few days on the road should cure him of his odd compulsions; it was impossible to stay clean while traveling.

"We're riding west to Folgen Sienie," announced Bedeckt, "just across the border into Reichweite. It's a big city-state. It'll be easy to disappear."

"They found us here easily enough," grumbled Stehlen under her breath but loud enough for everyone to hear.

When they left, the swords remained on the bed where Wichtig had dropped them.

Morgen sat in front of Wichtig, sharing the saddle. The Swordsman rode with consummate ease. They wound their way west through the filthy streets of Neidrig. Stehlen and Bedeckt, each on their own horse, led the way while Wichtig followed behind. Morgen watched the filthy people along the street pretend not to follow their slow progress. He could smell them, even the ones he couldn't see, those hidden in the darkest alleyways. He listened to whispers of desperate thought. Cowardice kept the thieves at bay; stories of Wichtig's death and rebirth had spread quickly.

The Swordsman talked in a low voice, keeping up a continual chatter seldom requiring thought or answer from Morgen. Wichtig liked the sound of his own voice, and fair enough, it was a nice voice.

"We're not going to make it to Folgen Sienie, are we?" asked Wichtig, startling Morgen out of his dark thoughts.

Folgen Sienie? Though he didn't know where they would end up, Morgen knew they'd never make it anywhere near that city-state. He remembered the nightmarish visions he'd seen in the tavern in which he'd brought Wichtig back from the Afterdeath. What was that grotesque spider he'd witnessed sucking the life from Neidrig? It felt like a metaphor rather than an actual depiction of reality. Why had his reflections shown him that? Why hadn't they been clearer, like they often had been in the past? Were they hiding something? Why did everything end in pain and flames? *Where did I go wrong?* "I should have left the cat to die. I made the wrong choice." His choice would haunt his friends.

"Probably," said Wichtig, hiding an annoyed look. "The way I see it, it was something you needed to do."

"I ruined Bedeckt's plans."

Wichtig snorted in amusement. "The old goat's plans are always shite. So . . . *are* we going to Folgen Sienie?"

Afraid to answer lest he share something he shouldn't, Morgen stared at the ground, avoiding the Swordsman's eyes. Neidrig was doomed. It was his fault. Why couldn't he have seen it earlier? Another, scarier thought occurred: Who decided when the reflections shared things with him? It certainly didn't feel like he was in control.

"I take it we're supposed to at least head in that direction?" When Morgen nodded, Wichtig continued. "Fine. I'll follow your lead. You let me know what you need me to do."

Wichtig was fishing for information. Should Morgen tell him what he'd seen? No.

"There's no dodging fate," Wichtig whispered into Morgen's ear.

Head down, Morgen stared into scummy brown puddles as they rode through them, the horse's hooves shattering the images he saw mirrored there.

Had Konig lied about Morgen's creation, had he been born to a woman just like everyone else and not brought into being by the united faith of Selbsthass? Morgen lifted the hem of his shirt and stared at the small belly button. He'd read about birthing cords and the connection between mother and child. *Why do I have a belly button?*

A group of children, clad in stained remnants of tattered rags, dashed across the street before the mounted riders. Faces stretched in grins soon to turn to terror, the children played at some indecipherable game. *Strange,* thought Morgen, *how the looks could be so similar.* Should he warn them? If he did, would anyone listen?

He thought not.

# CHAPTER 33

*The delusions of the elder gods gave birth to man, the mad animal.*
*Though we struggled against our legacy of insanity, civilization*
*is anathema to creatures thriving on worship and fear. United, we*
*grew mighty and the gods knew fear. They toppled us from the*
*pinnacle of our achievement, laid us low. The Menschheit Letzte*
*Imperium shall forever be humanity's first and last true empire.*

—Vermächtnis des Wahnsinns

Acceptance and Trepidation stood shoulder to shoulder, watching those within the massive mirror. The reflections huddled, bald heads almost touching, over the reflection of Konig's desk, writing and arguing.

Acceptance watched, tonguing the broken shards of teeth that were always catching at his lips. The eye patch covered the ragged wound Abandonment had left when he tore out his eye, but he wished there was something he could do about the mess Trepidation had made of his mouth kicking his teeth in. He glanced to the Doppel at his side. *I'll have my vengeance.*

"They know something," said Trepidation.

"They will share it with me," said Acceptance, hiding the ruin of his mouth with a hand. Hadn't Aufschlag done much the same? The thought was unpleasant. He'd hated Aufschlag not because he couldn't be trusted, but rather because he had been the closest thing Konig had to a friend. Revealing the scientist's betrayal would truly have been a coup for Abandonment had Acceptance not acted first. "They know the balance of power in this relationship."

"Abandonment's words before they dragged him into the mirror," Trepidation muttered.

Acceptance ignored the Doppel, gesturing to the mirror. "See?"

The reflections turned from the desk to face the Doppels in the room and held up pieces of paper covered in hasty scribbles, the letters and words all backward.

"Gods," muttered Acceptance, "Konig's penmanship is atrocious."

Trepidation, keeping a safe distance from the mirror, squinted at the spidery swirl of reversed letters. "I can't read a thing."

"I have an idea." Acceptance drew out the small mirror he used to examine his ruined face. "I'll read the message in my own mirror. This way the words won't be backward."

He could feel Trepidation's eyes on him as he turned his back on the large mirror and held up a small hand mirror of the sort ladies carried about.

Acceptance stared, mouth hanging open, at his hand mirror. The reflection of the reflections gathered in Konig's mirror all wore eye patches and sported the battered visage he saw daily in his own mirror. They held up a sheet of paper with their own badly written message. Acceptance slammed his mouth shut, hoping Trepidation—somewhere on his blind side—hadn't seen the look of confusion. He tasted blood as ragged teeth tore fresh wounds in tender lips. He craned his neck, looking over his shoulder at the reflections in the big mirror. They looked as they always had, exactly like Konig. Unmarred by the beating Acceptance had suffered. He spun to look at Trepidation, but the Doppel still squinted at Konig's mirror, trying to puzzle out the backward message.

Trepidation glanced at him. "Does your mirror help?"

"Not much," he said, returning his attention to the hand mirror.

The reflection of himself holding the mirror stared at him intensely with a single eye. Behind his reflection, in the reversed mirror image of Konig's mirror, Acceptance's eye-patch-adorned reflections held up a message of their own.

Acceptance read the message: *Konig's reflections plot against you.*

"This is still hard to read," muttered Acceptance, stalling to gather his thoughts.

"I think I can read it," announced Trepidation. "It says the assassins failed. The Schatten Mörder and Tiergeist are dead." He turned to face Acceptance. "Asena is dead."

Acceptance ignored Trepidation and stared at Konig's reflections. *Do they tell the truth? Is Asena dead?* What could they gain from lying? If he reported this to Konig, and it later turned out Asena was alive, Konig would think Acceptance had lied. He shuddered at the thought of suffering another beating.

"Do we tell Konig?" asked Trepidation.

Acceptance put away his hand mirror and walked to Konig's heavy oak desk. He took hold of the chair and dragged it out into the center of the room, leaving lines in the rich carpeting. "I have another idea," he said, and threw the chair into Konig's massive floor-to-ceiling mirror. He had time to see the eyes of Konig's reflections grow wide with terror as, with a deafening crash, the mirror shattered. Snatching up the chair, he wielded it like a war club, pounding first at the fragments clinging stubbornly to the mirror's brass frame, and then systematically reducing the shards on the ground to glinting dust.

Trepidation, eyes wide, watched in terrified silence.

Finally, confident that nothing remained of the mirror or its reflections, Acceptance dropped the chair and stood wheezing. Never before had he exerted himself to such an extent. *Is Konig this out of shape?*

"There," he gasped as he righted the chair and examined it. Though somewhat chipped and scuffed, it seemed undamaged by its mistreatment. "Good chair," he said, collapsing into it.

"There?" Trepidation asked, keeping a safe distance.

"Yes. It's a good thing *we* destroyed the mirror," he said, flashing Trepidation a broken smile. "The reflections tried to escape."

Trepidation frowned at the glinting dust on the floor. "I didn't see—"

"Or did *you* destroy the mirror for no reason?"

"*We* were just in time," agreed Trepidation. "I saw one reach out beyond the frame. It made a grab for you."

"Yes. They knew taking me would weaken Konig." He watched Trepidation through his single narrow eye. "There was no message."

"Of course not. I do hope Asena and Anomie are well."

"Indeed."

The two remained silent for a moment, Acceptance watching as Trepidation looked at everything other than his fellow Doppel.

"You realize what this means," said Trepidation, gesturing at the shattered remains of the mirror. "Konig's Mirrorist powers are growing. His reflections could see what was going on elsewhere." He glanced at Acceptance. "Perhaps they could even see into the future."

"I think if they could, they'd have done something to protect themselves."

*But what if they had?*

# CHAPTER 34

*You can lead a horse to water, but drowning it is surprisingly difficult.*

—HOFFNUNGSLOS

Huddled under her blankets, waiting for the dismal dregs of stained sunlight to slump beneath the horizon, Gehirn smelled Neidrig long before it came into sight. What she first took to be outlying slums turned out simply to be the city. Even Gottlos—which by Selbsthass standards was the kind of place you hurried through in order to get somewhere interesting—seemed like a glistening jewel in comparison. With some longing, the Hassebrand thought back to the time when she crossed the Flussrand River into Gottlos, driven by the knowledge that she served her Theocrat. How long ago had that been? A week? It seemed like forever.

Surrounded by the twenty-some-odd townspeople who had survived both the journey and the Slaver's voracious appetite, Erbrechen's litter moved deeper into Neidrig. As they passed decaying hovels, crumbling shanties, collapsing shacks—and the many inhabitants apparently not lucky enough to possess even that much—Erbrechen called out his invitation. The fat Slaver's retinue grew quickly as curiosity brought even more of the city's destitute and downtrodden within range of his voice and influence.

Within the hour more than a thousand people were following Erbrechen's litter, drawn by vague promises and ensnared by his desperate need for worship. The more people who believed in him, the stronger he became and the farther his influence reached. No doubt some fled the city, those few deranged enough to to think they saw the future or smart enough to understand the danger, but the vast majority remained.

Erbrechen's friends set up camp in the center of the city. Gehirn, standing beside the litter, examined the view. This was clearly the most prosperous part of town; most of the buildings retained their roofs and some even had a second floor.

Fearing any building he might enter would collapse under his weight, Erbrechen commanded a score of men and women to construct a large tent—made mostly of stained sheets hastily stitched together and tied to poles, buildings, or anything else handy. One corner was held up by a man Erbrechen told not to move. Though his arms quivered with the strain, he stayed loyally at his post, apparently thankful for the opportunity to serve.

Erbrechen wrinkled his nose and smacked pink lips at Gehirn. "They certainly are a ripe bunch."

"A little fire would cleanse the lot," muttered Gehirn.

"Don't you dare!" Erbrechen commanded with mock outrage.

The Hassebrand scowled and turned to hide the small pouch of seeds and nuts she drew from within her robe. Even with the pompous Mayor dead, someone still sought to poison her. She picked at the seeds, nibbling like a starved bird. Who could it be? Did Konig have agents in Erbrechen's camp?

Erbrechen watched the tall Hassebrand with concern. The woman was growing ever more unstable. *Not that she had ever been particularly sane,* he thought with a small giggle.

The dilemma vexed him greatly. The Hassebrand was frighteningly powerful and thus as useful as she was dangerous. Erbrechen considered sending Gehirn away on some make-work task. Preferably one ending in her death.

And yet he hesitated.

*Once away from me, she'll be susceptible to the influences of others.*

But that wasn't it; he couldn't bring himself to let go of her.

He examined the Hassebrand's hunched shoulders, the glistening dome of her bald skull. Why did it matter so much that she love him?

*Everyone loves me!*

They had to.

*But she wants to!*

And didn't.

With a grumbled sigh Erbrechen folded chubby hands across his gelatinous belly and cast his gaze about for the remaining blond sister. *Where is the damned girl?* She couldn't have gone far without his permission.

"Did we eat the girl in last night's stew?" he called to Gehirn's back, hoping his joke would break her foul mood.

The Hassebrand shrugged without turning. That stung. *Why is she ignoring me?* He gave her a place at the center of his grand design, saved her from burning herself alive, and she repaid him with rudeness. And lies, he reminded himself.

*But I am resilient. Truly kindhearted and forgiving. Already the pain of her betrayal fades.*

Why wouldn't she turn and look at him? Was she angry? What could she possibly be angry about?

Allowing himself to feel something for the woman had been a mistake.

*She's lucky she's useful,* he told himself, *or I'd send her away.*

He giggled and then stopped, annoyed. Where was the damned girl? He needed attention.

"How do we keep losing them?" Erbrechen aimed his question to the gods above. Though there was no answer, he knew someday, someday soon, there would be.

A few hours later, once it became obvious Morgen was not numbered among those who had fallen under Erbrechen's influence, the Slaver sent teams to scour the countryside. Instructed to bring back, unharmed, any young boy they found, these desperate men and women devastated the towns and farming communities surrounding Neidrig. They murdered families in their sleep, stealing young boys and girls away to be dragged back to Erbrechen's tent. Though a few of the groups didn't return, perhaps a result of regaining some sanity once they were free from Erbrechen's direct influence, most did.

In a few hours Erbrechen's army of children outnumbered the adults. He was more than comfortable with this. The young were so malleable, so easy to teach and twist. And those few finding their way into the evening stew were tender and tasty.

EARLY THE NEXT morning word arrived that two men and a woman had fled west with a young boy rumored to have brought a cat and a Swordsman back from the dead. Erbrechen, sure this must be his prey, ordered the the thronging thousands surrounding his makeshift tent to break camp.

As his new friends packed up the few belongings they'd be bringing—mostly food and blankets—others worked to hastily improve his litter. Both Erbrechen and Gehirn rode within its canopied interior as scores of men struggled to manipulate it down the narrow and winding streets of the soon-to-be-abandoned city.

WHEN THE SUN once again fell, Erbrechen's retinue had barely traveled beyond Neidrig's outer slums. After they knocked down a few homes for firewood, the orgy lasted late into the night.

The Hassebrand sat in glum silence at Erbrechen's side, uncommunicative and no fun at all. *Perhaps I should let her roast a few of my more annoying friends.* Fire always seemed to lift her mood. *Yes, perfect idea!* Perhaps then she'd see how giving he was.

Erbrechen leaned toward Gehirn and suddenly became aware of the heat emanating from the woman. He'd thought this a lovely warm evening, but when he noticed how his followers huddled around their campfires, he realized Gehirn kept him warm.

*Better not play with fire,* Erbrechen decided. The Hassebrand was too unstable.

He heard the piteous yowling of a cat. Moments later the answering yowls of a crowd of voices echoed through the vacant streets.

"What in the hells is that?" Erbrechen asked of one of his nearby friends.

"Cult of the Dead Cat," the woman answered, beaming with the opportunity to talk directly to him. "They crawl where the cats crawls, repeat everything it says."

"Are there a lot of them?"

"Hundreds," she answered.

"Why aren't they following *me*? I say things much more interesting than *meow*."

The woman, wearing nothing but a filthy yellow shirt, blinked up at him stupidly.

With a grunt Erbrechen sat back. Why *weren't* they following him? What did the cat have that he didn't?

Flickering orange shadows danced upon the remaining walls in sinuous mimicry of the rutting and writhing of those closest to the raging bonfire.

"There's some cult worshiping a dead cat," Erbrechen told Gehirn, hoping to break her uncomfortable silence. "Imagine," he mused, "if enough people follow it, it might Ascend."

"Am I in the Afterdeath already? Is this punishment?" Gehirn asked as if she hadn't heard him.

*What the hells did* that *mean?* What was going on in this woman's deranged mind? "Is this so bad?" he asked. "Is being with me such a burden?"

Teeth bared in a canine snarl, she spun to face him "Yes! I . . ." Her words trickled to silence as she looked into his eyes. "No. Of course not." She swallowed, turning away. "I'm sorry."

*How could she be unhappy, sitting here right next to me?* It was impossible! "You do love me, right?"

"Yes. Of course."

"And you're happy, right?"

She nodded without speaking.

"Say it aloud," he commanded.

"I'm happy."

She didn't look happy.

"You don't look happy."

Gehirn smiled sweetly, her eyes full of love.

"Better."

# CHAPTER 35

*He said I would never know what tender emotions lurked hidden beneath his fragile sanity. So I peeled him like a grape. He was right. I still don't know.*

—Wahnsinnig Gemahlin, Otraalma

Wichtig talked with Morgen as they rode west, maintaining a continual flow of inane chatter with consummate ease. Though he pretended to be relaxed and jovial, his eyes never stopped scanning the dark forest to the north of the road. The sky overhead was so thick with cloud he couldn't guess the time.

*What the hells is this forest called?* He had no clue, but disliked its look with the instinctive distrust of the city-born. Forests always hid things. Spill blood, and the ground soaked it up in seconds, forever hiding the violence. At least on a city street the blood stayed around for a few days, giving testament to the work done. And forests always seemed to bring out the darkest his soul had to offer. Bad things happened in forests at night. He shuddered as he remembered the night Bedeckt saved their lives when he should have fled.

Of course the memory was somewhat tainted by the much newer memory of Bedeckt abandoning him in the street.

The sky darkened, the world's colors fading to monochromatic. He darted a glance toward Bedeckt, who rode several yards in front, but said nothing. When the sky darkened further and he could barely make out Bedeckt ahead, he finally sighed with exasperation.

"Bedeckt, this is stupid. It'll be dark soon. We should make camp."

"A little further," grunted Bedeckt.

Wichtig didn't want to say what really bothered him. Albtraum. If they waited too long, it would make starting a good fire more difficult. *Damned if I'm skulking about in that damp forest looking for burnable wood in complete darkness.*

Any thought that Wichtig might still owe something to Bedeckt left him uncomfortable. So, a diversion. "The boy is tired," he said, placing a comforting hand on the lad's shoulder. "Hells, I'm tired too."

It didn't work. If Bedeckt heard he showed no sign.

Glancing at Stehlen, Wichtig gave her a worried look, which she returned. As much a product of the city as Wichtig, she understood immediately. She too had reason to fear the gloomy forest.

The Kleptic cleared her throat and spat thickly at the legs of Wichtig's horse, which flattened its ears and uttered a small complaining whinny. "I wouldn't mind stopping either," she said.

"A little further," repeated Bedeckt.

"Don't be an idiot," Stehlen snapped. "We almost died yesterday. One of us *did* die. This is no night to be without a good fire." She flared nostrils at Bedeckt's back. "What do you think seeing the Afterdeath has done for Wichtig's sanity?"

"Me?" Wichtig protested. "I'm fine! I was just thinking of the boy!"

"We could do without visits tonight," said Stehlen.

Bedeckt's shoulders hunched, but he said nothing.

"My sanity is fine," said Wichtig defensively, even though this was exactly what he worried about. "Stehlen is just looking for a little rematch of whatever happened the other—"

"Fine," interrupted Bedeckt. "We'll stop here. You two make camp." He gestured with his half hand. "Out of sight of the road. I'm going to find something to kill." He rode into the forest without another word.

"He meant for dinner, right?" asked Morgen.

"Probably," answered Wichtig.

HALF AN HOUR later they had a good-sized fire and a makeshift lean-to blocking it from sight of the road. Stehlen fussed around with her pack, rearranging whatever stolen trinkets she had stashed in there into a kind of order that would make sense only to the deranged. Wichtig had watched her do this so many times it had long since stopped being worthy of comment or mockery. He was more interested in the boy.

"I saw you watching as we made camp," said Wichtig as he spread his sleeping roll near the fire. "Would you like to learn how?"

Morgen looked doubtful.

"It's easy," Wichtig continued. "I can show you everything; how to make your own char cloth, what kind of tinder to use, and what stones make the best sparks."

"Is it dirty?"

Wichtig held up stained hands. "Most things are," he said with a casual shrug. "These skills keep you alive. I can teach you useful things, like how to skin and prepare game." He chuckled. "Now, *that* is dirty work."

Morgen, still standing, shuddered.

*Perfect!* Crouching near Morgen, Wichtig gave him a reassuring smile. "Don't worry. As long as you have me at your side"—he treated the boy to a grave look—"I will always do your dirty work." Staring into the woods beyond, he said quietly, as if to himself, "People like you need people like me."

"I'm sorry," said Morgen.

Wichtig pretended to look startled. "What? Oh, it's nothing." He flashed a brilliant smile and set about carefully clearing a spot for Morgen's sleeping roll. "You know what they say about the life you save."

The boy looked comically serious. "You are responsible for it. It *belongs* to you."

Wichtig didn't quite like the last part or the way the boy said it, but let it go. Sometimes the lad had a strange way of speaking. He glanced surreptitiously at Stehlen. The Kleptic remained absorbed in reorganizing her pack. Good. With Bedeckt away, this would be Wichtig's best chance. He wished he'd had more time to plan, but knew he wouldn't have done so anyway. He worked best when under pressure, when the slightest mistake could cost everything.

*If Bedeckt had half a clue how clever I am, he'd have killed me years ago. Or put me in charge.* Still, it was entertaining to let Bedeckt think he ran this sorry little troop of thieves.

"Morgen?"

The boy looked up, met his eyes. "Yes?"

"How much did Konig tell you of his plans?"

"Aufschlag, my teacher, told me more than he was supposed to." Morgen gazed sadly into the fire. "I think he felt guilty."

"But they told you that they groomed you to be a god?"

"I was *born* to be a god."

Wichtig accepted the correction without comment. "Do you know why?"

Morgen looked confused. "To serve the people of Selbsthass."

Wichtig let a little doubt show on his face. "You understand what the Geborene Damonen believe, right?"

"Man created the gods, and not the other way around."

"Sure," agreed Wichtig as if he'd known, "but there's more. Though they believe man created the gods, until very recently, they still worshiped those gods. The Geborene were little more than a crazy splinter sect from the Wahnvor Stellung. They worshiped the same gods." He had no idea whether this was strictly true, but figured the lad most likely knew even less than he. In his experience, half-truths sounded more believable than whole truths anyway. He mixed in bits he remembered from Bedeckt's rambling at the bridge. "The Geborene only became a serious religion when Konig took over. Previously they'd been something of a joke. Konig saw the truth."

"The truth?" Morgen asked when Wichtig let the pause grow long.

"The truth: if humanity created the gods, they can create more gods. New gods. He knew if he shaped the beliefs of the people worshiping this new god, he could shape how the god turned out. He understood a god could be *planned*."

Morgen licked his lips thoughtfully. "Makes sense, I suppose."

"Konig may be a powerful Gefahrgeist, but he is not without"—Wichtig did his best to look genuinely apologetic—"faults. Sorry, but I see this more clearly than he did. Don't get me wrong, I could never have started what he did, or had the vision to set things in motion. But I see what he missed."

Eyes wide, Morgen asked, "What did he miss?"

"It's a lot like one of Bedeckt's plans," Wichtig mused philosophically. "The bigger the plan, the longer you think about it . . . the more the plan will go to shite."

"And?"

"At some point the Geborene god will grow beyond the control of those who made it. They could shape it, but nobody can force a god to do something it doesn't want to do."

"It," said Morgen flatly.

"Sorry. You. People can do their best to manipulate you, but no one can force you to do anything. At least not once you're a god. Until then—"

"When I Ascend," said Morgen.

Wichtig hid a flash of annoyance at the interruption. He hated having his flow disturbed. "Right. Until you Ascend you are vulnerable to manipulation." He left the implied "by people other than me" unsaid.

A thought occurred to Wichtig. "How *do* you Ascend?"

Morgen hunched his shoulders as if he were cold. "Aufschlag says I have to die." A burning stick rolled to the edge of the hastily dug pit as the fire shifted, and Morgen gently nudged it with a toe. "I see a lot of fire."

Wichtig hid his confusion, nodding with a concerned frown. "Yeah, I see a lot of fire too." *Right there in front of me,* he thought sarcastically. He changed tack again. "Hey, I just thought of something. Those assassins, the things in Neidrig."

"Tiergeist."

"Do you think they tried to kill you so you'd Ascend?"

Morgen tensed. He nodded once.

"But why?" Wichtig let the question hang. He sat beside Morgen, pretending to stare into the fire in thoughtful contemplation. "Only one thing makes sense: they're afraid you might learn something."

The boy remained silent. Damned annoying. The more people talked, the easier it was to read and manipulate them.

"The question is," Wichtig continued, "did they work on their own, or were they doing Konig's bidding?" He picked up a stick and poked at the fire, using the distraction to check that Stehlen was still consumed with her pack. "What could the Tiergeist hope to gain from forcing your Ascension? No," he said quietly, as if musing more to himself than talking to Morgen. "They must have been following orders. Konig wants you dead. He's afraid you'll learn something, turning you against him." Wichtig placed a comforting hand on the boy's shoulder and felt the lad tense. "Bedeckt is a fool, a brainless moron. But every now and then he says something of such simple wisdom it stuns you. Knowledge is power. Bedeckt told me that. I know," agreed Wichtig to the lad's silence. "You'd never expect such insight from a thoughtless block of wood. What I'm saying is this: you need to learn whatever it is Konig doesn't want you to learn. You must know as much as you possibly can before you Ascend." He paused to look thoughtful. "Have you read much history?" he asked.

Morgen shook his head.

Gods damn, he wished the boy would say something, give him some insight into what was going on in his little skull. Ah, well. *At least the boy isn't well read.* Talking to the well educated was always so much more of a pain in the arse.

"A shame," admitted Wichtig, "because then you'd know all gods have heroes. For each god there is one hero who does the god's bidding here in the mortal world." He shook his head in mock disgust and sighed. "I can't believe Konig didn't tell you this stuff. It isn't right. No, I can't leave this wrong . . ." He couldn't think of the word. ". . . un-righted." Wichtig turned to face the boy, leaning down to look Morgen in the eyes. "I, Wichtig Lügner, the Greatest Swordsman in the World, will be your protector. Your hero for so however long as you need me. This I promise you: you shall live to learn all you need to know before you Ascend. You must learn what Konig seeks to hide from you. Knowledge is power, and truth is a weapon." *What a beautiful sentence! I'll have to remember it for later.* "Truth and my sword. These are the weapons you will need to become the god you must become. Your own god, not the plaything of a Gefahrgeist who doesn't respect you enough to tell you everything. The Geborene don't seek to create a wise god, they want an obedient god, an ignorant god. You don't want to be an ignorant god, do you?"

The lad shook his head.

"Good," said Wichtig. "You are safe at my side."

Stehlen looked up from her pack as if coming out of a trance.

Wichtig smiled his most innocent smile. "No one has stolen anything from you, I trust?"

Her eyes narrowed. "No one steals from me."

⁙

As Wichtig babbled, Morgen watched small figures, little more than oddly shaped sparks, dance and jump in the fire. He saw Konig pounding his fists against a wall of glass, screaming at the Konig beyond. Bedeckt he saw writhing in searing agony. Who was this grotesque spider, hunched, glistening in the center of a web of ravenous need? Glimpses of those he knew flickered teasingly before his eyes. Though he knew not how, he was sure these were visions of a not-so-distant future.

Not until Wichtig finally stopped talking did Morgen realize he hadn't seen the Swordsman in the flames. For all his promises of protection, Wichtig was nowhere to be found.

The flames flickered as if in response to his thoughts, building a scene he recognized. *That's this camp.* Wichtig lay sleeping, wrapped in a thin blanket. *No, he's not sleeping,* Morgen realized, seeing the Swordsman's wide, staring eyes. *He's dead.*

How could this happen? A falling-out with Stehlen? *Should I warn him? Wait, why does his death matter if I can just bring him back?*

381

The answer was obvious: *Because I don't bring him back.*

But why wouldn't he?

*Because I want him dead.*

He stared into the fire, watched as the dancing flames replayed every conversation, every word he'd ever shared with the Swordsman. Everything Wichtig had said contained undercurrents—now, looking back, not even particularly subtle—of manipulation. If Wichtig ever spoke a word of truth, it was an accident.

Morgen's jaw clenched; his fist tightened until the muscles in his thin arms felt like they would pop.

*Wichtig thinks he can use me. Is there anyone in all the world I can trust?*

The flames reached toward him, offering warmth and love. Just like the reflections, they showed the future, told him the truth when no one else would. The fire and reflections, they were one and the same. And they never lied.

Were Aufschlag here, Morgen felt sure the Geborene scientist would have been a source both of comfort and of wisdom. He missed the old man. At times like this he could almost hear what Aufschlag would have said.

Aufschlag's face stared at him from the flames. The scientist's lips moved, and though Morgen heard nothing, he understood.

*Think this through.*

Something Wichtig said bothered him: *Konig wants you dead. He's afraid you'll learn something that will turn you against him.* Was this the only explanation?

In the fire Aufschlag shook his head and then faded from view.

*No,* thought Morgen, *there is another explanation.* He watched Wichtig and Stehlen bicker. Though the Swordsman was relatively clean, at least in a physical sense, Morgen could feel something of the filth lurking in the man's soul. For all Wichtig spoke of trust, he trusted no one. For all he spoke of wisdom, he learned nothing. Every word he uttered was done so with an eye toward manipulation. Wichtig's tongue dripped poison. *He infects me with his lies.*

Stehlen was worse. She was disgusting from head to toe. Her clothes reeked of back-alley garbage, her yellow eyes burned with hatred for everything and everyone—herself included. She'd kill Morgen without hesitation. At least it was something he could trust. She was a thieving murderer and never pretended otherwise. Morgen would have felt a spot of warmth for the Kleptic had he not been terrified of her. Stehlen was easily the most dangerous of his three companions.

Again Morgen came back to the question: *Why would Konig send the Tiergeist to kill me?* Wichtig's assertion that Konig feared Morgen would learn something wasn't the whole truth, but it wasn't completely wrong either. Morgen scowled at the filthy ground beyond his sleeping roll. No matter what he did, no matter how careful he was, he always managed to get dirty again. *There is no escaping contamination.*

The thought stopped him.

Infection. Contamination.

Did Konig fear he would somehow be contaminated by the people he traveled with? But then why would Konig send them to . . .

A rush of fear raced cold fingers tickling down Morgen's spine. He thought back to the many bodies of Viele Sindein, his Mehrere bodyguard. Had the woman died protecting him, not trying to kill him, as Wichtig claimed?

*What are the odds Wichtig told the truth about this and lied about everything else?*

He'd been a fool. Morgen's sheltered life within the confines of the Geborene Damonen church left him ill prepared for dealing with the grime of reality. *Why did no one teach me to ask questions?* Prior to his time with Bedeckt, Wichtig, and Stehlen, he'd had no experience with lies. Now, though, he'd seen enough to know the three continually lied to themselves and each other. Subtext and alternate meanings lurked in everything they said. Few words weren't attempts at obfuscation and distraction. And Morgen was learning from them. He couldn't help it. He listened to their talk. Watched them steal and kill. They soaked through his skin like poison.

*Is it too late?* Was he already infected with their distrust, polluted by their greed, corrupted by the death following them?

Morgen thought back to Konig and life with the Geborene. The High Priest had been a stern taskmaster, but—as far as Morgen knew—he had never lied. And Morgen *never* lied to Konig. Was this part of what Konig sought to create, an honest god?

Morgen felt ill to his stomach. He'd lied when Wichtig had asked if he'd read much history. At the time he'd just wanted Wichtig to leave him alone. The small lie slipped out before he'd even thought about it. It had been easy.

"It's too late," Morgen said aloud. "I've been—"

"What?" interrupted Wichtig. "What's too late?"

"It's too late for me to be still awake," he lied. "I've been tired for ages. I'm going to sleep now."

Morgen crawled into his sleeping roll as Wichtig watched with a contemplative frown. Did the Swordsman suspect? Morgen doubted it; Wichtig was far too self-absorbed to notice someone else's discomfort.

"Sweet dreams," said Wichtig, patting him on the shoulder with an ash-stained hand. If he noticed Morgen's distaste at the contact, he made no mention of it.

Morgen lay curled with his eyes closed, anger twisting his stomach until he thought he would retch. He listened as Wichtig and Stehlen returned to arguing. He'd seen something in the fire as he once again lied to Wichtig. Bedeckt wouldn't return tonight, and Stehlen would slink away to find him. Wichtig would be the only one watching over him.

Morgen understood now why he never saw Wichtig in the future.

Contaminated. Corrupted. Lies.

And soon violence.

Morgen understood. *I must never Ascend.*

The Geborene experiment was a failure.

# CHAPTER 36

*As long as I can remember who I am, I'll be fine.*

—Einsam Geschichtenerzähler

Konig stood at the entrance to his personal chambers, examining the thickly carpeted floor, which sparkled with mirror dust. Within, the two Doppels stood shoulder to shoulder, facing him. Only Acceptance's wounds differentiated him from the other.

"You lie," said Konig, the threat unspoken.

Acceptance, head bowed low, shivered.

"No," said Trepidation. "We do not. We . . . I wouldn't dare."

"What *exactly* did you see in the mirror?" Konig demanded.

"They were escaping," said Trepidation, licking his lips nervously. "They would have replaced us."

Acceptance merely made a small whimpering sound and kept his face lowered.

Konig watched the two carefully. *Was* this a lie? Had something else happened? Nothing but dust remained of the mirror's reflective surface. Could this have been true, could his Mirrorist tendencies have suddenly grown in power? He knew he couldn't trust Acceptance, but surely Trepidation would be too terrified to lie. In the end, he just couldn't chance yet more delusions running amok.

"You." Konig pointed at Trepidation. "Have all the mirrors in the church destroyed. *All* of them. Cover anything reflective. I want no shining brass, no bright knives. Curtain all windows." Konig paced into the room, ignoring the gritty crunch of broken glass beneath his shoes. He stopped before Acceptance. "You," he said to the top of the Doppel's bald head. "Explain to me how my reflections became so powerful, while my Doppels, a much older delusion, seem to have dwindled. Seems unlikely, does it not?"

Acceptance looked up to meet Konig's eyes with his own single bloodshot eye. The Doppel looked beaten and dejected beyond his physical injuries. His clothes hung badly, wrinkled. He smelled like he hadn't bathed in days.

"We are broken," Acceptance said. "When you turned Abandonment and Trepidation against me, you weakened us all. Then, when Abandonment faded away, we were further diminished. We are but a shadow of what we could have been." A little anger crept into the Doppel's voice with the last sentence.

Konig scowled and turned his back contemptuously on the Doppel. "You made your play for power. You failed."

"There was division among your reflections," Acceptance whispered just loud enough to be heard.

Stopping, with his back still turned to the Doppel, Konig asked, "And?"

"They had a message."

"And?"

"Asena and her Tiergeist have the boy."

"Alive?"

"Yes," answered Acceptance. "Asena means to bring the boy home."

"She disobeyed me?"

"As Abandonment would have said, everyone betrays us in the end."

"Me," corrected Konig, distracted. "Everyone betrays *me* in the end." He stood, lost in thought. "If she brings him here, it must be for a reason. Either she fears the boy is not ready to Ascend, or she fears . . ."

He left the thought unfinished. He couldn't say it aloud. If Morgen was sufficiently corrupted by his contact with the outside world, all Konig had worked for was ash. His delusions were growing in number and power. Morgen *had* to Ascend before Konig lost control and was consumed.

Konig's remaining Doppels gathered behind him. He felt their gaze like a weight on his shoulders. Killing Morgen had always been the plan, but he'd intended the boy to die willingly. If Morgen loved or worshiped Konig enough, if he'd believed everything about serving the people of Selbsthass he'd been told, he'd willingly sacrifice himself. A naïve god, desperate to please, had been Konig's goal. Why build a new god to worship when Konig could build a god who'd worship *him*? Love and worship, what differentiated the two? He felt like he should know, but saw no distinction, and as everyone else acted as if there was a difference, it worried him.

*It doesn't matter.*

If the boy had been corrupted, the plan would have to change. He'd still have to die, but afterward he'd serve as a slave and not as a . . . what? Friend?

*You always meant to enslave the god.*

True, but it would be different if the boy was willing.

*Really? How so?*

Konig forced himself to relax, unclenching fists he hadn't noticed making. *I will kill the boy the moment he returns.* He had little choice; hiding from his reflections was at best a temporary measure. Konig remembered the feel of Meineigener's knife sliding into Aufschlag's chest, the gasp of air escaping a torn lung, the slow glazing of his friend's eyes. He swallowed doubt and revulsion.

*Can I do it again?*

The god must serve.

*He's just a boy.*

Konig straightened his shoulders and took a deep breath. He must not show weakness before his Doppels. "We move forward. When Asena returns with the boy we will see to his Ascension." He left the room before his Doppels could answer.

‖‖‖‖‖‖‖‖‖

Acceptance watched Konig leave, noticing the exaggerated set of the shoulders.

"*We* will see to his Ascension," Konig had said. Not I. A small slip, but an important one. *He shies from what he must do. He needs me.*

The man's will wore thin. Little by little the failure of Konig's plans were breaking him. *Soon I will step forward and replace him.*

"A good idea?" asked Trepidation.

"A gamble. He'll wait for Asena to return. He trusts her far more than he trusts us," he muttered vehemently.

"Not entirely unwise," said Trepidation with what almost sounded like humor.

Acceptance studied the Doppel for a moment. "True. By the time he realizes she isn't returning, he will have waited too long. We will make our move."

"We?" Trepidation asked with obvious doubt.

"We. I am no fool—I cannot do this without you."

"And we shall be equals, once we have taken Konig?"

"Don't be foolish."

Trepidation bowed slightly, accepting the admonition without comment. "Konig commanded me to destroy all mirrors."

"And?" asked Acceptance, mirroring Konig's earlier tone.

Trepidation gestured to where Acceptance's mirror remained tucked within his robes. "*All* mirrors."

"I think I shall keep this one," said Acceptance with a tight smile.

Trepidation looked doubtful. "Seeking to use Konig's reflections is unwise. They cannot be trusted."

"We too are Konig—or at least aspects of him. Who is to say we cannot develop our own Mirrorist talents?"

Acceptance saw dawning comprehension on Trepidation's face. How he hated that untouched, unbroken countenance. *Someday I will have my revenge. Someday soon.*

"Your reflections, they told you something." Trepidation, the least socially skilled of the Doppels, made no attempt at hiding his curiosity. "What did you see?"

Acceptance grinned evilly, though he hid the broken teeth and ruined lips behind a shielding hand, his insecurity spoiling the intended effect. "All in good time, my cowardly co-conspirator. All in good time."

# CHAPTER 37

*My sword! Bring me my sword, you cretinous wretches!*

—King Verblassen's last words

Morgen feigned sleep and soon Wichtig and Stehlen broke off their futile argument. It was as if without an audience there was no point. He didn't have to wait long before Stehlen began fidgeting with nervous tension. Sitting quietly at a fire didn't suit her. Wichtig didn't do much better. With no one to impress or manipulate, he sank into a dark depression. Morgen understood: for people like Wichtig and Stehlen, moments of quiet contemplation were anathema.

Through slitted eyes he watched the two, waiting for the moment he knew would come.

Stehlen glared at Wichtig—who ignored her—and spat into the fire. "Where's your sparkling wit now?"

"Probably out searching for your personal hygiene." Wichtig didn't look up from the fire.

Nostrils flared, she seemed to take a moment to consider this.

"You are poor company," she stated as if just discovering she'd invited a boor to a fine social event.

Wichtig finally glanced up, flashing her a sweet smile. "Stop pretending you want to fight with me and go find Bedeckt."

"I doubt he wants company."

Wichtig turned his face back to the fire and Morgen watched the sweet smile transform into a mischievous grin. "Why do you think he hasn't returned? You think he wants to freeze his arse off alone in those woods?" He snorted with mock disgust. "No. He's *waiting* for you."

Stehlen scowled uncertainly. "Liar."

"Suit yourself," said Wichtig, pretending he cared not one whit whether Stehlen believed him.

Morgen watched the Kleptic's innate paranoia wrestle with her desire. Even knowing the outcome, he found it interesting to watch her convince herself she was not doing exactly what she would soon do, and that the doing was all her own idea.

*An important lesson,* he thought. *Trust your fears. When a quiet voice whispers,* You are being used, *listen. Ignore your baser desires.*

Thinking back, he saw that the two most important men in his life, Aufschlag and Konig, never gave in to their more vulgar appetites. Apparently some lessons went unspoken. How many other subtle teachings had he missed?

"I'm going for a walk," announced Stehlen to the night sky. "You bore me."

"Only boring people get bored," said Wichtig to the fire. "Enjoy your *walk*."

"I'm just walking."

"Of course. Enjoy it"

"Arsehole." Stehlen disappeared into the trees without a sound.

Wichtig sat in silence for several minutes, occasionally poking at the fire with the charred tip of a long stick. "I know you're watching me," he said without looking up, and for a moment Morgen thought he'd been caught. "Stehlen, you're a minor Kleptic at best."

No answer came from the forest. Wichtig seemed not to care. Half an hour later the Swordsman tossed the stick into the dwindling fire with a petulant sigh.

"Gods, I am bored," he muttered so quietly Morgen barely heard.

Stehlen, hidden in the woods, slunk away with a victorious smirk. Though he could neither hear nor see her, Morgen knew she was there and sensed her emotion. She would go in search of Bedeckt. Though he hoped they would enjoy the short time left to them, he knew they wouldn't. They were as incapable of taking comfort in each other's company as they were incapable of honesty. *Happiness,* he thought, *is beyond reach for some.* Fate didn't stand in the way. Rather, they themselves were their own worst enemies.

Morgen watched Wichtig grow increasingly restless. The Swordsman briefly entertained himself by having one-sided arguments with imaginary Bedeckts and Stehlens in which he was devastatingly witty (sometimes on the third attempt) and his opponents were stunned by his intellect. After a petulant argument with himself that he somehow managed to lose, though, the Swordsman once again grew despondent and quiet. With a grumbled curse at Bedeckt and Stehlen for leaving him here alone, he finally lay down, curling up in his sleeping roll. Seconds later the man was snoring gently, sleeping the sleep of the innocent. *Or at least of those incapable of feeling guilt,* thought Morgen

When Wichtig's breathing slowed, Morgen crawled from his sleeping roll and slid quietly to Stehlen's pack. He knew what he needed would be there; the dancing flames had shown him.

Wichtig's deep breathing never changed. It took Morgen only seconds to find what he sought. The oiled knife slid free of its sheath with less noise than breath from a snake. Everything about it epitomized Stehlen. A narrow blade, razor sharp and dangerous. The knife glinted in flawless perfection. No tarnish showed anywhere. It felt light in his hand, agile. He'd expected more weight, some heft to something so final.

For several minutes Morgen watched Wichtig breath. Was this really what had to happen? Was he sure?

He wasn't even sure there was a *supposed*. Those glimpses of the future, were they written in stone? It certainly seemed so. He wished Aufschlag had taught him more of the various Geisteskranken powers he would develop. Did the Geborene scientist seek to somehow shield him in ignorance? Or had Aufschlag simply not known . . . or had there been darker reasons?

*Always looking for the concealed truth now, aren't you?* But it made too much sense. He couldn't deny he'd been kept ignorant of things he should likely have known. How different would things have turned out had he known to question? Had he learned distrust sooner, perhaps he wouldn't be here now. He might still be back in Selbsthass with Aufschlag and Konig.

Waiting to die.

Morgen's breath caught. *How blind have I been?* To Ascend, he'd have to die. But no one had ever told him how his death would be achieved.

*Konig wants what's best for the Geborene and for all Selbsthass.* He would have figured out the best, safest way for Morgen to die. Konig would have planned everything to the last detail. Except even that somehow rang false. Aufschlag was the planner, Konig . . . what did Konig actually do?

He glanced again at Wichtig. Questions leading to more questions, and no answers to be found. Morgen craved assurance he made the right choices, but couldn't even be sure there were right choices to be made anymore. What if the reflections merely showed possibilities and the future was chaos? He shuddered at the thought of disorganization on such a colossal scale. Reality should be neat, tidy. It should follow rules.

Unable as he was to see his own future, certainty remained something he could never achieve. Still, some things can never be undone. Murder definitely counted among those things.

Morgen glanced at the dwindling fire. *Are you sure?* he asked. His anger hadn't faded—far from it—but contemplating violence wasn't the same as actually doing it.

Again the flames showed Wichtig's endless manipulations. *He thinks you're an idiot,* the fire seemed to hiss. *He uses you. Everyone uses you.* The fire replayed dimly remembered conversations Morgen had shared with Konig. *He also doesn't love you. He doesn't know how.* Morgen saw Konig awkwardly tussle his hair and the concealed look of distaste as he hugged the boy.

Morgen's heart broke. His breath came in short gasps and he felt strangely dizzy. What was this emotion gripping his heart, strangling every thought, collapsing his vision to a dark tunnel with but a single red ember throbbing at the far end?

He was nothing to Konig and he was nothing to Wichtig. These men thought him little more than a means to an end. Morgen stared at the sleeping Swordsman, tears smearing his vision.

Wichtig. The selfish bastard betrayed his trust, twisted his innocence to his own purpose. *He cares nothing for me.*

Did anyone?

His chest constricted like it was trying to throttle his heart, suffocating rational thought. He'd never felt anything like this before, had nothing to compare it to.

What was this maelstrom of emotion?

Sadness?

No, that wasn't quite right, though there were echoes of despair.

*They're using me, all of them.* He tasted the words in his mind and his teeth clenched so tight his jaw ached. *I feel . . .*

Rage.

The fire sputtered, throwing sparks into the air like spattered blood. The knife felt hot in his hand. Hungry.

Morgen knelt beside Wichtig.

Did this really have to happen the way the fire showed?

It didn't matter.

*I* want this.

━━━━━━

Stehlen found Bedeckt with ease. The old man had made no effort to disguise his tracks, and besides, it was damned difficult to hide something from a Kleptic when she wanted it badly enough. He'd lit his own fire and made himself comfortable. Clearly he had no intention of returning to their camp. *Was Wichtig correct, does Bedeckt wait for me to join him?*

She stayed in the dark, watching. Much like Wichtig, Bedeckt poked at the fire with a stick. She wondered if the need to poke things was some kind of stupid *man* thing. Unlike Wichtig, however, Bedeckt seemed at peace with the solitude and quiet. Stehlen envied his comfort.

"You might as well join me," Bedeckt said without looking up from the fire.

Stehlen stepped from the dark. "How many times have you said that tonight?"

"Dozens."

She snorted. "Why does everyone think I have nothing better to do than spy on them?"

"Maybe we know you."

She squatted by the fire, feet flat, elbows resting comfortably on knees. She could sit like this for hours and knew just watching her made Bedeckt's knees ache. She chose a spot not quite across the fire from Bedeckt. She wanted to see his face.

"It's going to get cold tonight," she said.

Bedeckt grunted.

"We've got a good-sized fire back at the camp." She twitched something between a sneer and a smile. "If the moron hasn't let it go out. Though after the last time he—"

"I'd like to be alone."

"Me too."

Bedeckt gave her a strange look.

"What?" she asked. "I thought we could do it together."

His brows furrowed but he said nothing.

"Be alone, I meant. Not what you . . . unless . . . you wanted to . . ."

"With you and no one else," said Bedeckt, "I think we could be together and alone."

Stehlen felt a rare glow of warmth in her chest. "That's what I thought."

He let out something between and groan and a sigh. *What did that mean?*

"We can sit quietly, right?" he asked.

"Of course. As long as Wichtig isn't here. I tell you, he—"

Bedeckt scowled, his scarred face all scrunched up with the effort.

"Sorry," she said.

They sat in silence for a handful of minutes before Stehlen stood and muttered something about getting more wood. When she returned with an armload of twigs and branches, she sat closer to Bedeckt. When he didn't comment she shuffled closer, saying something about her butt being uncomfortable. When he remained quiet she moved closer until their elbows touched.

Bedeckt finally glanced at her. "I have to piss," he said.

Stehlen watched him disappear into the trees and gave a philosophical shrug. Perhaps he wanted to relieve himself before . . . She smiled wistfully. It'd be nicer here than in some dark, puke-filled alley.

An hour later Bedeckt still hadn't returned.

"Gods damn it!"

Morgen crouched over Wichtig, knife clenched in both hands. Where should he stab the bastard? He had no idea. Wichtig and Stehlen made it look so easy. He thought about the throat. How long did someone take to die from a throat wound? The heart? There seemed like an awful lot of bone in the way. The softness of the guts seemed like an easy target. Lots of important organs, and no bone to get in the way. Morgen raised the knife, focusing on a spot just under the sternum. Surely a central strike would be best.

"What the hells are you doing?" Wichtig drawled, sounding unconcerned.

Morgen drove the knife downward with all his strength.

Bedeckt wandered in the dark until he felt sure Stehlen wasn't following. It was pointless. If she really wanted to trail him, he'd never know. The woman moved like a spider. This time he refrained from lighting a fire. *No point in making it easier for her.* Sure, he'd be cold and miserable, but at least he'd be alone.

Once he'd settled in and the local fauna accepted his presence, the forest noises returned to their normal nighttime level with the tree frogs leading the way.

"You might as well join me," he called to the trees to no effect.

If Stehlen was watching, she remained quiet and hidden. *Perhaps the best I can hope for.*

He sat in the dark, the damp earth slowly soaking the arse of his pants. It was so rare to have the time or quiet to think. The constant bickering of his companions was a distraction. He found himself thinking about Morgen. There was something about the boy Bedeckt couldn't help but like. The lad's innocence was a nice change from the brutal, self-serving violence of Wichtig and Stehlen—hell, of himself, for that matter. The boy listened, feigning attentiveness, when Wichtig blathered on in his never-ending attempts at manipulation. In truth, Bedeckt doubted the Swordsman was even aware of what he did. Instinct and habit drove him more than any directed desire. Wichtig had neither the brains nor the attention span to maintain a plan for longer than it took for the next shiny idea to cross his path.

Morgen, suspected Bedeckt, saw through Wichtig's endless crap. It was like the boy humored the Swordsman rather than hurt his feelings. Bedeckt couldn't think of anyone else who would be so kind.

Bedeckt bent and picked up a nearby stick. He poked at the ground as if working a fire.

He owed the boy a debt. Morgen had saved his life. He'd been dying after they'd taken him from Selbsthass, bleeding out his life from scores of wounds. Stehlen and Wichtig would have left him to die. Sure, they would have raced about, ineffectually trying to save him, but too much damage had been done. Stehlen, ever the pragmatist, would have seen it first. Bedeckt had been teetering on the edge of stepping into the Afterdeath. He remembered seeing his father. A dream?

The boy never talked of saving his life. He'd returned Bedeckt to health and not once made mention of a favor owed. Then Morgen had literally brought Wichtig back from the dead. The lad acted as if the deeds were beneath notice, not worthy of comment. Something he'd done and promptly forgotten about. Much as he wanted to, Bedeckt couldn't forget. He owed the boy his life.

"You might as well join me," Bedeckt again said to the night. Nothing. Either Stehlen hadn't bothered to follow, or chose, for whatever reason, to remain hidden.

Bedeckt chuckled. "There isn't really a plan," he admitted to the dark. "I don't know how to ransom the boy back." He sighed. "I had an idea, but it went to shite when Konig sent his Tiergeist to kill the boy."

*Maybe Wichtig is right. Maybe my plans are all shite.*

"I don't know what I'm doing anymore," he said to the tree frogs as he poked at the damp soil with his stick. "This was supposed to be the end, a last big score to make up for all the colossal failures." He shook his scarred head. "It won't work. If Konig wants the boy dead, who the hells can we sell him to?"

Water dropped from the leaves above and ran trickling down his neck. He shivered and scowled into the caliginous canopy above. He sat up suddenly.

"That's why Konig wants the boy dead. Gods damn it to all the hells, I can't believe I didn't see this before. The boy has to die to Ascend. Konig doesn't have to pay ransom, all he has to do is kill the lad." He thought it through to the only logical end he could see. He felt the tug of old scars as he bared his teeth in a grin. "If Konig wants the boy dead, we keep him alive! We threaten to keep him alive forever. No dead Morgen, no Geborene god. Konig will pay us to kill the lad!"

So simple, so perfect!

And then his shoulders slumped.

*It can't possibly work.*

The more he thought on it, though, the more his confidence returned. Yes, the new plan wasn't without its faults. But he felt he could bring it off. Luckily, his companions would never think to question him.

*You owe Morgen your life. Are you really going to kill him?*

Bedeckt shoved his worries aside. Promising Konig he'd murder Morgen for money didn't mean he actually had to kill the boy. Bedeckt had lied once or twice before.

DAWN FOUND HIM cold and damp and covered in snails. In the dewy morning light he easily followed his tracks back to where Stehlen had joined him, and from there to their original camp.

Launisch and the other horses looked dejected and sodden; their saddles and blankets hadn't been removed from the previous night. Launisch gave Bedeckt a reproachful glare as he entered the clearing. Wichtig still slept, wrapped tight in his sleeping roll, and Stehlen sat crouched nearby on her haunches. The fire had long since gone out and she stared into its soggy remains.

"Gods damn it," growled Bedeckt. "Can't you two idiots think to care for the horses when I'm not around? Do I have to tell you everything?" He gestured at the dead fire. "Thanks again. I was looking forward to a hot breakfast." He noticed Morgen's empty sleeping roll. "Where's Morgen?" he asked Stehlen.

"Gone," she said without looking up.

"Gone? That's bad. We kind of need him. Sort of integral to the whole kidnapping and ransom plan." He scowled at Wichtig's sleeping form. "Wake the idiot up. Let's go looking for the boy. He can't have gone far."

Stehlen finally looked up, her eyes rimmed red with tears. She looked exhausted, like she'd been crying for hours. "Wichtig is dead."

Bedeckt studied the motionless Swordsman. The blanket didn't rise and fall with the intake and exhalation of breath.

"He's not faking?" he asked. "If this is one of his pranks . . . if I check and he attempts to startle me, I'll kill him."

"Dead. Stabbed in the guts. He took hours to bleed out." She snorted and blew a wad of snot from a nostril. "He was wrapped too tightly in his sleeping roll. Couldn't defend himself."

Bedeckt stepped across the dead fire and gave Wichtig a shove with a booted toe. The Swordsman rolled onto his back and stared, eyes unblinking, into the overcast sky. His skin shone pale, glistening with the morning dew. A fly landed on an open eye, pausing to drink from the dampness gathered there.

*Dead like the fire,* thought Bedeckt. His mind, still sluggish, struggled to accept this. "Who?" he asked.

"Morgen," said Stehlen. "No other tracks. Used one of my knives." She shook, her entire body shuddering with jerky spasms. Bedeckt couldn't tell if it was submerged rage or anguish. "He's dead." Somewhere between lamentation and threat.

Bedeckt looked away, uncomfortable with her show of emotion but even more uncomfortable with his own feelings. Wichtig had spent years trying to manipulate Bedeckt, always seeking advantage. And yet . . .

"Stupid bastard," Bedeckt swore under his breath, unsure if he meant Wichtig or Morgen . . . or himself.

"He looked up to you like a father," muttered Stehlen.

"Horse shite. I was just another person he could use."

"Why do you think he stayed with you so long? All the manipulation crap was for his own benefit."

"I know—"

"No," she said, chopping the air with a sharp wave. "Not like that. I mean . . . he needed to *think* he didn't need you. He needed to think he used you. Wichtig lied to himself more than he lied to anyone. He needed you. Your direction. Your guidance." She swore quietly and spat into the ashes. "Your approval."

*Have I lost another friend to pointless violence?*

"No," he said. "You're wrong. Wichtig is a lying, manipulative, self-serving bastard."

"Was," Stehlen corrected angrily.

"You saw how he acted around the boy. I'm guessing he pushed it too far, wasn't as glib and silver-tongued as he thought. Morgen saw through him. Killed him for it."

"He was just a boy," she whispered, and Bedeckt wasn't sure whom she meant.

Stehlen crouched, arms wrapped tightly around her chest, rocking slowly. She made a high-pitched keening.

"We go after him," Bedeckt said.

"We go after him," she agreed.

What they would do once they caught him, he didn't know, but there was definitely a lack of plan without him. "Which way did he go?" he asked.

She pointed east, back toward Neidrig.

Bedeckt opened his mouth to speak and then remembered Morgen saying they'd end up going east. When had he said that? Back in the inn where he'd brought Wichtig back from the Afterdeath? Bedeckt wished he could remember more of what had been said, but the hangover he'd suffered at the time obliterated almost everything.

"You've already been through his stuff?" Bedeckt asked.

Stehlen gave him a disdainful look.

"Did he have much coin?"

She spat into the sludgy ash of the dead fire. "Cretinous turd died a pauper."

No doubt she lied, she couldn't help herself. He didn't care.

Bedeckt thought back to the previous night. *Another plan turned to shite.*

"Fine," he said. "We ride east."

Wichtig sat up in a sudden convulsion and clutched at his guts. Nothing. No stabbing fire. No icy steel. Only the distant memory of pain.

*Hell of a dream,* he thought, kicking aside his sleeping roll and standing. The fire had long gone out and naught remained but damp ash. Morgen, Bedeckt, and Stehlen were nowhere to be seen, their packs and gear gone too.

"They left me here! Took my damned horse too."

No. Something didn't feel right. He stood and gazed east. East. He had to go east.

"Why east?" he asked the gray sky. "We headed west toward Folgen Sienie in Reichweite." And then he remembered asking Morgen if they'd make it to Folgen Sienie and the answering look on the boy's face. "Right. We were never going to make it anyway. So . . . I'm going east."

Wichtig bent to pack his gear and sleeping roll and stopped when he saw the bloodstained sheet. His guts tightened. He looked to the gray sky. He looked to the bent and grizzled trees. No life. No real color. Everything appeared gray, faded.

*Only a true artist,* he told himself, *would notice the difference.*

It helped that he'd been here before.

"I'm dead," he said flatly. "Again."

Die with your boots on, they always say. That which is buried with you or is on your body when you die will be there in the Afterdeath.

Since his last death he'd taken to sleeping with his boots on. This time he was ready. He'd stashed some gold in each boot and slept wearing his swords.

Wichtig pulled off his boots and searched about within. Empty. He stared dumbly into them. Nothing in there but foot odor.

"Oh, Stehlen, you gods-damned bitch." She'd robbed him.

But when?

*Does it matter?*

No. Not really. The last time he had been here, it wasn't like he'd needed money anyway.

He stared east, knowing now why he had to go there.

"And so soon after the last time." He thought he'd have longer. He thought he'd have a *lot* longer. "I'm not finished yet!" he called to the eastern sky. "The boy-god may think he's done with me, but I am not finished with him!"

"Hey, arsehole."

Wichtig spun, startled. A considerable crowd stood gathered behind him, watching and listening. Had he not been so confident he looked great, he'd have been tempted to be embarrassed.

A scarred brute of a man stepped forward, rolling muscled shoulders and glaring at Wichtig. He looked familiar.

"Ah," said Wichtig. "Vollk Urzschluss, we meet again."

"You took even less time than the last time," the scarred man growled. "Still think you're so great?"

"Of course." Wichtig smiled at the crowd of people he'd slain over the years, avoiding the eyes of a few and nodding cockily at others. "We go east to await the death and Ascension of a new god." He felt the need to start moving, a relentless tension, like he'd swum too deep and his ears would soon pop. "We won't have to wait long." He laughed at their doubting faces. "This is not the end of Wichtig Lügner, the Greatest Swordsman in all the World. Oh no," he said, wagging a finger at the crowd. "This is but the beginning, another step down the path to greatness. This is destiny!" Wichtig watched them watch him. They still looked doubtful. "This soon-to-be-god owes me!"

Vollk sneered but didn't have the wit not to look curious. "Why does this god owe you?"

"Two reasons, my dead friend. One, I helped shape him. I made him the boy he is today."

"And?" asked Vollk.

"The little bastard killed me."

Vollk grunted. "Good luck."

Wichtig collected his swords—at least Stehlen had left those—and walked east. Vollk jogged to catch up and walk at his side.

"At least you brought your own swords this time," the scarred warrior muttered, patting the sword hanging at his hip. "I had a hell of a time getting this after you disappeared with my last one."

Wichtig and his army of victims hadn't walked for more than an hour when they saw an even larger mob of people ahead, also heading east.

"Not good," said Wichtig.

The other crowd saw their approach and stopped to wait.

"No point in putting this off, is there?" Wichtig asked without expecting an answer.

"They might kill us," pointed out Vollk.

"But we're already dead."

"In my experience," said Vollk, "there's always more death."

Wichtig grunted.

A large woman stepped out of the crowd and stood waiting. Her hair, hewn short and rough, was a pale orange bordering on strawberry.

"The gods are truly smiling on me today," she said as Wichtig approached.

He stopped before her and bowed low. "You have me at a disadvantage," he said.

"Yes. There are quite a few more of us."

"I meant, rather, that you know me and I don't know you." He looked her up and down. "Though you do look familiar."

"I am Lebendig Durchdachter, the Greatest Swordswoman in Neidrig."

"Ah yes. We almost fought. A shame. Not that we almost

fought, but rather that we *almost* fought. I was looking forward to killing you."

"Your friend did it for you," snarled Lebendig.

"Not for me. A minor quibble, but an important one. She did it to piss me off."

Lebendig gestured at the gathered crowd behind her. Many looked familiar, but Wichtig couldn't put names to the faces.

"We have you outnumbered," she said.

"Yes, as you've mentioned."

She nodded at his swords. "Those are mine."

"Oh."

Wichtig handed the swords over with a philosophical shrug. *Easy come, easy go.*

"Vollk," he said, "it seems I'll be needing your sword again."

# CHAPTER 38

*Sanity. Insanity. Genius. Rampant stupidity. Frankly, I can no longer tell them apart.*

—Fehlende Wahrheit, Geisteskranken Philosopher

The sun crept ever higher in the sky, replacing the damp chill with comfortable warmth and chasing away the thin morning clouds. Birds flew lazy circles overhead, and to the west something larger circled above where they'd left Wichtig's body.

*Idiot, idiot, idiot,* Stehlen cursed over and over. How could the half-wit donkey-sticking fool let himself be killed by a child? *Gods, I hope he's writhing in embarrassment in the Afterdeath.* When she found him, she'd never let him live it down. And once she'd killed the boy and avenged Wichtig, the idiot Swordsman would owe her. She'd lord it over him forever!

Bedeckt, riding in front, looked back over his shoulder. "We should have buried him," he said.

Stehlen snorted and spat noisily. Her horse's ears twitched away from the sound. Wichtig's horse, tethered to her own and

408

following behind, tried to slow but gave up when she turned her gaze on it. "The arsehole is dead," she said. "Don't waste effort on spoiling meat."

Bedeckt grimaced and said nothing.

"Seriously?" she asked. "Wichtig is suddenly more deserving of respect now he's dead? Is that what it takes for you?" She hawked and spat again. "Gods, you're a moron."

Bedeckt, turning away, pretended he hadn't heard. He rested a calming hand on Launisch's neck. The coal-black war-horse's eye rolled as it tried to keep Stehlen in sight.

*Just as well,* she thought. Sometimes the answers weren't worth having.

They rode in awkward silence for several minutes.

"We'll catch Morgen before the day is up," said Stehlen.

"You sure?" asked Bedeckt, scanning the trees. "He could be anywhere."

Stehlen rolled her eyes at Bedeckt's back. "No one hides anything from me. Not when I want it bad enough. And I want this—no one steals from me." When Bedeckt nodded she figured he understood. Wichtig may have been a manipulative arrogant prick, but he was their friend. Morgen would die for killing him. If anyone got to kill Wichtig, it should be her. Morgen took that from her.

"Anyway, he won't go into the forest, he's afraid to get dirty. He'll stick to the road."

Stehlen pushed the pace, driving her horse to take the lead. Bedeckt lagged behind. It was like the old goat—*damn, Wichtig always called him that*—didn't really want to catch the boy. Fine. If he didn't have the stomach for it, she was more than capable of killing the little bastard. She'd do it for Wichtig. She'd do it for Bedeckt. The old man was getting soft.

She slowed to let him catch up.

It was well into the afternoon when Bedeckt finally spotted the boy, a small, shuffling figure several hundred yards down the road. He knew a moment of regret. Why couldn't the lad have walked off into the trees and simply disappeared?

"Stehlen."

"Hmm?" She broke off from glaring at the back of her horse's head.

"There's the boy. Let's do this carefully. Approach slowly, no threat." When she scowled he added, "We don't know what he's capable of."

She said nothing, just stared at him, her yellowy eyes narrow shards of anger.

They spurred their horses into a gentle trot and caught up with Morgen. If the boy heard them, he didn't react. He walked, head bowed, picking flecks of dried blood from his hands and arms. His fingernails were stained with gore. Bedeckt wheeled Launisch around to block the boy's path.

"Morgen," he said gently, dismounting to stand before the boy.

The lad looked up to meet his eyes. "Sorry," he said. "I tried to warn . . ." His eyes red, he glanced about as if searching for something. Nodding toward the side of the road, he said, "There it is."

Bedeckt looked. *Nothing but a bunch of rocks.* "There what is?" he asked.

Morgen waved a hand as if trying to encompass everything. "Sometimes, there's just no knowing. Still, you have to make a choice. At some point you have to decide who—or what—to trust."

Stehlen slid off her horse and stood beside Bedeckt, a hand resting menacingly on the pommel of her sword. "You killed Wichtig, you little bastard."

"I had to. The fire showed me."

Morgen glanced at Bedeckt, his eyes flat. *Gods, Wichtig's eyes looked just like that.* "Fire?" Bedeckt asked.

"He thought he could use me," Morgen snarled with startling vehemence. Never before had Bedeckt heard anger from the boy.

Stehlen shoved Bedeckt aside.

"Can you bring him back?" she asked. Bedeckt saw naked hope on Stehlen's pinched face.

"Yes. But I'm not going to."

Stehlen's sword hissed free of its sheath and glinted in the sun, and Bedeckt wondered if she took as good care of anything else as she did her blades.

"You might want to reconsider," she said with cold calm.

"No."

"I'll kill you."

"You'll try."

Bedeckt watched the meaning of Morgen's words dawn across Stehlen's face like a fire raging through dried leaves. "Shite."

Stehlen moved.

With no time to draw a weapon, Bedeckt slammed into her from the side, his greater weight sending her sprawling in the dirt of the road. "Stehlen—"

She was up before he finished speaking her name. Bedeckt wished he'd spent time getting his ax from where it hung off Launisch's saddle instead of talking.

Stehlen advanced, death in her eyes. "He killed Wichtig," she hissed. "He dies."

Bedeckt stepped between her and the boy. He spoke fast, desperately trying to reason with her, or at least appeal to her greed. "We need him. Like you said, Wichtig is just spoiled meat. This boy will make us rich. But only if he's alive." He saw in her face that he'd said the wrong thing. Because now she no longer looked like she'd kill the boy; she looked like she planned on killing Bedeckt instead.

*Gods. Women. Who could understand them?*

"You bastard!" she spat, pointing the sword at his heart. "His *body* is spoiled meat. Wichtig is still our friend. He's one of us. He died when you ran away." She advanced and Bedeckt retreated before her, keeping the boy behind him.

*Shite, she's still angry about that?* "I didn't kill him. Then *or* now. This isn't my—"

"Coward."

"Coward?" Bedeckt laughed. "How long have you known me? You think running away is on the list of things I won't do? When half a dozen Therianthrope come after you, only an idiot stands his ground."

"The idiot was our friend." She leaped forward, stabbing, and Bedeckt threw himself sideways. He landed hard, crushing the air from his lungs. When he rolled to his feet blood streamed down his side, pouring from a deep gash along his ribs. *Gods, she is fast.* He darted a look toward Launisch and the ax and she laughed evilly. "Forget it, old man."

Bedeckt circled away and she followed, her sword darting and dancing. "I saved your life," he said desperately. "Remember? The albtraum."

"Which is why killing you is going to hurt." She launched another series of blistering attacks, stabbing and slashing.

Bedeckt retreated before the onslaught, ducking and spinning. When she let up, Bedeckt, wheezing, bled from a dozen long wounds. His lungs burned fire. *She's toying with you.* The old murderous rage built within. He fought to strangle it, to bury it deep. He had to reason with her.

"Stehlen," he gasped, "if you kill the boy, the Geborene win. He Ascends and becomes a god. We get nothing. Wichtig's death was for nothing."

She stopped advancing and stared at him with a look of pity. "Moron," she said. "Wichtig's death *was* for nothing. You making money off the boy doesn't give it meaning. And the Geborene . . ." She laughed, a short bark of disgust. "They're as dumb as you are. Those you slay serve in the Afterdeath. That's the rule." The words poured out of her in a torrent. "I kill the boy, he serves *me*. I will be served in the Afterdeath by a god." Her voice cracked into a wet sob. "You think you're the only one with plans? You think I haven't thought this through? This was always the way it would end, from the moment we took him. How could you ever have trusted me? I am a Kleptic, I take. From everyone. No matter how much I love you." Tears streamed freely down her face. "Wichtig's spirit is here now watching, waiting for its vengeance. I will give it to him."

"No, you're wrong," said Morgen from behind Bedeckt. "Wichtig's spirit is—"

"Damn it, shut up!" Bedeckt snapped.

Too late. Stehlen launched herself at Morgen with a snarl, all thought of killing Bedeckt washed away in a tide of hemorrhaging emotion. Bedeckt saw it as if time had slowed to a crawl: her rage made her careless. He sidestepped her charge, slamming the hardened fingers of his half hand into her throat. The force of the blow lifted her feet from the ground, sent her crumpling to the hard dirt of the road. She curled into a tight ball and made a raw choking sound as she fought to suck air past her crushed trachea. Bedeckt stood over her, unsure whether to bend to see if she was all right, or take this opportunity to run and get his ax.

He knelt beside her and rolled her onto her back, ready to defend himself. Her face turned blue, her eyes and tongue bulging. She shuddered with the attempt to draw air past her collapsed windpipe. With clawing fingers she grabbed at his sleeve, supplicating.

Bedeckt laid a calming palm on her forehead. "It's going to be okay," he said. "Morgen, heal her. Quickly. She's dying."

Morgen neither moved nor spoke. He stood watching, eyes wide.

"Gods damn it, child! Heal her. Heal her like you healed me." Bedeckt reached for the boy but the lad backed away.

"This is as I saw it," whispered Morgen. "The reflections didn't lie."

"Heal her!"

"She dies here." Morgen backed farther away. "She'll be waiting for you."

Bedeckt cursed at the boy and turned back to Stehlen. Her spasms weakened, her face and tongue an angry, mottled purple. She grabbed weakly at Bedeckt's sleeve.

"One chance," he said. "One chance." He pushed Stehlen flat and drew one of her small knives from its place of concealment. Her eyes widened with dawning fear. "It's all right," he said softly. "I saw this done once. On the battlefield. A long time ago." He paused with the blade held to her throat, just below where he'd crushed it. *Will this work?* He couldn't remember how it had turned out last time. "Morgen," he asked, desperate. "Will this work?"

Morgen fetched the rock he knew would be there at the side of the road. He hefted it with a grunt of effort and approached Bedeckt from behind. It took two hands and all his strength. He tried desperately not to think of the filth on the bottom of the rock. He tried to ignore the crawling feeling as something slimy and wriggling slipped across his fingers. Everything he'd seen had come true. This too must happen.

"Morgen, will this work?" Bedeckt asked.

He stared at the grizzled warrior's broadly muscled back and hefted the rock above his head. "Yes, and no."

Bedeckt turned and Morgen brought the rock down with all

the force he could muster. There was a sickening crunch and Bedeckt collapsed forward to land on top of Stehlen. She struggled to push him away, but his weight and her weakness made the task impossible.

Morgen stepped forward to where Stehlen could see him over the bulk of Bedeckt sprawled on top of her.

"I'm sorry," he said. She ceased her struggle and glared venomous hatred. "Had you killed me, we would have been the scourge of the Afterdeath. You're not well. You're . . . you're *crazy*. You hate everyone, even the people you love. And you hate yourself most of all." She bubbled saliva, probably trying to spit at him. "But it isn't too late. The Afterdeath is just another life but with different rules. It's a chance to atone, to correct past mistakes.

"There *is* redemption to be found there. If you want it."

Stehlen's yellowy eyes grew dim, unfocused. She reached a supplicating hand toward him as if begging for one last moment of human contact before she passed on to the next world.

Morgen frowned at the filthy hand and ragged, dirt-stained fingernails. Those hands had spilled so much blood over the years.

"No," he said, backing away. "I know you have a knife in your other hand."

She died silently with a strange smile.

When he felt sure she was dead, Morgen gingerly took the knife she'd held concealed; the fires had once again shown him the truth. In many futures she succeeded in killing him when his pity for her drew him near. Those futures were too dark to contemplate. Life beyond death spent in servitude to someone incapable of loving themselves . . . there was no redemption there.

To the west the sun set in a beautiful display of swirling oranges and reds, a soft pastel smear of warmth. The rolling hills of Reichweite beckoned, promising freedom from the future. Morgen turned his back on that promise. It was an illusion anyway.

Bedeckt groaned but didn't otherwise move and Morgen was glad the big man was still alive. The reflections had promised he would be.

"Your head must be harder than stone," Morgen whispered.

His arms ached with unaccustomed effort. His pampered life with the Geborene Damonen had not prepared him for such physical hardships. In truth, they hadn't prepared him for much of anything.

*It's of no matter: my reflections guide me true.*

Morgen put the setting sun behind him. Dark took the eastern sky. There lay fire and pain, slavery, and maybe, just maybe, redemption. Holding Stehlen's blade before his eyes, he stared at the reflections gathered there. "Should I walk, or take one of the horses?" As he watched their pantomimed performance, his shoulders sagged with exhaustion. He would continue on as he must.

MORGEN STUMBLED EAST, leaving Bedeckt behind. His feet felt like leaden weights. His legs were sodden wood. The old warrior would rise and follow. Why, Morgen couldn't begin to guess. Knowing the future didn't grant the sight to see the reasons giving it birth. He saw outcomes, nothing more. It was a weakness, a lack. Decisions mattered. Or they should. Might he not react differently to the possible futures he witnessed if he knew the reasons of the people involved? Perhaps he had already extinguished someone's chance at redemption. He couldn't know.

# CHAPTER 39

*The voices in my head just told me they were hearing voices. They said the voices wanted them to do something dangerous.*

—H<small>OFFNUNGSLOS</small>

Searching from top to bottom, smashing every mirror he found, dulling every reflective surface, Trepidation finally arrived in the bowels of the ancient church. He had no idea what god or religion previously walked these halls, but sometimes he felt the ghosts of dead faiths following him. Today was one of those days. Shadows danced on the edges of his vision, but no matter how fast he spun, there was nothing there. He'd doubt his sanity, except he knew beyond a doubt he was delusional.

The only question: Did he believe what he saw strongly enough to make it real?

The thought of his delusions becoming real was less scary than being tracked through dark halls by dead gods. Or so he told himself.

"If you're angry we made our own god," he told the stalking spirits, "take it up with Konig. Leave me be."

There was, of course, no answer.

In the farthest recesses of the deepest basement, Trepidation found a room. The door, thick oak bound in rusting iron, opened with great screeching protests.

He stood waiting, the lantern in his hand all but shuttered, for half an hour. No one came to investigate.

Dare he hope?

No. Fear would never allow him anything so hopelessly silly as hope. Still, fear would keep him alive. It was the only sane emotion in an insane world.

Trepidation unshuttered the lantern and lit the room. Wood benches and pews from at least three different time periods sat piled haphazardly against one wall. Half buried under a mound of rotting tapestries, broken chairs, and strangely shaped idols lurked a massive statue carved from some dark wood. When Trepidation worked up the nerve to raise the lantern to better see, the wood turned red like drying blood. The statue, depicting a woman with viciously curved blades protruding from orifice, limb, and joint, stared at him with hollow eyes.

*Gems probably once filled those sockets,* he thought. She looked blind now, though judging from the way she stared at him, he wasn't so sure.

"I'm not here to further desecrate you," he promised. "Maybe later, when Konig is dead and I rule, I can bring you back upstairs and into the light. I could use a god, even one as old and dead as you."

This seemed to appease her and she left him alone.

Trepidation swallowed his fear and drew a cloth-wrapped bundle not much bigger than the palm of his hand from within his robes. Carefully he folded the cloth back, revealing the small hand mirror cushioned within.

Did Acceptance really think Trepidation would be okay with him being the only one with a mirror? Did he think Trepidation would just *trust* him? *If so, he is a fool.* Trepidation trusted no one.

Slowly turning the mirror, Trepidation looked within, unsure what he would see and poised and ready to smash it to the floor should it prove dangerous.

His face stared back at him. But it wasn't his face. He was missing an eye, dark bruises mottled his cheeks, and his teeth were shattered ruins. Acceptance.

*No,* he realized, *Acceptance's reflection;* an important distinction.

Trepidation blinked at it in confusion. *How can I see Acceptance's reflection? Unless . . .*

"You seek to betray him," he said to the mirror. The reflection nodded. "Because he broke Konig's mirror and you fear he'll smash the one he has as soon as he's won." Again the reflection nodded. "He'll kill us both, won't he?" The reflection nodded.

Trepidation sat in silence, thinking. The reflection watched, waiting.

"You know I don't trust you," he told the mirror, and the reflection within laughed silently. "Good. So what is it you suggest I do?" he asked.

The reflection showed him and he watched in horror.

"It's too dangerous," he told the mirror.

The reflection stared at him, unblinking.

"What if it goes wrong?"

It just stared at him.

*What choice do I have?* Acceptance would never share power, not even the smallest fragment.

The reflection grinned, showing broken teeth.

*Right. I did that to him.* Acceptance would never forgive.

"And how will Konig react?"

The reflection showed him.

Trepidation folded the mirror back into its cloth and tucked it away under his robes.

## CHAPTER 40

*I think most people are too stupid to go truly mad.*

—Hoffnungslos

"Are you going to lie there all day?"

Stehlen looked up and saw Wichtig standing over her. Behind him the sky was a pale gray even though no clouds could be seen.

She needed to go east.

"I have something better to do?" she asked, just because agreeing with Wichtig set her teeth on edge.

"There's always vengeance," Wichtig suggested. "I would have thought revenge topped your list of reasons to get up even on a day you hadn't been killed."

Vengeance. Not long ago she would have happily sworn vengeance for the mildest slight, real or imagined. What was the point now? She grimaced up at Wichtig's handsome face.

"I'll just lie here awhile," she said to the sky.

Another man moved forward to stand beside Wichtig. He

looked vaguely familiar. "Who is this?" he asked, staring down at Stehlen with disgust.

"She's my friend," answered Wichtig. He offered a hand to pull her up. "We are still friends, right?"

Stehlen accepted the hand and Wichtig lifted her easily to her feet. "Death changes nothing," she said. "I still can't stand you."

"Good. I'd hate to think it made you soft."

Now standing, she saw hundreds of men and women gathered around them.

"If I'd known dying would get me an army, I might have done it ages ago."

Wichtig's eyes lit with glee. "You don't get an army, remember. At least not for long. Whoever killed you gets the army."

She felt the life drain from her. *I'll have to see him again. I'll have to serve him.* After all he'd done to her. "I'll kill him," she swore.

Wichtig patted her reassuringly on the back and then retreated when she glanced up at him. "I'm guessing you have the need to go east, eh?"

Stehlen growled an affirmative.

Wichtig looked very pleased with himself indeed. "The little bastard got you too. I wouldn't have though it possible."

"Bedeckt. It was Bedeckt."

The Swordsman's face lost all humor. "Oh."

"He killed me to protect the boy."

"Oh."

"You have nothing else to say?"

"I'm glad I'm not Bedeckt."

"Gods-damned right," snarled Stehlen.

"But you're going east too."

"Yes."

"How strong is the pull?" Wichtig asked.

"Strong."

"So Bedeckt is going to die soon."

She stared at Wichtig until he fidgeted uncomfortably.

"So is the boy," he said. "I have to go east too. He's going to Ascend."

"Not if I kill him first."

"He'll already be dead," pointed out Wichtig, though he sounded none too sure of himself.

"There's always more death," said Vollk from behind Wichtig.

"I heard you last time," said Wichtig. "Stehlen. This is it. Your chance at redemption. Tell Bedeckt how you feel."

*The bastard never gives up.* She should kill him now and be done with it. *No. Too easy.* Better she beat him at his own game. Better he realize she could better him in all ways.

"Maybe," she said, looking him over. She poked him in the chest with a filthy finger. "Where are your swords? Don't tell me you lost them already."

Wichtig gestured at a large woman standing nearby. "She took them."

Stehlen recognized the woman. "And you just let her?"

"Well, there's more of them than us," Wichtig said defensively.

"I know," said Stehlen. "I just wanted to hear you admit it."

"Bitch."

"I've killed more people than you. I win. And now we *both* know it."

"You cheated. Anyway, half of yours are total nobodies. Most of mine are great Swordsmen."

Stehlen wafted his complaints away with an airy wave of her hand. "Doesn't matter. I have more." She turned to Lebendig Durchdachter. "Those two swords, give them back to Wichtig." Lebendig opened her mouth to argue. "Now," said Stehlen.

Lebendig's shoulders fell and she handed the swords back to Wichtig, who accepted them and returned his sword to Vollk.

"Don't think this means I owe you," he said.

"Think of it as a prize for coming in second," she said.

"This leaves me without a sword," said Lebendig. "I need a sword."

Stehlen pointed at Vollk. "You. Give her your sword."

"I'm not one of yours to command," growled Vollk, drawing the blade he'd just sheathed.

"If I were you," said Wichtig, "I'd do as she says. You're the one who keeps saying there's always more death."

"Shite," said Vollk, handing Lebendig his sword.

"Anyway," said Wichtig, "I've got the feeling there's going to be a lot of extra swords lying around soon enough. Death follows Stehlen everywhere." He stopped, and suddenly grinned happily at Stehlen. "Speaking of swords, where are yours?"

"Lying on the road somewhere," answered Stehlen with a twisted grimace.

"Bedeckt didn't . . ."

"No. He didn't get the chance. The boy hit him in the head with a rock."

"Oh."

"Not to worry. Like you said, there will be a lot of extra swords lying around soon." Stehlen spun and stabbed the nearest sword-bearing man through the heart with one of her hidden daggers. He made a surprised gurgle and dropped like a stone. "Oh, look, here's one."

Wichtig scowled disapprovingly at the corpse.

"What?" she asked, disgusted.

"Was he one of mine or one of yours?"

Stehlen glanced at the corpse. He didn't look familiar, but few of these people did. "Does it matter?"

Morgen staggered east. The morning sun had yet to crest the horizon and the sky was lit bloody with fire. It would be a red, red day.

With each step he felt a damp squelching in his shoes. Some time during the night his feet had begun to ache. Then, for many hours, each step had been its own raw agony. Now they were numb and he was grateful. He dreaded what he would find when he removed his shoes.

*Why didn't Konig give me real shoes instead of these silly slippers? Why hadn't Bedeckt or Stehlen or Wichtig pointed out how useless they were?*

Because no one wanted him to stray far.

Even his shoes were a prison. He should take them off.

No. He didn't want to see his feet. They'd be a mess, and there was nowhere to clean them.

Gods, his hands were filthy. He picked the dried blood from under a fingernail.

One foot after the other. *Squelch, squelch.*

Morgen looked up from his hands. The sun, hidden behind a thick layer of cloud, sat somewhere well above the horizon. East. Why east?

WHY WOULDN'T HIS reflections show him something useful? Did they hide truths just like everyone else? Who could he trust?

*No one.*

He blinked. His hands stung. He lifted one hand from the road to stare dumbly at the stones embedded in the palm. The hand was dirty. Spots of red soaked through a layer of fine road dust.

*How long have I been kneeling?*

Morgen pushed himself to his feet and looked for somewhere to clean his hands. Nothing. He tried wiping them on his pants, but they were filthy too.

Ahead he saw a crowd approaching. They looked something like what he'd expect a traveling circus to look like. He could hear songs of worship sung in high and strained voices. A traveling church, maybe? He'd read of such things. Had he seen this in the reflections? He couldn't remember. He was so thirsty. Maybe they'd give him water.

Morgen sat on the road to wait.

⸻

Erbrechen swayed in his canopied litter, his monstrous belly, slick with sweat, moving in time to the measured tread of those who carried him. His arse cheeks felt slippery and he wondered if he'd shat himself again. No matter, it was a pleasant enough sensation for now. He'd have one of his lads look into it later.

He kept a careful eye on Gehirn. The Hassebrand sat hunched, picking at something she kept hidden from sight. Even under the canopy on this cloudy day, the woman radiated heat. Her skin flaked red and raw, blistering as if she'd lain in the desert sun for days. The air around her rippled.

*Shame this isn't winter,* thought Erbrechen. *I'd be toasty warm instead of swimming in arse sweat.*

How had he not seen the danger the Hassebrand would become? He'd been blinded by his need for love. For real love. He glanced past Gehirn and watched two children fight over the scrawny corpse of a plucked chicken. *Not the empty worship of fools.* Was she any different? He'd almost believed she was. He peeled back his lips, baring his teeth at the Hassebrand's back. *No, she's just like the others.*

The snarl died, leaking from his face. *Gods, I'm so lonely.*

The sight of two men leading a blond boy—filthy, but soft and fresh-faced—toward the litter interrupted Erbrechen's thoughts. Even under the coating of road dust, he could tell this lad had been well fed and pampered his entire life. Lust surged in him and he crushed it down.

Not now. If this was the boy Gehirn told him of, he must make him his.

Erbrechen called a halt and those carrying the litter stumbled to an awkward stop. The approaching men marched the boy forward to stand before Erbrechen. The lad, trembling from exhaustion, seemed barely aware of where he was.

"Oh, you poor boy," purred Erbrechen. "I see blood. Are you hurt?"

"Thirsty," croaked the boy, staring at his blood-encrusted hands. "Need to get clean."

"Of course, of course. I understand completely. You!" Erbrechen thrust a pudgy finger at a woman waiting nearby. "Fetch the boy water. Now!" The woman scurried away.

"Morgen?" said Gehirn.

The lad's head came up slowly and he stared dumbly at the Hassebrand. "Gehirn Schlechtes? Konig sent you to—"

"We're here to help," interrupted Erbrechen before Gehirn could say something stupid and ruin everything. "We're here to protect you. You can trust us." He shot the Hassebrand a meaningful look. "Right, Gehirn? Tell him he can trust us."

Gehirn's face tensed and a wave of heat washed over Erbrechen. "You can trust us," she said.

The boy looked confused, lost. "I thought Konig . . . He sent the Tiergeist."

"Tiergeist?" Erbrechen hissed at Gehirn.

"Therianthrope assassins," the Hassebrand answered.

Erbrechen spat, drool spattering his belly. "Damned shapeshifters." He returned his attention to Morgen. "You're safe with me. I won't let anyone hurt you."

"I can't be allowed to die," said Morgen, staring at Erbrechen with hopeful eyes.

"No one shall touch you. I promise," Erbrechen lied. "I've already defeated Konig's Schatten Mörder, his filthy Cotardist assassins."

"Konig didn't send you?" the lad asked, dumbfounded, directing his question at the Hassebrand.

A shock of fear stabbed through Erbrechen. *How can the child ignore me? He must be a formidable Gefahrgeist.* He needed to find the child's weakness, some way of engendering gratefulness.

"Gods, no!" exclaimed Erbrechen, thinking quickly. "Gehirn is here to save you. She's your friend, right? And I'm her friend. And a friend of a friend is . . . a friend!"

The woman he'd sent for water finally scurried up and offered a chipped mug to the boy. Erbrechen watched Morgen hesitate, take a sip, and then splash water onto his hands and attempt to scrub them clean. *Aha!* This was what he'd been looking for, some way into the child's mind.

"More!" commanded Erbrechen. "A tubful of hot water!"

The woman fled.

"Thank you," said Morgen, tears of gratitude streaming down his face, cutting tracks through the caked filth. "It's been so long. Dirty. Everything."

"Don't you worry," Erbrechen purred comfortingly. "Never again. I'll keep you clean. Forever."

The boy smiled tentatively, eyes glistening with hope. "Forever?"

"Forever. I promise." Erbrechen poked Gehirn with a fat finger. "Tell him I keep my promises."

"He keeps his promises," muttered Gehirn.

"Yes, I do," agreed Erbrechen. "And I take care of my friends." He beamed happily at the boy. "We are friends, right?"

Morgen looked uncertain. *Damn, he must be strong! Anyone else would have been begging to lick my feet by now.* Better make sure he had the boy under control.

"A bath will feel so good, won't it?" Erbrechen asked.

The boy nodded eagerly. "Yes."

"You'll feel much better, won't you?"

"Yes, I will."

"Are you hungry?"

"Very."

"We have delicious stew."

Morgen licked his lips. "Stew would be nice. After."

"After you're clean. Of course." Erbrechen smiled fondly. "It feels good to take care of your friends, doesn't it. Friends always take care of friends. I'm taking care of you. Right?"

"Yes."

"So we're friends?"

"Yes."

"Really? We are?" Erbrechen allowed himself to look uncertain, hurt.

"Yes," said Morgen quickly. "We're friends."

"Good!"

Erbrechen turned to command Gehirn to warm some water for the boy's bath, but the Hassebrand's clenched jaw, canines exposed in something just shy of a deranged snarl, changed his mind. The woman's cold blue eyes bulged and sweat streamed down her blistered face. Her mouth opened and she looked as if she desperately wanted to say something but couldn't find the words.

"You stay where you are," Erbrechen commanded Gehirn. "You need to rest." A pulse of heat washed over him as Gehirn clenched her fists. "Rest," he said forcefully, and the Hassebrand lay back, closing her eyes.

Erbrechen caught Morgen watching with open curiosity. "She worried about you," he explained. "It exhausted her."

A dozen men and women dragged a huge iron tub into view. Where they'd found it, Erbrechen had no idea. *Did they drag it from Neidrig on the off chance I'd want a bath? Fools.* He'd never fit into such a small tub. In moments, a chain of bedraggled peasants filled the tub with steaming water.

The boy stood staring at the tub, hesitating for some reason. *Ah, of course. Privacy.* Erbrechen was always alone, even in the thick of a crowd. It was so easy to forget such social niceties.

"You." Erbrechen pointed at a man squatting nearby, pants down around his ankles. "Two things." The man stared up at him, eyes round with terror. "Never shite in my presence. It's rude. And put a curtain around the tub. The young lad needs his privacy." Morgen sagged with gratitude. *Excellent!*

The crouched man stood, hiking his pants up.

"Wait!" said Erbrechen, suddenly feeling jovial. "I change my mind. Never shite again. Ever. Anywhere."

The man winced and nodded. He looked pained, like he was clenching.

*Hilarious,* thought Erbrechen. *How long will the the poor bastard hold it?* It was a small thing, but of such small things were life's joys truly made. The thought, he knew, would keep him smiling for days.

⸻

Bedeckt, face down on the road, woke with a pained groan, his eyes glued shut with dried blood from the wound in the back of his throbbing skull.

What the hells had the Morgen hit him with, a mountain? He lay moaning for some time before finally struggling to his feet.

How long had he been unconscious?

The sun was high, but obscured by thick cloud. There was no sign of the boy.

Bedeckt crouched over Stehlen's corpse. Her eyes were open and she wore an odd smile, as if pleased with how things had turned out.

*Pretty damned unlikely.*

She'd been dead for a while, definitely long enough to have made the journey to the Afterdeath. At this point, anything she carried was fair game. He stopped when he saw her sword lying in the dust of the road. She'd died without a sword in her hands.

"Oh, hells."

She'd never forgive him.

Well, seeing as he'd killed her, his failure to make sure she died with a sword might not be the first thing on her mind. Then again, with Stehlen, you could never be sure.

*She'll be waiting for me*. Never before had he wanted immortality so badly.

"Sorry," he said to the corpse as he bent to search her pockets. He found a small fortune in gems and several gold coins. Maybe not enough to retire on, but enough to keep him in comfort for a few years. It wasn't stealing, he figured. Most of this had probably once been his. It didn't matter. Even if it hadn't been his, he'd take it anyway.

Stealing from friends wasn't on the list of things he wouldn't do.

Friends.

*What a fool*. Men like him didn't have friends.

He should walk away now. Take this loot and find a small house somewhere quiet. Maybe he could invest in something safe and useful like a whorehouse. Forget Morgen. Forget ransoming the boy's life—or death—and call it quits while he still could.

It wasn't enough, though. He knew he'd never invest it. He'd drink and whore it away and be left with nothing. He needed more.

Konig would pay well for Morgen's death.

Bedeckt pushed the thought away and rifled through the rest of Stehlen's clothes and meager belongings.

Hidden under her awful-smelling shirt, he found an unbelievable number of tattered and faded scarves looking like they might once have been brightly colored. He'd never seen them before.

How long had she carried these? A long time, judging from their sour smell and sorry state. The scarves looked old enough to date back to her childhood. Try as he might, Bedeckt couldn't picture Stehlen as a child. She'd been a crazy murderous thieving bitch every second of every day he'd known her. He couldn't imagine her elsewise.

*Except in the alley.* She'd been warm and alive. Had she said she loved him? He couldn't remember; that night was an alcohol-induced blur.

*She said she loved you just before you killed her.*

Oh, shite.

Bedeckt cursed the gods and jammed the faded scarves into a pocket. What the hells he planned on doing with them, he had no idea. Dumping the coins and stones into his left boot, he stood with a groan. His knees made wet popping noises and his back ached from crouching. He should say something.

Spoiling meat, Stehlen called Wichtig's corpse. Was she nothing more?

He couldn't be so lucky. Someday he'd die and there she'd be . . . waiting.

Strange, he hadn't felt the need to say something as he'd stood over Wichtig's corpse. Maybe Stehlen was right. Maybe he was growing soft.

"To hells with you," he told the corpse. He had the feeling he'd see her soon enough anyway.

He examined his surroundings and spotted Launisch and the other horses. *His* horses, he supposed. They hadn't wandered far, and pulled at the tough grass nearby.

Launisch approached and gently nuzzled at his chest.

"Sorry," said Bedeckt. "I don't have any apples."

"Ppfft!" answered Launisch.

# CHAPTER 41

*My mirror never shows me what I want to see. I can't possibly be
that fat and ugly!*

—FETT HÄSSLICH, MIRRORIST

Having swept the mirror dust from the floor, Acceptance
and Trepidation stood in Konig's chambers. Acceptance's
hands were bleeding from countless slivers, whereas Trepidation
seemed to have managed not to cut himself at all. Acceptance
hated him; the cowardly Doppel was far too careful.

The Theocrat was elsewhere, trying to find out why none of
his spies in Neidrig could be contacted.

Acceptance watched Trepidation's nervous twitching with annoyance. "What are you afraid of?" he demanded.

"Konig," answered Trepidation, staring at the floor. "If he
finds your mirror, he'll kill us both."

"Best he not find it. My reflections have shown me something
disturbing."

Trepidation's head came up suddenly. *Interesting.*

"They've shown me the boy," Acceptance said, watching his fellow Doppel closely. Trepidation might have relaxed fractionally, but it was difficult to tell. The fool was always wound so damned tight. "Morgen will never return here."

"So Konig is doomed."

"Yes," Acceptance agreed. "We will soon rule."

"You will rule," Trepidation corrected. "I will follow."

"Do you fear me so?"

"Yes."

"Good."

"How will we dispose of Konig? He is still dangerous."

Acceptance laughed nastily, hiding the ruin of his mouth behind a slim-fingered hand. "Easy. I will do what he would never expect from me."

"Which is?"

"Violence."

"Just you?" Trepidation asked. "Not we?"

"Yes. He will serve me in the Afterdeath."

Trepidation's lip quivered and he blinked rapidly. He looked like he was struggling to hold back tears. *Pathetic.* Living his entire life in terror of every choice made him weak. Once Konig was dead, killing Trepidation would be easy.

"You are with me?" Acceptance asked.

"Yes," answered Trepidation.

"Good. He will be here soon."

<hr />

As soon as Konig stepped into his chambers, he knew something was up. Acceptance smiled openly, for once not hiding his mouth behind his hand. Trepidation looked to be on the verge of tears.

"What happened?" Konig demanded.

Acceptance sketched a mocking bow. "You have failed."

"Failed? How?" *What the hells is the gods-damned Doppel talking about?*

"It is too late." Acceptance laughed, drooling through the broken gaps in his teeth. "Morgen is not returning."

Konig's gut soured. "No," he said in desperate denial.

"And he has been infected. Poisoned," said Acceptance, moving closer.

Tears stung Konig's face. "No," he whispered. "You lie. He will be our god. We made him."

"Oh, *we* is it now?" Acceptance demanded sarcastically. The Doppel stepped forward, closing the distance between them. "Morgen is no god! You've made nothing! He's an insane child riddled with delusion."

"You—"

Acceptance lunged forward, knife in hand, but stopped just shy of thrusting the blade into Konig's chest. Konig stared into the Doppel's eyes, surprised.

"They showed me . . ." Acceptance slid to the floor, a knife protruding from the base of his skull.

Trepidation stood behind him, watching with terrified eyes.

"You saved me," said Konig.

"No," said Trepidation.

Konig backed away warily but the Doppel didn't follow.

"You're no match for me," hissed Konig. "I'll kill you in a heartbeat."

"I know. It doesn't matter. Morgen knows you sent assassins to kill him. He knows you used him. He knows you never loved him. You are incapable of such emotion. It's over. Your man-made god is in ruins. When he Ascends he will come for vengeance."

"How . . . how do you know?"

Trepidation knelt by Acceptance's body, rolling the corpse onto its back. From within the dead Doppel's robe he drew forth a small mirror. He held it up and Konig flinched away.

"The reflections showed Acceptance what will happen."

"How did you know he would try and kill me?" Konig asked.

"He made a mistake," answered Trepidation. "He underestimated my fear."

"Acceptance lied?" Konig asked, annoyed at how desperate he sounded.

Trepidation shook his head sorrowfully. "No."

"If I can return him to Selbsthass—"

"You cannot change who he has become."

"Then we shall start again," said Konig, with more confidence than he felt.

"You cannot stop what you have set in motion. He will be our god, but he will not be the god you wanted."

Konig glared at Trepidation and the Doppel quivered in fear. "I am not finished yet. If I kill the boy he will have to obey me."

Trepidation bowed his head meekly. "True. But we are too late—"

"You don't know. Not for sure. Only a fool trusts Doppels and reflections."

The Doppel licked his lips and Konig saw the resolve fade as Trepidation's shoulders dropped and the fight seemed to leak from him.

"We go to fetch the boy."

"We?" asked Trepidation.

"Of course. You didn't think I'd leave you here alone, do you?"

"Of course not," said the Doppel, sagging further in on himself.

"Ready my Dysmorphics."

"Of course."

Trepidation hated the Dysmorphics and Konig knew it. The great lunks were as massively stupid as they were massively muscled. Any one of them—men and women alike—could crush him dead in an instant. Fearing such obscene strength seemed only sane.

"What should I do with this mirror?" Trepidation asked.

Konig flinched again as Trepidation lifted it toward him, and the Doppel quashed the urge to gloat.

"Break it," commanded Konig. "Shatter it to dust."

"Of course."

Without a second glance at Acceptance's corpse, Konig left the room.

Things had almost gone according to plan. The reflections hadn't shown Konig chasing after the boy, but then maybe they hadn't known. Or maybe they'd sought to hide something from him.

*Does it change anything?*

Sadly, yes. It meant Konig still had some breath of hope. It meant the man was not yet finished.

Konig's hope would have to be extinguished before Trepidation could take his place as Theocrat. But how to extinguish a man's hope?

Trepidation placed Acceptance's mirror faceup on the floor. From his pocket he drew his own mirror and, unwrapping it, placed it beside the first. Two of him—one in each mirror—stared back. Neither showed the damage Acceptance had suffered. *What the hells does that mean?* With Acceptance dead, had his reflections died too? Were these now Trepidation's own reflections? He saw no way to know for sure.

"Which of you shall I keep?" he asked the reflections, and they glanced nervously at each other.

One began pantomiming elaborate actions while the other watched with fearful eyes. There was his answer. He never would dare something so bold as what the capering reflection suggested. He would have watched with dawning terror, much as the second mirror was doing.

The second reflection glanced nervously at the first and pantomimed whispering in someone's ear. Secrecy born of fear. Trepidation understood perfectly. He lifted the mirror to his ear to listen and screamed when small hands clutched at the lobe. He yanked the mirror away but the hands remained and a small copy of himself forced itself ever deeper into his ear.

Trepidation screamed again. Impossible agony. It entered his skull.

The reflection in the other mirror clapped happily.

⸻

*Free!*

Konig's reflection stood tall, stretching his arms. It felt good to finally be real. Or at least as real as a Doppel.

The charade could end. There had never been any reflections but those of Konig. It had been an act from the very beginning. Everything the fools had seen and listened to had been Konig's reflections all along. They'd beaten each other to match Acceptance's wounds and feigned fear to trick Trepidation. The Doppels had never been Mirrorists, only Konig.

The reflection glanced down at the second mirror. The reflection within waited, hand held up, ready to be pulled free. He laughed at the reflection and brought his heel down on the mirror. He stomped it again and again. Then he fetched a hammer to reduce it to dust. When finished with the mirror, he tossed the hammer aside.

The second mirror, the one he'd crawled from, he lifted from the floor. When he held it up to his face, he saw nothing but the room behind him.

*It's empty. Perfect.*

Slipping the mirror into his robes, he left to prepare the Dysmorphics as Konig had ordered Trepidation to do. The reflection had no fear of the huge brutes. He saw them as tools, little more.

"I am Konig," he said, testing the words. "I am Konig. Konig Furimmer. High Priest of the Geborene Damonen. Theocrat of Selbsthass." He narrowed his eyes, facing an imaginary audience. "I am Konig." *Yes, perfect.* "My Doppel plots treason."

Morgen lay curled on Erbrechen's litter, sleeping. Gehirn studied him. The boy's face twitched and he moaned quietly, plagued with worries and nightmares Gehirn could all too well imagine. She had to save him. One clean act before insanity took her. She needed something to cling to, something not tainted by the filth of Erbrechen's soul. The Slaver would twist the boy, foul him to the core of his being, and then kill him.

"No." Gehirn stood, turning toward the Slaver. She'd turn the fat bastard to ash before—

Erbrechen smiled childish innocence at Gehirn's wrath. "Heat the stew, would you?"

Gehirn hesitated. *Kill him now.*

"Heat the stew," said the Slaver more forcefully, all warmth gone from his voice.

*He never loved you. Not one gentle touch.*

Gehirn turned her attention on the huge cauldron slung over the dying fire. She raised a hand and let slip a tiny fraction of her self-loathing.

She was a failure, in every conceivable way.

The fire surged to life.

Morgen would die at Erbrechen's hand, worshiping the Slaver, twisted to his grotesque will.

The stew boiled over.

Erbrechen said something but Gehirn didn't hear it. Her blood was boiling with hatred. Her whole life she'd served men who used her, who cast her aside. She was nothing. She'd achieved not a single untainted act.

With a flash the cauldron melted and was blasted to ash before the molten metal touched ground.

"Stop!" screamed Erbrechen, and the fire guttered. "Enough! Sit. Be silent. Say nothing. Do nothing," the Slaver commanded.

Gehirn sat in the hot mud.

Erbrechen's heart fluttered with fear, straining to shove blood through his corpulent body. *Too close!* Had he not been staring at the Hassebrand, wondering what to do with her, he might not have seen the threat until it was too late. Erbrechen let out a slow sigh.

"Damned if you do, damned if you don't," he muttered. *Wait! Genius! What a catchy saying!* He'd have to remember to repeat it in front of others. Sometimes it felt like he was the only reasonably intelligent person in all the world. He looked out over the scattered wreckage of his camp. These people had no pride, no will to better themselves. They were disgusting, pathetic. Useful in numbers, but still detestable.

The man he'd told not to shite lay curled moaning on the ground, clutching at his stomach. Erbrechen giggled. At least something was still funny. His laughter woke the boy.

"What's so funny?" Morgen asked, blinking and glancing around the camp as if seeing it for the first time.

"The world is a comedy," intoned Erbrechen, tittering, "and each must play his fart." The stupid boy looked confused. "Never mind. Hungry?"

Morgen nodded quickly. "Very."

"Well then—" Erbrechen glanced at the ashen remains of the stewpot. *Damn it all to the hells!* Getting the boy to eat some human stew had been part of his plan. He must soil the boy's soul, weaken his self-assurance. Bend him.

Erbrechen pointed at a group of men sitting nearby. Thin and filthy, they were covered in windblown ash. "You lot. Start a new fire. Make me my stew." He saw the Hassebrand's head come up at the mention of fire. "No, my friend, you stay where you are."

Gehirn glared hatred and Erbrechen felt a wave of heat wash over him.

"You'll hurt the boy," he warned softly.

The heat guttered and the Hassebrand sagged forward to stare into the mud.

The more he thought about it, the more Erbrechen saw only one escape from Gehirn: the boy must die, and he must die soon. There was no time for the slow erosion of self. Erbrechen must crush him, and fast. But how to do it? *Gods, I'm so hungry I can hardly think!*

"Hurry with the stew!"

"Is everything okay?" asked the boy.

"No." Erbrechen pointed at another group of men and women who were loitering nearby, hoping for the chance to serve their master. "You." They stood immediately, their backs straightening. "Beat the boy. If you kill him, you're all going into the stew. Break fingers and toes. Cause him terrible agony."

Morgen scrambled to his feet. The look of confused betrayal beyond comedic, his mouth hung open. "Why?"

"Not to worry," Erbrechen reassured the lad. "Once you are begging for mercy, I will save you from these terrible people. You will thank me. You'll do anything to make it stop."

"I thought . . ." The boy trailed off. "But I saw fire."

"Sorry, your friend cannot help you. She is mine." Erbrechen grinned wet lust. "As will you be."

A man stepped forward and landed a crushing blow to the boy's face, shattering his nose. Morgen crumpled to the ground.

"Gods damn it, make sure he stays conscious. There's no point in torturing an unconscious victim, you idiot."

"Sorry," said the man as he kicked Morgen in the stomach.

For several seconds the boy was hidden by milling legs and flailing punches.

"Okay, okay," called out Erbrechen, and they stepped back.

Morgen, face streaming blood and spattered in filth, stared up at Erbrechen from the mud, his expression dazed. "I saw fire."

The lad was tougher than he'd expected. With an imperious wave of Erbrechen's hand, the men and women returned to thrashing him.

# CHAPTER 42

*The doing is the easy part. It's the deciding to do that is difficult. I
most regret the decisions never made.*

—HOFFNUNGSLOS

Night fell fast and Bedeckt led Launisch and the other two
horses away from the road and into the shelter of the trees.
Alone, he didn't want to run into the kind of trouble often found
wandering roads such as this. With his two deranged friends
dead, he had no fear of albtraum, nightmares of the insane giv-
en flesh. But he'd be easy pickings for the wandering gangs of
thieves who haunted dark roads.

Tying the horses to a nearby tree, he set about lighting a small
fire.

Once it got going, he sat at the fire, warming his feet. He ate
well. With Wichtig and Stehlen gone, Bedeckt had more food
than he could possibly eat. Come tomorrow, he'd carry what he
could and leave the rest to the scavengers.

It was quiet. No one was bickering.

It was also lonely. He'd traveled with the two cretins for years. Their constant arguing had been a background hum he'd become accustomed to. Gods damned if he didn't miss it.

Bedeckt climbed into his sleeping roll and stared into the twisting flames of the fire.

He'd see Wichtig and Stehlen again, no doubt.

Those whom you slay shall serve you in the Afterdeath: the Warrior's Credo. Stehlen would be waiting, but he couldn't imagine her in a role of servitude. *She'll find some way to kill me*. And if she couldn't, she'd find some way of making him wish she'd killed him.

"Wake up, you little shite."

"What?" Bedeckt opened a crusty eye. Had he fallen asleep? He could have sworn he just heard a voice, one he recognized from—

"You're still a lazy shite. You haven't changed. Useless cunt."

Bedeckt sat up. There, across the fire, sat his father.

"I've killed you once, old man. I'd happily do it again."

The old bastard grunted a dismissal. He didn't look as huge and scary as Bedeckt remembered. The old man sat hunched forward, his eyes rimmed red with exhaustion, his back bent with an age he'd never lived to see. This was his father as he would have looked had Bedeckt not slain him all those decades ago.

The old man waved a hand as if shushing him and prodded at the dying fire with a stick. "I'm not here to beat you—much as you deserve it. I'm here to talk."

Bedeckt watched the old man warily. "Begone, albtraum."

"Ah, still clinging to your much-vaunted sanity, I see. Well, here I sit. Perhaps you aren't as sane as you think."

"I am sane," growled Bedeckt.

"Or perhaps you are too sane, or believe in your sanity a little too strongly. Such belief, my son, would make anyone crazy."

"I'm not your son." Bedeckt scowled at the dream spirit. "Nothing you say will make me doubt my sanity."

"My point exactly."

"My father was never this smart."

The albtraum waved away his words. "This isn't about you. This isn't about your father."

"What then? Will you tell me I feel guilty for killing Stehlen? She left me no choice."

His father spat into the fire, much as Stehlen would have done. "Nice try, spirit."

"It's the boy."

"Morgen?" Bedeckt asked, surprised. "What do you know of him?"

"He will die soon."

Bedeckt's chest tightened. The boy had saved his life. "Tell me something I didn't know."

"You and you alone pursue him with no thoughts of killing him to your own ends."

"Not exactly true," Bedeckt pointed out.

"Wichtig manipulated the boy from the beginning, once he understood his significance. Even Stehlen, who loved you enough to follow you to the very ends of the world, planned to kill him."

Bedeckt shifted uncomfortably. "Stehlen didn't love—"

"She loved you so much it blinded her to the threat you were."

"Horse shite."

"Really?" The albtraum snorted derisively. "You think you could have beaten her, unarmed? Even armed, you were never her match." The albtraum poked again at the fire, rolling a log into the reddest embers. "She had a knife in her hand the entire time you sat near her. She could have killed you in an instant."

"Horse shite." But his words lacked power.

"Even as she tried to kill the boy, she never believed that you would kill her. She trusted you. Totally."

"Horse—"

"Shite," finished the albtraum, again gesturing as if it didn't care what Bedeckt thought. This wasn't right; the creatures were supposed to attack, to feed off their victim's fears and lusts and dreams. This creature succeeded only in making him uncomfortable. *What kind of nightmare feeds off discomfort?*

"Morgen has fallen into the clutches of a powerful Gefahrgeist," said the albtraum. "A Slaver of the worst order."

*A Slaver?* The boy was beyond reach, then. Nothing Bedeckt could do would save him now. He watched his plans sink away into the depths of the foulest shite-hole.

Wichtig and Stehlen, dead for nothing. Everything he'd been through and he was worse off now than when this began. *Typical.*

He ran a hand over his weary eyes. "Why would I care?" Bedeckt asked the albtraum. "I'm tired. Go stick pigs."

"You are old," said the albtraum. "You are slowing down. On this path you will die sooner rather than later. What then? Paradise is not for men like you. All those you wronged, all those you killed and damaged; all await you in the next world. You are a man without redeeming features. You will have no allies in the next world."

Bedeckt laughed, a snort of derision. "I have none in this world."

"Stehlen loved and worshiped you."

"She tried to kill me."

"You pushed her until she had no choice. Wichtig saw you as a father. He thought you his only friend."

"Wichtig was a manipulative fool."

"True," agreed the albtraum, poking again at the fire. "He tried to use you. But only to better himself. Yes, he was a fool for hoping you might find something worth liking in him when he saw nothing. He loathed himself and clothed it in bravado. All he ever wanted was to impress you, hear a kind word. He got nothing. He and Stehlen await you in the next life."

"I'll deal with them when I get there."

"No doubt. You'll probably, having learned nothing, kill them both. But it doesn't have to be this way."

"Ah, I *can* be redeemed?" Bedeckt asked sarcastically. "My soul can be saved so I may frolic among fields of virgins in the next life?"

"Morgen saved your life. You owe him."

"Shite on my debts."

Again the albtraum ignored his words. "The worst of what trauma humanity has to offer awaits Morgen. If the Slaver has his way, the child will Ascend in such a damaged state he will absolutely worship the one who caused him so much pain. And the beliefs of gods are powerful things."

"I don't care. I'm done."

"Save the child and—"

"Redeem myself?" Bedeckt barked a harsh laugh and found himself sitting alone in the dark, the fire long since gone out.

He sat blinking at the ashes. What had Morgen said about heading east? Bedeckt couldn't remember.

"Shite and hellfires."

Redemption. What a laughable concept. When he looked back over his life, he couldn't see where he had first stepped off the righteous path. More important, had he even ever laid a single foot on that path?

Was this destiny? Was he doomed to a hellish Afterdeath of slain friends and lovers.

"She wasn't a lover," he said aloud, his words hollow with doubt.

Somewhere far off to the east he heard the screams of a child.

"Not my problem. I go west."

447

The screams went on, unending agony.

"Who cares if the child dies and becomes the plaything of some foul Slaver? Who cares if he Ascends to be a twisted new god?"

The scream cut off suddenly, leaving Bedeckt sitting in silence. He sat, listening.

Nothing.

Bedeckt pushed himself to his feet with a groan, his knees and back popping.

"My arse was getting damp anyway."

After setting Stehlen and Wichtig's horses free and sending them west with a slap on the hindquarters, he turned to Launisch. He spent half an hour removing the saddle and tack and brushing the destrier's black coat until it was silky and smooth.

"You've been a good horse, the best."

Launisch snorted as if to say, *Tell me something I didn't know.*

"You can't come with me this time. I think it will end badly."

Launisch stared at him.

"I'm serious."

The massive war-horse looked over Bedeckt's shoulder to the east, turned, and headed west. Bedeckt watched it for several minutes. Expecting an emotional good-bye from his war-horse had probably been foolish.

Bedeckt collected his ax. Everything else he left behind.

He walked east.

When Konig finally made his way to the great courtyard, he found Trepidation waiting with a dozen massive Dysmorphics. Gods damn it, he'd wanted the Doppel to gather *all* of the overly muscled morons. If he was to leave the safety of Selbsthass, he would do so with an army at his back.

He approached quickly, intending to berate the Doppel. As he closed the distance he found himself staring up into the square-jawed face of a Dysmorphic. Gods, they were huge. Even the man's neck—if indeed it was a man, Konig couldn't be sure—bulged with muscle. He felt a surge of fear and turned away from the giant, avoiding eye contact.

*Wait. I have no fear of these muscled fools.* He glanced at the Doppel; Trepidation looked unusually smug.

"What's going on here?" demanded Konig, his quivering voice undercutting the authority.

"It is as I said," announced Trepidation loudly, as if orating to all in the courtyard.

Konig's gaze darted about the open area. All the highest-ranking priests were in attendance. Why had so many people gathered here? Everyone watched, waiting.

Something was wrong. They stared at him with loathing. But why? They loved him! He was the High Priest! He'd made them their very own god!

"Where are the horses? I told you to get all this ready. We have to ride . . ."

No one moved.

"He pretends," said the Doppel. "But he can't hide the fear in his eyes."

Konig backed away and then caught himself. He squared his shoulders and tried to stand tall, but all stared at him. They hated him.

"I am Konig!" Konig screamed, his voice cracking. "I am the High Priest!"

"It is as I said," Trepidation repeated. "He will come and pretend at being me. This weak sham. This desperate ploy. But look at him shake with fear. All can see his trepidation. I named him well."

"No!" Konig backed away. "I am Konig. *He*"—he thrust a finger at the smirking Doppel—"is Trepidation!"

Trepidation shook his head sadly. "Do any here see an ounce of fear in me?"

For a moment all eyes turned to the Doppel, and Konig sagged with relief, but in a flash they returned to him. Trepidation stood tall, fearless.

Konig's heart quailed. "No . . . I'm the real me." His voice shook, weak and pleading.

A hugely muscled hand landed on his shoulder from behind and forced him to his knees. He looked up, saw the massive face glaring down at him, and squeaked pitifully.

*No. Not like this.* He was Konig. Wasn't he? Gods, he was so scared. He couldn't think straight. This wasn't right. Konig knew no fear. Trepidation was his fear manifest. If he felt fear . . . either he *was* Trepidation or the Doppel was dead.

*Why don't they love me?* He'd done so much for his people. He needed their love. He'd *earned* it. They owed him worship!

Trepidation drew a mirror from within his robes and held it up for Konig to see. The mirror reflected the room, but none of the people within it.

Konig stared up at himself standing tall and fearless. "Who?"

And he stared down at himself. "I am who you would be. Konig Furimmer, High Priest of the Geborene Damonen, Theocrat of Selbsthass. You are but a pale reflection." With the last word he winked at himself.

*Reflection?* Had a reflection somehow escaped a mirror? *Impossible! Trepidation and Acceptance destroyed the mirrors!*

Except Acceptance had kept one for himself. Had Trepidation done the same? Of course he had.

He gestured down at himself, and the weight of the hand lifted from his shoulder. Konig's relief was flashing brief. A fist closed about his bald skull with crushing force and lifted him off his feet. He hung dangling like a child's doll.

"He has become too dangerous," he said.

No, wait. He hadn't said it, the other had, the impostor. Gods, he was so scared, so confused.

"And yet I have use for him. He must serve." He stood before himself, mirror raised and held just before his face. The mirror reflected naught but an empty room. "Push him in," Konig commanded the Dysmorphic.

Konig's face pressed hard against cold glass, the narrow rim of the mirror crushing an ear.

*It's too small! I can't fit in here!*

Slowly the surface of the mirror gave way beneath his cheek, sucking at him like thick, cold mud. His skull groaned from the pressure.

*You're killing me!*

The surface of the mirror collapsed and he tumbled into an empty room, landing badly. His skull throbbed with pain and each breath shot stabs of agony through his chest; he'd broken something inside. He stared about the empty room. Where had everyone gone?

Turning, he saw the room ended suddenly at a wall of glass. Beyond that wall, the people, Dysmorphics, priests, and acolytes, stood gathered, staring at him. They were huge, giants. The view through the window was spinning alarmingly and Konig found himself staring up at himself.

"What shall I call you?" the Konig beyond the wall asked.

Konig screamed, hurling himself bodily against the glass, pounding at it with his fists until the finger he'd broken beating Acceptance broke a second time.

The Konig beyond grinned, eyes wide and insane. "They can't hear you," he whispered. "No one can hear you."

Konig collapsed to the floor of his empty room. His prison.

"I think I shall call you Failure," he said, tucking the small mirror into his robes. He said more, but with his voice muffled by the thick crimson robes of the Theocrat, Failure couldn't hear him.

*No, that isn't me. I'm in here.*

Sprawled on the floor, cradling broken ribs, Failure giggled and wept.

*You may be free, but now I am the reflection. I see what you cannot.*

The giggle broke into crazed laughter and then choked off into sobs of pain.

Konig's freedom would be short-lived, Failure knew.

*Morgen will return.*

# CHAPTER 43

*Those who live without a great fire in their soul live in darkness.*

—BRENNENDE SEELE, HASSEBRAND

Morgen lay curled in mud hot enough to raise blisters. The sun had gone down and night had fallen. He hadn't seen it happen. The camp flowed around him as if he weren't there, as if he were beneath notice. And maybe he was. Mud and blood caked his mottled skin, formed crusts in his hair. He could open only one eye, and then only enough to peer through a thin, throbbing slit. His face was aflame in pain, and when he tried to reach a hand up to touch his bent nose, he found he couldn't. His arms hung like insensate lumps of dead flesh. They refused to obey his commands.

*Are they broken?*

With a whimper he tilted his head enough to look the length of his body. The one arm he saw was bent the wrong way at the elbow. Farther down he saw his fingers splayed at impossible angles. When he drew breath something grated deep inside his chest and he felt a stabbing pain in his guts.

*They've broken me.*

But why had they stopped?

It didn't matter; he was beyond grateful for the respite. Even if everything hurt, at least no new pain was being added, no new indignity heaped upon his shattered frame.

Erbrechen's face filled Morgen's view. He looked worried.

"You're still alive, thank the gods! I thought those idiots killed you. I can stop them. Do you want me to stop them?"

Morgen coughed out sharp fragments of teeth. "Pluh," he said. *Please. No more. Anything.*

Erbrechen touched his face gently. "Poor boy. Poor, poor boy."

"Pluh."

"Poor, poor boy. I'll protect you. You want my protection?"

Morgen tried to nod but nothing worked. "Pluh."

"What? You want me to protect you?"

"Yush," he sobbed. "Pluh!"

"They'll hurt you again if I let them."

Morgen cringed. "Nuh muh. Pluh."

"No one here loves you more than I do," purred Erbrechen. "You know this, right?"

Morgen tried to speak but a spasm of coughing interrupted him. When it passed, he saw he'd coughed blood into the mud.

"Gehirn wants to burn you with fire. Only I can stop her. You don't want to be burned alive, do you?"

Burned. Fire. Those two words punched holes in Morgen's scrambled thoughts, punctured the fog of agony. He'd seen fire. There had to be fire.

Nothing else mattered.

"Fuh," he said, desperately trying to make his mouth and jaw work.

"Fire?" asked Erbrechen. "Fire is scary. Painful."

The fat bastard went on, but Morgen wasn't listening. He didn't know what to do. Gehirn terrified him, but he'd seen fire. The reflections had been right about everything. There *had* to be fire. He knew what he needed to do but shied away from it. There would be no going back.

"Fire," he whispered.

Erbrechen leaned in to better hear. His earlobe swung fat and greasy, filling Morgen's vision.

Morgen, remembering Stehlen, spat a bloody glob of phlegm into the Slaver's ear.

Erbrechen turned to look at him, a long streamer of thick red drool swinging from his earlobe. "Oh, child. That was a mistake. A terrible mistake." He glanced at two men who appeared out of the darkness. "He's not ready yet. Beat him some more." The men nodded happily, rapturous to be given the chance to serve. "If you kill him, you'll suffer beyond anything."

*No! This isn't right! Erbrechen threatened fire! There's supposed to be fire! Not more—*

Someone kicked him in the face and his vision shattered apart like a broken mirror. White agony. Blows fell upon his body from everywhere. There must have been more men he hadn't seen.

*Where is the fire? The reflections showed me fire.*

Oh gods. Had they lied?

⸻

Bedeckt came as close to the camp as he dared. He stood watching, hidden in the trees, covered by the dark of night. The camp followers were uniformly filthy. At a quick guess, he estimated thousands occupied this camp. Most milled about aimlessly or rutted in the mud or fought over something he couldn't see. Many weren't even wearing boots and most wore no more than a few strips of ratty clothing.

He'd seen this before, a long, long time ago. This was what

happened when people fell under the influence of a powerful Slaver-type Gefahrgeist; they lost all sense of self. These people were barely capable of feeding themselves, much less bathing or grooming. If it went on long enough, most would starve to death unless the Slaver thought to remind them to eat. And how rarely did Gefahrgeist think of others?

"You aren't going to get anything done from here," he whispered to himself.

*Well then, maybe you should just leave.*

Bedeckt stood motionless. He saw nothing of the boy, but then the camp was the size of a small city, albeit one consisting solely of vagrants.

"Well, if you aren't going to get anything done from here, why not do it from somewhere farther away and much safer?"

Gods, he hated Slavers. Few things terrified him more than losing oneself in the self-aggrandizing delusions of another.

*Walk away. Put this scene behind you.*

He stripped off his shirt, tossing it aside. Won't be needing that again. The air felt cold on his bare chest.

*Go back and find Launisch.* With a few days riding he could be in Folgen Sienie.

Bedeckt reached into the mud and dug up a great fistful. He smeared it across his body and into his hair.

To hells with the boy and everyone who wants to use him. This was none of Bedeckt's problem.

He looked at his boots. Die with your boots on. Damned if he would take them off. When he figured he looked as much like one of the Slaver's pitiful drudges as he cared to, he scooped up his massive ax, slung it over his shoulder, and set off into camp. The ax would make him stand out in this crowd, but no way was he going anywhere without it.

Boots and ax. He needed nothing more.

He marched through the camp, pushing his way through mobs

drunk on worshiping their Slaver master. The air grew warmer the farther into the camp he got. Something or someone near the center of the camp was heating the atmosphere for acres around and he immediately knew what was causing it. *Shite.*

Slavers might be frightening, but Hassebrands were down-right dangerous.

When people saw him coming, they scattered out of his way like a flock of startled chickens. Most, however, were too lost to notice him. These he shoved rudely through. Few paid him any attention, but those who did stared unabashedly. As he pushed forward the air grew thick with heat, and soon he was sweating profusely.

Ahead he saw a huge litter, and sitting upon it a gelatinous mountain of a human. He couldn't tell from here if it was male or female; fat hid everything. A dozen men and women sat or stood near the litter, many muttering to themselves, picking at their flesh, or twitching at things unseen. The Slaver had gathered a cadre of Geisteskranken about him, and gods knew what delusions and powers they possessed. No way he could kill them all.

A young woman with shards of mirror glued to her flesh glanced at Bedeckt, eyes widening in apparent recognition. She looked to the Slaver, opening her mouth as if about to speak, and then stopped. Turning, the mirrored woman hurried away as if attempting to surreptitiously flee for her life.

*What the hells was that about?* Had the Mirrorist woman seen something in the reflections?

Sitting cross-legged in the filth was a tall woman with a glistening bald skull. The air around her shimmered. Every now and then the woman's fists clenched and a wave of blistering heat swept off her. This then was the Hassebrand. Four men stood nearby, thin and hungry-looking. They were nothing, drudges of the Slaver. Dangerous only if they got in the way.

Bedeckt stopped. *Slaver or Hassebrand?* With a camp of fol-

457

lowers like this, the Slaver must be at the peak of his power. The Slaver could take him with a single word.

He glanced at the sitting Hassebrand. This was a woman beyond the pinnacle, well into a swift descent to madness. She might last days, but it could just as easily be minutes.

Who should he kill first?

*The Hassebrand.*

"So, boy," said the Slaver, gesturing a massive arm at a pile of dirt. Fat swung underneath the arm like billowing curtains. "Do you wish for more? They're itching for more, you know. They keep asking if they can beat you further."

From the pile of gathered filth Bedeckt heard a soft moan. A single glistening eye cracked open and stared directly at him. His mind fit the pieces together. There, bent at an impossible angle, a child's arm. Those weren't branches sticking from the mud, they were splayed fingers.

Morgen.

They'd broken the boy. Tortured the purest soul Bedeckt had ever met. They had crushed him to the filth, sullying more than just the boy's faith, but his very being. Bedeckt couldn't help thinking—knowing what he did about Morgen—that he knew what bothered the god-to-be more.

The ax came off its resting place on his shoulder as Bedeckt moved forward.

He would kill them all. Every single miserable living wretch without the will to turn against this Slaver or the wisdom to flee Bedeckt's wrath.

The drudges saw him and screamed something incomprehensible. Red bloody rage washed away all sound. His head filled with the slamming beat of his heart and the pulsating need to do death. The Slaver strained to turn his head far enough to see Bedeckt, eyes wide and wet, fat lips quivering. The mouth opened and said something.

Bedeckt didn't understand a word.

The Slaver's power was nothing compared to his rage. It wasn't delusion, but something more than that—a belief in himself based on experience and pride and fear and all the things that make a sane person able to cope in this mad world. He had one purpose and one purpose alone. He stepped past the Hassebrand, who glanced up at him but didn't otherwise move. He felt the hair on his head shrink and curl as a pulse of heat washed over him.

The Slaver's fat arm swung slowly around and pointed at Bedeckt. Fat lips writhed in terror and the drudges came at him. Bedeckt didn't slow. With a swing of his ax he cut the first one down. The man didn't try to defend himself, running straight into the blow. Bedeckt spun, slamming an elbow into the nose of the next as he ripped the ax from the chest of the first. Someone clawed at his muddy torso and he drew a dagger with his half hand, driving it into flesh in one swift motion. The body fell away, taking his dagger with it. The fourth dove at Bedeckt, seeking to tackle him, and met Bedeckt's raised knee. Nose shattering with a damp crunch, the drudge fell heavily into the mud, clutching at his face.

The whole camp came alive. Thousands of scrawny men and women surged forward, each desperate to be the one to reach Bedeckt. He couldn't kill them all. They'd drag him down.

But not before he did what he came to do.

〰〰〰

Gehirn Schlechtes, once Hassebrand of the Geborene Damonen, loyal servant to Konig Furimmer, sat in the steaming mud, her arse soaked through, the skin blistering from the heat. She could do nothing to better her position. She watched a huge old man, back rippling with scarred muscle, step past her. Watched as the double-bladed ax, held in one massive scarred fist, swung effortlessly off a broad shoulder. Watched as Erbrechen noticed the man. Saw bright fear blossom in the Slaver's eyes as the old man ignored his screamed commands and plaintive appeals for worship. The old man was stone-deaf or even more insane than Erbrechen.

"Kill him!" Erbrechen screamed at the nearby men when he realized his Gefahrgeist powers were having no effect. The four who had been beating Morgen charged forward, hurled themselves at the grizzled old man. The scarred warrior was liquid death. He flowed around and through them, leaving corpses and shattered bones in his wake.

Erbrechen screamed at Gehirn, "What are you doing?"

The Hassebrand, arse soaking in the mud, stared up at the Slaver.

*Sit. Be silent. Say nothing. Do nothing.* Erbrechen's last commands. Gehirn would follow them until told otherwise.

She grinned at the Slaver, showing sharp canines. *Die, you—*

"Burn him burn him burn him!" Erbrechen pointed at the approaching man.

With a sob Gehirn pushed herself to her feet. She gritted teeth until they creaked and groaned in her jaw. It was useless. She would obey. She would burn the old man. She lifted a hand. Beyond the scarred warrior she saw the gathered thousands of the camp rushing in. No way she could burn just the warrior.

No way she *wanted* to burn just the warrior.

What little control remained frayed apart.

"I loved you!" she screamed at Erbrechen. "I just wanted to matter. Just a little!"

Gehirn unraveled.

⸻

Bedeckt stood over Morgen, ax hanging comfortably in his hand. They came at him, screaming insensate rage. Thousands of men and women racing to be the first to bring him down. This was a shite death, but then what kind of death had he expected? Certainly nothing better. Truth be told, he had always hoped to die in a brothel with a smile on his face.

*No one ever gets what they want.*

Wichtig and Stehlen certainly hadn't, though it could be argued that they got what they deserved. Shaking those thoughts aside, he couldn't help think that, for the first time in a long time, he felt good. No regrets. Maybe dying with one good deed to his credit was no match for a lifetime of robbery and murder, but he didn't care. This wasn't about balance. This wasn't about doing good. He wasn't a good man, so there would be no redemption. The list of things he wouldn't do was far shorter than the list of crimes he was willing to perpetrate.

But *this* he could not allow.

Bedeckt screamed, "You'll serve in hell!" and threw his ax at the fat Slaver.

⸻

Fire boiled up from Gehirn's seething guts, seared her tongue, before spilling past clenched teeth. Her robes, long since fouled and fallen to decay, ignited. The mud at her feet bubbled and boiled.

The scarred old man threw his ax, splitting Erbrechen's skull in two. The chains of obedience binding Gehirn fell away and she laughed aloud.

*Free!* She cried, and the tears of flame began as relief, but quickly dissolved into anguish and . . . joy.

For she was not free. There was no putting this fire back, no shoving her self-loathing back down into the dark depths of her soul.

This would be her last fire. She knew it.

She welcomed it.

The mob of Erbrechen's followers still streamed forward, screaming and crying. The Slaver's death may have freed them, but nothing could free them from the memories of their actions. Appalled terror stretched faces in haunted screams. They wanted death as much as they wanted to kill the scarred old man for opening their eyes.

*There's a lesson here,* thought Gehirn as control fled. *No one thanks you for showing them the light.*

She'd show them her light nonetheless. Welcome or not. She'd set them all free.

Truly free.

The ground shook with a pulse of power and a few hundred desperate souls became ash. All around, the earth boiled and steamed. She couldn't control it. Her chest split from the fire within. Blood boiled in her veins.

"Run!" she screamed at the old man.

‧‧‧‧‧‧‧‧‧‧

Bedeckt stared at the Hassebrand. The woman's skin glowed and darkened as if scorched from within.

"Take the boy and run!" yelled the Hassebrand, startlingly bright blue eyes wide and pleading.

A wave of heat raised blisters on Bedeckt's skin and blasted away what little hair he had left. He'd never make it to the woman in time to kill her before fire turned this whole stinking valley to molten stone.

Bedeckt bent and scooped Morgen into his arms. Blistered skin tore on his fingers and wept. He ignored the pain. It was nothing. He turned his back, sheltering the boy with the bulk of his body as the Hassebrand screamed and twitched and let loose another searing blast of heat, scattering the ash of a few hundred drudges.

Bedeckt stumbled away, barely aware that what little clothing he wore was ablaze. His back was one large raw wound, the flesh crisped and cooked ashen white. He moved, one foot in front of the other, crushing Morgen to his body as if he could protect the boy from all that had happened. If the boy made noise, Bedeckt couldn't hear it. The men and women who had been rushing him were gone. A wide-open field lay ahead, ankle-deep in sodden ash. His feet burned as he pushed through boiling mud. A foot sank deep and he dragged it free, leaving the steaming boot in the mud. One foot in front of the other. The skin on his back melted and sloughed away in great hanging threads.

"It's okay," he told Morgen. "I have you. You'll be okay." For once he hoped he wasn't lying to the boy.

As Bedeckt stumbled down a hill the sky behind him lit as if from a thousand bonfires. An explosion slammed him to the mud and endless flame roared around him. He huddled Morgen underneath him, shielding the boy from the fire as best he could. His skin charred. Any part touching earth felt like it was being boiled. Endless agony. He had to stand. He had to keep moving. He had to get Morgen away from here.

His legs didn't work. The smell of burned flesh filled his nostrils. Darkness took him.

<hr />

Gehirn fought to control the flood of emotion and fire spilling out of her soul. The scarred old man stumbled out of sight down a hill, carrying Morgen.

*Move, damn it! Run!*

She couldn't hold it any longer!

Fire burned her to nothing. She was soft ash, caught spinning in a tornado of flame. The world fell away and the heavens lit bright.

One last fire. One last beautiful fire. The gods would see this and know.

# CHAPTER 44

*I think if you walk toward the Afterdeath thinking it is a chance at redemption, it's already too late.*

—Hoffnungslos

Bedeckt awoke with a groan.

This wasn't so bad. He'd expected more pain.

He moved, and burned skin everywhere cracked open and bled. He lifted his left hand and stared at it. Charred bone. Strange he couldn't feel it, but just as well.

*It should probably hurt,* he thought numbly.

He tried to stand, but nothing happened. He glanced the length of his body and saw his legs too were charred ruin.

*That should hurt too.*

A cough caught his attention and he used his remaining arm to turn painfully. Morgen stared at him through one swollen eye, the boy's face battered beyond recognition, his arms bent at impossible angles. Every joint looked to have been savagely broken or twisted out of place. Bedeckt had known grown men to die from lesser wounds.

"I saw the fire," whispered Morgen so softly Bedeckt had to lean in close to hear.

"There was a big fire," Bedeckt agreed. Oh, there was the pain he'd expected. Talking was agony, his throat raw and seared. It felt like his lungs had been boiled.

"Gehirn?"

"Who?" Bedeckt croaked.

"Hassebrand."

"Dead. All dead."

"Good."

"Morgen."

"Yes?"

"I'm done. Your Hassebrand friend has slain me."

"Not yet."

"Soon." Very soon. Bedeckt felt his grip on life weakening. Darkness beckoned, its cool embrace growing more attractive by the second.

"I'm dying," said Morgen. "I don't know which will kill me first."

"Which?" asked Bedeckt, confused.

"The wounds I suffered at the hands of Erbrechen's men, or the Hassebrand's fire."

*What is the boy saying?* Bedeckt struggled to follow. It was difficult to think. "So?"

"Those whom you slay serve in the Afterdeath," whispered Morgen.

"Shite." Bedeckt understood.

"You have to kill me."

Bedeckt laughed, a dry cough of smoke. "Forget it. It's on the list. I don't kill children."

"You have to. Gehirn hates herself. I'd be too dangerous under her control." Bedeckt glared at the boy as the single swollen eye cracked open to stare at him. "And the Slaver . . ." The boy shuddered. "*You* have to," whispered Morgen, begging.

"But then I . . . You'll have to serve me."

"You're fallible, but you won't use a child."

"Fallible?" Bedeckt asked, dumbfounded by the boy's naïveté.

"Means you make mistakes."

"I know what it—"

"It's on your list now. You won't use children. I'll be free."

Maybe, but free to be what? What kind of god would this child be? No, that wasn't what Bedeckt cared about. He really wanted to know how Morgen could be so sure Bedeckt wouldn't make use of the fact that a god was serving him in the After-death. What kind of man did Morgen think him? Which begged another question:

*What kind of man am I?*

There was no answer. Instead, Morgen whispered, "Soon I will know."

"Know what?"

"If Konig lied. Born of faith or . . . mother." The boy's eye closed. "Hurry. Not much time. Going."

"Can't. Ax gone. Left my knife in someone."

Morgen cracked a small smile, showing the shattered remains of teeth that were startling white in his burned and filthy face. "I have one. Belt."

Bedeckt found the knife hidden under Morgen's torn clothes. Reaching it was difficult with only one working limb, and by the time he had it, his vision had narrowed to a collapsing tunnel. The knife, spotless, glinted in the fading light. It looked familiar.

"Where?" asked Bedeckt.

"Stehlen," answered Morgen.

"Oh."

When had the boy taken it? After Bedeckt killed her? He supposed it didn't really matter.

Morgen's eyes widened as he saw the knife. *That's not fear,* Bedeckt realized. *That's understanding.* What did the boy see?

"Oh, *shite*," Morgen said clearly, gaze never leaving the blade's mirrored surface. "They're laughing. They lied to me. This whole time . . ." His swollen eyes, leaking tears, slid closed. "The future, it was never set in stone. I killed . . . They led me to this . . . tricked me." The boy's small, broken body shook with sobs. "They'll Ascend with me."

"They?" Bedeckt asked, confused.

"Konig was wrong," whispered Morgen, his voice cracking. "Aufschlag was wrong. I'm no god; I'm just a . . . a . . ."

"Morgen?"

The boy didn't answer, though his chest still rose and fell in short, shallow breaths.

"Morgen!"

Nothing.

*What the hells was he talking about?* It didn't matter. "I don't kill children. It's on the list."

Nothing.

But if he didn't . . . and then he understood.

*Oh, shite!*

The very same Hassebrand had slain Bedeckt. He too would soon die of his wounds. Even if he killed the boy, Morgen would still wind up serving the insane woman.

Unless . . .

Bedeckt pushed Stehlen's knife through Morgen's chest and into his heart. When he tried to pull the knife free, it stuck.

*Oh, gods sticking hells, no!*

Bedeckt tried again, straining with all his remaining might. The knife moved slowly, grating where it caught on a rib—*Come on!*—and finally slid free.

Bedeckt wept tears of joy. He held the knife clutched to his own chest, huddling it there like a lover. He strained to catch sight of the bloody blade. Stehlen. So much death they'd seen together. How many backs had she put this very knife into? How many throats had she cut in dark alleys?

Bedeckt drew the knife upward along his chest until the tip pricked the soft skin under his chin.

One more. One more death.

She'd be waiting. Stehlen would be there and he'd have to see her again. What would he say? What *could* he say?

"Sorry for killing you," hissed Bedeckt, and drove the knife up through his throat into his brain.

# CHAPTER 45

*What I want to know is what happens when you are killed in the Afterdeath? Is there an Afterafterdeath? How long does this go on? Who dreamed this insanity?*

—Einsam Geschichtenerzähler

A crowd of thousands stood before Erbrechen. He looked them over appraisingly. This was no gathering of the weak unwashed. These were warriors, dangerous, each and every one.

"Well, well, well. This is handy indeed," he said.

A short scrawny woman with yellowy eyes, a sickly complexion, and teeth that made him want to avert his gaze stepped forward. A cocky-looking dandy with a matched pair of swords peeking over his broad shoulders stood at her side, as perfectly beautiful as she was hideous.

The woman spat at Erbrechen's feet. "And how is this handy, you jiggling puddle of fat?"

Erbrechen smiled his best innocent and disarming smile.

"Why, to have you all waiting. Though I've caused my share of death, I never expected so many."

"He thinks we're waiting for *him*," the dandy said to the woman.

"It doesn't really matter who you're waiting for," Erbrechen said gleefully. "You're here, and now so am I. You are mine. You are *all* mine. You love me, don't you."

ıııııııııııı

Stehlen killed the fat slug, spinning a knife into an eye socket, before he annoyed her further.

"Why did you kill him?" Wichtig asked. "He seemed nice."

"Idiot. Bedeckt killed him."

"So?"

"So I didn't want to listen to him prattling on about himself while we wait. It's bad enough I have to listen to your inane drivel."

"Inane?"

"Ask Bedeckt what it means. And look how big the fat sow is. No way he . . . she . . . it can walk far. Someone would have had to carry it."

Wichtig examined the fat slug. "What a corpulent corpse," he said, dashing a smirk at Stehlen.

She rolled her eyes. "I watched you think that one up. Your face gets all scrunchy when you're concentrating."

"Is he going to be long?" Wichtig asked, ignoring her.

She pointed downhill. "He's lying in the mud there."

Wichtig glanced in the direction she pointed. "Just looks like a big pile of dirt."

"It's him."

"Shall we say hello?"

She turned and strode down the hill without answering and heard Wichtig follow behind.

"What are you going to do?" he called out. "Are you going to kill him?"

Truth be told, she wasn't sure.

━━━━━━

Bedeckt lay in quiet peace. A soft breeze smelling of fresh clover caressed his skin. Nothing hurt, a blessed relief. The wind tickled the toes of his left foot. Damn. Where had he left his boot?

The left boot. *Shite*. The one with the money in it.

A boot nudged Bedeckt in the ribs.

"What is it with you and losing your boots?"

Wichtig's voice. No, couldn't be. Wichtig was—

Bedeckt cracked an eye open and looked up at Stehlen and Wichtig. The two stared down at him, Wichtig looking cocky as always, Stehlen . . . he wasn't sure what her expression was.

"You going to lie in the grass all day?" Stehlen asked.

"I expected a lot more people," said Bedeckt, not moving.

"They're up the hill, waiting," she answered, gesturing with a flick of fingers. "Seems you've got a bloody army gathered here."

Bedeckt wiggled his toes. They felt fine, not at all like they'd been charred to the bone. "Morgen?" he asked.

"Nowhere to be seen," answered Wichtig. "He's dead?" When Bedeckt nodded, he continued. "But I feel no compulsion. I had to come here, and here I am. But it's gone now. I feel . . . free." Wichtig looked confused, as if this wasn't what he'd hoped for or expected. "I can go wherever I want," finished the Swordsman.

"Morgen must have released you," said Bedeckt.

"Could he do that?" asked Stehlen, her eyes lighting with hope.

Ignoring the question, Bedeckt sat up with a groan. His spine popped and cracked and his lower back ached. Somehow he'd thought he'd be starting again here, a young man at the very least. He glanced up at Stehlen; she watched him with intense yellowy eyes.

"Forget it," said Bedeckt, pushing to his feet. "If I release you, you'll kill me for sure."

"I might not."

"Right," scoffed Wichtig, who fell silent when Stehlen glared in his direction.

"Stehlen, go fetch me some boots and an ax from the army over there. Someone must have something that will fit."

She spun away with a growl and he called, "Wait!"

Stehlen stood with her back to him, shoulders hunched. Bedeckt thought about what his father had said. Did she really love him? Had she really let him kill her? The possibility seemed crazy, but then it *was* Stehlen.

"I have something for you," he said.

"My freedom?" she growled.

"Uh . . . no. Not yet. Maybe later, once I think you won't kill me the very second I free you." *Why is this so damned awkward?* He felt like a damned teenager. Bedeckt drew the ragged and faded scarves from his pocket and held them out to her still-turned back. "These."

She turned with a snarl and stopped. The anger disappeared from her eyes, replaced by a look Bedeckt had never expected to see there. Tears welled up and she brushed them roughly away with a stained sleeve. Gently she took the scarves from his hand, folded them lovingly, and hid them back inside her shirt.

"This is yours too," said Bedeckt, lifting the knife he still clutched in his hand.

She took it without a word and it too disappeared into her clothing. "I'll go get your damned boots and ax," she said.

Stehlen spat on his bare foot, spun, and marched away, spine straight. Wichtig and Bedeckt watched her leave, exchanging confused glances.

"Where are you going now?" Bedeckt asked.

"No idea," said Wichtig. "Got quite the little army of my own, though nothing like what you and Stehlen have between you."

"In a straight fight I might give your lot the edge," said Bedeckt. "You've got a lot of excellent Swordsmen." Wichtig preened and Bedeckt let him have his moment. "Mine are mostly people I killed from behind in the dark or during drunken brawls. A sorry-looking lot."

"Greatest Swordsman in the Afterdeath," mused Wichtig. "Not quite the same ring, but it'll do."

"And that pursuit turned out well," said Bedeckt before he could stop himself. "Sorry. You're not going to start over? Not going to try something different?"

Wichtig snorted derisively. "And do what? Farm?"

"You were a pretty good poet," said Bedeckt.

"No. I am who I am."

"Good. I need the old Wichtig. I need the Greatest Swordsman in This or Any Other World."

"You have a plan?" Wichtig asked, showing perfect teeth in a wide grin. "A little something up your sleeve?"

"Better." Bedeckt met Wichtig's grin with his own. "I killed a god."

# CHAPTER 46

*The mirror ever lies.*

—Auf der Lauer, Mirrorist

Flesh, savaged by fire and made anew by Morgen's Ascension, remembered the agony. With each breath he felt the cold steel of Stehlen's knife as Bedeckt slid it between his ribs to pierce his heart. And the filth followed him. His hands would never be clean again. He'd spilled blood. He'd lied and murdered. He was contaminated, corrupted.

Morgen screamed and his reflections laughed and pranced and frolicked in his misery, for they too had Ascended alongside him. This, he realized, had always been their plan. They hadn't served him or shown glimpses of the future as a means of guidance. No, they'd led him by the nose to this moment. They'd manipulated his every choice.

Why hadn't Aufschlag or Konig told him not to trust the reflections? Surely they had known. How different would things have been if someone had been willing to educate him, just a little?

Morgen's reflections, each an aspect of the boy's shattered mind, bowed mockingly and fled into the world to pursue whatever capricious distractions they sought.

*I'll never be the god the Geborene wanted.*

Yet even that had been a lie. If the Geborene had wanted a good god, a pure god, then that is what he should have been; their beliefs should have defined him. But he wasn't. He was a *free* god. He could do whatever he wanted, play with lives, snuff souls on a whim, or send all Selbsthass marching to war. And they would, they'd obey his every command. For he, Morgen, a tortured little boy, was their god.

Morgen looked down upon Selbsthass City, watching the bustle of people going about their business. This seemingly omniscient view reminded him of playing with the toy soldiers and peasants in his model city. He remembered the bloodless battle between the two groups and joking with Konig that the peasants were revolting. At the time he'd thought Konig hadn't found it funny. Now he knew Konig simply hadn't understood it as a joke. As a god, he saw things differently, understood Konig's Doppels and reflections for what they were: manifestations of self-loathing, cowardice, and fear.

What kind of god could such a man make?

Morgen knew the answer: a broken god.

Morgen rose higher still. Far to the east he saw the jagged ridges of the Kälte Mountains and knew that beyond them lay the eternal wastes of the Basamortuan desert, the easternmost edge of the world. He could sense other gods, distant and vague. Some were relatively young, no more than a few millennia old, while others were ancient beyond reckoning. All, he realized, were Ascended mortals.

*Where are the old gods?* He sensed nothing of the creatures whose delusions were supposed to have created this twisted reality and birthed mankind. *Have they abandoned us, sickened by all we are?* It seemed possible. Likely, even.

*Or are they just another layer of lies?*

It didn't matter, he decided. They were gone or had never been.

Morgen turned his back on such thoughts and moved east, thinking to see for himself the vast wealth of Geldangelegenheiten, and stopped; the borders of man, defined by politics, war, and faith—all three manifestations of delusion—meant even more to gods. Morgen could not leave Selbsthass.

Beyond this city-state, no one believed in him.

*Even my omniscience is a lie.*

That, Morgen decided, would have to change.

He returned to Selbsthass City—the center of his power—this time focusing on the twisted castle the Geborene called home. For a time he watched, his skin burning, his heart shuddering with stabbing pain, as his priests scuttled about their business. In the tallest tower the new Konig, once a reflection and now basking in its illusory freedom, planned how he would use his new god.

Morgen laughed, a scornful sob of bitter pain. Konig—each and every aspect and manifestation—thought far too small. Their dreams were the dreams of pitiful, terrified men. The days of being used by such fools were done.

Manifesting in Konig's personal chambers, Morgen crushed the man to the thick carpeting with a savage and gleeful will. In a hand mirror on Konig's massive oaken desk, he saw Failure applauding joyfully. That joy wouldn't last.

Konig blubbered incoherently, begging and pleading and desperate to please.

"You are nothing to me," said Morgen, and Konig nodded,

agreeing. "I have many of you to chose from. You will be useful or I will snuff you from existence."

That too was a lie; he could not cause a soul to cease to exist. Limits and rules defined his power. The dead moved on. Where they went next might depend on their beliefs, or who killed them, but they always moved on. It was law.

*I am a god!* Morgen raged. *How can I be so limited?*

Pushing aside these thoughts, he returned his attention to Konig. "I am the culmination of all you have wrought, everything the Geborene have worked for. I have Ascended and I am your god."

Morgen again screamed as flames danced across his flesh and the memory of icy steel sought his heart.

Konig, blood trickling from his ears, pressed his face to the floor as if he sought to disappear into the carpeting. "Yes! Yes! Yes!" he wailed, his voice muffled. The pathetic wretch had soiled himself.

*How could I ever have looked up to this man? How could I have loved him?*

"I will not be limited," said Morgen, forcing cold calm.

Konig merely nodded dumbly.

"If I am to remake this world, I must be everywhere. I must be worshiped everywhere."

"We will spread the word," Konig said, cringing.

Morgen ignored the filthy mortal's words. "The Geborene will infiltrate every city-state. We shall bring holy war to all who resist." *This time the war will not be clean and bloodless.* "I shall scour this world. It shall be clean, immaculate. Forever."

"The old gods—"

"Stick the old gods."

Konig's eyes widened comically at Morgen's coarse language. "The Wahnvor Stellung will resist us."

"We shall eradicate them *and* their gods." Morgen drove Konig against the floor until he heard the man's ribs groan in protest. "There will be only one god."

"One . . . god . . ." gasped Konig.

"Geborene temples in every city. Each shall be a pinnacle of purity." He grinned madly at Konig's prostrate form, basking in the man's terror, savoring the taste of his abject worship. "White. I want spotless, white pyramids. Everywhere."

"Purity" was all Konig managed to force from his compressed lungs.

Morgen released the man and listened to the shuddering intake of breath. "We are no longer a Theocracy."

"We . . . we aren't?" Konig stared at him, eyes brimming with tears, though whether from gratitude or awe or sadness Morgen couldn't tell.

Morgen gestured at Failure, the previous Konig, watching from within the mirror. "I promised you I'd bring back the days of empire. Unlike you—" He bared his teeth as another searing stab of agony sought his heart. "Unlike *all* of you, I keep my promises. No mere *Theocrat* rules here. I do. This is a nation ruled by a god. This is the Holy Empire of Selbsthass."

Once again Konig nodded dumbly.

"Make it happen," Morgen commanded, and fled the corrupt stench of the soiled man's apartments.

GHOSTS OF TORMENT savaged Morgen's flesh. He remembered Erbrechen's followers beating him, snapping his fingers like green twigs. He was drowning in filth, mud clogging his eyes closed, suffocating his broken nose. Gods, he wanted to torture that foul slug. But when Morgen reached out he sensed nothing of the Slaver. Even in the Afterdeath nothing remained of the man. Was it just that Erbrechen didn't believe in Morgen and thus the boy-god had no power over him, or had something else happened to the grotesque man?

*How can a god be so limited?*

Was he defined by the beliefs of his worshipers? Could he free himself of these rules simply by changing what people believed, or did something else, something greater even than he, enforce these laws? And if so, where was it? He sensed other gods, but nothing with the power to so utterly and unequivocally define reality.

Morgen cloaked himself in false flesh and walked Selbsthass City. They believed in him now, but soon they would worship with absolute conviction. His Geborene would hunt and crush all hints of doubt and dissent. Then, once he owned these grimy little souls, he would send them to war, march them like toy soldiers.

But he needed more than soldiers, he'd learned that much from Konig. He needed assassins and spies.

Morgen reached out for Asena and her Tiergeist and found them wandering the Afterdeath, still a pack, bound by the young Therianthrope's need. Anomie and her Schatten Mörder he found too. They believed in him, each and every one of them.

The assassins answered his call.

He wasn't finished, for he needed dangerously insane people willing to do dangerously insane things. He needed raw savage power, someone willing to burn the world for the one they loved.

There was one person who even at the end, her sanity incinerating, had sought to protect him with her final act. She loved Morgen as she had loved no other.

Morgen searched the Afterdeath for Gehirn and found her, a small child no older than himself, a delicate girl who just wanted to be loved, desperately seeking redemption.

"I'm sorry," he told her, reaching a hand toward the girl. "I need you."

Morgen watched as Gehirn aged before his eyes, growing in height and weight, her long red hair singeing and blowing away like ash in the wind. When she nodded and took his proffered hand, his heart shattered. He knew what this would cost her.

*I've done a terrible thing.*

He brought his assassins and his Hassebrand back to Selbsthass.

And then he felt the pull, the need to return to the Afterdeath. A man there demanded Morgen's presence, and he had no choice but to answer.

Even gods are bound by rules.

# CAST OF CHARACTERS

‖‖‖‖‖‖‖‖‖‖‖‖‖‖‖‖‖‖‖‖‖‖‖‖‖‖‖‖‖‖‖‖‖‖‖‖‖‖‖‖‖‖‖‖‖‖‖‖‖‖‖‖‖‖‖‖‖‖‖‖‖‖‖‖‖‖

**Abandonment:** Doppel of Konig Furimmer.

**Acceptance:** Doppel of Konig Furimmer.

**Anomie:** Leader of the Schatten Mörder, Konig's Cotardist assassins.

**Asena:** Leader of the Tiergeist, Konig's Therianthrope assassins.

**Aufschlag Hoher:** Geborene Chief Scientist.

**Ausfall:** A young girl bred by the Geborene Damonen to be a god.

**Bär:** Tiergeist assassin. Therianthrope with the ability to become a bear.

**Bedeckt Imblut:** Warrior, liar, thief, killer.

**Erbrechen Gedanke:** Slaver.

**Fluch:** Son of Wichtig.

**Gehirn Schlechtes:** Hassebrand.

**Geschwister Schlangen:** Dead sister of Masse, the Tiergeist assassin.

**GroBe Klinge:** Widely considered to the the best Swordsman in Selbsthass.

**Halber Tod:** Cotardist poet.

**Keil Zwischen:** Founder of the Geborene Damonen.

**Konig Furimmer:** High Priest of the Geborene Damonen, Comorbidic (Doppelgangist, Mirrorist, Gefahrgeist).

## CAST OF CHARACTERS

**Kurzschluss Gegangen:** Bishop of the Geborene temple in Gotloss.

**Launisch:** Bedeckt's war-horse.

**Lebendig Durchdachter:** Swordswoman in Neidrig.

**Masse:** Tiergeist assassin. Snakes.

**Meineigener Beobachter:** Head of Konig's personal guard.

**Morgen:** The god/child.

**Ohne Seele:** Master Krieger.

**Regen Anrufer:** Formerly shaman of a small Schlammstamm tribe, Regen is now a favored pet of Erbrechen Gedanke. Regen has delusions of being able to control the weather and talk to animals.

**Schwacher Sucher:** Young Geborene Mirrorist.

**Selbstmörderisch:** Konig's Comorbidic bodyguard, she is a Dysmorphic Mehrere. Selbstmörderisch appears as two different but equally large and massively muscled women.

**Stehlen Siealles:** Violent Kleptic.

**Stich:** Tiergeist assassin. Scorpions.

**Tragen Nachrichten:** Geborene priest.

**Trepidation:** Doppel of Konig Furimmer.

**Verblassen:** King of Einletztes Keuchen, defeated at Vergessener and slain.

**Verlorener Spiegel:** Mirrorist in Unbrauchbar.

**Versklaven Schwache:** Gefahrgeist philosopher.

**Vertrauens Würdig:** One of Konig's personal guards.

**Viele Sindein:** Mehrere. Bodyguard to Morgen Held.

**Vollk Urzschluss:** The Greatest Swordsman in Unbrauchbar.

**Wahrheit Ertrinkt:** Philosopher.

**Wegwerfen:** Geborene priestess, assistant to Aufschlag Hoher.

**Wichtig Lügner:** Swordsman and minor Gefahrgeist.

**Wütend Alten:** Friend of Bedeckt's, lost at the battle of Sinnlos.

**Zuerst Geborene:** Founder of the Geborene Damonen. The first man to deny the supremacy of the gods, Zuerst was cursed and reportedly banished from the Afterdeath.

**Zweifelsschicksal:** Mehrere philosopher who eventually lost control of his multiple personalities and fragmented. Legend has it that he is still alive and traveling as a large crowd of people in search of the original.

**Zweiter Stelle:** Second-best Swordsman in Selbsthass.

# GEISTESKRANKEN
# (THE DELUSIONAL)

||||||||||||||||||||||||||||||||||||||||||||||||||||||||||||||||||||

**Capgrast (Capgras Syndrome):** Believe that a relative or spouse has been replaced by an impostor (often demonic in nature).

**Comorbidic (Comorbidity):** A person with multiple delusions that have reached the manifestation stage. Konig is a Comorbidic, as he is a Gefahrgeist, Doppelgangist, *and* a developing Mirrorist. Comorbidity often marks the final days of a Geisteskranken, as it signifies an increasingly decaying mental state.

**Cotardist (Cotard's Syndrome):** Believe they are dead. Often combined with the belief that they are rotting or missing internal organs.

**Doppelgangist (Syndrome of Subjective Doubles):** Believe a double of themselves is carrying out independent actions.

**Dysmorphic (Dysmorphic Syndrome):** These folks are overly worried about a perceived defect in their physical features. They want to look different so badly that their appearance actually changes. Due to their obsession, they are unable to see the changes and still think themselves defective. Many believe they are so unspeakably hideous that they are unable to interact with others. This will eventually spiral out of control. Most Dysmorphics eventually withdraw from society and end in suicide. Many become abnormally thin, muscled, large-breasted, or exaggerated specimens of physical perfection . . . in one area.

## GEISTESKRANKEN (THE DELUSIONAL)

**Fregolist (Fregoli Delusion):** Believe various people are actually the same person in disguise.

**Gefahrgeist (Sociopath):** Sociopaths lack empathy (the ability to feel for the pain and suffering of others) and morality. They are driven by their need to achieve and rule in social circles.

**Geisteskranken (Delusionist):** Reality is responsive to the beliefs of humanity. Under normal circumstances, it requires large numbers of people—all believing the same thing—to effect change. The more people who believe something, the more real their belief becomes. Geisteskranken are capable of believing something so utterly and completely—are insane enough—to effect noticeable changes in reality all by themselves. Most are only mildly neurotic and can cause minor or subtle changes. A Geisteskranken's power is directly proportional to the strength of his or her delusions.

**Halluzinieren (Hallucinations):** These folks are capable of manifesting hallucinations in one or more senses. Minor Halluzinieren might just cause people to smell whatever the Geisteskranken is thinking about. Powerful Halluzinieren can hallcinate in all five senses and twist local reality.

**Hassebrand (Pyromaniac):** Set fires as an outlet for their repressed rage and loneliness.

**Intermetic (Syndrome of Intermetamorphosis):** Believe people swap identities with each other while maintaining the same appearance.

**Kleptic (Kleptomaniac):** Are compelled to steal things (usually of little or no value). They are often not even aware they've committed the theft.

**Mehrere (Schizophrenic):** Are so sure they are more than one person . . . they actually are! The various people they become can have wildly varying physical and mental traits. The truly deranged can be an entire crowd of people; either one at a time, or all at once.

**Mirrorist (Eisoptrophobia):** Some believe the reflection in a mirror is someone other than themselves. Some Mirrorists believe their reflections know things, can see the future, or travel freely between different mirrors (useful for long-distance communication). Others believe mirrors are portals to other worlds or dimensions. Some Mirrorists fear their reflections are trying to escape, while others fear their reflections are trying to drag them into the mirror.

**Otraalma:** Think they are possessed by demons or evil spirits.

**Phobic:** Anyone suffering a strong phobia.

**The Pinnacle:** The ultimate leveler of the playing field. Embracing one's delusions comes with a price. Sure, holding one's emotional scars tight and constantly picking at one's mental wounds might cause a Geisteskranken to grow in power, but embracing insanity is not healthy. As Geisteskranken lose their grip on reality, they become stronger, more able to utterly believe all manner of insane shite. As their sanity crumbles apart, the range and strength of their delusions increases. Eventually, however, those delusions come to completely define that Geisteskranken's reality. They take over. That moment, that teetering instant when delusion crushes sanity, is the Pinnacle, and for a brief instant, the Geisteskranken might become so powerful as to challenge the gods. Unfortunately (at least for them) they are no longer sane enough to do anything with that power. What happens after depends on the delusions in question. A Mirrorist might be dragged into the mirror by his reflections. The Doppelgangist might be replaced by a Doppel. The Hassebrand might incinerate herself in an orgy of flame.

**Somatoparaphrenic (Somatoparaphrenia):** Believe one or more limbs (sometimes an entire half of their body) belong to someone else. Often this means they have no control over that limb. In extreme cases, the limb develops a "mind of its own," with its own agenda.

**Therianthrope (Therianthropy):** Believe they are possessed by (or sometimes were born with) animal spirits. Many believe they can transform partially (or completely) into their animal form.

**Wendigast (Wendigo Psychosis):** An insatiable craving for human flesh. Typically the person will become a demonic monster, though still recognizable as having once been human. This is more common in the tribes to the far north, where every winter, starvation becomes an issue. In appearance they combine the emaciation of severe starvation—along with open sores—with demonic strength. They also stink of death and decay. Some turn into massive giants, growing in strength and size as they eat.

# GLOSSARY

||||||||||||||||||||||||||||||||||||||||||||||

**Abgeleitete Leute:** Semimythological city populated solely by copies of a single Mehrere.

**Albtraum:** The nightmares of man given flesh. These creatures take shapes relevant to those they haunt. They feed off the delusional and mostly attack Geisteskranken.

**Aufenthalt:** Independent city-state.

**Auseinander:** A city-state defeated by the Sieger clans. A Sieger Geisteskranken lost control during the battle of Sinnlos after raising an army of the dead. The city-state is now populated by the raised undead and ruled by what was the strongest of the Geisteskranken's inner demons.

**Basamortuan desert:** The easternmost edge of the world. Home to the Basamortuan tribes.

**Flussrand River:** The physical boundary defining the border between the city-state of Gottlos and the Theocracy of Selbsthass.

**Folgen Sienie:** Small city on the eastern border of Reichweite.

**Geborene Damonen:** A religion/Theocracy based in Selbsthass, headed by Konig Furimmer. The Geborene believe the universe was not created by the gods, that somehow it came before them, and that humanity created the gods out of its desperate need to believe in something.

**Geldangelegenheiten:** Small but extremely prosperous city-state. Center of the Verzweiflung Banking Conglomerate.

**Gottlos:** Grubby little city-state run by King Dieb Schmutzig, who had been the previous king's greatest general. Dieb is a fairly powerful Gefahrgeist.

**Grunlugen:** Independent city-state ruled by a family of petty Gefahrgeist.

**Kälte Mountains:** A range of mountains far to the east of Selbsthass and north of Geldangelegenheiten. Beyond these mountains lies the Basamortuan desert, the easternmost edge of the world.

**Krieger:** The warrior sect of the Geborene Damonen.

**Leichtes Haus:** Tavern in Selbsthass City.

**Menschheit Letzte Imperium:** The last of humanity's great empires to fall. This entire continent had once been united under a single despotic ruler, perhaps the greatest Gefahrgeist ever to live.

**Mitteldirne:** Capital of Gottlos.

**Müll Loch:** Birthplace of Stehlen.

**Neidrig:** City just beyond the northwestern border of Grauschloss.

**Rand:** City belonging to the Auseinander city-state.

**Reichweite:** Small city-state west of Selbsthass, beyond the free cities (including Neidrig).

**Ruchlos Arms:** Inn located in Neidrig

**Schatten Mörder:** Cotardist assassins of the Geborene Damonen.

**Schlammstamm:** Nomadic grassland tribes whose society is organized around whoever of its members owns the most horses. At the center of each tribe is a deranged shaman who thinks he can control the weather and talk to tribal ancestors.

**Schwarze Beerdigung:** Tavern in Neidrig.

**Selbsthass City:** Capital of Selbsthass. Home to Konig Furimmer, High Priest of the Geborene Damonen.

**Selbsthass:** Theocratic city-state. Ruled by Konig Furimmer, High Priest of the Geborene Damonen. Originally an independent state with its own royal family, Selbsthass fell under the sway of the Geborene.

**Sinnlos:** Small city located on the border of Auseinander and the lands held by the Sieger clans. Famous due only to the fact that the final battle between the Sieger and the Auseinander occurred here.

**Tiergeist:** Therianthrope assassins of the Geborene Damonen.

**Traurig:** City in the city-state of Geldangelegenheiten. Birthplace of Wichtig.

**Unbedeutend:** Backwater city-state that's been at war with itself for three generations.

**Unbrauchbar:** Small city just within the borders of the city-state of Gottlos.

**Verrottung Loch:** The worst tavern in all of Neidrig.

**Verschlinger:** A tribe of savages in the far north who believe they gain strength and wisdom by devouring their foes. The Verschlinger do not believe in an Afterdeath.

**Verteidigung:** Garrisoned city to the north of Selbsthass City.

**Verzweiflung:** Organized banks/moneylenders based in the city-state of Geldangelegenheiten.

**Wahnvor Stellung:** The largest and most powerful religion. They believe the gods are crazy. Crazy enough, in fact, that through sheer divine belief, they created the universe and everything within it. Only truly insane creatures could believe strongly enough to create something this complex. They worship the old gods that pre-date recorded history.

# ACKNOWLEDGMENTS

||||||||||||||||||||||||||||||||||||||||||||||||||||||||||||||||||||||||||||||||||

Where to start? Well, I guess at the beginning . . .

My parents passed along their love of books. Without them I wouldn't be here. Literally *and* literarily.

Being the spouse of a writer cannot be easy. We're moody, lock ourselves away for months on end, and often get grumpy when reality drags us from the fantasies we're building in our demented little minds. Or maybe that's just me. And so . . . Emma, my love, thank you.

Someone once said a wise man can count his true friends on one hand. Actually, I think it was the bassist from Iron Maiden. Anyway, I have to use a second hand, so I guess I don't qualify. Truth be told, no one has ever accused me of wisdom. I have been blessed with a truly amazing and supportive group of friends: Richard Height, Ken Iliadis, Hans Leuschner, Rich Little, Dave Stephenson, and Peter "Zed" Zosimadis. A better group of dudes in all the world there is not.

Thanks to my test readers, Richard Little (who read the book almost as many times as I have), Richard Height, and Kristopher Neidecker, who pushed me to create the wiki for this novel (http://michaelrfletcher.com/beyondwiki). Check out Kristopher's blaagh at http://klneidecker.com/. Their feedback helped make this book what it is.

I left a fifteen-year career as an audio engineer to write books, and promptly became destitute. SpringGage hired me on as a project coordinator and continues to employ me even though I spend most of my time writing books. Apparently the idea of patronizing the arts is not yet dead. Thanks!

A special thanks has to go out to my amazing agent, Cameron McClure. She called my novel *viscerally disgusting,* my characters *repulsive,* and then offered to represent me. I knew then I'd found the right agent!

I'd also like to thank executive editor David Pomerico at Harper Voyager for taking a chance on an unknown. You spend a few years writing a book and you think you know everything about it and then David comes along and shows you what you missed.

Last but certainly not least, I'd like to thank everyone at Harper Voyager. I haven't met you all yet, but let's do pints. And soon! Seriously, I'm thirsty.

Cheers!

—Michael R. Fletcher

# ABOUT THE AUTHOR

Michael Fletcher is a Canadian writer whose first novel, *88*, was published by Five Rivers Publishing, a small Canadian press. His short fiction can be found in *Interzone, On Spec, Daily Science Fiction, Heroic Fantasy Quarterly,* and *Arcane.* This novel grew out of his desire to write something outside of the normal tropes of fantasy, and his contemplation of rare mental disorders (like Cotard's Syndrome) in a fantasy context.

Michael can be found at www.michaelrfletcher.com.